THE DEATH OF PICASSO

THE DEATH OF PICASSO

new & selected writing

by GUY DAVENPORT

Shoemaker & Hoard, *Publishers*

Washington, DC

Library of Congress Cataloging-in-Publication Data is available.

ISBN: 1-59376-002-7

Cover and interior design by Kimberly Glyder
Printed in the United States of America on acid-free paper

Shoemaker & Hoard 🏛
A Division of the Avalon Publishing Group
Distributed by Publishers Group West

10 9 8 7 6 5 4 3 2 1

"The Owl of Minerva" originally appeared in *The Georgia Review;* "The Playing Field" in *Hotel Amerika;* "Ruskin" in *Harper's Magazine;* "The Concord Sonata" in *A Table of Green Fields* (New Directions, 1993); "The Death of Picasso" in *The Kenyon Review;* "The Hunter Gracchus" in *The New Criterion;* "Every Force Evolves a Form" in *Zyzzyya;* "Boys Smell Like Oranges" in *The Cardiff Team* (New Directions, 1996); "Belinda's World Tour" in *The Santa Monica Review;* "The Messengers" in *The Cardiff Team* (New Directions, 1996); "The Aeroplanes at Brescia" in *The Hudson Review;* "The Chair" in *Apples and Pears* (North Point Press, 1984); "Wide as the Waters Be" in *Harper's Magazine;* "Gunnar and Nikolai," "Mr. Churchyard and the Troll," and "And" in *A Table of Green Fields* (New Directions, 1993); "Dinner at the Bank of England" in *The Paris Review;* "Christ Preaching at the Henley Regatta" in *The North American Review;* "Pergolesi's Dog" in *The New York Times;* "Horace and Walt in Camden" in *Harper's Magazine;* "We Often Think of Lenin at the Clothespin Factory" in *Conjunctions;* "The Anthropology of Table Manners" in *Antaeus;* "Veranda Hung with Wisteria" in *The Cardiff Team* (New Directions, 1996); "The Jules Verne Steam Balloon" in *Facing Texts* (Duke University Press, ed. Heidi Ziegler, 1988); "The Bicycle Rider" was first published as a book by Red Ozier Press in a different version; "Wo es war, soll Ich werden" in *The Drummer of the Eleventh North Devonshire Fusiliers* (North Point Press, 1990); and "The Ringdove Sign" in *Parnassus.*

FOR BONNIE JEAN

CONTENTS

I

A meteor from beyond our sun's family of rounding worlds hit the upper air of Kalaallit Nunaat in the night of 9 September 1997 going 125,000 miles an hour. An Inuit who saw it said that it was as big as the moon and as bright as the sun. With a noise like time splitting away from space it broke into four burning thunderstones high in the air and then into a hail of white-hot coals that rained into the snow that has covered Greenland for a million years.

The first mate on a trawler off the Qeqertarsuatsiaat coast said that night became day. Two instruments followed its track for a few seconds each. One was a camera guarding Kristian Heilmann's snow scooter at Nuuk. The other was a sensor on a United States satellite that registered an explosion equal to sixty-four tons of TNT in the air over the Frederikshab Isblink.

—And they can't find it is what I said in my class report, Adam said. And Frøken Jorgenssen's mouth fell open when I said I knew all about it from my uncle Magnus Rasmussen who's on the team looking for the pieces.

Adam Rasmussen at twelve was the spit image of his father Mikkel at that age. His brother Henry, walking home from school with their mother, was almost eleven, and was sometimes taken for Adam's twin.

—Everybody hates me, Henry said, for having an uncle in the Geodesic Survey who's in Greenland looking for the meteor from outside the solar system.

—And you can't find it? Adam asked.

—Snow covered the pieces as soon as they fell, Onkel Magnus said.

—A biggy like that offed the dinosaurs. If the Niels Bohr Institute can't find it, who can? We've seen the moon rock there. One right here now would make hash of us.

—That's for sure, Henry said. No more long-shanked marsh hens. No more Sortemosen.

—The ice fields, Magnus said, are riven by deep crevices as treacherous as hell to move about among. The German geologist Alfred Wegener who figured out continental drift and tectonic plates is at the bottom of one of them.

—We know *him*, Adam said. Some day they'll find him and he'll be like the Ice Age man in the Alps in Italy who was frozen five thousand years ago.

—Pitseolak the old Innuit grandma said in her book that there are people nowadays who *cook* polar bear, Henry said.

—*Kabloona*, Adam said.

—Sand and snow make the same kind of desert, Henry said.

Adam's preponderate green eyes moved from Henry to Onkel Magnus to the door through which Mama would come from the greenhouse to the window where he would see his father Major Mikkel Rasmussen arriving through the snow. At school Adam had explained to his friend Wolf while they were dressing in the locker room that Technical Sergeant Magnus Rasmussen of the Geodesic Survey in Special Forces had raised his father, who was an orphan. It was a lovely joke at home that a major was the adopted son of a sergeant. The joke was funnier in that Onkel Magnus is also a professor of geology at the Niels Bohr Institute and is looking for the stupendous meteor that smashed into Greenland and has written all sorts of books about sand. He's still only a sergeant as he once was in the army so's he can be on army pay when he works with Papa, who writes orders saying he's indispensable.

—I was telling my friend Wolf about you and Daddy, Adam said, that neither of you knows now which of you went crazy when you saw each other. I hear Mama.

Susanna Rasmussen, her hair tied in a ponytail the color of honey, a denim smock over her dress, said she'd seen Mikkel marching through the snow from the bus. Henry and Adam scrambled up from the floor in front of Magnus and followed her to the door.

—Rats! Susanna said, you're not dressed for going out. You'll catch your death of cold.

—*Marching* through the snow? Magnus laughed.

—Head up, shoulders back, Susanna said. For you.

Before Magnus Rasmussen arrived in the middle of the afternoon, Susanna home from her Folk High School and Adam and Henry from their Georg Brandes Mellemskol had scarcely been home a quarter hour when the local vicar Poul Anderson paid a call.

—Oh my! he said. I'll come another time.

—No, no, Susanna said. You're new, aren't you? We can at least get acquainted, though there's no one here with more religion than a buck hare. I'm Susanna Rasmussen.

To Adam, who'd galloped downstairs and bounced into the living room, she said:

8

—Go back and find some clothes. You'll have the vicar blushing.

—We're inventing things, Adam said from behind his mother. A badger alderman, a dignified hog, a lady tree. For Onkel Magnus when he comes.

—This is Adam, Susanna said. His brother Henry will be along. Adam, this is Vicar Anderson.

—At night, Adam said, when the buses are in the car barn, seals come and sit in them, pretending they're passengers looking out the windows. Walt Whitman lived in Mikkelgade in New Jersey, the village of Camden.

—What he means, Susanna said, is that his father's name is Mikkel.

—Major Rasmussen, the vicar said, consulting a list of parish names and addresses. I'd venture to say, Fru Rasmussen, that you're not Danish by birth.

Susanna laughed.

—I'm Scots, and worse than Scots, Hebridean. My two outlaws are obstreperous because their uncle is coming later today. He's been in Greenland looking for the meteor that fell there. He's our only family. Mikkel and I don't exist when he's here.

—Major Rasmussen's brother or yours?

—Neither. The *uncle* is honorific. I have scattered kin back in Scotland but no brothers. And Mikkel has no kinfolk. He's an orphan Magnus took in and raised. Professor Rasmussen, I should say, though he's also attached to Mikkel's army group. He's much too young to be Mikkel's father. More like an elder brother. Jonathan and David. Mikkel says that he and I are remote cousins from the days of the Vikings.

—What's your name? Adam asked the vicar.

—Poul Anderson. You're Adam, a reader of Walt Whitman.

—We're reading Whitman at the Folk High School, Susanna said. Mikkel reads along with me, and the boys take in everything within a mile around them.

—And Magnus will explain everything when he gets here, Adam said. He always does. He was Daddy's teacher a long time ago. They lived together in a big long room over the stables, at the Oak Hill school over in Jylland, and did everything together, and had an island off the coast of Sweden one summer and didn't wear any clothes at all.

—If you can credit it, Susanna laughed, my scalawags imagine themselves deprived by having two parents.

Adam looked puzzled.

—We do?

Henry ventured into the room wearing the most exiguous underpants the vicar had ever seen.

—I heard you hollering at Adam to get dressed, he said. So I've put something on. Hello.

—Hello, the vicar said. You're Henry Rasmussen.

9

—Yes, Henry said. What's a vicar?

Vicar Anderson looked to Susanna for guidance.

—I'm an oatmeal-fed Presbyterian, she said. I read these savages stories from the Bible. Mikkel's a pagan, like Magnus. They like the folk tales: David and Goliath, Jonah and the whale, Balaam's talking donkey. And the parables that I myself can understand. I'm afraid I edit it all terribly. They'll read it for themselves when they're older and curious. I was raised to think that character is what's important.

—You're right, of course.

And turning to Henry:

—A vicar tries to help people who are unhappy, in trouble, or in need of someone to talk to. I'm visiting simply to meet your mother, you, and Adam. As far as I can see, I have no business here at all. I hear, Fru Rasmussen, that you have a greenhouse where you grow African violets, that you and the major are keen ornithologists.

—Amateur geologists, too, because of Magnus. You can talk maths with the boys if you're so minded.

—We're going to have a sister, Henry said. Adam and I are going to teach her to talk as soon as she's rested up from being born. And change her nappies and take her for walks. She's going to be *so* surprised when she meets us, Mama, Daddy, me and Adam, and Onkel Magnus.

—She'll be lucky to have a name, Susanna said. Every one we think of gets vetoed by somebody. We want one that's Danish and English, as with the boys.

And no sooner had the vicar shaken hands and left than Magnus arrived, hugging Susanna, Adam, and Henry all in an armful, and then Susanna to herself, with a kiss, and Henry to himself, lifted into a squealing hug, and Adam, who climbed like a monkey into Magnus' arms.

—I need coffee, Magnus said. Stay where you are, Susanna. Henry makes an excellent cup of coffee.

—Better still, Susanna said, let's all go to the kitchen. Adam, now that you've had your joke with being naked, go put on underwear and a sweater, and bring a sweater for Henry. Magnus, you look wonderful.

Henry and Adam, both astride Magnus' lap, the one talking over the other's shoulder, discussed the Frederikshab Isblink meteor, its provenance from outside our solar system, a wanderer in unimaginably deep space when earth had methane for an atmosphere and the South Pole was in Sydney, Australia, its disintegration into fiery rubble as it fell on the world's oldest rocks, the Danish helicopters that flew back and forth looking for signs of it, without any success at all, the weather station where the search party bunked, Magnus' and Daddy's conversations on the radio-telephone hookup, their skateboards, their sister still inside Mama, her kicking when they spoke to her in her amniotic pod, the dimensions of Magnus' and Daddy's long room over the stables at Oak Hill, their friends by the fire with Ovaltine, Daddy's triumphs in algebra and gymnastics, how they met (all over again) and how Magnus went to Oak Hill because Colonel Rask asked the colonel at Kastellet to send him somebody who could teach biology and geography, how Corporal Redclover looked after Daddy until Magnus sent for him, how Corporal Redclover took Daddy, who still looked like a ragamuffin, to a big department store and bought him school clothes, and dressed him in a Faeroe Islander's idea of what boys wear at a posh school, how Magnus simply put him in with his other students and added his name to rolls without the administration being any the wiser, how Daddy couldn't read or write worth a hoot, how he set fire to everybody's curiosity by suddenly being there in nifty brass-button jeans and English shirt and broad yellow galluses, speaking dockside Copenhagen Danish, how Daddy took the name Rasmussen, how an older boy who had a crush on Magnus put the fear of God into various bullies who tried to pick on Daddy, the film of Anderson Nexø's Pelle, Mama's African violets, their violin lessons, Magnus' new apartment near the Botanisk Have and when they were going to see it, Isak Dinesen's house at Rungstedkust and her grave under a giant beech in the forest behind it, until Susanna returned to the kitchen and said that from the greenhouse she could see Mikkel getting off the bus and marching home through the snow.

II

Colonel Rask in a deck chair, asleep in his garden with a newspaper over his face, was aware of the bees in the hollyhocks, of the kind warmth of the late summer sun, and of steps along the garden path. Old men nap lightly.

—Sir? said Birgit the maid, there's a man says he would like to see you. He's in uniform, an officer I would guess.

Colonel Rask removed *Politiken*, blinking, rubbing his eyes.

—An army man, Birgit?

—His uniform is dark blue, a beret on his head. Uncommon handsome, and proper spoken. Took off his beret when I answered the door.

—Ask him to come on out. Did he give a name?

—That he didn't. Would you like tea brought out, sir?

—Tea, yes. And my pill, Birgit.

A tall officer approached from the back door with deference, beret in hand. His hair, a bronze blond, was cropped close, his shoulders broad, his hips narrow. Rask, swinging his legs off the deck chair, using a cane to stand, held out a hand.

—Arthritis in the knees, he said, tottering and balancing with his cane. You're the youngest major I've ever seen in my life! Are they promoting you earlier, or do you have the secret of eternal youth?

—We move up quickly in Special Forces, colonel. Actually, I'm Geodesic Survey, a branch so new they've had to staff it with anybody even vaguely qualified.

—You're being charmingly modest. Birgit's bringing out tea for us, but perhaps you'd like something livelier? And you haven't come on military matters, surely, Major? I go back to airplanes with propellers and 75 mm field guns.

—Tea's fine, sir. I realized how close I was to the school and thought I'd look in. You're retired, I'm told.

—Oh Lord yes! I've stayed on as Headmaster Emeritus, meaning that I have this house. Once in a while, when they remember I'm not long dead, I have to get dressed up and attend a board of directors, where I usually fall asleep. Are you one of our boys?

—I was, yes. Some, let's see, fifteen years ago.

—I absolutely cannot place you. But then hundreds of boys have been here since then.

—Do you remember a geography and botany teacher who was also a sergeant of engineers, Magnus Rasmussen?

—Rasmussen. Yes, I do, of course. Came as a substitute to fill a post suddenly vacant, up from Kastellet. Very capable young man. But he disappeared, you know. Here for about two years, I think, and then vanished. He bought a car, a kind of station wagon thing, Japanese make. Lived up over the old stables out near the spinney. Very popular with students and an excellent teacher. One morning he simply wasn't there. Had cleared out his belongings and, without a word to anybody, left. How do you know him?

—Do you also remember, sir, that he lived with a boy who wasn't really a student here, but attended classes all the same?

Rask, trying to remember, shifted his attention to the folding table Birgit had brought out, helping her snap down its legs.

—Lived with? Do you mean he was out over the old stables, too? A rather charming boy with a proletarian voice, bosom friends with young Marcus Havemand, the industrialist and arts fancier? He gave us our museum, you know, and endowed a chair in the art department for which the school is now so well known. All the Havemands have been generous to us. His oldest son's coming here year after next, Mikkel Havemand.

—That's lovely. The name, I mean.

—You know the Havemands? Ah, here's tea, and sandwiches and biscuits. Thank you Birgit. And, oh yes, my pill.

—The boy who lived with Magnus Rasmussen was from Copenhagen. Who his father was, God knows. His mother was a streetwalker, not to put too fine a point on it. To this day he doesn't know his age or his birthday. By the greatest luck in the world he met Magnus Rasmussen, whose name he eventually took, and who brought him here to Oak Hill. Mikkel could scarcely read and write, having never been to school. Do you remember that he won the Algebra Prize his second year?

—It's coming back, yes. Mikkel was the name. He wrote remarkable papers in an art appreciation class.

—And a silver cup for his age group in bodybuilding.

—Yes, yes! The year we were in all the newspapers for having the boys nude at the presentation do.

—That was Magnus' and Sten Solveg's idea. We loved it.

—Who's *we?* Were you here then, Major?

—Sir, I'm Mikkel Rasmussen.

—My God! You're Rasmussen's little rascal?

—Himself.

—And already a major! What a credit to the school! I could burst with pride. Look here, you must stay for dinner. I'll have the new head and his good wife over, and some other faculty.

—I'm afraid I can't accept, sir. I'm on duty, not leave. I have to be in Helsingør this evening. And, sir, I was never really a student here. Magnus put my name on various class rolls, and I went to class. I don't think anyone dared call Magnus' bluff.

—He had a way, didn't he? But can you tell me why he left so mysteriously?

—Well, I left with him. One night he said that he and I were the happiest people in the world. We were. That's a true statement. He then said that happiness has to be *spent*, that we couldn't wallow in it. That was his word, *wallow*. So we packed the station wagon in the middle of the night. I remember crying as we left, as our wonderful big room over the stables was the only home I'd ever had, and I was in love with Marcus Havemand, and with Holt Rasvinger, remember him? But I loved Magnus more than anything in the world. He was my mother and father and best friend. He loved me.

—How blind I was.

—I don't think so, sir. The reason I've stopped by is to thank you for how kind you were to us. You knew I wasn't a student.

—I think I did, yes. I trusted Sergeant Rasmussen to know what he was doing.

—That's what I'm thanking you for.

—But where did you go when you left? What did you do?

—That's too much to tell. Magnus said later that he felt that something awful would have happened if we'd stayed, that the relationships we'd gotten into were potential disasters. They were daring adventures depending on trust and comradeship, and were more accident than design. We were, as he said, too happy. We had, the next two years, a wonderful life together. Nobody could ever understand.

—Where is he now, do you know?

—Of course I know. He's at the moment in Greenland, on one of my geodesic teams, looking for the awesome meteor that impacted last September. We couldn't do without him. He lectures on geology every other term at the university. My wife understands that we are very special friends, and my two sons adore him. I sometimes think they like their Uncle Magnus better than their father. His book on sand and quartz was well reviewed. I told him on the phone the other evening that I was going to drop by. So we both thank you for your great kindness.

—This is all quite startling, Major. Out of the blue, so to speak. An event from a past I thought I knew, but didn't. It explains, I think, yet another mystery I'd forgotten. There was an English teacher here, Pol Eddeke, who came to me once with a lot of folderol about Sergeant Rasmussen corrupting the morals of a boy who, and he said he had evidence, slept with him. He said he'd seen the bed. I suppose that was you and Rasmussen?

—It would have been, yes. Sound logic: two people, one bed. He came over one morning when Magnus and I were back from our summer vacation in Paris and on a Swedish island, no happier summer any two people in love with each other ever spent.

—You have no regrets, then?

—None.

—Good. Eddeke, rather a sad case, persisted in dithering and making accusations, until one day the physical education master—what was his name?

—Sten Solveg, Sir.

—Solveg, yes. He came to my office, what a handsome fellow he was, too, he came to my office and said enigmatically that he had shut Eddeke up. I hadn't a clue what he was talking about. But, sure enough, about an hour later Eddeke, pale as a sheet and trembling, came and resigned, saying he was leaving immediately. When I asked why, he said he'd rather not say. I had to take his English classes myself. I've always been fond of Milton and Wordsworth.

—This would be after we left.

—Yes. As soon I'd got somebody to take over Rasmussen's classes, I had to take over Eddeke's.

—Good old Sten! Is he still here?

—Went to America, I believe. Look, if you'll put up with my hobbling along on my cane, we might take a turn around the grounds, for old times' sake. Shall we?

—I don't think I can, sir. I would see a twelve-year-old in a red-checked shirt, wide yellow braces, and stone-washed jeans with a brass-button fly. I want to remember the quadrangle as he knew it. He was a very happy little boy.

III

Now I Yosef was walking and I walked not. And I looked up into the air and saw the air in amazement, for the clouds were standing still, a hawk was fixed in its flight, neither going forward nor falling, and the earth had stopped turning on its axle. And I looked about me and saw workmen at their dish, some with their spoons halfway to their mouths, motionless. And I saw sheep being driven but they were not and stood still, and their shepherd had raised his staff and it came not down. And at the river where his kids had gone to drink, their mouths were upon the water and they drank not. And the smoke from a fire under a pot in a yard rose not and was like a picture on the wall of a house of the Romans. A waft of dust that the wind had lifted hung in the air. Then of a sudden all things moved forward in their courses.

IV

—I tell you, Adam Rasmussen, it's there.

Sholto Tvemunding put a finger on the tip of Adam's nose and pushed.

—I saw you wandering off, a thing you do, to pee or get a better look at a butterfly, and you saw this house and said absolutely fucking nothing about it.

—Right. Had all sorts of cool ideas. It couldn't belong to anybody who's been there in years. It's all but invisible. Trees crowded up to the windows. Weeds up to our chins. It's on a jut of the woods onto the lake, a peninsula. If it hadn't been for the tin roof I'd have missed it. A straight line in trees. Then I made out the chimney. A windowpane catching the sun.

—And inside, skeletons, grinning skeletons.

—Two of 'em. They shot each other.

—And nobody missed 'em.

—They robbed a bank and had a fight over divvying up. The money's still there. We turn off where we left this road with the troop, the big oak and the red cows looking over the fence.

—You say it's a house, not a cabin? Somebody's summerhouse on the lake, abandoned and all, for years maybe?

—What if it's not there? A ghost of a house.

—I wonder if you can see it from the other side of the lake? If not, it's as good as invisible. Whether we can get in is another matter.

—Housebreaking. But we'd only be borrowing it for a while. A house just sitting there that nobody's using.

The house was there. They pushed their bikes through the thick of tall weeds and bushes, saplings and convoluted briars to the front door, over which a vine, one of the wall climbers, had fastened itself on its way to the eaves, under which it had branched left and right. The back door was inside a screened porch. The windows were shuttered.

Adam followed Sholto, neither speaking. After two circuits, Sholto, pushing aside branches, whistling softly to himself, found the lake shore.

—We should have worn long pants, Adam said.

—And brought an ax, a saw, a crowbar, and a glass cutter. Voices carry across water.

They followed the outline of the short peninsula until they came back to their bicycles near the house's front. Only then did Sholto turn to face Adam and stare at him.

The coast of Greenland, if you straightened out the wiggles, is as long as the equator.

—We haven't tried all the shutters.

—There's a tree on an island in the Gulf of Aden that's the only species of its genus. They're fastened on the inside, the shutters.

Sholto pushed Adam's nose again, causing him to grin and close his eyes.

—There's not even a path from the road.

—Not anymore. How long would you say it's been since anybody was here?

With three fingers Sholto pushed Adam's nose and the corners of his mouth.

—They're still in there.

—It's fucking lovely out here. We're like ants down in the grass with all these trees. Inside there'll be clues as to whose house it is and if they're ever coming back. So let's look at the shutters again.

—Back screen door. A small snip in the wire, a finger through, lift the latch, and we're in.

—As far as the backdoor.

Sholto ran a finger down Adam's nose.

—Yucatan. We've landed our pontoon Piper Cub on the lake. The Mayan temple is tied up in lianas. Pumas and alligators are watching us from under leaves as big as ponchos.

—Monkeys, parrots, boa constrictors.

—Since when are heathen temples more interesting than other people's houses?

—You're the one who's Sholto Tvemunding.

—But you're Adam Rasmussen.

They looked at each other smiling.

—Backdoor.

—Backdoor.

With the bottle-cap opener on his scout knife Sholto pried away the lathing strip that secured the screen half its length, freeing a way for his fingers, found a sliding latch, and disengaged its bolt.

Adam, his chin on Sholto's shoulder, blew softly in his ear. The door would not open until they had sliced holding vines. They went through together, shoulder to shoulder.

—Hold your breath, Adam said, trying the knob of the backdoor.

—Push.

The door opened onto a musty dark kitchen. Beyond, through an open door, a room with furniture in dense shadow. Off to the right, another room, its door partly open. Adam kept a hand on Sholto's shoulder, squeezing.

—Housebreakers is what we are, Adam said.

—Adam and Sholto is what we are. Let's open shutters and windows. What does it smell like in here? Mildew, dust, woodsmoke, and something peculiar. How many skeletons do you count?

—They're in the other room.

—If they are, they're under the bed.

Opened shutters showed a dusty, cobwebbed two rooms and kitchen.

—Oxygen! Sholto said, unlatching and raising a window. Do the front door while I get the windows up. Bring in the bikes. Talk about scuzz. But it's a homey place, you know?

—I saw a broom in the kitchen, Adam said from outside.

—Don't talk so loud.

—You can tell a grave by the wildflowers on it. Remember that film? How old are the trees closest to the windows?

—Two years, five years. A yellow house with a red-tin roof. A bed, made, with sheets and blanket.

They found plates and cups in a kitchen cabinet, a pair of jeans, a sweat-shirt, towels, and a man's bathing brief in the closet. Outside they found an outhouse even more hidden by weeds and vines, a one-seater and with a bag of quicklime on a shelf, petrified into a hard lump.

—There's a pail in the kitchen, Adam said. Let's get the spider webs down, clear this room of the chair and settle or whatever you call that in front of the fireplace, this Finnish folk-art throw rug that ought to be whipped outside, and with everything out, slosh down the floor.

—Better still, let's shake the bed blanket outside first. Then we'll have a place to put our clothes, so's we can strip down for pitching pails of water and sweeping it out as mud.

—Smarter still: sweep first, slosh afterwards.

—Well then, let's do all the rooms. Roll up the mattress on the bed.

—What about putting it outside, over a bush, for sun and air?

—Sheets, too, pillow and pillowcase. We're not scouts for nothing. As big Hugo says, brains get more work done than arms and legs.

—So. Togs off and over the bikes. Keep your underpants on for going to the lake, and your shoes.

Sholto swept dust into rills, stirring up a mist of motes that spun sunlit in the air. Adam brought pail after pail of water, swirling it in a circle. They began in the bedroom, moved to the kitchen's linoleum, and finished with their washing down in the big room, by which time they had muddy legs and dusty arms and faces. From time to time they halted to laugh, get their breath, and mouth mimic kisses.

—Are you still feeling immoral? Adam asked.

—I wouldn't be me if I didn't. Another three buckets ought to do it. I'll bring 'em.

—Shouldn't we rinse it down?

—Fresh as a lumberyard it's beginning to smell. Us next, then, after the rinse.

—And after whomping a bushel of dust out of the rug and blanket and pillow.

—And after a dip in the lake, sammidges, apple, and coffee.

—Way to live. Are we, by the way, spending the night here? Thought I'd ask.

After splashing his third fetched pail across the floor in a leaping surge that drenched Adam's knees, Sholto padded over to push Adam's nose, dance fingers on his chin, and draw a circle around his navel.

—Our folks know we're camping out. I think they imagine it's with the troop.

—We're on patrol.

In the lake, which was cold, they took off their briefs, batted the water with them, and wrung them out.

—Housecleaning, laundry, Sholto said. How moral can you get?

—You're beautiful, Sholto, wet and shiny. Put our wash on that bush there. One zigzag yellow green orange with white piping underpants, one blue micro. Mom bought the zigzag. She says boys ought to be dazzling.

—I'm a year older. Shouldn't I be the one to get fresh?

—In friendly numbers the divisors of the one that add up to the other, and vice versa, are a new assembling of the other number's components. Pythagoras. A friend is yourself in another person.

—If you say so. Anyway, I like you. You're scrumptious.

—Our dicks are the same size.

—Mine had better grow. The friend who's another self is not just like you, that would be silly, but is different in ways that add up to a kind of sameness, so friends can be unlike each other in all sorts of ways and still get along just fine.

—Lisbeth Holberg was at a girl party where some dumb bint explained that dicks hang down soft only on little boys and stand up stiff all the time on teenagers and fathers.

—Don't they?

—Girls! What we did, Sholto Tvemunding, is transfer a houseful of dust and cobwebs to us, which we've now transferred to the lake, and we're clean and the house is clean, and I'm hungry. Lunch is in my backpack, supper in yours.

—Word has gone around among the butterflies that we're here.

—Who have told the mosquitoes and gnats.

—It's their place. We're intruders.

—No we're not. We're going to fit in. Everything's a matter of learning how to belong. Two specks of *brint* and one of *ilt* join up to be water. And way up in the clouds goes in for being hexagonal crystals.

—Snow, Sholto said. Or in the summer gets blown around when it means to be rain, but gets rolled up in balls and comes down as hail.

—Can also be fog and dew, ice, steam, oceans, rivers.

—Lakes and icebergs. A speck of *kulstof* married to two specks of *ilt* shoved into it gives us Perrier *vand*.

—And Onkel Magnus says there's no way an atom can be an accident, or a cell.

—What are the sammidges? I see ham and Swiss. So how do we get atoms and cells? They're sort of everything that is, aren't they?

—Slice 'm all on a diagonal, and we'll have the same. Is that Pythagorean buddy numbers? Unscrew the thermos. Magnus thinks we never will know, except maybe to figure out that there's no nothing, that the whole fucking clockworks is *stuff*, with the intervals between things a different kind of stuff that we poor ignoramuses call nothing. He says Walt Whitman understood this, and chose grass as his favorite example of atoms and cells. Cows eat grass and give milk, and horses eat grass and pulled buses and plows and wagons.

—Also stitches topsoil together so that we don't get buried under sand dunes. If Mr. Whitman had been a Dane his book would have been *Red Clover* instead of *Grassblades*. Magnus looks at me as if I were a candy bar.

—You are. Neither Daddy nor Magnus say they can remember which of them lost their minds when they first saw each other. They're hilarious. Magnus keeps his rank of sergeant even though he's a lecturer at the Niels Bohr Institute so that Daddy can send him on geodesic surveys. A civilian would have to be appointed. They both use *civilian* as a cuss word.

Sholto, chewing and grinning, pushed in Adam's nose. Adam, grinning and chewing, pushed in Sholto's nose.

—Hugo would say that for heavy-breathing comradely immorality we're in rompers sucking our thumbs.

—We're eating lunch.

—We have a house. I don't believe it. Look at all the windows. The trees have been trying to get in for years.

—The floor's dry enough to bring in that peasant runner rug. We don't need to sit here in the damp on our bare bottoms.

—The mattress back on the bed, too. Next week, window cleaner.

Sholto brushed a crumb from Adam's top lip. Adam brushed an imaginary crumb from Sholto's lower lip. To see what would happen, Sholto circled Adam's left nipple with his middle finger. Adam punched Sholto's right nipple.

—Pushing buttons, Adam said.

Navel, navel, laughing.

—It's not as if we haven't shared a sleeping bag and a bed.

—Henry, the little bugger, got into bed with us, expecting God knows what.

—Leave Henry out of it. We're brothers.

Rubbed knee, rubbed knee. Spidery fingers inside thighs.

—Let's bring all the stuff on bushes in.

—Our underpants won't be dry. Lean in, like, so's I can play with the back of your neck.

—Fine by me. Tickles. Feels good. All this is going to my balls.

—Napes are sexy. So are shoulder blades, the groove down the spine, butts.

—Hair, tummies, legs, toes, peters.

—Ears, noses, eyes.

—Mom says she married Daddy for the fun of it, but mainly for his eyes.

—I thought you and Henry were bastards.

—*Born* bastards, like Daddy. Family tradition, he says. But when he made major and they had to go to dinners and things, they got married.

—Our tans are pinking over. Check your shoulders. The pink seems to be *under* the tan, wouldn't you say?

Adam, staring over Sholto's head, a tactic signaling a need to be forgiven, into his laughing eyes, and running spread fingers along his shins, said that the mattress was aired enough to be brought in, the sky was incredibly blue, the sunlight as good as Denmark ever gets, and that the island in the Gulf of Aden with the monotypic tree is Socotra.

—Do we put the sheets back on the bed? Sunlight kills germs.

—Whoever built this house hasn't been here in years. We snapped enough dust out of the blanket to start a garden. How long do germs live?

—No electricity, only a pump for running water. They must have brought a lantern, for nights.

—The dinky little stove in the kitchen burns wood. I'm going to feel you, OK?

—I'll feel back. Girls *practice* kissing, as they call it, French kissing, hands in each other's knickers and all. Asgar Vollmer, classmate of Henry's, cute as a puppy and with all his hopes set on being a policeman, gets to act as a kissable boy, passed around like a rag doll. For hours. They keep him tractable by petting his peter. He says he hates it but that it's sort of fun.

—Pukey, Adam said, but maybe not. The *green* out all our windows! And the light through the door, forest light, no, *woods* light, as we're in second-growth trees and underbrush, on a spit of land. Does Asgar's sister kiss him too?

—She's the one who thought it up. He can play with himself all he wants to, and does, without his sister snitching. Do we have everything in?

—Underpants still drying. Bedroom's damp and the mattress is whiffy. But we're *here*, Sholto Tvemunding.

They walked around the rooms, looking out each of the windows in turn, staying away from each other, arms out for balance, as if they were on the deck of a rolling boat, gazing at each other from time to time, grinning. They walked quietly, one foot before the other, Iroquois fashion. Sholto stopped, listening.

He tiptoed to the door, beckoning Adam to follow.

—What's up? Adam whispered.

—I thought I heard something. Somebody, maybe.

—A badger looking for grubs.

—They're nocturnal.

Sholto's hand on Adam's nape slid its way, halting in hesitation, down his back to his butt. Adam snuggled his chin onto Sholto's shoulder.

—Feels neat, he said. There are too many trees out there for their own good, I mean. They're all in each other's way.

—Making us a house all to ourselves.

They nudged noses. They rubbed cheeks, like horses and cats, mute. Sholto smoothed his foot along Adam's calf. Adam squeezed Sholto's shoulder.

—Golly, Adam said.

Sholto swiped the tip of his tongue across Adam's lips.

—Friendly numbers crunching in, Adam said.

Sholto kissed Adam's left ear, then his right.

—What we do, he said, is head for the lake, feeling like billy goats. We've got all night. You know Ejnar Kolderup? His big brother with balls like a grapefruit jacks to within a half stroke of coming, does his math homework gritting his teeth and feeling wonderful, returns to his dick, which is happier than a Lutheran marching band, up to a quarter pull of splatting the ceiling. Then he carefully eases on shorts and mows the lawn. Cold shower, a brilliant conversation with his father about politics and whichwhat, kicks a soccer ball around with Ejnar, and then back to his dick.

—We don't have a lawn mower, Adam said, or math homework, and our fathers are miles away.

Halfway to the lake, walking sideways in tall weeds, checking to see how their underpants were drying on their bush, batting away gnats, Adam pushed Sholto's nose, hugged him, and kissed both ears. They waded into the lake, arms over each other's shoulders, and watched their penises wilt.

—Sven Kolderup's cold shower, Adam said.

He swam a few meters out, dove under, bobbed up sputtering, and crawled slowly back, passing Sholto on the way out.

—Square root of ten!

—Sum of the first nine primes!

—Oof! Sholto, said, trolling the water with his hands, we've stirred up enough leaf trash from the bottom to need a bath. Where did those clouds come from?

—Norway, Adam said. Lakes are middens of muck. Hundreds of autumns. Here, I'll get some of it off you.

—Best of friends, Adam Rasmussen, is what you are.

—I like immorality. It's neat.

—We haven't even begun. Right now we're as wet as rats and it's clouding over. Let's find dry sticks before the rain starts so's we can have a fire. And bring in our underpants. I'm going to wear yours if we ever put on clothes again. I suppose they'd send the police looking for us if we spend the next ten days out here.

—All for it. Living on what?

—Hugo says that German scouts jack off into a pan, scramble it into an omelette, and eat it with blueberries.

Adam crossed his eyes and grabbed his crotch.

—The world's a wonderful place, Sholto said. Get sticks like this, easy to snap.

—Do we have matches?

—Does a scout forget matches? You have beautiful eyes, you know, Adam Rasmussen? Your butt is as cute as they come, your hangdown that's now lifting its head is eye-catching, and you're not ribby.

—What the fuck's *not ribby*?

—Not bony-backed or all ribs in front. You're smooth, hard meat all over. And the eye-catcher has stuck its head out like a turtle looking around.

—With good reason. Two armloads apiece by the fireplace ought to do it.

The firewood stashed, they stood looking at each other. Sholto pushed Adam's nose, both nipples.

—Foreplay, he said.

They shrugged, laughed, and fell into a hug.

—Let's start our fire, and think supper, as when twilight sets in we're in the dark.

—And in bed. We could do bed first, and eat by firelight, listening to the owls.

—What I really want is to jack off for the rest of my life, goofy and happy, fed by social workers, and with a like-minded friend.

—Who's right here, name of Sholto. You're a devil, you know?

—Bed, then.

—Right. But it's getting dusk. Bring in our underpants off the bush. More sticks would be a good idea. I'll secure the back. Do we close the shutters?

—To keep out mosquitoes, bears, and bats.

They brought in dry underpants, more firewood.

—Plops of rain beginning.

—Another wall against the world outside. Wind getting up, too.

Rain beat on the roof. Wind rattled the shutters. They heard neither. The night was deep dark when they got up to pee out the front door, side by side. Adam blew his breath into Sholto's face, Sholto his in Adam's. They rubbed noses, breathing together.

—There's a flashlight in my backpack against the far wall, if I can get to it without barking a shin. It's as dark as inside a cow in here. I'm happy, I'm cold, I'm hungry, and we're friends like no others, ever. And it's the middle of the night. Did you bring a flashlight, too?

—Here's matches. The sandwich papers will do to start the fire. Hey! Mom snuck in a can of Vienna sausages. And three almond-chocolate bars.

—Moms worry a lot about their children starving.

—Small sticks at the bottom. It's going to smoke a bugger before it catches good.

—Who cares? With you, Sholto Tvemunding, to look at, bare-assed and nifty, to smell and taste, I'm in love something awesome, the fire can act up all it wants to, the roof can leak, the shutters rattle, Denmark can declare war on Sweden, Russia can nuke America.

—My dick smells like seaweed and is only half down. It thinks we're still in bed. The fire's trying.

—Blow on it. It's midnight, do you know?

—Golly it's wonderful in here, out here, whooshing wind and rain. Sandwiches, apple juice, Vienna sausages in a pull-tab can. Do you want your shirt and socks? I do. Why is half dressed, cocks wagging and lolling, sexier than naked?

—It teases. You're scrumptious by firelight.

—The wind's scary. Makes it cozier. Scary things have their uses. An owl hooting most mournfully got a spadger into my sleeping bag one night out camping. Scouts. He had no more underpants on than a dog.

—Paper napkins. Mom put in paper napkins. A spadger in your bedroll.

—I was sharing a tent with Tom Nielssen. We'd just jacked off before calling it a day, the kind scouts recognize, he in his sleeping bag, I in mine, without taking any notice of what we each knew the other was doing. Grunts of pleasure in our talk from time to time. We'd come, sighed boastfully, said good night, and were asleep when the owl started in. Good sandwiches, aren't they? Finger me out another Vienna sausage.

—Starved is what I am. The owl hooted.

—And here, from nowhere, was Pascal, our understudy mascot, butting into our tent, saying he was scared shitless.

—Understudy mascot?

—Billy, who'd been our mascot for two years, was growing hair in his britches and talking like a frog. So Hugo recruited this tadpole Pascal, whose folks are some kind of Green Party radicals. Tom told him to fuck off, but I, without giving it a thought, welcomed him into my bedroll and hugged him.

—I told him the owl was advertising for a wife, singing a love song. Mooses do a trombone aria, birds play the flute and whistle, cats do an automobile trying to start when you've flooded the carburetor, elephants trumpet, whales bellow. None of which impressed Pascal in the least. So I hugged him and may even have kissed him. His mama would have. His hair smelled like tar soap, and his T-shirt unaccountably of vanilla. I patted his pert little behind. It was when I felt his miniature erection prodding my stomach that I knew for a fact that boys are my flavor.

—Like that, huh?

—Like that. He asked me if he could stay. I said sure, and he gave *me* a hug. I could just see his eyes by starlight, his jug ears and gopher teeth. He was up against me like wallpaper.

—Golly. Put some more sticks on the fire. What did you do?

—We whispered directly into each other's ear, driving me crazy. I said we mustn't wake Tom. He whispered that I was a real pal to save him from the owl. I ran a hand around on what I could reach of him, and tweaked his nose, what a grin I got, and asked him why he had a boner. He said he just did. I said that a hard-on meant either that he had to pee or to masturbate. He said he didn't have to pee.

—Rain's coming down harder. I'm jealous of Pascal.

—We made friends, learning about his school, folks, about whom he had only the scantiest information. His father was his father and his mother was his mother, and what they were otherwise he hadn't the first clue. He kept nudging my chin with his noggin, explored around, found what interested him, said it was awesome big. So I felt his, casually inquisitive. This met with his full approval.

—I'll bet. Where is he now, this Pascal?

—Moved away, I think. He followed me around like a puppy that summer, year before you joined the troop and became the apple of my eye, when you turned up in the world's shortest denim pants. We've eaten everything we brought, haven't we?

—All but the oranges. They're breakfast.

THE PLAYING FIELD

SOLDIER AND BOY UNDER A TREE

On the willow oak under which Mikkel and Magnus were lying one summer afternoon there rained down every second on every square centimeter of long sunlit leaf a quintillion photons.

—A thousand quadrillion photons.

—What's it look like as a number? Mikkel asked. And what are those midges *doing*, bouncing up and down in the air and turning like a wheel?

—They're happy, Magnus said in a drowsy voice. You write quintillion with a one and eighteen zeros. That's nothing compared to the neutrinos falling through the leaves rather than onto them, through us too, and the dithering gnats. They are so little that to them the spaces between the leaf's atoms is like from here to the moon.

—Midges. Gnats are bigger. You think they're happy, like us?

—They have minds. They're frolicking in existential ecstasy, dancing and spiraling. The old Greeks put mind everywhere, as things have to know how to be. This tree knows how to be a tree. It eats light and drinks water. It breathes out what we breathe in.

—And breathes in what we breathe out.

—It makes seed. It has gender. Like a boy I know. We need to give you a haircut. A corporal asked me who the pretty girl is in such short pants who waits for me when I go off duty.

—The green-eyed corporal with carroty hair? He winks at me.

ROOM WITH AFTERNOON LIGHT

Magnus was talking about fields of greengold algae in western Australia three million five hundred thousand years ago and meadows of cyanobacteria in Cuba, Siberias of bluegreen organisms neither plants nor animals, hat-

25

ing oxygen, alive to carbon monoxide and the archaic light that sifted through white mist, tundras of red bacterial gulfs of sulfur and mud, silent as time.

—Golly, Mikkel said from his pallet on the floor, around which his comicbooks were spread, and elementary botany text, sneakers and jeans.

—This was the old life that gave, still gives, all other life its being, for these animal plants, or vegetable animals, learned how to eat light and by photosynthesis convert themselves into carbohydrates exhaling oxygen. They were there for a million years, alone, the only beings in the whole of creation.

—Breathing oxygen into the air.

—What we call disease may be this old anaerobic order of things, on which we will be dependent forever.

—How can you stand me, moving in, sort of, like this, with my pallet and my corner, my *place*, which I keep neat, don't I? What kind of god would create this purplesilver gunk and lay it down for a foundation, one million years, to get things ready for Silurian catfish the size of submarines, the silly dinosaurs, and us? You can throw me out, you know.

—The kind of god who did. I don't want to throw you out.

SLEET AGAINST THE WINDOWPANE

The first night Mikkel slept on his pallet in Magnus's room he rolled himself naked in two blankets and was sleeping soundly at six the next morning. Magnus put a hand on his forehead to see if he had a fever. Mikkel opened his eyes and smiled.

—Why would you think I had a fever?

—I don't know. It's a thing you do with children. They seem to get every disease in the book, whooping cough, measles, mumps, asthma. Nature trying to see if you're tough enough to make it. Are you used to sleeping on hard floors? And where are the pyjamas we bought you?

—I didn't want to wrinkle them.

—Winter's here. Sleet. Ice mush. Tonight you sleep in the bed with me. In your pyjamas.

—Something, Mikkel said with his raisin roll and coffee, to think about all day.

ELBOWS AND KNEES

Magnus's experience of sleeping with friends was of two hot naked bodies in a sleeping bag designed for one, comfortable because companionable, tolerable because sensual, delightful because naughty, and sleep was not why they were there.

—We're strangers, you know, he said to Mikkel bathed and in his pyjamas. That is, though we're making friends fast, we know very little about each other. I don't see why you should spend the night on the hard floor when there's the bed.

—I squirm, Mikkel said. Do I have to keep away from you?

Magnus, sitting by the last of the fire, still dressed in fatigues and heavy military socks, patted the hearth rug for Mikkel to sit beside him.

—You've run away from wherever you belong, right?

—I thought you said you weren't going to ask questions.

—No questions. You don't know who I am, either.

—You're a soldier and my friend, and last summer you were some kind of scoutmaster who was not like our keeper. You were different.

—I'm a soldier doing my national service for a year, out at the Fort. I'm also at the university, where I'm going back when I've served the Queen. These quarters, officers' housing back a century or so, are for married personnel, though nobody likes them, they're too much like a movie set for Napoleonic times, with their old fireplaces and archaic plumbing. This big room is actually not part of a unit, and was being used for storage when I asked to have it. So here we are.

—Ha! Mikkel said, putting a finger to Magnus's cheek.

—You look great in your pyjamas, and with a haircut. And smell like a bar of soap. I'll find a clean T-shirt, which is what I sleep in. Is that OK with you by way of protocol?

—What's that, protocol?

—The way things are done. The way two people, or lots of people, agree on how to act toward each other, speak, dress.

—Protocol, protocol. It sounds like cough medicine. And protocol is what you wear to bed. Your underpants are littler than mine, I mean for somebody your size. I don't know what I mean.

—Buy you Mikkel-sized underpants tomorrow.

Mikkel ran his hands along the clean sheets and felt his pillow, furtively watching Magnus taking off his briefs and pulling on a T-shirt.

—I almost got up last night to pick you up off the hard floor and stick you in the bed, but thought it might scare you. I also figured you were proving something, and that you needed to prove it. And now we have to learn to sleep together. We can't be in the same bed without rolling against each other, so let's get used to being close, to be comfortable about it.

Mikkel wriggled closer, feeling Magnus's legs with a foot, putting splayed fingers out to explore. Magnus put an arm around his shoulders and a hand on his small butt. Mikkel snuggled tighter, nudging Magnus's chest.

—You're not edgy that we're being puppies in a basket?

—Not me.

—What are you doing, scamp?

—Taking off my pyjama pants, to be like you.

Magnus with a long reach turned on the table lamp.

—What kind of knot is this you tied in the string?

—Pull both ends and watch it fall apart. I'll teach you lots of knots. And the protocol of shed clothes is that you fold them, like this, and put them where you can find them. Not wad them up and throw them on the floor. We're soldiers.

—I'm a goof.

PEAPODS

Magnus and Mikkel eating peapods from a paper bag.

—The animals, where are they?

Mikkel thought about this, rubbing his nose with a knuckle.

—No polar bears on the equator, no giraffes in the Faeroes, is that it?

—Tigers in New Zealand?

—Where's New Zealand?

—Maoris, mountains, one island north, one south. The atlas we bought is, I know, terrific for keeping your drawings in, but it also has maps.

—Can we go and stand on the Arctic Circle? There's a picture of that, scouts who look like Swedes, camping on the Arctic Circle.

—Tomorrow. Today we're doing laundry, buying groceries, looking in at a bookstore, maybe a good long walk out to Ordrupsgaard.

SUNDAY IN THE PARK

—With friends, real friends, Magnus said, the space they fill belongs to them both, as at home in the other's space as in their own. I don't think you got a burn. You're going to radiate heat for awhile, but this lotion should soothe the more scorched parts. Do I include your piddler, or is that reserved space?

Grin and unbelieving look.

—Smear me everywhere. I'm cooked. I get to do you next, right?

—When I was a Scout shining with industrial-strength testosterone and full of sperm, we explored each other in honest Danish ways, wore our buddy's underpants, sniffed, licked, and hugged. We were companionable animals.

—Your briefs would fit me like socks on a rooster. I can wear your sweatshirt. It smells like you.

—You didn't get on with that bunch you were with last summer, did you?

—They picked on me. I heard what their teacher said. He said they had to make allowances for me as I'm lower class.

—Yes, but does this paragon of the consuming classes have a handsome soldier smoothing cucumber almond salve on his legs and bottom, and has he spent all day with his best friend, and has he eaten a banana split *and* a sausage and pepperoni pizza at Mama Gina's?

—Nah. And neither are the snot-nosed sissies I was with. I quit talking to them after awhile. They said back to me whatever I said.

—Other people, Magnus said. That says it all, *other*. We have to look around

and find the people we're really kin to. They're only rarely our family.
Mikkel looked at Magnus out of the side of his eyes. ..

—Leonardo da Vinci, Magnus said, the painter and inventor and the most intelligent man in all history, owned and operated a boy your age, and liked him so much he made him a bicycle three hundred and ninety-eight years before the next boy had one.

WINDFLOWERS

Mikkel and Magnus snug before their fire, Mikkel on Magnus lap.

—The first four are pretty hopeless. No other gods, no idols, no saying God's name except when praying, no working on Sunday. As we don't talk about your parents and I've promised not to ask, you can't do much about the fifth except be nice to others' parents.

—Not me.

—Fine. You're your own man. You may not even be human at all, but the godling Eros with smuts on his nose, in disguise as a Dane.

—You'd better believe it.

—What do you make of number six?

—What it says. Don't kill. It's mean to kill anything. Everything wants to live. What's the next, Magnus, being grown up?

—Adultery means fucking another man's wife, or the wife fucking a man she's not married to.

—What if they want to?

—Well, God says they shouldn't.

—Big deal. But the next one is good. Stealing is mean. You might take something somebody needs, or likes a lot.

—False witness is fibbing when you ought to tell the truth.

—Like in court.

—Anywhere. *Covet* means to want something so bad that you're liable to steal it, or seduce, or be sneaky about getting it.

—But all that's already in the other *don'ts*.

—So there are really only three commandments. Don't kill, lie, or steal.

—Yes, but you might have to do all three. We have to kill Germans in a war, and you might have to kill somebody who's trying to kill you. You lie if the truth is going to get you or somebody you like into big trouble. You steal if you're hungry. If you were sick, Magnus, and needed a medicine, I'd steal it and be proud of myself.

—What a moralist!

—What's a moralist?

—Somebody who knows what's right and what's wrong.

—But everybody knows what's right and what's wrong, don't they?

—No.

—They don't?

—Absolutely not.

—So they don't. Where's that leave us?

—Well, there's the rule for fair play: don't do to anybody what you wouldn't like them to do to you.

Silence. Scrounging in paper bag for more peapods.

—And there are laws.

—Don't walk on the grass.

—Exactly. And then there's the undeniable fact that some of us love each other.

—Is love sex, Magnus?

—Nope.

Silence. Wiggling.

—Love is eating peapods out of the same bag.

RIETVELD TABLE

—You've played it so fucking cool, Magnus, that half the school is in shock, gossip swarming like bees. You come into class with Mikkel here, and nobody knows who he is or where he comes from, and him neat as an ad for kiddy togs, in a red-and-blue-checked shirt, stone-washed jeans we would all kill for, black trainers, and, oh sweet Jesus, those wide yellow braces the likes of which nobody's seen, *and* with the textbook and a notebook that maybe the Crown Prince gave him, and him as cool as Daniel strolling into the lions, taking a seat not in the front row, where you could save him when we started to eat him, but back in the third, with Asgar, Ole, and Ejnar.

—Is Ole the big round specs and flop of hair down to his nose? Mikkel asked. *Just who the fuck are you?* is what he asked me. I said I was Mikkel Rasmussen and did he want to make anything of it?

—Holt is a social critic, Mikkel. He likes to talk.

—*And* the disappearing act after class, when there was practically a queue to quiz Mikkel, smell him, find out what his jeans cost and where the yellow braces come from, but he'd melted away into thin air.

—To be decanted again in geography, Magnus said, with the same effect, except that word had already spread that a new boy of unknown origin and status had been turned loose into the order of things.

—You *made* this table, Magnus? Dutch De Stijl design, you say? And this room, apartment I suppose it is, O wow! You realize that I'm the most hated person in the whole school, getting invited here for lunch with Mikkel and you, getting to ask all the good questions. Start answering with the nifty yellow braces.

—They're a present from Corporal Redclover, who was with Magnus at the Fort. We came up for the weekend once. He's from the Faeroes. He's my other best friend. Magnus sent him lots of money and told him to take me around to Jespersen's and say that I was going to Oak Hill Boys School. Thomas, that's Corporal Redclover, was in his Class A uniform, parade dress with all the insignia patches and stripes and buttons, and for the fun of it a big pistol in its white holster, and his baton. And I was in my rattiest jeans, my barracks rat's pants as Magnus calls them. Well, and well, *ha!* this snooty department-store snob would have been happier if I weren't there, and when he asked, to make sure he'd heard right, *the Oak Hill School?* Thomas gave him a look that meant that if he didn't get on with it the Royal Artillery, Second Battalion, Company B, would not like it at all.

—It's great to have friends. I've never had the Army with me to buy socks and shirts.

—Eat up, Holt. You're our second guest, after Solveg.

—Solveg's been up here? I suppose he took in the one bed, which, by the way, I know I'm not to peddle as paparazzi dirt, none of anybody's business.

—Hr. Solveg showed me how he's dressed for teaching swimming, wearing a red cap and whistle and nothing else. Magnus says his red cap and size XL hang-down are all the authority he needs.

—That's for sure, Holt said. If I know Sten, he asked to see yours.

—Because I haven't been to his gym yet. He's an empiricist. That means somebody who has to see for himself.

—I'll bet it does.

—Sten, Magnus said, says that Phys Ed is the only place for a philosopher anymore.

A SENSE OF PLACE

—I like Holt, Mikkel said. He's neat. I like all the trees and the walks. I guess there's every kind of person in the world here. Everybody's from somewhere else, aren't they? Some boys talk real funny. There's a library with about a thousand books in it.

—We can check out any we want.

—They call barracks dorms, and when people ask me what dorm I'm in I say I'm in private quarters. Most of the boys I've met are friendly, but some are snooty, you know. And some try to talk English to me.

—You aren't feeling out of place, are you, Mikkel? I am, sort of.

—I don't think so. I'm at home, here, with you. Everybody else is away from home.

—We're going to make our big room here a home like nobody's ever had before, a place that's all ours, exactly the way we want it.

A ROSE IS ALSO ITS THORNS

—Well, Mikkel said, I was going from your classroom over to the gym, and there was this shit, I think his name's Peder Hanssen, said something real nasty to me. I wasn't even looking at him. What I didn't know was that Holt heard him. I didn't know Holt was anywhere about. I suppose I said something nasty back at him.

—We're not asking what, Magnus said. Meanwhile, he's in the infirmary and Holt is in Rask's office. I have several versions. What did happen?

—Well, before I knew what was going on, Holt was on him like a tiger, had his face against the walk and was kicking his butt, I mean hard. *Ka-whop! Ka-whop!* Hr. What's-his-name, the Social Studies rabbit with the little eyes, threw his books down, actually up and they fell in front of him, and he danced around trying not to step on them. He came over and demanded that Holt stop *this brutality*. Well, Holt looked knives at Social Studies, and gave Hanssen one more kick, for good measure. Hanssen by this time was crying and saying that he was being killed. His legs didn't work when they tried to walk him, to the infirmary I suppose, and some snitch had gone to bring back the Headmaster. Nobody knew I had anything to do with it. Poor Holt. Is he in big trouble?

—I'm going over to find out. You stay here.

—I'm going with you. I've got to thank Holt, if only through a window. He can read my mind.

SOLDIERS

—Sergeant.

—Colonel.

—What do you know about any of this?

—Hearsay only, Sir. But I know Holt Rasvinger to be a boy of excellent character, and can't think that he would attack another student without real provocation.

—He won't talk, you know. He's in there. He won't say a word to me, stubborn as a mule. Hanssen, the boy he kicked, quite viciously I understand, is in a bad way, under sedation. So we have nothing from him, either. Is Hanssen one of your students?

—No, sir, but Rasvinger is. I know him quite well. He's in the discussion group I'm advisor to, and we run together cross country regularly. He'll talk to me, but perhaps not with you or anybody else present.

—Will you tell us what he has to say for himself?

—No, sir, I will not.

Colonel Rask moved some pencils on his desk, rubbed his chin, and stared out the window.

—I'm certain you have an excellent reason for refusing? Is it that you know more of all this than you're letting me know?

—I don't know if I do, Colonel. What I mean is that I can't betray to you what he won't tell you himself. That's common decency. I want to talk with him, privately, to see what happened, and to discuss with him what he ought to do.

—Why do you think he will talk to you?

—I know he will.

—Very well. But perhaps, in some indirect way, you can tell me why he kicked Hanssen, and if Hanssen started it. Through here.

Holt was in a locked reception room, sitting on a leather couch, his hands on his knees. Magnus sat on the floor, with his hands over Holt's.

—I'm not ashamed of myself, and I'm not sorry, Holt said. He called Mikkel a pukey little faggot. I'll kick him again when I can get at him.

—Why won't you talk to Rask?

—Because it's none of his fucking business who you love. And anybody you love, I look after. The next shit who wants to smart off and call Mikkel names will think twice about it.

—Mikkel is outside. He says to thank you. He was hoping he could thank you with cryptic signals through a window.

—Sweet little squirt. Kiss his dick for me.

—Right now Rask wants to put you before a firing squad. I will of course tell him nothing you're saying, and told him I wouldn't. But may I say you were teaching a bully a lesson? Will you come into Rask's office and listen to what I say?

—He called me a barbarian, and said *I'm* a bully.

—Headmasters and colonels don't always get things right. What I want, Holt, is to take you over to my place where Mikkel and I can make on over you. Counselling, we'll tell Rask. Let's go.

—I'm saying nothing.

Magnus had his hand on Holt's shoulder when they entered.

—Well? Have you come to your senses, young man?

—He has not come to his senses, Colonel. He doesn't feel that he should have to defend himself in what he considers an honorable act of chastising a foul-mouthed bully. I will put in as from myself that his chastising Hanssen was indeed barbaric in the sense that a recourse to violence was the only response. To call the bully names would have resulted in a slanging match. To have reported the incident to you would have pitted one word against another. Barbarity is outside the law because the law is not interested in its honorable rages. Holt heard an obscene insult gratuitously inflicted on an innocent younger boy who was leaving my geography class to go to the gym. He felt that the bully needed to be taught a lesson, and kicked him in the behind.

—Is this the truth of the matter, Rasvinger?

Holt stood mute, looking straight ahead.

—Rasvinger, sir, does not feel that he needs to explain, or excuse himself, when he has come to the defense of someone being hurt.

—Should we hear this younger boy's account?

—Whether we should or not we aren't going to. I've talked with him. I don't want him to relive the experience by telling it as a witness. And now, sir, if Rasvinger is willing, I'd like to take him over to my place to play checkers, or have a walk, or whatever it occurs to us to do. As for Hanssen, it's my experience as a scout and soldier that a kicked behind is very sore, and very bruised for some days, but is not otherwise harmed.

—Thank you, sergeant. The two of you may leave.

DAFFODILS FROM HOLLAND

—The world's wonders pile up, Magnus said, unbuttoning Mikkel's shirt.

—Now what?

—Well, Dr. Havemand, Marcus's mama, had lunch today with the Rasks and sang praises about the school. Seems that her once shy son, and once fastidious about his clothes, met her in a pair of scruffy jeans, deplorable sneakers, and a sweatshirt that has been a stranger to detergent and hot water for several months.

—My clothes, Mikkel smiled.

—She said he smelled like a gymnasium, and that his ruddy face, much more mature conversation, and confident walk gave him the authority to wear anything. I'm quoting Rask, who was considerably bucked. He was, however, a bit confused by her approval of Marcus's best friend who lives in a neat place with a soldier. This shirt's good for another day. Dr. Havemand seems to approve of boys being whiffy. We don't have her opinion on underpants.

—These go to Marcus, and are just getting good and nasty.

—Marcus will be with his mama until about five. Do I stand in for him, or do we have a walk, or draw, read, or go shopping for groceries?

—Feels great, what you're doing.

—A friendly working in of tone, for later.

—Nobody's objecting. Marcus says he doesn't know *who* his folks are. His father notices once in awhile that he exists, and talks cars and soccer scores with him, boring Marcus into a fit. His mama talks clothes and being popular.

ORANGE AND BLUE

A sheer mist made the players look as if they were behind gauze. The soccer field was still summer green, though the trees on the far side were bronze and yellow.

—All the playing fields in the world on an autumn afternoon must remain the same forever, Major Mikkel Rasmussen said to Colonel Rask.

—You feel that, do you? Rask said. I wholly agree. You put it very nicely.

The ball flew wide out of the mist toward them. Major Rasmussen butted it back, losing his beret. A player in an orange jersey and blue pants caught the neatly returned ball between his knees, rolled it down his shin to his boot, and waved thanks.

—Look here, Major, Colonel Rask said, it's wonderful that you've dropped by like this. I've not completely recovered from your surprise visit back in the summer, when you filled me in on your extraordinary time as one of us, as Sergeant Rasmussen's lively rascal and your friendship with the Havemand boy. My old eyes water every time I think of it.

—There's the whistle, Major Rasmussen said. Olfactory memories persist, you know. I'm remembering the smell of the showers they're headed toward, wet tin and that soap the school provided, surely meant for horses. Would it be *mal apropos* for me to look in, as a visit to the past?

—You'll find it all thoroughly modern, thanks to the generosity of the Havemands. Tile instead of wood, lots of hot water, and would you believe washing machines?

The boy who'd taken Major Rasmussen's butted return came grinning out of the mist and gave a high sign of solidarity.

—Oh, Mikkel, Colonel Rask called. Come and meet your namesake Major Mikkel Rasmussen, an alumnus who's dropped by to have a look at his old school. Major, Mikkel Havemand.

—*Hej!* You were Dad's best friend! I'm *named* for you!

They shook hands.

—Sorry about the mud, Mikkel Havemand said.

—Mikkel, Colonel Rask said, Major Rasmussen would like to see our new lockers and showers. He was remembering just now the wooden shed and ice-water showers from his heroic days here. Me, I've been out longer than my arthritic knees will thank me for. We'll expect you for tea, Major, after you've quenched your nostalgia.

On the way to the locker room, Mikkel Havemand said with searching, anxious eyes:

—Don't you recognize me?

—Of course I recognize you, Major Rasmussen said. How not?

—I saw Magnus on television, the search in Kallalit Nunaat for the meteorite from outside the solar system. He doesn't look older, you know?

—He isn't. He sometimes forgets I'm not eleven anymore, but he has my boys Adam and Henry to adore.

—Our boys. And I'll have a Scottish wife from the Hebrides. Dad talks about you, and keeps up with you. He doesn't want to meet you. He still feels the hurt of our going away in the middle of the night, with Magnus and without a word to him.

—You've reconstructed it all from Marcus's talk? You and I have a budget of things to discuss. But you need your shower and warm clothes.

Steam vapor in the shower stalls took up where the fog had made a screen of mist outside. There was a muddled controversy afterwards as to whether there had been a tall soldier (beret, blue uniform, infantry boots, dog tag, athletic build, the grandfather of all chronometers on his wrist) who undressed quickly and got in a shower with Mikkel Havemand, the two of them speaking Copenhagen dockside Danish. Some hadn't seen any tall soldier, and charged those who had with being psychotic.

—The soap in my day was carbolic, Mikkel Rasmussen said, and we smelled decidedly chemical. The water was at best tepid.

—To discourage self-abuse, Mikkel Havemand grinned.

—Didn't discourage your dad.

—Grandma tells about visiting dad in his first year. When he went off to school he was shy, vain, and stuck-up. Old Colonel Rask, the Head back then, sent for dad, who turned up looking like an urchin and smelling like a gymnasium (I'm quoting Grandma) in ratty jeans and filthy shirt.

—Mine, Major Rasmussen said. He would have had on my underpants, too.

—Grandma was delighted. She said Dad was confident, full of self-esteem, and was speaking *real Danish!* So you're responsible for the Havemand Endowment. Soap my back, huh?

—So do you want to know what Magnus and I did after we skedaddled in the middle of the night?

—I know some. You kept me, and grew up around me. There was that trigonometry exam in officer's school, when you asked me to help, and I did. And when you told Magnus that you were going to marry Susanna you used my voice.

—I couldn't have done anything without you. I thought for years that I couldn't be out of Magnus's sight. We still talk almost daily on the phone. He's in my command, you know, in Special Forces. Every time, in front of others, he calls me *Major Rasmussen*, a lizard runs up my spine.

—We can't see the long room over the stables. There's a young couple there now, with a baby. Dad says it was the most wonderful room in the world. It was.

—We'd had no other home.

—I think I've seen the Sortemosen house, not clearly. I could recognize Susanna in a supermarket. You'll have to show me pictures of Adam and Henry.

—The willow oak at Kastellet.

—A quintillion photons on every square centimeter of leaf per second.

STILL LIFE WITH TEA POT

—You must think me daff, Major, introducing you to a boy whose name I cannot think of as Mikkel Havemand. Havemand sprained his ankle early on this afternoon and was in the infirmary when we walked over to the practice field.

A hundred years ago the eighty-year-old John Ruskin died at Brantwood, his home on the shores of Coniston Water in Lancashire, the Lake District made famous by Wordsworth and Coleridge. For ten dark years he had been out of his right mind, only intermittently recognizing his cousin Joan Severn, a long-suffering woman who had been adopted by the Ruskin family thirty-six years before to nurse Ruskin's aging mother. In 1871 Joan Agnew, as she then was, had married the son of the Joseph Severn who closed Keats's eyes. Ruskin had met Joseph Severn on a staircase in Rome in 1841, Ruskin ascending, Severn and George Richmond descending. Richmond had closed the eyes of William Blake.

Ruskin's life was like that, a fortuity of encounters. As a child he had seen Wordsworth asleep in church. Later, at Oxford, Wordsworth would hand him the coveted Newdigate Prize for Poetry. He came to think of his life, and all life, as a maze of unexpected turns, a labyrinth (or *crinkle-crankle*, the Chaucerian word Ruskin liked to use) of fortunate passages and obstructing dead ends. From 1871 to 1884 he elaborated this idea in a series of monthly essays addressed to the "labourers of Great Britain." *Fors Clavigera* he called this work (he liked Latin titles). This is a pun as elaborate as the work itself: a *claviger* is the bearer of a *clava* (a cudgel, like Hercules'), or of a *clavis* (a key, like that of Janus, god of doors), or of a *clavus* (a nail, like Jael's in the Bible, which she drove into the head of the tyrant Sisera). *Fors* means "luck" and is, Ruskin said, the "better part" of the English words "force" and "fortitude."

When the club-bearing Theseus ventured into the Cretan labyrinth to slay the monstrous Minotaur, his key to getting back out was a ball of thread, or *clue* (etymologically kin to *clava, clavis,* and *clavus*), paid out by Ariadne.

The Cretan labyrinth was built by the archetype of all builders and designers, Daedalus: sculptor, architect, aeronaut, inventor of sails and ship rigging, designer of mechanical cows in which the Cretan queen Pasiphae could mate with a bull. The offspring of this trans-species coupling was the Minotaur, who ate Athenian children. He lived at the center of the maze Daedalus built for him, the Labyrinth. This myth has figured in European poetry and painting for three thousand years.

Little John Ruskin's first labyrinth, as Professor Jay Fellows explained in his brilliant *Ruskin's Maze*, was the back garden at Herne Hill, the London house in which John Ruskin grew up, where long brick walls enclosed trees, flowers, grass, and walks. Here the red-haired, blue-eyed boy thought acorn cups and snail shells the most delightful things in the world. He also liked keys and pebbles.

His father, a rich wine merchant, importer and wholesaler of sherry, port, and bordeaux, was a handsome Scot, also named John. His mother, Margaret, was a strict Calvinist who unflinchingly faced up to the Bible's being "so outspoken." The Ruskins began every day with reading aloud from Scripture, right through, year after year, from Genesis 1:1 to Revelation 22:21, at which point they began again. Ruskin knew the Bible by heart.

Ruskin's upbringing, so beautifully remembered in his fragmentary autobiography, *Praeterita* (Shakespeare's "things past," Proust's *temps retrouvé*), was a careful and loving education in piety, character, and intellectual curiosity. His parents hoped he would be a clergyman; Ruskin was all for being a geologist. He was a brilliant child. He was taken around England in comfortable coaches, and on European tours to see paintings and cathedrals. He fell in love with crystals, glaciers, alpine valleys, landscape painting, poetry, Greek and Latin, Gothic architecture, a daughter of the Domecq family (the wine business's French connection) and played with her in the Hampton Court topiary maze (Ruskin's first *real* labyrinth, though he'd seen the mazes on the floors of French churches, at Amiens and Chartres, and the Italian one at Lucca). He learned everything except the facts of life.

When, after Oxford, where he wrote two books as an undergraduate, he married Effie Gray, he did not know what to do on the wedding night, and— for six years—did nothing. Effie was beautiful, charming, and perhaps as ignorant as Ruskin about where babies come from. Ruskin's most recent biographer, Tim Hilton, author of the magnificent new *John Ruskin: The Later Years* (sequel to *The Early Years: 1819-1859*) and of a forthcoming volume on *Fors Clavigera*, treats this peculiar marriage with understanding and tact. He makes it clear that Ruskin, with awesome ignorance or unconscious planning, put Effie and the pre-Raphaelite painter John Everett Millais in such deliberate proximity on a painting excursion that nature would do what it always does with twenty-year-olds sharing a bedroom in a rustic cabin. Effie filed for divorce, married Millais, had a large family, and lived happily ever after.

Ruskin in a deposition to the divorce court said that the female body was not what he thought it was. Hilton puts it bluntly: "He was a paedophile"— four laconic words in an 875-page work. This naked fact, however, becomes the leitmotif of the rest of Hilton's biography, as it was of Ruskin's life. Sexual obsession can, as in Nabokov's *Lolita,* lead to a blinding madness. It can also give us the Alice books of Lewis Carroll, Ruskin's fellow don at Oxford, or create chuckling pagans like the English novelist and travel writer Norman Douglas, voluptuous satirists like Frederick Rolfe, or ironic Germans like Thomas Mann. Or, for that matter, the philosophy of Socrates and the mind of Leonardo.

When Ruskin fell in love with the ten-year-old Rose La Touche, the sprite-like daughter of a well-to-do evangelical Anglo-Irish family, he was meeting his daimon. Hilton shows how Ruskin began to fancy prepubescent girls in 1853, when he was thirty-four: an almost naked Italian peasant girl luxuriating in a sand pile acted as an epiphany, as when Dante first saw Beatrice, age nine, on the Ponte Vecchio, or when Stephen Dedalus was transformed by a girl wading in the sea's edge, in Joyce's *Portrait.*

Rose, and others like her to follow, was purest symbol. She was a petulant, teasing, illiterate religious fanatic wholly unworthy of Ruskin's adoration. We know nothing of Beatrice Portinari, or of Petrarch's blonde Laura; it's a good guess that they were practical Italians, afraid of owls and the evil eye, good cooks, and strong-armed beaters of dirt out of laundry on washing day at the river. And Shakespeare's Mr. W.H. probably couldn't follow the plot of *Hamlet* and smelled like a wet dog.

The girl in the sand pile was an event on Ruskin's road to Damascus. He had long before ceased to believe in the historical truth of the Bible. The study of the English Romantic painter J.M.W. Turner, a "sun-worshipper," and of Italian art had humanized his fundamentalism. The Victorian period saw an earnest questioning of Biblical truth and of Christian doctrine. Matthew Arnold thought that the apostles, none of whom were Eton and Oxford material, misunderstood what Jesus tried to teach them. Geology, Darwin, Bishop John William Colenso (author of *The Pentateuch and the Book of Joshua Critically Examined,* 1862), and German scholarship were outing closet atheists by the dozen. Ruskin's religion began to admit an appreciation of how God appeared to Egyptians, Greeks, Romans, even Catholics. He progressively came to see his Protestantism as restrictive, mean, and perhaps inhuman.

If Ruskin's erotic emotions were fixed in a perpetual preadolescence, his genius for the synthesis of knowledge derived from perception became as extensive as that of Leonardo. His *Modern Painters,* begun as a survey of landscape painting in order to place Turner foremost in that art, grew through four more volumes to include Renaissance and medieval painting, and to be a richly eccentric study of geology, botany, and geography. The other two multivolume works among Ruskin's books, *The Seven Lamps of Architecture* and *The Stones of Venice,* grew in the same branching way, putting out digressions that are books in themselves, the main text pushing along through an undergrowth of footnotes, waving a dragon's tail of appendices.

There are 250 titles in Ruskin's complete works, not counting many volumes of letters and diaries. Some are technical pamphlets about drawing and perspective; some are about geology, weather, political economy, glaciers, history, wildflowers, the morphology of leaves. All of these passions flow into *Fors Clavigera,* where they are enlisted into the service of a vast enterprise, an all-but-imaginary Guild of St. George, a widely varied round of activities distributed all over England, duly registered as a corporation, the purpose of which was no less than to return to the culture of medieval handicraft (in an England that was supplying the world with locomotives and rails) and medieval values: the lord in his manor, the peasant in his cottage. Its purpose was also to cleanse the air, rivers, and streets. Friends of the Guild swept the pavement in front of the British Museum (in Ruskin's pay), ran a London tea shop with the best tea, cream in daily from the country. Guild members wove linen in Yorkshire, translated Xenophon, copied details of French cathedrals, measured buildings in Venice, illustrated manuscripts, set type, collected crystals, milked cows, and taught drawing. The Guild began with Ruskin's Oxford students (Oscar Wilde among them) in the 1870s, the dawn of the Aesthetic Movement, when Walter Pater urged the young to "burn with a hard, gemlike flame."

Ruskin chose to live in an old stagecoach inn outside Oxford when he became the first Slade Professor of Art. He rose before dawn, read his Bible and prayed, translated a page or two of Plato (Jowett's translation being "a disgrace"), walked into Oxford with his dog, gave a lecture on Carpaccio (with visuals held up by a servant), repeated the lecture (out of necessity, for no hall at Oxford could hold the crowds who came to hear him), then rolled up his sleeves to work with spade and pickax on the road to Ferry Hinksey that he and his students were building. The long evening of reading and writing lay ahead.

His energy was boundless. He never passed up a game of chess (and kept games going by mail). He loved the theater (the more vulgar the play, the better), the Christie minstrels, military bands, dancing (he could do a memorable highland fling). He knew everybody: Prince Leopold and Sir Edward Burne-Jones, Rosa Bonheur and Charles Eliot Norton, Carlyle and Dante Gabriel Rossetti. He loved visiting girls' schools. He loved rowing and mountain climbing. If there was a subject he was not knowledgeable about, Hilton hasn't found it.

Ruskin relaxed with Euclid (in Greek) all his life. He built scaffolds in Italian churches and climbed them to inspect frescoes that hadn't been seen close-up for centuries. He collected manuscripts and books, maps and paintings. He endowed and built museums. (At one time I thought I knew the range of Ruskin's interests, only to be surprised by an exhibit, at the Ashmolean in Oxford, of archaic Greek sculpture of the kind that became appreciated after World War I, when Gaudier-Brzeska, Brancusi, and Modigliani made us aware of its severe, primitive beauty. Ruskin had got there first, bought it Lord knows where, and given it to the museum, to be appreciated when the world's eyes caught up with his.)

It took a while for the world to catch up with Ruskin's discoveries. He recognized, for example, the Countess of Pembroke's and her brother Sir Philip Sidney's metrical translation of the *Psalms* (each psalm in a different meter) for the splendid work it is, "the most beautiful book in English," forgotten and critically neglected, and republished it. His familiarity with Dante was, for the time, daring and unusual, as was his love of Chaucer.

A story of Edith Wharton's "False Dawn" (1924), nicely illustrates Ruskin's aesthetic pioneering. The story is about an old and wealthy New York family that sends a son abroad to buy Old European Art as the basis for a museum. In Switzerland he meets up with Ruskin at an inn, is captivated by his talk, and is advised to collect not Baroque but Trecento and Quattrocento Italian paintings. So he returns to New York with Carpaccios, Cimabues, and Giottos. His father is horrified. The newspapers are satirical. The paintings are hidden in an attic for two generations, until a dealer is shown them and they sell for millions, a Piero della Francesca returning to Europe, others going to California. The sweet irony of the story is that the son had a list of advisers to show him what the Americans like. Worse luck, he falls in with this nobody John Ruskin.

Ruskin's influence on his contemporaries was pervasive. Proust worshiped him and translated two of his books, *The Bible of Amiens* (with his mother's help) and *Sesame and Lilies*. The presence of Ruskin in the Modernist movement is evident in the similarity of Pound's *Cantos* to *Fors Clavigera:* their labyrinthine twists and turns, their concern with economic systems that benefit from frequent wars, their interest in Venetian history and the Italian Quattrocento in architecture, poetry, and politics.

Beatrix Potter recorded in her diary seeing Ruskin at the Royal Academy. He was showing some friends around, commenting on the paintings. Seeing Ruskin in public was a jolly surprise, but what fascinated her artist's eye was that Ruskin's trouser leg was caught in the top of his boot and that he was surreptitiously trying to shake it loose. Kafka, too, would have noticed Ruskin's plight. It is a detail that exposes the protocol of biography, which must decide what's relevant and what isn't. The life of a person born 180 years ago was lived in a world wholly different from our own. We no longer respond to some of the most important things in Ruskin's life; his drawing, for instance. He founded a school of drawing at Oxford. He drew all of his life, taught drawing (at Working Men's College in London, as well as by correspondence for many years), wrote about drawing, breathed drawing. Hilton keeps us aware of this, but I wonder if, in an age when drawing is something artists are ashamed of and masterful draftsmen like Norman Rockwell and Paul Cadmus are considered despicable, this attention won't prove invisible.

Then there's Ruskin's world. His Venice, every stone of which he knew the history of, may as well be a different place than the one backpackers look in on. Our Venice is another Italian city; Ruskin's was another world. He traveled in a comfortable carriage, like Montaigne in his day. He stopped to draw wildflowers, clouds, rivers.

In all of Ruskin's travels there is an urgency—not like ours, to see notable places before we die or are too old to travel, but to see them while they yet exist, to see Venice before it sank into the sea, before Austrian shells destroyed more of San Marco, before fire and earthquake and renovation had their way. He had a prophetic sense that the darkening of European skies by industrial smoke portended some disaster. He rages in *Fors* at the burning of the Tuileries Palace in 1871. Within a few years of his death the Germans burned the medieval library at Louvain and German shells began to hit the cathedral at Amiens, about which he had written his most fervent study of Gothic architecture. Seventy French cathedrals were blown to rubble by German artillery in the First World War.

When Sir Edward T. Cook and Alexander Wedderburn brought out their *Works of John Ruskin* between 1903 and 1912 (thirty-nine volumes), a masterfully edited and annotated work, Ruskin's popularity was in sharp decline. In his lifetime he had attracted all manner of idealists, from a bottle-cork-cutter who belonged to the Guild of St. George, to Prince Leopold, who attended his Oxford lectures. We need only look at his centrality to Henry Adams's *Mont-Saint-Michel and Chartres* (1904), at the romantic Socialism of William Morris and Oscar Wilde, at Adrian Stokes's *Stones of Rimini,* at Pound's early *Cantos.* We need a study of Ruskin's *rayonnement*: Rodin's study of French cathedrals, Charles Sheeler's photographs of Chartres, Proust's preface to his translation of *Sesame and Lilies* (1905), three lectures on the availability of culture to everybody, in libraries ("Kings' treasuries") and nature ("Queens' gardens"). It can be demonstrated that the Arts and Crafts Movement that spread across Europe and the United States was largely inspired by Ruskin, and that his medievalism and championing of organic design flowered in Art Nouveau (the first international style since the twelfth century). One might even argue that this century's Modernism, whose theories were incubated at the Bauhaus and in Moscow—Art Nouveau with the lines straightened— comes out of Ruskin and Morris.

As finely textured and interesting as Hilton's biography is—as interesting in its plot and characters as a George Eliot novel—it is still, problematically, a life of a Victorian giant whose work is nowadays unread. Hilton himself admits that he has met practically no one who has read more than a few pages of *Fors Clavigera.* Who reads *any* of Ruskin? There are set pieces in antholo-gies ("The Nature of Gothic," for instance). Yet all of Ruskin was one big rambling work, and a real familiarity with him is practically equivalent to a university education. Hilton's most tempting offer for readers is to follow the fated derivation of each of Ruskin's books from *Modern Painters,* written in five volumes from 1843 to 1860. This first and seminal work, with its empha-sis on landscape painting, leads to studies of actual landscape, and from there to cities and cathedrals. Already in *The Stones of Venice,* completed in 1850, Ruskin's attention was turning to the interplay of art and economics, and to the sociology and politics of the Middle Ages as medieval people experiment-ed with small republics.

When Victorian readers opened *The Stones of Venice* in 1851 they learned on its first page that three great island cities—"three thrones, of mark beyond all others"—had ruled vast empires. They were Bible readers all, and if they could not readily remember just where Tyre, the first of these cities, had been located, Ruskin's allusion to Ezekiel's description of it (the most glorious description of a city in all of literature) reminded them. The desolation of the second city, Venice, had been mourned in a sonnet everyone knew, "On the Extinction of the Venetian Republic," by Wordsworth (whose death the year before, in 1850, was fresh in English minds). We do not think of Venice as a "ruin," but Ruskin and the Victorians did. That God would eventually smite the third island city, London, was a romantic idea that nobody believed—the British Empire fall!—but readers were thrilled to hear the pious warning that it assuredly would "if it forget" the fate of Tyre and Venice. Later in the cen-tury an ardent reader of Ruskin and nephew of Ruskin's friend Sir Edward Burne-Jones would repeat this warning in a knell to Ruskin's England, Rudyard Kipling's "Recessional."

Venice is not really sinking: the sea is rising up over it. It is a city built on wooden piles driven into sand. Its origins bespeak the fact that the barbarians who poured into Italy in the early years of the first millennium came on hors-es. If you built a city offshore, you had foiled these fur-clad, long-bearded Huns and Goths. The city's name may echo the people mentioned in the sev-enth century B.C. by the Greek poet Alcman: the Wenetioi, who bred long-maned horses as beautiful as girls. Their knack for wandering became a Venetian talent: a Venetian merchant named for the evangelist who lies entombed in the chapel of the Ducal Palace, Mark, and for the wandering missionary, Paul—Marco Polo in the local dialect—is the first European to visit China. For trade was the source of Venice's wealth. Its navy denuded the Dalmatian coast for masts. Its people became rich, as Shakespeare knew, beyond all imagining. They ate not with their fingers, like Queen Elizabeth, but with forks. Their warehouses were laden with silk, spices, weapons, Egyptian cotton, Sicilian wheat, silver, and gold. After 1450 they printed the world's most beautiful books, in Hebrew, Greek, and Latin. It was this perfection of civilization that Ruskin studied in fine detail. Its energy had lasted for well over a thousand years, always perilously and always brilliantly, holding off Turks, mainland Italians, enemies from over the Alps. When Ruskin first saw Venice, an enormous painting by Tiepolo hung in shreds inside the Ducal Palace (which had been hit by Austrian artillery) and the roof was open to rain.

Ruskin's Newdigate Prize poem at Oxford had been about Romantic ruins (those at Salsette and Elephanta in India). John William Burgon's "Petra"—with its one memorable line: "A rose-red city half as old as time"— is the best known of the Newdigates. For many years their subjects, set by the chancellor, were meditations on Volney's prose work *Les Ruines* (1791), which had inspired Shelley's "Ozymandias." Even Macaulay imagined a future New Zealand poet gazing on the ruins of London Bridge. Archaeology in Ruskin's lifetime gave the history of civilizations a deeper past. Geologists were tracing strata of rock with coherent fossils of flora and fauna from Siberia to Michigan: orders of nature that, like civilizations, had flourished and disappeared millions of years ago. The past seemed to be not one creation, as in Genesis, but many, each canceled by awesome catastrophes followed by a new beginning.

What Ruskin saw in all this was that civilizations that took thousands of years to mature could be destroyed in a second. One Austrian shell through the roof of San Marco could make ashes of a Veronese. Time itself is enemy enough of the arts: watercolors and photographs are irrevocably fading. Automobile exhaust in our time is eating the Parthenon. Turner's paintings, as Ruskin observed, kept their brilliant colors for a few hours only, losing their intensity as they dried. The skies of Europe were darkening. Venice was disappearing into the Adriatic.

Ruskin had traced European painting from Turner back to its medieval beginnings, architecture back to the Romanesque. He had consistently laid down an ethics and a morality for individual works and styles. Egyptian art was executed by slaves; how could it be good? Greek art was sensual and therefore morally suspect. Ruskin burned Turner's pornographic drawings (and Charles Eliot Norton, after Ruskin's death, burned Ruskin's correspondence with Rose La Touche). Victorians thought in categories of foul and fair. The aristocracy knew "what's done, and what isn't done"—a taboo system much stronger than law.

Ruskin's mind evolved, book by book. He thought and *felt* his way out of Victorian constraints, or tried to, and went mad in the process. Hilton charts this dramatic change, an awakening that was as tragic as Lear and as triumphant as Spinoza's escape from dogma and superstition into crystalline reason. Ruskin did not abandon his evangelical fundamentalism; he transformed it. He evolved a philosophy of religion in which morality and art were complementary and mutually vital.

His sense of the foul and fair became a new energy. England's economic system was foul. It created more *illth* (a word he coined) than wealth. Its proponents, moreover, didn't know what real wealth was. They had lost their sense of moral decency (Ruskin resigned his professorship at Oxford rather than countenance vivisection in the medical school). Ruskin decided that Turner's glorious paganism had been fair, that the soul does not survive the death of the body, that the grace of God was as evident in Aristotle as in St. Paul. The England he began to imagine in *Fors Clavigera* was to be organized in accordance with this new value system: a socialist society devoted to justice, significant work (handicraft rather than manufacture), administered by benevolent "captains" of guilds, with happy clean children and noble stonemasons like the ones who had raised Chartres in French fields.

Hilton promises us a study of *Fors* as a sort of third volume of his biography. The book still belongs to the distinguished list of worthy and influential works that are almost never read even by those interested in literature and ideas: Burton's *Anatomy of Melancholy,* Doughty's *Travels in Arabia Deserta,* Horace Traubel's *Conversations with Walt Whitman in Camden,* Thoreau's *Week on the Concord and Merrimack Rivers,* the Bible. The one book of Ruskin's that people seem to read, *Praeterita,* began as a part of *Fors.*

A more eccentric work than *Fors Clavigera* had never been written (unless it is *Tristram Shandy*). The book's original purpose, to found the Guild of St. George, becomes incidental. Its hero is Theseus; its Ariadne, Rose La Touche; and its Minotaur is the economics of capitalism, laissez-faire business, banks, usury, and the kind of advertising that makes the inferior product seem to be the best. In short, our own world of engineered obsolescence, scoundrels in high places, and eleven different taxes and surcharges on one telephone bill.

One of the oldest images in world art and literature is that of a hero—Gilgamesh, Odysseus, Samson, Beowulf, St. George, and perhaps the one hunter on the cave walls at Lascaux—facing a monster, a dragon, a demon. On the night of February 22, 1878, at Brantwood, the fifty-nine-year-old Ruskin fought with the Devil. He took off all his clothes, to be armorless like

David before Goliath. Being Ruskin, he wrote it all down in his diary, before and after. Hilton analyzes these cryptic, terrifying, and pitiful pages with subtlety and insight. It was a battle of symbol against symbol—a St. Anthony contending with hallucinations. Faith fought with doubt, fair fought with foul, sanity with insanity. Ruskin's servant found him at dawn, naked and freezing, out of his mind.

These paranoid seizures would return with increasing ferocity. Ruskin, the most decent of men, would curse Joan Severn (whom he normally wrote to in baby talk), accusing her and her husband of being freeloaders and layabouts. He thought the cook was Queen Victoria. He gathered the household on their knees at the front door to confess to Cardinal Manning. He became so impossible that Joan agreed to his leaving Brantwood for a boarding house in Folkestone, where he was lonely, disoriented, and a stranger among strangers.

The great mind that had been so skilled in perception in Ruskin's youth and so omnidirectional in his maturity flared into an incandescent irrationality, and went out. For his last ten years he sat in his room at Brantwood, shielded by the Severns. Turner, too, had gone batty, Swift and Nietzsche, Emerson and John Clare. Ruskin's madness had a kind of logic to it: his frustrated loves, his failure to make people understand his vision of a just society, and his religious doubts compounded his despair. Add old age, a cruelly trussed hernia (from dancing a jig), loneliness, and disembodied voices.

Biographies grasp the exteriors of lives and give what account they can of their interiors. These can be wholly different realities. The existence in space and time of the art historians Max Raphael and Erwin Panofsky, two great inheritors of what Ruskin began, will be dramatic and interesting when we have biographies of them as complete as Hilton's of Ruskin, but until we read their books our knowledge of them is little better than ignorance. Curiously, we don't believe this. I know several intelligent people who have read biographies of Joyce and Wittgenstein but not Joyce and Wittgenstein. Hilton's immensely readable and meticulously researched life of Ruskin will be read by hundreds of people who have never read a word of Ruskin and probably won't.

What they will miss is Ruskin's voice. It is, even at its most querulous and preacherly, not writing but speaking. It is, in a beautiful sense, thinking aloud, at its most congenial, conversational, richly anecdotal, and always observant. He is the world's best companion for looking at a Venetian building or Gothic carving. He can tell you that the stone flowers that seem to be mere decoration at the top of a cathedral column grow wild in the fields round about. He takes nothing for granted; his readers are children to be taught, to be beguiled into learning. For one of his Oxford lectures he brought a plow, to make certain that his students knew what one looked like. (The lecture was on sculpture.) He could make passages from the Bible sound like words you had never heard before. A lecture that began with Michelangelo ended with the proper shoes for little girls; one on landscape painting ended with the industrial pollution of rivers and what to do about it. Most of the problems Ruskin addressed are ours as well. The century that began in the year of his death saw the most terrible wars in all of recorded time; and cruelty, without shame or pity, has gone on disgracing humanity. For fifty years Ruskin tried to show us how to live and how to praise.

THE CONCORD SONATA

AN AUTUMN AFTERNOON

At his small sanded white pine table in his cabin at Walden Pond on which he kept an arrowhead, an oak leaf, and an *Iliad* in Greek, Henry David Thoreau worked on two books at once. In one, *A Week on the Concord and Merrimac Rivers,* he wrote: Give me a sentence which no intelligence can understand. In the other, *Walden, or Life in the Woods,* he wrote three such sentences, a paragraph which no intelligence can understand: I long ago lost a hound, a bay horse, and a turtledove, and am still on their trail. Many are the travellers whom I have spoken concerning them, describing their tracks and what calls they answered to. I have met one or two who had heard the hound, and the tramp of the horse, and even seen the dove disappear behind a cloud, and they seemed as anxious to recover them as if they had lost them themselves.

JOHN BURROUGHS

Thoreau did not love Nature for her own sake, or the bird and the flower for their own sakes, or with an unmixed and disinterested love, as Gilbert White did, for instance, but for what he could make out of them. He says: The ultimate expression or fruit of any created thing is a fine effluence which only the most ingenuous worshiper perceives at a reverent distance from its surface even. This *fine effluence* he was always reaching after, and often grasping or inhaling. This is the mythical hound and horse and turtledove which he says in *Walden* he long ago lost, and has been on their trail ever since. He never abandons the search, and in every woodchuck hole or muskrat den, in retreat of bird, or squirrel, or mouse, or fox that he pries into, in every walk and expedition to the fields or swamps or to distant woods, in every spring note and call that he listens to so patiently, he hopes to get some clew to his lost treasures, to the effluence that so provokingly eludes him.

This search of his for the transcendental, the unfindable, the wild that will not be caught, he has set forth in this beautiful parable in Walden.

GEESE

Well now, that Henry. Thursday one of the Hosmer boys told him he'd heard geese. He wants to know everything anybody can tell him in the way of a bird or skunk or weed or a new turn to the wind. Well, Henry knew damned good and well that it's no time to be hearing geese. So, always assuming his leg wasn't being pulled, he sat down and thought about it. And after awhile, didn't take him long, he got up and walked to the station. He didn't ask. He told Ned that at half past one on Thursday a train had passed through with a crate of geese in the baggage car. That's a fact, Ned said, but I don't recollect anybody being around here at the time.

STANLEY CAVELL

I have no new proposal to offer about the literary or biographical source of these symbols in perhaps his most famously cryptic passage. But the very fact that they are symbols, and function within a little myth, seems to me to tell us what we need to know. The writer comes to us from a sense of loss; the myth does not contain more than symbols because it is no set of desired things he has lost, but a connection with things, the track of desire itself.

THE JOURNAL: 1 APRIL 1860

The fruit of a thinker is sentences: statements or opinions. He seeks to affirm something as true. I am surprised that my affirmations or utterances come to me ready-made, not fore-thought, so that I occasionally wake in the night simply to let fall ripe a statement which I never consciously considered before, and as surprisingly novel and agreeable to me as anything can be.

6

And yet we did unbend so far as to let our guns speak for us, when at length we had swept out of sight, and thus left the woods to ring, again with their echoes; and it may be many russet-clad children, lurking in those broad meadows with the bittern and the woodcock and the rail, though wholly concealed by brakes and hardhack and meadowsweet, heard our salute that afternoon.

7

Solitude, reform, and silence.

8

In *A Week on the Concord and Merrimac Rivers* Thoreau wrote: Mencius says:
If one loses a fowl or a dog, he knows well how to seek them again; if one loses
the sentiments of the heart, he does not know how to seek them again. The
duties of all practical philosophy consist only in seeking after the sentiments
of the heart which we have lost; that is all.

9

Duke Hsuan of Qi arranged his skirts and assumed a serene face to receive
the philosopher Meng Tze, and who knows how many devils had come with
him? The magicians had drilled the air around the gates with incessant
drumming, and the butlers were burning incense.

The duke could see wagons of millet on the yellow road. The philosopher
had apparently travelled in some humble manner. From the terrace he could
see no caravan. There was no commotion among the palace guard.

Sparrows picked among the rocks below the bamboo grove.

A merchant was handing in a skip of persimmons and a string of carp at
the porter's lodge. The weather was dry.

The philosopher when he was ushered in was indeed humble. His clothes
were coarse but neat, and his sleeves were modest. He wore a scholar's cap
with ear flaps.

They met as gentlemen skilled in deference and courtly manners, bow for
bow. The duke soon turned their talk to this feudal baron or that, angling for
news. There had for years been one war after another.

—And yet, Meng Tze said, the benevolent have no enemies.

Duke Hsuan smiled. Philosophers were always saying idiotic things like this.

—The grass, Meng Tze continued, stands dry and ungrowing in the seventh
month and the eighth. Then clouds darken the sky. Rain falls in torrents. The
grass, the millet, the buckwheat, the barley turns green again, and grows
anew. Nothing we are capable of can control this process of nature. And yet
men who ought to be the caretakers of other men kill them instead. They are
pleased to kill. If there were a ruler who did not love war, his people would
look at him with longing, loving eyes. It is in nature to love the benevolent.

So there was to be no gossip about Hwan of Ch'i, or Wan of Tsin. So the
duke asked politely:

—How may a ruler attain and express benevolence?

—He should regard his people as his charges and not with contempt.

—Am I one, the duke asked slyly, who might be so benevolent?

—Yes.

—How?

—Let me tell you about a duke. I had this from Hu Ho. A duke was sitting
in his hall when he saw a man leading an ox through the door. The duke

asked why, and was told that the ox was to be slaughtered, to anoint a cere-
monial bell with its blood. Just so, said the duke, but don't do it. I cannot bear
the fear of death in its eyes. Kill a sheep instead.

—This is a thing I did, the duke replied. You have learned of things in
my court.

—Yes, Meng Tze said with a smile. And I see hope for you in it. It was not
the ox but your heart you were sparing.

—The people thought otherwise. They said I begrudged an ox. Qi is but a
small dukedom, but I can afford the sacrifice of an ox. It had such innocent
eyes and it did not want to die.

—And yet you sent for a sheep. You knew the pity you felt for the ox. How
was the sheep different?

—You make a point, the duke said. You show me that I scarcely know my
own mind.

—The minds of others, rather.

—Yes. You are searching for compassion in me, aren't you? In *The Book of the
Odes* it is written *the minds of others I am able by reflection to measure.* You have
seen why I spared the ox and was indifferent to the misery of the sheep. I did
not know my own mind.

—If, Meng Tze said with great politeness, you will allow me to play that lute
there by the bronze and jade vessels, I will sing one of the most archaic of the
odes, as part of our discourse.

The duke with correct deference asked him by all means to sing it.
Meng Tze, finding the pitch, sang:

The world's order is in the stars.
We are its children, its orphans.
Cicadas shrill in the willows.

It is not fault, it is not guilt
That has brought us to this. It is
Disorder. We were not born to it.
The autumn moon is round and red.
I have not troubled the order,
Yet I am no longer in it.

In the first waywardness we could
Have gone back. In the second we
Began to confuse lost and found.

Had we been angry to be lost,
Would we have taken disorder
For order, if any had cared?

Cicadas shrill in the willows.
There was a time we had neighbors.
The autumn moon is round and red.

Men without character took us
Into the marshes, neither land
Nor river, where we cannot build.

Order is harmony. It is
Innovation in tradition.
The autumn moon is round and red.

Elastic words beguiled our ears.
What is the courage worth of fools?
Cicadas shrill in the willows.

Fat faces and slick tongues sold
Us disorder for real estate.
The autumn moon is round and red

The young lord's trees are tender green.
Saplings grow to be useful wood.
Hollow words are the wind blowing.

Cicadas shrill in the willows.
There was a time we had neighbors.
The autumn moon is round and red.

10

The dove is over water in Scripture: over the flood with an olive twig in its beak, the rainbow above; over the Jordan with Jesus and John in it, upon the sea as Jonah (which name signifieth *dove*), up out of the sea as Aphrodite (whose totem animal it was). It was the family name of the Admiral of the Ocean Sea.

The horse is the body, its stamina, health, and skills. The hound is faith and loyalty. But symbols are not sense but signs.

Mencius's Chinese cock (tail the color of persimmons, breast the color of the beech in autumn, legs blue) and unimaginable Chinese dog have become under Concord skies a biblical dove, a Rover, and a bay horse. The one is a pet, one is a friend, one is a fellow worker.

We lose not our innocence or our youth or opportunity but our nature itself, atom by atom, helplessly, unless we are kept in possession of it by the spirit of a culture passed down the generations as tradition, the great hearsay of the past.

11

Thoreau was most himself when he was Diogenes.

12

One ship *speaks* another when they pass on the high seas. There is a naval metaphor in the paragraph (misprinted as *spoken to* in modern ignorance). Thoreau and his brother John had sailed around the world in August of 1839, all on the Concord and Merrimac, and you could see him in his sailboat on the Concord with a crew of boys, or the smiling Mr. Hawthorne, or the prim Mr. Emerson.

CONVERSATION

The mouse, who left abruptly if Thoreau changed from one tune to another on his flute, was a good listener.

—A man who is moral and chaste, Mr. Thoreau said to the mouse, does not pry into the affairs of others, which may be very different from his own, and which he may not understand.

—Oh yes! said the mouse. But the affairs of others are interesting. You can learn all sorts of things.

—The housekeeping of my soul may seem a madman's to a Presbyterian or a bear.

The mouse twitched his whiskers. Offered a crumb of hoe-cake, he took it, sitting on Mr. Thoreau's sleeve, sniffed it, and began a diligent chewing.

The mouse knew all about the lead pencils and their inedible shavings, the surveyor's chain, the Anakreon in Greek (edible), the journal with pressed leaves between the pages, the fire (dangerous), the spider family in the corner (none of his business), but it was the flute and the cornmeal that bound him to Mr. Thoreau. And the friendliness.

14

The man under the enormous umbrella out in the snow storm is Mr. Thoreau. Inspecting, as he says. Looking for his dove, his hound, his horse.

15

Diogenes was an experimental moralist. He found wealth in owning nothing. He found freedom in being a servant. He discovered that owning was being owned. He discovered that frankness was sharper than a sword. If we act by design, by principle, we need designers. Designers need to search. Mr. Thoreau discovered that the dove is fiercer than a lion when he sat in the Concord jail, like Diogenes. Why should a government come to him to finance its war in Mexico and pay a clergy he could not listen to? Let them find their own money. Let them write laws an honest man can obey. He would write his sentences. That was his genius. Others might find them as useful as he found Diogenes's. The world is far from being over. When Mr. Emerson came to the jail and said, *Henry, what are you doing in here?* And he replied, *Rafe, what are you doing out there?* The words slipped loose like a dove into the spring sky, and were remembered in a London jail by Emmeline Pankhurst, in a South African jail by Mohandas Gandhi, in a Birmingham jail by Martin Luther King, and cannot be forgotten.

MEADOW

I remember years ago breaking through a thick oak wood east of the Great Fields and descending into a long, narrow, and winding blueberry swamp which I did not know existed there. A deep, withdrawn meadow sunk low amid the forest, filled with green waving sedge three feet high, and low andromeda, and hardhack, for the most part dry to the feet then, though with a bottom of unfathomed mud, not penetrable except in midsummer or midwinter, and with no print of man or beast in it that I could detect. Over this meadow the marsh-hawk circled undisturbed, and she probably had her nest in it, for flying over the wood she had long since easily discovered it. It was dotted with islands of blueberry bushes and surrounded by a dense hedge of them, mingled with the pannicled andromeda, high chokeberry, wild holly with its beautiful crimson berries, and so on, these being the front rank to a higher wood. Great blueberries, as big as old-fashioned bullets, alternated, or were closely intermingled, with the crimson hollyberries and black chokeberries, in singular contrast yet harmony, and you hardly knew why you selected those only to eat, leaving the others to the birds.

17

This text has been written first with a lead pencil (graphite encased in an hexagonal cedar cylinder) invented by Henry David Thoreau. He also invented a way of sounding ponds, a philosophy for being oneself, and raisin bread.

W.E.B. DUBOIS

Lions have no historians.

WITTGENSTEIN

If a lion could talk, we could not understand him.

20

Fear not, thou drummer of the night, we shall be there.

THE DEATH OF PICASSO
Het Erewhonisch Schetsboek:
GERMINAL, FLORÉAL, PRAIRIAL 1973

12 GERMINAL
Anderszins 2 april. Fog until almost noon. Wild glare in lakes over the sea. It has been but a month from putting in the eight-by-threes, treated with creosote and laid a foot and a half apart in the long northernish rectangle of our cabin's base, construction fir let into grey marl on the chine of an island, to the last sheet of shingling on the roof. An island that, as Archilochos said of his Thasos, lies in the sea like the backbone of an ass, Thasos a ridge of primrose marble in the *wijndonker Zee,* our Snegren a hump of old red sandstone in the cold North Sea. Plain as a shoebox, it is little more than a roof, chimney, and windows. The Eiland Commissaris did not bat an eyelash when I registered it under the name Snegren, *grensbewoner* being the allusion he supposed. Sander has already coined *snegrensbewoner,* Erewhonian pioneer. If I had explained that it is *nergens* reversed, he would have made a joke about so remote and *lilliputachtig* an island being precisely that, nowhere.

Parmenides is wrong: the nothing he will not allow to be is time itself. Time is the empty house that being inhabits. It may well be the ghost of something in the beginning, before light became matter. But it went away, so that something could be.

13 GERMINAL
Coffee, journal, a swim with Sander, just enough to count as a bath, the water Arctic. We built the Rietveld tensegrity table, razored labels off windowpanes, squared things away so that for the first time the long room begins to look like home, practised Corelli on our flutes, Telemann and Bach. Baroque progressions, the wind, the waves. Thoreau had a flute at Waldenpoel I think.

14 GERMINAL

Vincent's *Stilleven met uien*. It is the first painting he did after cutting off part of his ear according to the Sint Mattheus Evangelie. In a rage at Gauguin, a blusterer like Tartarin de Tarascon. They had a kind of marriage, those two, a companionship as chaste as that of the apostles Paulus and Barnabas. All their talk was of color and form, of *motif* and theme. But Gauguin would talk of the hot girls upstairs over the café and Vincent would stop his ears, and rage, and pray, and resort to Raspail's camphor treatments to ward off impurity. To talk of the Christus only generated blasphemies in Gauguin. What indulgence in the flesh did to the creative spirit was what syphilis did to the flesh itself; worse, to the mind. And Gauguin only laughed and called him a big Dutch crybaby.

The painting is a resolution, a charting of the waters after almost foundering. A drawing board in a room at Arles. It is as if we have zoomed in on a table top that had hitherto been a detail in all the scenes of Erasmus writing, of Sint Hieronymus with his books. The two things that are not on the board are a bottle of white wine and a jug of olive oil. The board is a bridge from one to the other.

The doctor's diagnosis of Vincent's hot nerves was based on learning that Vincent's diet for some weeks had been white wine and his pipe. Malnutrition! Look, *mon vieux,* anybody who subsists day after day on cheap wine and shag tobacco is going to cut off his ears. Nervous prostration: it is no wonder that you are out of your mind.

And in Raspail's *Annuaire de la santé,* there on the drawing board, the book that broke the doctors' monopoly and placed a knowledge of medicine in every humble home, it explains the nutritiousness of onions and olives, the efficacy of camphor in preventing wet dreams and lascivious thoughts.

The candle is lit: hope. Sealing wax: for letters to Theo. Matches, pipe, wine.

The letter is from Theo. It is addressed *Poste Restante* because Theo knew that Vincent had been turned out of his house. The postman, whose portrait Vincent had done, would know where he was. That is the postman's mark, the numeral 67 in a broken circle. The R in an octagon means that it is a registered letter: it contained a fifty-franc note.

There are two postage stamps on the letter, one green, one blue. The green one is a twenty-centime stamp of the kind issued between 1877 and 1900. The numeral 20 is in red. The only other French stamp with which Vincent's block of color might be identified is a straw-colored twenty-five centime one with the numeral 25 in yellow. Since the other stamp on the letter, however, is definitely the fifteen-centime of the same issue and is the only other blue stamp in use at the time, the post office in Paris would have affixed a forty-centime stamp to the letter rather than a fifteen and a twenty-five. There was no thirty-five centime denomination.

So unless the bureau had run short of the forty-centime denomination and unless petty exactitude is a new thing in French post offices, the stamps are the blue fifteen centimes, and green twenty-centime issues current at the time. The design on both, which Vincent made no attempt to indicate, was an ornate one: numeral in an upright tablet before a globe to the left on which stood an allegorical female figure with bay in her hair and bearing an olive branch. To the right, Mercurius in winged hat and sandals, and with the caduceus.

A harmony in gold and green.

15 GERMINAL

The Vincent *Onions* is the center of a triptych I think I have discovered. Vincent's chair, with pipe, is the right-hand piece, Gauguin's empty chair, the left-hand.

Sun burned through the fog quite early, and we rowed around the island in a wide loop, Sander stark naked. I had better sense: he was splotched with strawberry stains under the remnant of last year's tan, goose bumps all over. He stuck it out, though rowing with a will. In a blanket before a fire the rest of the morning.

16 GERMINAL

Warmer, and with an earlier lifting of fog. Even so, Sander turned out in jeans and sweater, sneezing. *Vrijdagheid als kameraadschap maar dubbelzinnig genoeg: men moet een gegeven knaap niet in het hart zien.* Caesar and Pompey look very much alike, especially Pompey. Sint Hieronymus with lion, breath like bee balm. Grocery lists, supplies. Reading Simenon: the perfect page for the fireside. Maigret is comfortable in a constant discomfort, wrapped in his coat, cosseted by food and his pipe.

In the post that old Hans had for us: Manfredo's *Progetto e Utopia,* with a note to say it will for the most play into my hands but has vulnerabilities (he means Marxist rhetoric) that I will go for with, as he says, my Dutch house-keeping mind. And Michel's *Cosmologie de Giordano Bruno.* Sander remarks that Italian looks like Latin respelled by an English tourist. Letters from Petrus and Sylvie, wondrous dull. Clerical humor, but it's worth knowing that Bergson went around calling the American pragmatist William Jones.

17 GERMINAL

Schubert's second quartet on the radio, fine against the mewing of gulls and the somber wash of the sea. A Soviet trawler in the channel.

Worked all day, off and on, at the iconographica. Neumann on Greek gesture, Marcel Jousse, Birdwhistell. Painter feels the body of the sitter as he works, two mimeses. Open hand in David, beauty of legs in Goya. Watch contours and see what else they bound other than the image we see: thus Freud found the scavenger bird. Philosophical rigor of moralists: Goya, Daumier, van Gogh. It has taken a century for drama to catch up with the painters. A line through Moliére, Callot, Jarry, Ionesco. Themes refine, become subtle and articulate from age to age: children who will become artists brood in window seats on art they absorb into the deep grain of their sensibilities: Mr. Punch and Pinocchio in the lap of Klee become metaphysical puppets in a series of *caprichos* to Mozart rather than the Spanish guitar.

Sander maps the island with compass and sighting sticks, reinventing geography and surveying.

18 GERMINAL

We hear on the radio that Picasso is dead. He was ninety-two.

19 GERMINAL

Sander in *Padvinder* boondoggle and Bike *skridtbind* rings the island double time. At the outcrop on the promontory he must scuttle up and spring down. The rest of his circumference is shore, shale, pebble, sand, his pace lyric and sweet. *Ah!* he gasps at the end of it, down on elbows and knees, panting like a dog. *Ah* is an undictionaried word implying joy, rich fatigue, accomplishment, fulfillment. How many such words are missing from the lexicon: the gasp after quenched thirst, the moo at finding food good, bleats and drones of sexual delirium, clucks, smacks, whistles, mungencies, whoops, burbles.

I ask why the boondoggle, out of waggish curiosity. I get a gape and stare and something like a bark. Patches of the young mind remain animal and inarticulate, not to be inspected by sophistication, such as a grave study of toes, heroic stretches on waking, the choice of clothes, the pleased mischief, lips pursed, eyebrows raised, of padding about in the torn and laundry-battered blue shirt only, *tumescens lascive mentula praeputio demiretracto*.

Een herinnering: Bruno at Sounion. August. Columns of the Poseidonos Tempel sublime and Ciceronian, purest blue the sky, indigo charged with lilac the sea, a brightness over all, light as clean as rain, every texture, stone, cicada, thorn, shards, pebbles, exact and clear. Vile Germans leaving as we arrived, laughing over some rudeness to a family of kind Americans. Two ironic French adolescents, boy and girl, playing at being amused by their own boredom. They shambled away. Another batch arriving, we could see, at the awful restaurant down the hill, adjusting cameras and sunglasses for the climb. Bruno set the reading on our camera and handed it to me. Pulled his jersey, then, over his head, *schadelijk*, bent and unlaced his sneakers, peeled off his socks, stepped out of his jeans, doffed his briefs, unbuckled his wristwatch. There are tourists coming, I said. One, he said, arms folded and legs spread.

Two: at easy attention by a pillar. Three: sitting, elbows on knees, a frank and engaging look into the lens. *Om godswil!* I cried. *O antiek wellustigheid!* he sang back. Four: profile, hands against a column. *Er vlug mee zijn!* Golden smile, glans roused and uncupped, left hand toying with pubic clump, right fist on hip. People, Japanese and British, Toyota executives and bottlers of marmalade, rounded the corner of the temple. Bruno into jeans as an eel under a rock, into shirt, buttoning up cool as you please as the first foreign eyes found him. Into socks and sneakers as they passed. British lady stared at his briefs lying on brown stone in brilliant light, their crop dented, convex, feral, male. Reached them over, slapped them against his thigh, and stuffed them in his pocket. And what in the name of God was all that? *Grieks,* he said.

20 GERMINAL

His 75 years of meditation on a still life: this is like a sonnet cycle, the progression of Montaigne's essays, Rembrandt's and Van Gogh's self-portraits. A natural rhythm, as all the variations of fish and leaf make a coherent harmony. A fish is a leaf.

Wine, bread, table: his Catholic childhood. Perhaps his Catholic life. Lute, guitar, mandolin: the Spanish ear, which abides life as a terrible dream made tolerable by music.

Spain and Holland. Felipe's expulsion of farmers and bankers, whom he saw with fanatic eyes as Muslims and Jews, shifted the counting houses to Holland. Spain dreamed on in its pageant of men dressed in black and women in shawls, surrounded by agonies they kept as symbols to validate, as ritual, the cruelty they claimed as their piety: the lynching of ecstatics, heretics, and humanists, the slaughtering of bulls, the sending of navies and armies against all other cultures of the Mediterranean.

Silver to the east, pepper to the west, silver and pepper, wool and cloves, gold and wheat, cannon and Titians. And on this theme the old man ended, with a vision of sworded gallants idiotic in the cruelty of their pride, women as a separate species, available by property deeds, a blade through a gut, a trunk of coins, a point of honor precluding reason or forgiveness.

His study of Velazquez parallels the researches of Braudel; his intuition of a deeper past rivals the century's classical studies, the prehistorians, the anthropologists.

21 GERMINAL

Een herinnering: Paris 1947. A glimpse, a mere passing sight of Picasso inside the Deux Magots, before a bottle of Perrier at a table, his hair combed across his bald head in a last desperate coiffure, already grey. But there he was. Bruno has seen Max Ernst walking his poodle on the Avenue Foch.

Sander begins a notebook of our island's natural history, climbs trees to include our neighbor islands in his map, exercises like an acrobat. How smoothly he is beginning to forget I dare not guess.

22 GERMINAL

We row over for newspapers and mail, a cold and blustery voyage, and wet. Water and wind are a havoc of power. We are colonists who can make an excursion back to Europe, shopping list in hand.

A blind old Minotaur pulls his household goods along in a cart, washpot, skillet, quilts, mangle, bust of Lillie Langtry, framed lithograph of Napoleon, rotary eggbeater, bread board, Raspail's *Home Medical Practitioner,* a felt hat from Milan, a map of Corsica, a sack of roasted chicory, the key to a barn, tongs, a reading lamp mounted on a porcelain parrot, bulbs of garlic, a tobacco tin containing fishhooks, brass centimes from the Occupation, buttons, a bullet, a feather from the tail of an owl.

Sander says he discovers that shopping can be fun, and I try to penetrate his meaning. Is it that the ordinary becomes known only as the unusual? It is the convenient we are giving up, what he agreed to, with diffidence, when I offered him the stint on the island.

23 GERMINAL

O well, says Sander, *O well.* He organizes himself at various times of day by turning in circles, batting the air with his hands. An inventory of energies. He glances at the pages of this journal, briefly, as if to register that writing is a thing I do, like reading, walking. I keep thinking that he is a median between Bruno and Itard's Victor, between urban sophistication and benign savagery. He has a penchant for botany and zoology. That is, those subjects caught his fancy. Spells badly. Found all the sociological courses meaningless and history is still so much hash.

24 GERMINAL

Jean Marc Gaspard Itard, *De l'Education d'un homme sauvage, ou des premiers developpemens physiques et moraux du jeune sauvage de l'Aveyron,* Vendémiaire an X.

The pathos is one all teachers feel, all parents. Repeated now by the American psychologists training chimpanzees to sign with deaf-and-dumb hand language. Itard's Victor had had his attention fixed by his own strategies for survival in a forest. So are all attentions fixed. His skills were animal and they were successful. Eat, scutter to safety, hide from enemies, sleep, forage. He was unfamiliar with fire, with warmth, and loved in Paris to roll naked in the snow.

De Gaulle remarked, from under that nose, that we raise our own Vandals. What is the grief I feel when I admit the truth of that? I also deny it.

25 GERMINAL

The feeling again yesterday afternoon that the hour belonged to a previous, perhaps future, time, but was decidedly not *now*. I was looking out of the window, at afternoon light on bushes, in an elation of melancholy, savoring one truth and another without fear or anxiety, at peace with myself. Then this deliciously strange feeling that time is nothing, or is my friend rather than my enemy.

Time, like the sea, is layered into nekton, plankton, and benthos.

Long deep rhythms like the turning of the planets and the drift of the stars, the decay of matter, the old-turtle creep of continents around the globe. Evolution. Over which lie the adagio rhythms of history, the play of fire over burning sticks.

Picasso at the last was gazing at the immediate pressures of Renaissance Spain on the France of Georges Pompidou: moth flicker of individual sensibilities around a flame of money, cherished proprieties, romance, a dreaming life with no notion of what it is to be awake, the sleep of reason. He felt the tension between the Netherlands and Madrid, north and south, prudence and passion. Titian and Rembrandt, and yet his heart was with those foragers who suffered the violence of making sense of these extremes, Van Gogh and Rimbaud, Rousseau le Douanier.

His genius was satisfied with two forms only: still life and tableau. He stepped over the moment of Cézanne, Manet, Courbet like a giant negligently striding over a garden whose order and brilliance were none of his concern. All of his tenderness is like a Minotaur gazing at a cow. There was sweetness in the regard, submerged in a primal animality. He was like a grandee from the Spanish courts trying to behave himself among people with polished manners, books, philosophy, graciousness. He played their game, assumed French liberalism, pledged brotherhood with Marxist babblers, commanded charm enough to make friends with civilized people like Gertrude Stein and Cocteau, Apollinaire and Braque. Barcelona stood him in good stead.

26 GERMINAL

Roads, paths, and rivers in XIXth Century painting. And windows. Corridors was their theme, and corridors for the eye. Picasso sidestepped this brilliant understanding of the world, and returned to the theatrical, the Spanish room that is not properly a room but a cell, a dark place. The Spanish have no love for or understanding of roads. They are perilous in *Quijote,* bandit-ridden in Spanish history. Suspicious stay-at-homes, the Spanish. A public place is still vulgar, one's dignity can be exposed to the affront of a stare. A morbid pride, which Goya saw as insanity.

How lovely Paris must have seemed to the young Picasso, with its guileless Max Jacob, laughing Apollinaire, rich Americans who were affable, friendly, and intelligent: Miss Stein, Miss Toklas, the sisters Cone, John Quinn, people who knew nothing of the dark anguish of the Spanish mind. Sander making a list, with characteristics, of our birds. We cannot identify the half of them.

Hò siokómos skaphiókouros orchídionon monózonos.

Corelli sarabandes, good talk by the fire, the wind in a huffle after sunset making a humpenscrump of the waves and trees.

27 GERMINAL

De dageraad met rooskleurige vingeren. Coffee, journal in a seat on the rocks, warm enough for shorts and *visnet jersey.* Fine iodine kelpy green smell of the sea. No fog at all, a sharp sight of all the islands around us. Yachts. *The life!* crowed Sander naked.

Itard failed with Victor (assuming that Victor was not an idiot, which no evidence indicates) because he was trying to teach him manners.

He should have allowed himself to be taught by Victor, as the cat teaches us the rules of a companionship, as Griaule learned from the Dogon.

Teacher as student, an inside-out idea. Useful where applicable.

Art is bad when it is poor in news, dull, and has no rich uncle to boast of. Culture abhors a plenum and has its finest moments hunting on a lean day.

Philosophy is the husband of art: the civility they beget is not a hostage to fortune but our fortune itself.

Nature has no destiny for us: our boat is upon her ocean and in her winds, but she has expended as much ingenuity designing the flea as she has expended on us, and is perfectly indifferent to Hooke's conversation at Garroway's Coffee House. We, however, perish the instant we take our eyes off nature.

28 GERMINAL

One of the things Hooke said at Garroway's was that he suspected insects of being the husbands of flowers. Fourier was capable of believing that as fact.

Schets: Quaggas at noon under mimosa green and gold, graceful and grey like mules by Gaudier-Brzeska, with boughs of silver silk, stripeless zebras, gazelles with heft.

Does Fourier's uncluttered imagination belong to philosophy or art? I see him surviving in the verve and color of Roger de la Fresnaye, Delaunay, Lurçat. Was he a philosopher at all? Braque is the better epistemologist.

Something of a serious talk with Sander. I tell him that he can go back to Amsterdam anytime he wants, but to Dokter Tomas. The terms and happenstance of the custody, which is entirely informal and fortuitous.

I suggest that we are on a voyage, the island our ship, that we are Crusoe and Friday, two characters out of Rousseau living civilizedly as savages.

29 GERMINAL

We learn on the radio that Picasso was painting a picture when he died. Water and land. When they found the first dinosaur track in America, a three-toed footprint in old red sandstone, the *predikant* (top hat, frock coat, buttoned leggings) said it was the *voetspoor* of Noah's raven. Grey troubled waters everywhere, and the raven's cry the only sound over their tumult.

A red cry. And next the dove, olive sprig, and ground. The rivers went back to their beds, the sky to blue, a rainbow spanning the shining mud. Out onto which ventured goose and gander, hen and cock, quagga, mastodon, dik-dik, ostrich, tarpan, opossum, elk, baboon.

Sander notes that already we have our *schapewei* around the island, our movements preferring a path. I have not mentioned routine except to insist that beds be made, dishes and cookware washed, the lime turned and renewed in the outhouse, clothes hung up, and so on. Surprised that he likes sweeping a floor.

30 GERMINAL

Vreemheid en tovermiddel! A shore of gulls, quarreling and milling in a clutter of white. *Quark!* they squawk in Joyce, giving physicists a name for a hypothetical particle that has the hypothetical quality charm. Clustered and clinging to the nucleus of an atom, they congregate as hadrons, or if paired with an antiquark, a kaon, which is perhaps a charmed meson, or disintegration of light into matter, a process in which some quarks display strangeness, some display charm, with so ready an affinity that kaons and mesons exchange the one quality for the other as a firefly flicks off and on. It is thought that strange quarks prefer to couple with charmed quarks, electric bees quick for the rich of the nectar.

Tributes to Picasso on the radio: Malraux, Pompidou, Miró, Chagall, some functionary of the Spanish government in exile. He was not, it turns out, painting when he died. He had dined as usual, with Jacqueline and some friends, excused himself to go to his studio, painted a last canvas, presumably one of the courtcard cavaliers or duennas, and went to bed. He died in his sleep. Eighty-five years of drawing, painting, sculpting!

Sander comments that he finds chastity interesting, that word, interesting. *Moedernaakt, waarachtig, met een starende blik op zijn penis.*

I tell him, with coffee after supper on the shingle, the sea changing from its silver and rose of day's end to the flint and gleaming greys of dusk, about Ludwig Hänsel's *Die Jugend und die leibliche Liebe* that Wittgenstein found so strangely moving and Otto Weininger's *Geschlecht und Charakter*. The phrase *sexual purity of boys* got me a sideways glance of comic surmise. Why don't they know, he asks, after all this time? Mentioned Marcuse's perception of tolerance as repression, and bandied ideas about. Thought is enhanced by the tumble of waves, the sound of rain. I remark that so much forbidding sweetened the value of the forbidden. Man has always savored the irony of having to believe an idea and its opposite. All these furry old doctors, Sander says. Even so, I've had it with too much. Innocence is regenerative, he is teaching me.

I FLOREAL

Window washing, painting the trim outside, a swim, a run in the boat. We become brown.

Through the chryselectric green with goatstep, ramshorns curled, sharp of eye, satyrs. Their musk precedes them, armpit and honeysuckle. Quince flower descant upon a rackle of billy pizzle. Tuscan tan and with the visages of Italic gods, their pentathletic torsos flow with bestial grace into dappled haunches. Stag tails frisking up from the holybone wag above the flat of narrow butts.

One munches an apple, one buzzes his lips like a hornet, the third twiddles the radical of his stegocephalic posthon. Their knowledge of the gods is intuitive, fretful, dark. Of Zeus they know but the suddenness of the lightning and the thunder's hackling of its neck, hateful winds, snow, and rain. Artemis they know as the Mother of the Bears. Hera they do not know. Their Lord of the Dance is not Apollo but Pan, whom they call Humper. Asklepios is Snake, Demeter the apple, pear, and plum, Persephatta the poppy and the wren.

Their language is inhuman. They can chatter with the squirrels, using squirrel words among themselves to bound their peripatesis. For time they use the vocabulary of the grey wolf, for elegy and boast the nicker and whinny of the horse, for familiar discourse a patois of birdsong, fox bark, goat bleat, and the siffle and mump of their cousins the deer.

Hesiod first mentions them, *the race of satyrs about which nothing can be done.* In Sicily they are called Tityrs. Silenos the friend of Dionysos was one of them, prophet and drunkard. I see Asia in this detail, a transference onto the leafgod Dushara through whom the dead speak of some shaman whose trance came from wine.

The true satyrs were shy woods creatures whose only boldness was in mounting hamadryads, fauns, maelids, sheep and their snubnosed shepherd, goats and their darkeyed goatherd, country girls out berrying, pious wives at the spring, anything with penetrable *pterygomata* into which their impudent *saunia* might squeeze, poke, slide, prod, or slurp. Neither voluptuaries nor lovers, they never thought to mention in their talk of weather and time with the wolves that the day had seen them chase and hump a nimble wench and her cow, a brace of oreads whom they found in each other's arms, a pastureful of horses, and an hysterical swan.

Coffee and notebook on the heart. A fire of sticks and fircones feels good in the evening. A domestic animal, fire.

2 FLOREAL

Writing in our seat on the big rock, the day sweet and gentle, Sander beside me just out of the sea, out of wholly unconscious habit, scritched Sander's tummy along the mesial, nudged the lens of water from his navel, and was tracing absentminded patterns when he said with singsong parody that Dokter Tomas had vetted me as gentleman, scholar, and man of letters whose *beschaafde manieren* were supposed to be a model and an inspiration to a teenager with fried nerves and staring at the wall. Three weeks of carpentry had cured that, together with fresh air, the sea, and the company of a philosopher. *Niettegenstande dat,* he said, see the willful nosecone volunteer to join in.

3 FLOREAL

Scumble sienna over bronzen green, the ruddle gold. The wax is vermillion, to pick up the *vert Louis XV* of the bottle on the other end of the diagonal. With a charcoal stub he put in the lines of the drawing board. Two corners would be out of the picture, as in Degas, as Hokusai would want it, as the perspective frame indicated.

He will eat the onions, but first he will eat them with his eyes. He put two of them on the white plate, the third beside the plate. Two quick rectangles with the charcoal: letter and book. A fourth onion on the book, on Raspail. Box of matches.

Bottle in the lower left corner, both in and out of the frame, something for the eye to move over. A jug of olive oil beyond the drawing board, contrast and balance. Shag tobacco in its paper, open. His pipe.

The onion on Raspail's book begins the meaning. Then candle, lit, immediately above. Theo's letter with a burnt match laid against it. *Stilleven met uien, tabak, pijp, kaars, een brief.*

The still life is the painter's sonnet, the painter's essay. Did he dare to put in an allusion to Ricord as well? No, for Raspail was Ricord enough.

He had tried to make himself clear about Ricord in a letter to Theo soon after he cut off his ear, was it two weeks ago already? Three? It was in his reply to the letter with the fifty francs that he was putting in the still life. He had been oblique, comparing Raspail and Ricord. If Theo understood, he did not say. Delacroix and after him Seurat had sorted out the colors into their components, like ancient men sorting out the notes of the scale, the Goncourts were sorting out the emotions, and Ricord had distinguished between the two dread diseases caught through the genitals. One never went away, but moved through the system until it reached the spine and the brain. It caused madness. The other was a disease that could be cured, though never with complete certainty. He did now know which he had. But one could hope.

And one could make a vow, with the help of the Christus, to remain chaste and pure. The doctor had seemed to think that his madness was dietary, and that Raspail could bring him around to health, of body and mind, again. How the rich doctors and professors tried to suppress the *Annuaire de la santé*! No country other than France had such a book, a medical guide for the home, with all the science known about disease in clear prose that even the most simple could understand.

And what had he had for, say, an average meal, the good doctor had asked after he had cauterized and bandaged what was left of his ear? Meal, meal? He did not rightly take meals, he was ashamed to say. He lived off white wine and shag tobacco, with the occasional glass of Pernod. The doctor had buried his face in his hands. And blasphemed. We are commended not to blaspheme, he had said to the doctor.

We are also commanded, by Nature, if you will, Monsieur Vincent, to nourish our bodies with food and not with poison. We are also commanded not to mutilate our ears.

Raspail recommended onions for the poor as the most nourishing of foods for the least sous. And olive oil. He drew onions that were beginning to sprout. Green is the symbol of hope. And the olive jug must be green as well.

4 FLOREAL

Sander delights to sit suddenly and inventory his precocious and wicked past, knowing that mine is nothing like, amazed that he is shocked by it and cheerfully shocked by his amazement. Item, his best girl, as was, before she went off with hippy creeps in a tide of macramé, transcendental meditation, and organic meals that tasted like paper, sand, and whey, well he made it with her little sister one afternoon on the sly, scarcely thirteen, eager as a *poesje* rolling in catnip. Never mind *his* sister, since they were in rompers practically. He was an accomplished smoocher at ten, a rake at eleven, a Ganymed at twelve, a father, probably, at thirteen, outcoming Don Juan at fourteen. It was lovely, *slordig,* messy. Item, every girl in his set, too many out of it (what slobs! what smarm!), somebody's soused mother on a bed at a party, unwashed French sailors in dingy hotels, a divinity student with halitosis and hung like a chihuahua.

Impressive, I said, suggesting it was *kinderspel* and the evidence of a warm heart. A sigh and a dirty look. You don't even think I'm a monster, he said. Dokter Tomas wanted to hold his nose.

5 FLOREAL

That the world is a skin of air around a sphere of rock is so modern an idea that no culture knows it. We mites, the big roaming animals, inhabit this balloon much as microbes swim about in the film of a bubble, which must have its Asias and Alps, just as motes of dust have their moons, seasons, and geology.

The scale of *ubi* and *quando* is, as far as we know, one of the infinitudes so strangely interrelated, so perfectly harmonized, that we shall probably never perceive how time is knit with space, how the pulse of light is also the pulse of time, or how the energy of radiant stars can brake and still itself to become matter.

The stuff of a world, ant, iron, cantaloupe, is light ash accumulated over quadrillions of quadrillions of eons. Finished time, said Samuel Alexander, becomes a place. This is an angel's sense of things. Our attention is too frail to focus on it, however awful it is to admit that the nature of being is a boring subject.

6 FLOREAL

Chastity as contempt of the sensual. The word *sensual* troubles Sander, makes him wrinkle his nose. Chastity he may well never have heard of, though he keeps to it with a will.

Value as the judgment of a discerning mind, not as agreeing to the crowd's approval. Sander nods his seeing. Later: that things are what you are capable of making them. No cheating allowed.

7 FLOREAL

Shopping on shore. Our supplies over a choppy sea coming back. Sander took in a movie while I called friends: Keirinckx is doing some topnotch work he wants me to see soon. Bruno and Kaatje splendidly happy (Hans and Saartje crowed over the phone), but didn't believe the USA where they're just back from. Paulus says the summer students are duller than ever before.

Sander's film was a skinflick, French, in which mother and daughter seduce each other's boyfriends: too gooey, his verdict, but with lots of girl on show, some grunty bedwork, make believe in his expert opinion, and lots of neat cars. Had I ever been to Paris? Tried to give him some idea of how beautiful it is, how congenial, how orderly. He said his friends told him it was a cruddy place where you had to beg in the underground. Impulsively said I would take him to see it. When? he replied.

A place is defined anew even when returning to it after a few hours. My island, my cabin, my books, my sea.

See how the book of essays will fit together. What the pastoral does in Picasso, what a still life is, how the erotic, like wild ginger in the Seychelles, thrives domestically in a cultivated ecology. Goya and Theokritos, Jarry and Virgil converge in Picasso's last etchings. Cézanne comes from Virgil. Picasso takes up the Classical just when it was most anaemic, academic, and bleached of its eroticism.

8 FLOREAL

Finish painting the composition-board inner walls. Their white takes the sun beautifully. Pictures up, finally. The Marc Bauhaus calendar, several early Kandinskys thumbtacked up, arrangements of postcards.

Whitecaps, a warmish wind from the east. A storm brewing far out, could move in.

9 FLOREAL

A gale drenching the windows: can scarcely see out. Began in the night. We feel wonderfully isolated. The Island of Snegren, Sander says in a radio voice, completely cut off by North Sea storm from Europe and all the continents. The population of two, Professor van Hovendaal the noted philosopher, and Alexander Brouwer, the *schaamtellos tiener,* asked for a statement by the press, replied that they couldn't care less.

We go out and secure the boat, leaning into the wind and getting drenched. Toweled down, Sander wears a denim jacket only. So dark we need lamps: a comforting and congenial light.

Reading awhile, drawing awhile, Sander's up every five minutes or so to peer out the windows, out the door, getting dashed with rain. As often, he pokes his scrotum, which seems swollen, unsettles his foreskin, and counts the days of his resolute chastity. Something short of two months, he figures out loud, not counting a wet dream a month back.

Thought of Itard's Victor, who needed to escape from time to time to bat the water of the stream and howl at the moon.

Traverse Picasso with two vectors: the long tradition of the still life (eating, manners, ritual, household) and the pastoral (herds, pasturage, horse, cavalier, campsite).

10 FLOREAL

Strangeness and charm. After a convivial meal laid out in front of the fire late yesterday, the dark squall continuing, I had suggested that I read us a ghost story as befitting such a night. Suddenly, a slam of the door, and no Sander. Stood only half surprised, as I assumed he was making a dash for the outhouse. Half an hour, and no Sander. Either he was ill, or had not gone to the outhouse. Or was ending his chaste fast, more than likely. He would return spent and relaxed.

An hour. I dressed for the solid rain and slashing wind. Rapped on the outhouse door: no reply. Inside, no Sander. Called. Walked and called. Back to the cabin to see if he'd returned. No. An uneasy dread. One side of the island under an assault of champing, raging waves, the other awash. Walked and called.

Was sick with anxiety when I found him at the far end, standing braced against a tree, his face streaming in the beam of my flashlight. His eyes were closed, his mouth open. One hand kneaded his testicles, the other was satisfying his body's demand with profligate frenzy. I clicked off the flashlight as soon as I saw. See you when you get back, I said as cheerfully and as normally as I could.

Itard's Victor, I said all the way to the cabin, Itard's Victor, slipped loose into the elements, gone wild. Broke up two crates for the fire, got out a bathrobe and towels. It was another hour before he returned.

Dried him before the fire while he shivered, hair, body, sex, which stood, his streaming eyes, tears as I discovered. His teeth chattered. Wrapped him in the bathrobe and a blanket. Put him in my bed and held him until he was asleep.

13 FLOREAL

Sander still feverish but, I think, in the clear. The gale left our island tangled with detritus, the staves of somebody's dory, shells, limbs, tackle, nameless trash. Sea still high and boisterous, clouds scudding in glare.

14 FLOREAL

Calm. Sander for a walk with me to inspect the island. Though warm, and clearing steadily, insisted on jeans, sneakers, shirt and sweater. Has slept in bed with me since the wild night, sexless and cuddly as a puppy. Temperature normal. Will I tell Dokter Tomas? he asks. What's to tell? I say.

15 FLOREAL

Fine weather again. Sander sets to cleaning up. A storm, he says, is to provide firewood for islanders. I get back to writing. Sander in jeans, as if the nudity he loved so much were ruined.

16 FLOREAL

We study phyllotaxis, diagramming arrangements of leaves on stems, using a string to plot the Fibonacci proportions. Sander's good at this.

Each species of animal lives in its own world. Each being lives in its own world.

In Virgil the shrill cicada's cry is the symbol of appetence. It is the edge of desire that gives the pastoral its identity. The erotic moves along fine gradations and differences, Daphnis and Chloe discovering each other's bodies, the opposition of sheep and goats, sun and shade, summer and winter, grassland and rock, field and wood. Leporello's classification of charms begins in the *Anthology*: I kissed, says Artemon, Erkhedemos twelve, when he was peeping around a door, and then I dreamed that he wore a quiver, was winged, spry, and beautiful, and that he brought me a brace of bantams, awful omen, and smiled at me and frowned. I have walked into bees swarming. Twelve! Thirteen is the age preferred by adepts, fourteen is Eros in full blossom, fifteen sweeter still, none sweeter than. Sixteen is for the gods to love, seventeen, bearding out and well hung, is for Zeus alone. At twenty they go for each other.

17 FLOREAL

Euphoria. Sander's blue disc of eye is again calm, and he has returned to wearing water only. His chest runches out from chinning, heaping niftily where it reefs underarm at the nipples.

We row in great sweeps around the island, brown as Choctaws. Sander refuses a haircut and begins to look like Victor when Itard first saw him.

You know, he says, I've never really looked at things before, or tried to get alongside them in the right way. Selfish pig, he calls himself.

18 FLOREAL

The six essays are beginning to fit together just as I want them to. Find I can work on them all at once. I begin to find everything in Picasso in the Mediterranean past, of which he is the great custodian in our time.

Sander, sprag imp and stinker, turns up glossy with sweat from running, unties his sneakers on the edge of my worktable, and says with bright sincerity, you can have my body if you want it. A scrunch in my scrotum, but I'm speechless. Don't look so hacked, he says, I am the new Sander. I don't take, I give. I figured it out: give me credit for being smart. I'll stay horny in my head, ready anytime, for whatever.

But I love you just so, *liefje* Sander, charmingly naked and good natured. You keep my imagination alive. You've helped me write my book, you have beguiled all our time here into a kind of ancient ambiance, Damon the old shepherd I, Mopsus the young shepherd you, full of piss and vinegar.

I can always go jump in the sea, he says. You aren't old.

What if I wanted you, what would you want me to want?

Grown people are Martians, he says. They don't know nothing from nothing, but I mean nothing!

20 FLOREAL

Coffee and journal on the rock. Sander brings out second mugs of coffee. *Iets reusachtigs!* he says, adding a whistle and a shake of his ankle. Crouches on my knees and we sip our coffee. We could row over to the mainland and brag, he says, I mean just by walking around and laughing with our eyes.

71

22 FLOREAL

The dedication, if I dared, of the essays might be *Péoi Aléxandros Pentekaidekaétes.*

30 FLOREAL

Crushed green smell of fir needles, sweetgrass, bee balm in salty hair, tang of creosote at the roots, earwax faintly acrid, sweat licked from the upper lip, axial sweat the odor of hay and urine, olive and soda the pileum, celery and ginger the sac. You, Sander says, giving me look for look, bright as a wolf, smell like billy goat, tobacco, onions, *zaad,* Aqua Velva, licorice, and wet dog. Doesn't all that hair tickle?

1 PRAIRIAL

It was the Englishman John Tyndall who discovered why the sky is blue. What we see is dust suspended in our shell of air, quadrillions of prisms shattering pure sunlight into spectra. Blue is the color that scatters. The moon's sky is black, Mars' is red.

THE HUNTER GRACCHUS

On April 6, 1917, in a dwarfishly small house rented by his sister Ottla in the medieval quarter of Prague (22 Alchimistengasse—Alchemists Alley), Franz Kafka wrote in his diary:

Today, in the tiny harbor where save for fishing boats only two ocean-going passenger steamers used to call, a strange boat lay at anchor. A clumsy old craft, rather low and very broad, filthy, as if bilge water had been poured over it, it still seemed to be dripping down the yellowish sides; the masts disproportionately tall, the upper third of the main-mast split; wrinkled, coarse, yellowish-brown sails stretched every which way between the yards, patched, too weak to stand against the slightest gust of wind.

I gazed in astonishment at it for a time, waited for someone to show himself on deck; no one appeared. A workman sat down beside me on the harbor wall. "Whose ship is that?" I asked; "this is the first time I've seen it."

"It puts in every two or three years," the man said, "and belongs to the Hunter Gracchus."

Gracchus, the name of a noble Roman family from the third to the first centuries B.C., is synonymous with Roman virtue at its sternest. It is useful to Kafka not only for its antiquity and tone of incorruptible rectitude (a portrait bust on a classroom shelf, at odds and yet in harmony with the periodic table of the elements behind it) but also for its meaning, grackle or blackbird; in Czech, *kavka*. Kafka's father had a blackbird on his business letterhead.

The description of Gracchus's old ship is remarkably like Melville's of the *Pequod,* whose "venerable bows looked bearded" and whose "ancient decks were worn and wrinkled." From Noah's ark to Jonah's storm-tossed boat out of Joppa to the Roman ships in which Saint Paul sailed perilously, the ship in history has always been a sign of fate itself.

THE FIRST HUNTER GRACCHUS

A first draft, or fragment of "The Hunter Gracchus" (the title of both the fragment and the story were supplied by Kafka's literary executor, Max Brod) is a dialogue between Gracchus and a visitor to his boat. Gracchus imagines himself known and important. His fate is special and unique. The dialogue is one of cross-purposes. Gracchus says that he is "the most ancient of seafarers," patron saint of sailors. He offers wine: "The master does me proud." Who the master is is a mystery: Gracchus doesn't even understand his language. He died, in fact, "today" in Hamburg, while Gracchus is "down south here." The effect of this fragment is of an Ancient Mariner trying to tell his story to and impress his importance upon a reluctant listener, who concludes that life is too short to hear this old bore out. In the achieved story the interlocutor is the mayor of Riva, who must be diplomatically attentive. The authority of myth engages with the authority of skeptical reason, so that when the mayor asks "*Sind Sie tot?*" (Are you dead?) the metaphysical locale shivers like the confused needle of a compass in "*Ja, sagte der Jäger, wie Sie sehen*" (Yes, said the hunter, as you see).

A VICTORIAN PENTIMENTO

Between writing the two texts now known as "The Hunter Gracchus: A Fragment" and "The Hunter Gracchus," Kafka read Wilkie Collins's novel *Armadale*, which ran serially in *The Cornhill Magazine* from 1864 to 1866, when it was published with great success and popularity. A German translation by Marie Scott (Leipzig, 1866) went through three editions before 1878.

Along with *The Woman in White* (1860) and *The Moonstone* (1868), *Armadale* is one of the three masterpieces of intricately plotted melodrama, suspense, and detection that made Collins as famous as, and for a while more famous than, his friend Dickens.

Although its plot contains a ship that has taken a wrong course and turns up later as a ghostly wreck, a sudden impulse that dictates the fate of two innocent people (both named Allen Armadale), it is the novel's opening scene that Kafka found interesting enough to appropriate and transmute. Collins furnished Kafka with the ominous arrival of an invalid with a ghastly face and matted hair who is carried on a stretcher past the everyday street life of a village, including "flying detachments of plump white-headed children" and a mother with a child at her breast, to be met by the mayor.

Collins's scene is set at a spa in the Black Forest (home of the Hunter Gracchus in the fragment). He has a band playing the waltz from Weber's

Der Freischütz, which must have struck Kafka as a fortuitous correspondence. Among the archetypes of the Hunter Gracchus is the enchanted marksman of that opera. In Collins it is a guilty past that cannot be buried. The dead past persists. Kafka makes a crystalline abstract of Collins's plot, concentrating its essence into the figure of Gracchus, his wandering ship, his fate, and the enigmatic sense that the dead, having lived and acted, are alive.

Collins's elderly, dying invalid is a murderer. He has come to the spa at Wildbad with a young wife and child. In his last moments he writes a confession intended to avert retribution for his crime from being passed on to his son. *Armadale* is the working out of the futility of that hope.

Kafka, having written a dialogue between Gracchus and an unidentified interlocutor, found in Collins a staging. Gracchus must have an arrival, a procession to a room, an interlocutor with an identity, and a more focused role as man the wanderer, fated by an inexplicable past in which a wrong turn was taken that can never be corrected.

DE CHIRICO

The first paragraph of "The Hunter Gracchus" displays the quiet, melancholy stillness of Italian piazze that Nietzsche admired, leading Giorgio de Chirico to translate Nietzsche's feeling for Italian light, architecture, and street life into those paintings that art history calls metaphysical. The enigmatic tone of de Chirico comes equally from Arnold Böcklin (whose painting *Isle of the Dead* is a scene further down the lake from Riva). Böcklin's romanticization of mystery, of dark funeral beauty, is in the idiom of the Décadence, "the moment of Nietzsche." Kafka, like de Chirico, was aware of and influenced by this new melancholy that informed European art and writing from Scandinavia to Rome, from London to Prague.

Kafka's distinction is that he stripped it of those elements that would quickly soften into kitsch.*

"Zwei Knaben sassen auf der Quaimauer und spielen Würfel." Two boys were sitting on the harbor wall playing with dice. They touch, lightly, the theme of hazard, of chance, that will vibrate throughout. "History is a child building a sandcastle by the sea," said Heraclitus two and a half millennia earlier, "and that child is the whole majesty of man's power in the world." Mallarmé's *Un coup de dés jamais n'abolira le hasard*, with its imagery of

---

* For *nicceismo* in Böcklin and de Chirico, see Alberto Savinio's "Arnold Böcklin" in *Operatic Lives* (1942, translated by John Shepley, 1988) and de Chirico's *Memoirs* (1962, translated by Margaret Crosland, 1971). Savinio is de Chirico's brother.

shipreck and pathless seas, was published in 1897 when Kafka was fourteen. "God does not play at dice," said Einstein (whom Kafka may have met at a Prague salon they are both known to have attended). Kafka was not certain that He didn't.

There is a monument on this quay, a *säbelschwingende Held,* a sword-flourishing hero, in whose shadow a man is reading a newspaper. History in two tempi, and Kafka made the statue up, much as he placed a sword-bearing Statue of Liberty in *Amerika.*

A girl is filling her jug at the public fountain. (Joyce, having a Gemini in the boys, an Aquarius in the water jug, and a Sagittarius in the monument, would have gone ahead and tucked in the full zodiac, however furtively; signs and symbols have no claim on Kafka, who wrecks tradition rather than trust any part of it.)

A fruit seller lies beside his scales (more zodiac, Libra!) staring out to sea.

Then a fleeting Cézanne: through the door and windows of the café we can see two men drinking wine at a table *in der Tiefe,* all the way at the back. The patron is out front, asleep at one of his own tables.

Into this de Chirico high noon comes a ship, *eine Barke,* "silently making for the little harbor." The sailor who secures the boat with a rope through a ring wears a blue blouse, a French touch that makes us note that two French words have already turned up (*quai* and *barque*). It's the late, hard spare style of Flaubert, as in the opening paragraphs of *Bouvard et Pécuchet,* that Kafka is taking for a model and improving upon.

Gracchus, like Wilkie Collins's Armadale, is brought across the quay on a bier, covered by a large Victorian shawl, "a great flower-patterned tasselled silk cloth" perhaps taken from Collins's carpet speckled with "flowers in all the colours of the rainbow," and like Armadale he seems to be more dead than alive.

Gracchus's arrival is strangely ignored by the people in the square, as if he were invisible. A new set of characters—a committee of innocents—takes over: a mother with a nursing child, a little boy who opens and closes a window, and a flock of biblical doves, whose associations with fated ships fit Kafka's diction of imagery, Noah's dove from the ask, and Jonah's name ("dove" in Hebrew).

The mayor of Riva arrives as soon as Gracchus has been carried inside a yellow house with an oaken door. He is dressed in black, with a funereal band on his top hat.

FIFTY LITTLE BOYS

These *fünfzig kleine Knaben* who line up in two rows and bow to the Bürgermeister of Riva when he arrives at the house where the Hunter Gracchus has been carried remind us of Max Ernst's *collages,* of Paul Delvaux's paintings; that is, they enact the surrealist strategy of being from the dream world, like Rudyard Kipling's hovering ghost children in "They" or Pavel Tchelitchew's children in his painting *Hide-and-Seek*. Another horde of children, girls this time, crowd the stairs to the court painter Titorelli's studio in *The Trial*. Their presence is almost as inexplicable as that of the boys. They live in the mazelike tenement where Titorelli paints judges and where brokers gossip about cases in process. They are silly, provocative, brazen pests. Like the boys, they line up on either side of the stairway, "squeezing against the walls to leave room for K. to pass." They form, like the boys, a kind of gauntlet through which the mayor of Riva and K. have to pass to their strange and unsettling encounters.

In December 1911 Kafka, having witnessed the circumcision of a nephew, noted that in Russia the period between birth and circumcision was thought to be particularly vulnerable to devils for both the mother and the son.

For seven days after the birth, except on Friday, also in order to ward off evil spirits, ten to fifteen children, always different ones, led by the *belfer* (assistant teacher), are admitted to the bedside of the mother, there repeat *Shema Israel*, and are then given candy. These innocent, five-to-eight-year-old children are supposed to be especially effective in driving back the evil spirits, who press forward most strongly toward evening.

At the beginning of Armadale, the Bürgermeister of Wildbad in the Black Forest, awaiting the arrival of the elder Armadale ("who lay helpless on a mattress supported by a stretcher; his hair long and disordered under a black skull-cap; his eyes wide open, rolling to and fro ceaselessly anxious; the rest of his face as void of all expression . . . as if he had been dead"), is surrounded by "flying detachments of plump white-headed children careered in perpetual motion."

In 1917 Kafka wrote in his Blue Notebook (as some of his journals have come to be called): "They were given the choice of becoming kings or the king's messengers. As is the way with children, they all wanted to be messengers. That is why there are only messengers, racing through the world and, since there are no kings, calling out to each other the messages that have now become meaningless." (There is another sentence—"They would gladly put an end to their miserable life, but they do not dare to do so because of their oath of loyalty"—that starts another thought superfluous to the perfect image of messenger children making a botch of all messages.)

All messages in Kafka are incoherent, misleading, enigmatic. The most irresponsible and childish messengers are the assistants to K. in *The Castle*. (They probably entered Kafka's imagination as two silent Swedish boys

Kafka kept seeing at a nudist spa in Austria in *1912*, always together, uncommunicative, politely nodding in passing, traversing Kafka's path with comic regularity.)

THE NEW MYTH

Despite Kafka's counting on myths and folktales about hunters, enchanted ships, the Wandering Jew, ships for the souls of the dead, and all the other cultural furniture to stir in the back of our minds as we read "The Hunter Gracchus," he does not, like Joyce, specify them. He treats them like groundwater that his taproot can reach. Even when he selects something from the midden of myth, he estranges it. His Don Quixote, his Tower of Babel, his Bucephalus are transmutations.

Hermann Broch placed Kafka's relation to myth accurately: beyond it as an exhausted resource. Broch was one of the earliest sensibilities to see James Joyce's greatness and uniqueness. His art, however, was an end and a culmination. Broch's own *The Death of Virgil* (1945) may be the final elegy closing the long duration of a European literature from Homer to Joyce. In Kafka he saw a new beginning, a fiercely bright sun burning through the opaque mists of a dawn.

The striking relationship between the arts on the basis of their common abstraction [Broch wrote], their common style of old age, this hallmark of our epoch is the cause of the inner relationship between artists like Picasso, Stravinsky and Joyce. This relationship is not only striking in itself but also by reason of the parallelism through which the style of old age was imposed on these men, even in their rather early years.

Nevertheless, abstractism forms no *Gesamtkunstwerk*—the ideal of the late romantic; the arts remain separate. Literature especially can never become abstract and "musicalized": therefore the style of old age relies here much more on another symptomatic attitude, namely on the trend toward myth. It is highly significant that Joyce goes back to the Odyssey. And although this return to myth—already anticipated in Wagner—is nowhere so elaborated as in Joyce's work, it is for all that a general attitude of modern literature: the revival of Biblical themes, as, for instance, in the novels of Thomas Mann, is an evidence of the impetuosity with which myth surges to the forefront of poetry. However, this is only a return—a return to myth in its ancient forms (even when they are so modernized as in Joyce), and so far it is not a new myth, not the new myth. Yet, we may assume that at least the first realization of such a new myth is already evident, namely in Franz Kafka's writing.

In Joyce one may still detect neo-romantic trends, a concern with the complications of the human soul, which derives directly from nineteenth-century literature, from Stendhal, and even from Ibsen. Nothing of this kind can be said about Kafka. Here the personal problem no longer exists, and what seems still personal is, at the very moment it is uttered, dissolved in a super-personal atmosphere. The prophecy of myth is suddenly at hand. [Broch, introduction to Rachel Bespaloff's *De l'Iliade* (1943, English translation as *On the Iliad,* 1947)]

Prophecy. All of Kafka is about history that had not yet happened. His sister Ottla would die in the camps, along with all of his kin. The German word for *insect* (*Ungeziefer,* "vermin") that Kafka used for Gregor Samsa is the same word the Nazis used for Jews, and *insect extermination* was one of their obscene euphemisms, as George Steiner has pointed out.

Quite soon after the Second World War it was evident that with *The Castle* and *The Trial,* and especially with "In the Penal Colony," Kafka was accurately describing the mechanics of totalitarian barbarity.

PERPETUAL OSCILLATION
Kafka, Broch says, had "reached the point of the Either-Or: either poetry is able to proceed to myth, or it goes bankrupt."

Kafka, in his presentiment of the new cosmogony, the new theogony that he had to achieve, struggling with his love of literature, his disgust for literature, feeling the ultimate insufficiency of any artistic approach, decided (as did Tolstoy, faced with a similar decision) to quit the realm of literature, and ask that his work be destroyed; he asked this for the sake of the universe whose new mythical concept had been bestowed upon him.

In the Blue Notebooks Kafka wrote: "To what indifference people may come, to what profound conviction of having lost the right track forever."
And: "Our salvation is death, but not this one."
Kafka's prose is a hard surface, as of polished steel, without resonance or exact reflection. It is, as Broch remarked, abstract ("of bare essentials and unconditional abstractness"). It is, as many critics have said, a pure German, the austere German in which the Austro-Hungarian empire conducted its administrative affairs, an efficient, spartan idiom admitting of neither ornament nor poetic tones. Its grace was that of abrupt information and naked utility.
Christopher Middleton speaks (in a letter) of "the transparent, ever-inquiring, tenderly comical, ferociously paradoxical narrative voice that came to

Kafka for his Great Wall of China and Josephine the Singer: Kafka's *last* voice."
The paradox everywhere in Kafka is that this efficient prose is graphing images and events forever alien to the administration of a bureaucracy. Middleton's remark comes in a discussion of the spiritual dance of language.

I'm reading about Abraham Abulafia, his "mystical experience," theories of music and of symbolic words. There was a wonderful old Sephardic Rabbi in Smyrna, Isaak ha-Kohen, who borrowed and developed a theory, in turn adopted and cherished by Abulafia, about melody, a theory with obviously ancient origins, but traceable to Byzantium, melody as a rehearsal, with its undulatory ups and downs, of the soul's dancing toward ecstatic union with God: to rehearse the soul, bid your instrumentalists play . . . so melody is a breathing, a veil of breath which flows and undulates, a veiling of the Ruach (spirit). When you listen to recent re-creations of Byzantine music, the theory seems more and more childish, but the facts it enwraps become more and more audible—even the *touching* of flute-notes and harp strings enacts the vertiginous conspiracy, the "letting go," out of any succession of instants into an imaginable *nunc stans*, an ingression into "the perfect and complete simultaneous possession of unlimited life" (as dear old Boethius put it). Oddly enough, this (what's "this"?) is the clue to the narrative voice (I conjecture) . . . that came to Kafka for his Great Wall of China.

What Kafka had to be so clear and simple about was that nothing is clear and simple. On his deathbed he said of a vase of flowers that they were like him: simultaneously alive and dead. All demarcations are shimmeringly blurred. Some powerful sets of opposites absolutely do not, as Heraclitus said, cooperate. They fight. They tip over the balance of every certainty. We can, Kafka said, easily believe any truth and its negative at the same time.

LUSTRON UND KASTRON

Gracchus's *Lebensproblem*, as the Germans say, is that he cannot encounter his opposite and be resolved (or not) into Being or Nonbeing, as the outcome may be.

Opposites do not cooperate; they obliterate each other.

In 1912, at a nudist spa in Austria, Kafka dreamed that two contingents of nudists were facing each other. One contingent was shouting at the other the insult "Lustron und Kastron!"

The insult was considered so objectionable that they fought. They obliterated each other like the Calico Cat and the Gingham Dog, or like subatomic particles colliding into nonexistence.

The dream interested Kafka; he recorded it. He did not analyze it, at least not on paper. He knew his Freud. There are no such words as *lustron* and *kastron* in Greek, though the dream made them Greek. If we transpose them into Greek loan words in Latin, we get *castrum* (castle) and *lustrum* (the five-year recurring spiritual cleansing of Roman religion). Both words are antonyms, containing their own opposites (like *altus*, deep or high). *Lustrum*, a washing clean, also means filthy; the *cast-* root gives us *chaste* and *castrate*. And *lust* and *chaste* play around in their juxtaposition.

At the spa Kafka records, with wry wit, the presence of the two silent Swedish boys whose handsome nudity reminded him of Castor and Pollux, whose names strangely mean Clean and Dirty (our *chaste* and *polluted*). These archetypal twins, the sons of Leda, Helen's brothers, noble heroes, duplicates of Damon and Pythias in friendship, existed alternately. One lived while the other was dead, capable of swapping these states of being. They are in the zodiac as Gemini, and figure in much folklore, merging with Jesus and James.

When Gracchus claims in the fragment that he is the patron saint of sailors, he is lying. Castor and Pollux are the patron saints of sailors, the corposants that play like bright fire in the rigging.

Pollux in Greek has a euphemism for a name: Polydeukes (the Sweet One). When the Greeks felt they needed to propitiate, they avoided a real name (as in calling the avenging Fates the Eumenides). Pollux was a boxer when all fights were to the death.

Dirty and clean, then, tref and kosher, motivated Kafka's dream. The insult was that one group of nudists were both. Kafka was a nudist who wore bathing drawers, a nonobservant Jew, a Czech who wrote in German, a man who was habitually engaged to be married and died a bachelor. He could imagine "a curious animal, half kitten, half lamb" (derived from a photograph of himself, age five, with a prop stuffed lamb whose hindquarters look remarkably like those of a cat). He could imagine "an Odradek," the identity of which has so far eluded all the scholars.

We live, Kafka seems to imply, in all matters suspended between belief and doubt, knowing and ignorance, law and chance. Gracchus is both prehistoric man, a hunter and gatherer, and man at his most civilized. He thinks that his fate is due to a fall in a primeval forest, as well as to his death ship's being off course.

Kafka could see the human predicament from various angles. We live by many codes of law written hundreds or thousands of years ago for people whose circumstances were not ours. This is not exclusively a Jewish or Muslim problem; the United States Constitution has its scandals and headaches. Hence lawyers, of whom Kafka was one. He dealt daily with workmen's accidents and their claims for compensation. What is the value of a hand?

His mind was pre-pre-Socratic. His physics teacher had studied under Ernst Mach, whose extreme skepticism about atoms and cause and effect activated Einstein in quite a different direction.

Walter Benjamin, Kafka's first interpreter, said that a strong prehistoric wind blows across Kafka from the past. There is that picture on the wall that Gracchus can see from his bed, of a Bushman "who is aiming his spear at me and taking cover as best he can behind a beautifully painted shield." A bushman who has not yet fallen off a cliff and broken his neck.

"Mein Kahn ist ohne Steuer, er fährt mit dem Wind, der in den untersten Regionen des Todes bläst." (My boat is rudderless, it is driven by the wind that blows in the deepest regions of death.)

This is the voice of the twentieth century, from the ovens of Buchenwald, from the bombarded trenches of the Marne, from Hiroshima.

It was words that started the annihilating fight in Kafka's dream, meaningless words invented by Kafka's dreaming mind. They seem to designate opposite things, things clean and things unclean. Yet they encode their opposite meanings. The relation of word to thing is the lawyer's, the philosopher's, the ruler's constant anguish. The word *Jew* (which occurs nowhere in Kafka's fiction) designates not an anthropological race but a culture, and yet both Hitler and the Jews used it as if it specified a race. "The Hunter Gracchus" inquires into the meaning of the word *death*. If there is an afterlife in an eternal state, then it does not mean death; it means transition, and death as a word is meaningless. It annihilates either of its meanings if you bring them together.

The language of the law, of talking dogs and apes, of singing field mice, of ogres and bridges that can talk—everything has its *logos* for Kafka. (Max Brod recounts a conversation in Paris between Kafka and a donkey.) Words are tyrants more powerful than any Caesar. When they are lies, they are devils.

The purity of Kafka's style assures us of its trustworthiness as a witness. It is this purity, as of a child's innocence or an angel's prerogative, that allows Kafka into metaphysical realities where a rhetorical or bogus style would flounder. Try to imagine "The Hunter Gracchus" by the late Tolstoy, or by Poe. The one would have moralized, the other would have tried to scare us. Kafka says, "Here is what it feels like to be lost."

As Auden noted, *as if* in Kafka is treated as *is*. To bring *is* to bear on Kafka's *as if* will only annihilate them both.

FIFTY CHILDREN IN TWO ROWS

We cannot read "The Hunter Gracchus" without being reminded of all the refugee ships loaded to the gunwales with Jews trying to escape the even more packed cattle cars to Auschwitz, turned away from harbor after harbor.

One of the arrangers of some of these ships was Ada Sereni, an Italian Jewish noblewoman whose family can be traced back to Rome in the first century. In September of 1947 she was involved in secret flights of Jewish children from Italy to Palestine. A twin-engine plane flown by two Americans was to land at night outside Salerno. Ada Sereni and the twenty-year-old Motti Fein (later to command the Israeli Air force in the Six-Day War) were waiting with fifty children to be taken to a kibbutz. As the plane approached, the fifty were placed in two rows of twenty-five each, holding candles as landing lights in a Sicilian meadow. The operation took only a few minutes and was successful. The children were in orange groves the next morning. *"An der Stubentür klopfte er an, gleichzeitig nahm er den Zylinderhut in seine schwarzbehandschuhte Rechte. Gleich wurde geöffnet, wohl fünfzig kleine Knaben bildeten ein Spaller in langen Flurgang und verbeugten sich."* (He knocked at the door, meanwhile removing his top hat with his black-gloved right hand. As soon as it was opened, fifty little boys stood in formation along the hallway and bowed.) The SS wore black gloves.

DEATH SHIPS

Kafka does not decode. He is not referring us to Wagner's *Flying Dutchman* or the myth of the Wandering Jew, or to the pharaonic death ships that had harbors built for them in the empty desert, or to the treasure ships in which Viking lords were laid in all their finery, or to the Polynesian death ships that glided from island to island collecting the dead, or to American Indian canoe burials, or to Coleridge's Ancient mariner, or to any of the ghost ships of legend and folktale. There is a ghostly hunter in the Black Forest. Kafka's ability to write "The Hunter Gracchus" is evidence of what Broch meant when he said that Kafka is the inventor of a new mythology.

SIND SIE TOT?

At Auschwitz it was difficult to tell the living from the dead.

RAVEN AND BLACKBIRD

Poe's mind was round, fat, and white; Kafka's cubical, lean, and transparent.

RIVA

When Max Brod and Kafka visited Riva in September of 1909 it was an Austrian town where eight thousand Italians lived. It sits on the northwest end of Lake Garda. Baedeker's *Northern Italy* for 1909 calls it "charming" and says that "the water is generally azure blue."

AION

Time in Kafka is dream time, Zenonian and interminable. The bridegroom will never get to his wedding in the country, the charges against Joseph K.

will never be known, the death ship of the Hunter Gracchus will never find its bearings.

CIRCADIAN RHYTHM

The opening of "The Hunter Gracchus" is a picture of urban infinity. There is always another throw of the dice. Another newspaper is being printed while today's is being read; a jug of water must soon be refilled; the fruit seller is engaged in "the eternal exchange of money and goods" (Heraclitus on the shore shaping the sea, the sea shaping the shore); the men in the café will be there again tomorrow; the sleeping patron is in one cycle of his circadian rhythm. Play, reading, housekeeping, business, rest: it is against these ordinary peaceful things that Kafka puts the long duration of Gracchus's thousand years of wandering, a cosmic infinity.

A KIND OF PARADOX

Reality is the most effective mask of reality. Our fondest wish, attained, ceases to be our fondest wish. Success is the greatest of disappointments. The spirit is most alive when it is lost. Anxiety was Kafka's composure, as despair was Kierkegaard's happiness. Kafka said impatience is our greatest fault. The man at the gate of the Law waited there all of his life.

THE HUNTER

Nimrod is the biblical archetype, "a mighty hunter before the "Lord" (Genesis 10:9), but the Targum, as Milton knew, records the tradition that he hunted men ("sinful hunting of the sons of men") as well as animals. Kafka was a vegetarian.

MOTION

Gracchus explains to the mayor of Riva that he is always in motion, despite his lying as still as a corpse. On the great stair "infinitely wide and spacious" that leads to "the other world" he clambers up and down, sideways to the left, sideways to the right, "always in motion." He says that he is a hunter turned into a butterfly. There is a gate (presumably heaven) toward which he flutters, but when he gets near he wakes to find himself back on his bier in the cabin of his ship, "still stranded forlornly in some earthly sea or other." The motion is in his mind (his *psyche*, Greek for "butterfly" as well as for "soul"). These imaginings (or dreams) are a mockery of his former nimbleness as a hunter. The butterfly is one of the most dramatic of metamorphic creatures, its transformations seemingly more divergent than any other. A caterpillar does not die; it becomes a wholly different being.

Gracchus when he tripped and fell in the Black Forest was glad to die; he sang joyfully his first night on the death ship. "I slipped into my winding sheet like a girl into her marriage dress. I lay and waited. Then came the mishap."

The mistake that caused Gracchus's long wandering happened *after* his death. Behind every enigma in Kafka there is another. "The Hunter Gracchus" can be placed among Kafka's parables. Are we, the living, already dead? How are we to know if we are on course or lost? We talk about loss of life in accidents and war as if we possessed life rather than life us. Is it that we are never wholly alive, if life is an engagement with the world as far as our talents go? Or does Kafka mean that we can exist but not be?

It is worthwhile, for perspective's sake, to keep the lively Kafka in mind, the delightful friend and traveling companion, the witty ironist, his fascinations with the Yiddish folk theater, with a wide scope of reading, his overlapping and giddy love affairs. He undoubtedly was "as lonely as Franz Kafka" (a remark made, surely, with a wicked smile).

And some genius of a critic will one day show us how comic a writer Kafka is, how a sense of the ridiculous very kin to that of Sterne and Beckett informs all of his work. Like Kierkegaard, he saw the absurdity of life as the most meaningful clue to its elusive vitality. His humor authenticates his seriousness. "Only Maimonides may say there is no God; he's entitled."

EVERY FORCE EVOLVES A FORM

"Jesus said: Split a stick. I will be inside."
—*The Gospel of Thomas [77]*

"Split the Lark, and you'll find the Music,
Bulb after Bulb, in Silver rolled."
—Emily Dickinson

1835

A robin entered a Westmorland cottage in which a child lay ill with a fever and an old woman, senile, sat by the fire. The robin was greeted as a daimon, an elemental spirit, whose presence was understood to be a good omen. Of this event Wordsworth, who was sixty-four, made a poem, "The Redbreast."

1845

A raven entered the room of a man in grief and drove him to madness by replying "Nevermore" to all questions put to it, as the man, aware that the bird was in effect an automaton, a bird capable of vocal mimicry but with a vocabulary of one word only, persisted in treating the raven as if it were supernatural and capable of answering questions about the fate of the soul after death.

1855

An osprey, swooping and crying with a "barbaric yawp" (both words referring to sound, speech that is not Greek and seems to be *bar bar* over and over, *yawp*, a word as old as English poetry itself for the strident or hoarse call of a bird) seemed to Walt Whitman to be a daimon upbraiding him for his "gab and loitering." Whitman replied (at the end of the first section of *Leaves of Grass*, in later editions the fifty-second and closing part of "Song of Myself") that he was indeed very like the osprey, "not a bit tamed," sounding *his* "barbaric yawp over the roofs of the world." And like the hawk he speaks with the authority of nature. We must make of his message what we will. "If you want me again look for me under your boot-soles."

You will hardly know who I am or what I mean,
But I shall be good health to you nevertheless,
And filter and fibre your blood.

Failing to fetch me at first keep encouraged,
Missing me one place search another,
I stop somewhere waiting for you.

Thereafter in *Leaves of Grass* birds are understood to be daimons. Poe's man in grief was sure that the raven was a prophet, but whether "bird or devil" "Whether Tempter sent, or whether tempest tossed thee here ashore") he did not know. Whitman was remembering this line when in "Out of the Cradle Endlessly Rocking" he asked if the mocking-bird, the *daimon* of that poem, be "Demon or bird."

1877

In the fields around St. Beuno's College in North Wales a thirty-three-year-old Jesuit named Gerard Manley Hopkins observed a kestrel, or windhover, riding the air. Remembering the hawk that fixed a lyric vision in Walt Whitman's heart (Whitman's mind, he wrote later, was "like my own"), he took the moment to be a revelation of Whitman's spirit "somewhere waiting for you." That his prophetic words would stir the heart of an English poet to see Christ as a raptor of souls would have pleased Whitman. We can also assume that he would have admired the younger poet's obvious rivalry in the art of fitting words to images and rhythms to emotions. *Minion* is Whitmanesque. "Dapple dawn-drawn Falcon, in his riding/ Of the rolling level underneath him steady air, and striding/ High there" bests Whitman's "The spotted hawk swoops by," the "last scud of day hold[ing] back" for it. Whitman's osprey is seen with the last of the day's sun on it, its height enabling it to be still sunlit while Whitman at ground level is in the "shadow'd wilds" of dusk. Hopkin's windhover is seen catching the first of the sun before dawn has reached the Welsh fields beneath it.

ROBIN

The robin in Wordsworth is a herald of inspiration after a fallow time, of recovery from an illness, and of heaven itself. In Book VII of *The Prelude*, a renewal of poetic power is announced by

A choir of red-breasts gathered somewhere near
My threshold,—minstrels from the distant woods
Sent in on Winter's service, to announce,
With preparation artful and benign,
That the rough lord had left the surly North. . . .

The robin in "The Redbreast" has similarly come into the cottage by the on-
coming of winter.

Driven in by Autumn's sharpening air
From half-stripped woods and pastures bare,
Brisk Robin seeks a kindlier home. . . .

Note Robin: a proper name. Birds assigned names, as well as animals, constitute a series which Lévi-Strauss discusses in *The Savage Mind*, in a chapter
titled "The Individual as Species." In French the fox is Reynard, the swan
Godard, the sparrow Pierrot, and so on. *Erithacus rubecula* is already Robin
Redbreast in Middle English, by which time it was established throughout
Europe as one of the Little Birds of Christ's Passion (with much folklore
about how its breast was reddened by Christ's blood, hell fire, and the like). It
is obvious that Wordsworth hears its name as if it were analogous to Harold
Bluetooth, rather than to Jack Daw, Jim Crow, or John Dory. Hence its ruddy
breast is "a natural shield/ Charged with a blazon on the field." This align-
ment with chivalric insignia is important, as Wordsworth is articulating a tradition whereby the robin can be thoroughly of the matter of Britain: it has an
elf in it (Chaucer, Jonson); it is a kind of Red Cross Knight; it is equally
Christian and pagan (Spenser), while being principally the bird daimon that
we can trace to European prehistory, and which became the chief symbol
of poetic inspiration for the Romantics (Shelley, Keats, Tennyson, Poe,
Whitman).

PARROT OWL RAVEN

Poe's imagery resolves into three styles, each constituting a dialect with its
own grammar and poetic purpose. His own names for these styles were the
Arabesque, the Grotesque, and the Classic. In the early stages of planning
"The Raven" he considered a parrot and an owl. A parrot would have
required that the poem's dominant style be Arabesque; an owl, Classic. As it
is, he managed to have the parrot's echoic mimicry implicit in the repetition
of *nevermore* (which is not an echo, unless the bird is trying to say "Night's
Plutonian shore"); and the owl was translated into its divine equivalent, the
bust of Pallas on which the raven perches.

ONE CALVINIST CROW

Poe's raven is an automaton, a machine programmed to say a single word. If a man, half mad with grief, takes it for an oracle and asks it questions, he can see his error or he can persist in projecting onto the raven his desperate hope that he has the use of an oracle. Thus the raven, asked its name, answers, "Nevermore." The grief-stricken man observes bitterly and hysterically that not even his loneliness will be alleviated by the bird named Nevermore, for it, too, like his friends and hopes, will abandon him "on the morrow." To this the raven replies "Nevermore." It is here that the man realizes that the raven's vocabulary consists of one word. Madness, however, has its own logic. The bird, for instance, may have been sent by God to help him forget his grief, and if sent by God, may therefore have theological wisdom. So he asks it if there is balm in Gilead. Meaning? "Will I be comforted in my loss by faith? Will I be united with Lenore in Heaven? Is there a Heaven? Is there life after death? Is Lenore with God? Does God exist? The question is Jeremiah's, at 8:22, "Is there no balm in Gilead?" Jeremiah was asking, by way of rhetorical flourish, if Newcastle has no coal. Poe transformed the meaning to: is there really a Newcastle, and is there coal there? To which Nevermore replies, "Nevermore." The next question is blunter: will he ever be reunited with Lenore? "Nevermore." The speaker orders the raven out of his house, and the raven refuses ever to leave. And never is also when the speaker's soul will be disentangled from the raven's shadow; his despair is permanent.

Poe had met the situation before. In Richmond he had seen Maelzel's machine that played chess, and saw through it (guessing, rightly, that it had a man concealed in it). In both the chess-playing machine and the univerbal raven Poe was looking at Presbyterian theology: all is predestined, or some human intermediary wants us to believe that it is. Worse, we are disposed by our helplessness in grief, despair, or bewilderment to cooperate with the idea of mechanized fate. After reason has acted, we can still find a residue of superstition. There is a part of our reason willing to believe that automata have minds. In that dark space Poe wrote. The ape in "The Murders in the Rue Morgue" is an automaton, as Roderick Usher is a zombie when he buries his sister alive. Calvin and Newton both gave us a machine for a world, a gear-work of inevitabilities.

DARWINIAN MOCKING-BIRD

Whitman's reply to "The Raven" is "Out of the Cradle Endlessly Rocking." Again, an oracle is questioned. The answer (from bird and the sound of the sea together) is polyphonic, *love* and *death* together. Life and death are a Heraclitean rhythm, independent. Whitman returns to the Greek sense that love is deepest in its tragic awareness of the brevity of life, of youth, of beauty.

TIME

Time for Poe was the monotonous tick of the universe, the unstoppable tread of death, coming closer second by second (like walls closing in, the swing of a pendulum, the sealing up of a wall brick by brick, footsteps evenly mounting a stair). Whitman's time was tidal, migratory, the arousal and satisfaction of desire. Hopkins knew that time was over at the moment it began, that it had no dimensions, that Christ on the cross cancelled all adverbs. There is no *soon*, no *never*. There is only the swoop of the hawk, the eyes that say *follow me* to the fisherman, the giddy ecstasy of *I stop somewhere waiting for you*.

11 MAY 1888: WHITMAN IN CAMDEN, TALKING

"Do I like Poe? At the start, for many years, not: but three or four years ago I got to reading him again, reading and liking, until at last—yes, now—I feel almost convinced that he is a star of considerable magnitude, if not a sun, in the literary firmament. Poe was morbid, shadowy, lugubrious—he seemed to suggest dark nights, horrors, spectralities—I could not originally stomach him at all. But today I see more of him than that—much more. If that was all there was to him he would have died long ago. I was a young man of about thirty, living in New York, when The Raven appeared—created its stir: everybody was excited about it—every reading body: somehow it did not enthuse me." [Whitman had given "Out of the Cradle Endlessly Rocking" its final revision (it was written in 1859) the year before, and placed it at the heart of the new "Sea-Drift" section of the 1881 *Leaves of Grass*.]

QUICK, SAID THE BIRD, FIND THEM, FIND THEM

The history of birds taken to be daimons traverses religions, folklore, and literature, In Europe it begins with the drawing of a bird mounted on pole in Lascaux. In the New World we can trace it back to the Amerindian understanding of the meadowlark as a mediator between men and spirits of the air. Poe's raven, Keats' nightingale, Shelley's skylark, Olson's kingfisher, Whitman's osprey, thrush, and mocking-bird, Hopkins' windhover are but modulations in a long tradition, a dance of forms to a perennial spiritual force.

BOYS SMELL LIKE ORANGES

On a fine autumn afternoon in 1938 two elderly men met at the Porte Maillot, as was their habit, to walk together in the Bois de Boulogne, Professor Lucien Lévy-Bruhl, who was eighty and strolled with an easy dignity, his hands behind his back except to accompany a remark with rounded gestures, and Pastor Maurice Leenhardt, missionary and ethnographer, who was sixty, tall and white-haired, his usual long stride curbed to match the amble of his slower friend.

They knew all the paths and small roads, the playing fields and children's zoo, and each had favorites among them, the one making his choice without a word from the other.

—These Trumai we were talking about yesterday, Lévy-Bruhl said, who are known by their neighbors to sleep at the bottom of the river.

He stooped to greet and stroke a cat, causing a second and third to glide from the underbrush. Pastor Leenhardt took the occasion to light his pipe. Lévy-Bruhl held out empty hands to show the cats he had nothing to give them. There was an old woman laden with sacks who fed cats in the Bois. She was one of the regulars they met on their walks.

—Madame your friend will be along. We know that it is a waste of breath trying to explain to the Trumai's neighbors that nobody can sleep underwater. They *know* they do. The syllogism men cannot sleep underwater, the Trumai are men, therefore the Trumai cannot sleep underwater won't work.

—Perhaps, Pastor Leenhardt said, we are looking at their logic the wrong way.

—Their logic!

Footballers, their shoulders sagging, their feet heavy, straggled muddy and tuckered toward the goalposts, where they sat and lay, like tired soldiers making bivouac. Some were in jerseys so worn that the blue was slate and the red collars and cuffs pink, colors more fitting for a Chinese poet than for a French boy. Late-afternoon light burnished their hair, making flames of cowlicks. Time stood still.

The captain of the junior team, Jacques Peyrony, fifteen and a half, was pulling on his sweater when he saw that he was being spoken to by an older halfback on the senior team, Robinet, twenty-four.

—Went down four to one, ouch! Robinet said. I've been watching you for the last twenty minutes.

—I saw you.

Peyrony's face was gloriously dirty from being wiped with muddy hands. His hair tangled out over his ears. It spun onto his forehead from a whorl like a young bull's. He rubbed sweat from his eyelashes with his forearm. His mouth was half open with fatigue.

—So you noticed me? I like that, but didn't think you did. When you were barreling toward the touchline you gave me a quick glance as if I were a total stranger. No time for a hello, I know.

Peyrony flopped down on the grass. Robinet took off his jacket and laid it over his legs.

—Keep warm, he said. Cold muscles don't relax.

A dog who was being allowed by his person to romp galloped over to them, wagged his tail to ask if he could meet them, laughing, got called *bon bougre,* and came and sniffed Peyrony's crotch.

—*Connaisseur!* said Robinet. But to my nose Peyrony smells like oranges.

Peyrony reached across Robinet's legs, grabbed a dandelion out of the grass and ate it, yellow flower, stem, leaves, and root.

—Green, he said. Raw spinach is greener. The best part of the orange is the rind, a nibble of it with the pulp and juice.

Robinet's frank eyes watched Peyrony chewing.

—Girls suck lemons.

—It figures. Next they'll be playing rugby. Do they smell like lemons?

—We must suppose so.

—The greener the bitterer. Over there's licorice. The Bois is full of it. The young roots halfway up the stem are sweet. Apple's the best of tastes, pear next. The citrons are something else.

—Kumquats, Robert said.

—*Vraiment.* And peaches.

Lucien Lévy-Bruhl walked with his hands behind his back. He stopped, spread a hand on his chest, and bowed to Maurice Leenhardt.

—My father, Leenhardt had said, held a fact to be the word of God.

—And your father taught science and was a geologist and, like yourself, was a Huguenot pastor?

—He respected Darwin and Lyell with the same honor he paid to whoever wrote First and Second Samuel, a history without logic or consistency, a text so archaic that it makes Homer seem as polished as Balzac. Its names and places are confused, its narrative is frequently incoherent. The narrator is concerned with effect and high drama, with the terribleness of a bloody and arbitrary god and with human nature at its darkest.

—And is also, like a fact, the word of God?

—The poetry, perhaps. The music. Its truth, as with myth and folktale, is deep inside. That is why it is so beautiful.

Peyrony searched around in a pocket and found the pulpy and gritty remains of an orange.

—For you, he said. I didn't finish it at halftime, as I ran to the *bistrot* in the woods and got half a cup of milk.

—*Half* a cup! Robinet said laughing. You're learning.

—Butted that damned kick full force with the top of my noggin, and it still hurts.

—Take an aspirin when you get home.

—Maybe. It will go away when I've showered.

—I love the way you look after yourself, goose. A week ago you had a cold which, as I remember, you proposed to cure with a good rubdown.

—So what do you think of the team?

—Anything's possible. You have them in command. And it's to your credit that several of them play better than you.

—I know that all too well.

—Is it, Lévy-Bruhl asked, that they think differently, or that they don't think at all?

—Differently, yes, and it's what that difference can tell us that makes up ethnology as a subject. In New Caledonia *I* was the difference, my wife and children and I. We were intruders. We smelled peculiar, we spoke their language idiotically. We could not guess what we symbolized to them, what threats we brought. The English hope of exporting iron kettles, pots, and pans to Russia in the seventeenth century was dashed by the Orthodox clergy, who were certain that devils inhabited these utensils. We were lucky in that needles and thread were thought wonderful by our New Caledonians, who have clever fingers and like making things. My first great gift was arithmetic. The island traders had been cheating them for years. I taught adding, subtracting, and dividing. That five from eight was always three gave them assurance that in me there was sound doctrine somewhere. Of the multiplication table they made a hymn and sang it in church.

—*Mon dieu! C'est joli, ça!*

—They know, Robinet said, that a good captain isn't always the best player on the team. And even if you fuck up as captain, they'll play well right on, regardless. When in the last quarter you stubbornly badgered that winded

93

player instead of making a decisive breakthrough, you can be sure that Labbé and that kid with the English hair saw how wrong you were but went along with you because you've trained them to. That's fine. What in the name of God are you doing?

—Getting some leaves to eat. I'm listening.

—Off of a tree?

—They're good. And some sweetgrass, here, and whatever this frilly weed is. Nettles are good only in the spring.

—*Le forêt de Rouvray,* Lévy-Bruhl said. The oak forest, *roveretum.* I played here as a child. Do primitive people ever play?

—What else do they do?

—Some advice, Robinet said, replacing his jacket over Peyrony's legs, throw Guilhermet off the team. He's weak. Every signal you give him, he's parked on his butt like those streetcars that spend half their trip stopped.

Peyrony chewed a leaf, staring across the level late-afternoon sun on the field.

—But he's my only friend on the team.

—Einstein in an article I've been reading says that the eternally incomprehensible thing about the world is that it is comprehensible. The years I've spent trying to comprehend the primitive mind.

Pastor Leenhardt, smiling, relit his pipe.

—Einstein! he said. Gravity, light, magnetic fields, time, history are as unintelligible still. None of these trouble the primitive mind, or even come to its attention. There are subatomic particles, the physicists say, which can be in two places at once. We have discussed the unfortunate missionary accused of stealing a Micronesian's yams. The missionary was miles away at the time of the theft, picking up his mail at the port. This would have settled the matter for a French jury. It cut no ice in the Micronesian mind.

—You are confusing two things, Robinet said poking a finger against Peyrony's nose. The discipline of the team applies to Guilhermet too. The team has one ideal, as its motto says, to do its best. So throw Guilhermet off, gently, with some tact and grace, but throw him off.

—I wouldn't like playing without him.

—How do you know? Is his being on the team to have him near you more important than having another player who knows what he's doing?

—He stays. He's my best friend.

—You're sure?

—I'm not joking. He stays.

Robinet was quiet for awhile.

—In that case, keep a sharp eye on him. Make your friendship useful. Make him understand that he must play well, for you.

A ball, kicked by a player who had gone back to the field, was falling from high in the air toward two companions. Peyrony bounded up, as if catapulted, leapt, and caught it between his thighs and midriff, like a nut in a nutcracker. He released it to roll down one leg, balanced it on his toe, and then held his foot on it, David with the head of Goliath. He then jumped it into the air with both feet and kicked it with a solid dry *thunk* across the field, his leg at a perfect right angle to his body.

La liberté de cette jambe.

—Thought you were frazzled, Robinet said. You're worse than a dog that can't keep out of whatever fray's handy.

—It is as if the primitive mind thought with things rather than concepts and words, Pastor Leenhardt said. Our logic falls between things, and connects them, or dissociates them. We cannot believe that a young man who thinks himself ugly and unloved can become a bird and be befriended by the girl he longs for. You know the myth.

—Oof! Peyrony said. A good leg can't resist a hurdle. A leg that snaps into action and takes you along with it is a good leg.

—You've a fine leg, for sure.

Peyrony absentmindedly opened Robinet's small backpack, looking around in it.

—*Baume Bengué!*

He uncapped the tube, sniffed, and made a show of falling backwards.

—Comb, clean socks, experienced underwear, and *tiens!* A book. *De natura rerum* of all things. You read Lucretius at halftime?

—On the train, coming in. Speaking of which, shall we go back together?

Silence, with thought.

—I promised Maman I'd take the 6:32, and you stay later, don't you?

The rain that had been threatening began to fall as a light shower. Peyrony took his beret from his backpack. He found a twig and began to chew it.

Robinet, staring at Peyrony, paid no attention to the rain.

—I think I'll call you on your fib, he said, to see what's behind it. Just yesterday your mother told me that she never expected you before eight, or half past. I won't deceive you in keeping back that you're handing me a line.

Peyrony picked a blade of grass and ate it.

—The truth, then, he said smiling. I'd rather go back with the team.

—Than with me. And so's not to admit that, you fib. Remember last summer, when you asked me to go with you to the France-Angleterre match, and I said no, that I was going with Remond, just that, no explanation, thinking I was doing you the honor of imagining that you were above silly infatuations. There are times when I prefer to be with Remond than with you, so there are times you'd rather be with the team than with me. Absolutely natural and reasonable. But take care. You begin with a pretense of being nice, and then trickery gets into it, and then you find yourself fucking with people's feelings for the fun of it. Look, we're football players, not like those tennis players over there running in from the rain. Telling the truth is part of having a well-built body. So is letting it rain on you. Take your beret off. The rain wants to know who you are.

—Rain is a blessing, Lévy-Bruhl said, holding out his tongue to taste it. For my old bones, however, I think that copse with the benches is wise.

—Europeans rarely see real rain. They see gentle rain like this, and a cloud-burst now and again. Rain in the Pacific is a season all to itself. Napoleon only thought he had seen mud when he called it the fifth element.

—The light is beautiful here. Would the primitive mind think it beautiful?

—Why not? It would be sensitive to the pleasantness you're calling beautiful light, but it would be very interested in the spirit inside this old tree, and in events that have happened here, a murder or debate or words of power said here by a wise elder.

Peyrony, throwing aside the jacket over his legs and pushing his tall socks down to his ankles, stretched out and welcomed the rain.

—Your boots, Robinet said, Do they lace up to a proper fit?

—I think so. Yes.

—A good boot must be against the foot on all surfaces, snug.

He felt his boot all over, pressing with his fingers, like a doctor palpating.

—How are your cleats holding up? They feel firm. Let me see your other foot.

—No!

—You're not really saying no, Robinet said, seizing the other leg by the ankle and inspecting the sole while Peyrony, half-angry, protested. So you're of the race of soldiers who would rather face death than dig a foxhole? Better to lose a cleat, bungle a kick, and risk fucking up a play than make a boring visit to the cobbler, is that it?

He tore the wobbly cleat from Peyrony's sole.

—Now you have to replace this boot.

—You idiot!

—Before every match line up your little shits and inspect every foot, carefully.

—What we call myth, Pastor Leenhardt said, is the very essence of the prim-itive mind. The logic is of things, not ideas. In First Samuel it's the honey on the tip of Jonathan's spear and lost asses found by prophets that occupy a space we would fill with abstract nouns and verbs, or omit altogether. Unless, of course, we are poets and children.

—Not, then, an early logic but an alternative one?

—What, after all, *is* thought? And why should we French, who have given the world a Pasteur and a Voltaire, be so curious about the mentality of Trobriand Islanders?

—The mentality, ah yes.

—I play backfield exclusively, Robinet said. For an hour and a half I serve the ball to the forwards. Only that, nothing more. *I serve.* I must make up for the errors, stopping balls that have got past, converting weaknesses into strengths. It's a lively position. To block a strapping big bastard going like a cannonball before he can make trouble is to be alive. Your ordinary person in his daily round experiences nothing like it. To outwit galloping bulls in cleated boots coming at you like a freight train and come out in one piece, that's looking life in the eye. You have balls. You feel big. You're free of all the mingy littleness that makes people tightfisted and afraid.

—It's done you good, hasn't it? I mean, you're still in shape.

—I started out as a brawler, believe me, with fingers in eyes and elbows in ribs, but now I stick to the rules, like the clean English players, chest forward and shoulders squared. What's behind me is history.

—This light, this lovely light. Monet can paint light.

—These trees are a word of God. I learned that from the Kanaka. A leaf is a word. They have a tree that embodies forgiveness, and I gave its name to Jesus. They could have taken him for a word, except that he wasn't there. The tree was. Everything, *mon cher Lucien,* is a fiction we have supplied to complement nature.

—If we could know the history of gestures.

Pastor Leenhardt chuckled.

—Because people without history have a history. There is no event without a past.

Peyrony was eating a stick.

—There was a woman sitting near me at the Rouen match last week who said to her boyfriend that you play like a cow. You do keep your eyes lowered and shift about like somebody who has wandered onto the field.

—That way I can do inside the rules all sorts of things that could count as errors, like not responding to taunts, saving my revenge for later. That was the one pleasure in the war, getting even. I forget what writer said that the Roman circus was a focussing and containment of violence. If I don't take out my aggressions on the field I'd bloody noses in the streetcar.

—But there's the saying that we should do unto others as we'd like them to treat us. It's in the Bible, I think.

—And it's wrong. Have you ever heard me complain about a player who's rough and mean? Do to others what they're doing to you. When you're on top of a return, naturally you're going to feed it to the team, and naturally you're going to feint, right? You've got Beyssac's eye, and Beyssac is the last person you're going to kick the ball to, and then you kick it to Beyssac.

—And the Red Lions always fall for it.

—*Eh bien!* Beside that little ruse we can put a phrase of Aristotle.

—Aristotle! *Merde alors.*

—Don't laugh at Aristotle. It is precisely when we seem most modern that we are imitating the past. I love sport, its training and spirit, the more for knowing that the classical world loved it. Aristotle said of gymnastics that they make a strategic mind, a healthy and prudent soul, and shape a liberal and courageous character. Aristotle would have said that of football, yes?

—He makes it all very moral, doesn't he? Where's the fun?

—The beauty of it is in the word *liberal:* an openness of spirit, an acceptance of the world. For the hour and a half of a game you're freely consenting with a male and liberal heart to all the fire and sanctions of the game. You accept that the sun goes in when it might have got in the other team's eyes, and that it blazes out when it's in ours. You accept the wind going against you and its dying down when it might have been in your favor. You accept your team's doing the opposite of what you know is the right play.

Peyrony listened with big eyes. Eating grass.

The rain was letting up. Lévy-Bruhl stood, brushed his sleeves with his hands, and nodded toward their path.

—Have you read Swedenborg? I mean, some of him.

—I see what you're thinking. The primitive in his imagination, his globes of light and angels and geometrical heaven, can be found in poets and mystics, in Balzac and Baudelaire. Do you want primitive thought to be subsumed in the enlightened mind?

—Is there an enlightened mind?

—Leonardo, Locke, Voltaire, Aristotle.

—Darwin, the two Humboldts, Montaigne, none of whom built villages that are poems of symbols and ideas, like my Kanaka.

Peyrony smeared the rain on his legs, pulling his shorts back as far as they would wad.

—Your Labbé and the kid with the English hair obeyed your signals when they clearly thought they were cockeyed. In football you accept all the unnecessary strain and fatigue of going through hopeless plays, like when I tear off after a man I know is faster than I, for the satisfaction of knowing that I did my damndest, eh? You accept it when Beyssac makes an end run and scores, when it was I, I alone, who set up the play. You accept the referee's idiot rulings. You try to protest and Raimondou, the shit, shouts me down. He was eighteen and I was twenty-five, and he was wrong and I was right, but I was already learning the truth of what Goethe said: *an injustice is preferable to disorder.*

—Myth, my dear Lucien, is not a narrative. It is life itself, the way a people live.

Peyrony tried to wash his face with rain from the grass.

—You're merely rearranging the mud, Robinet said. It makes you look as wild as a savage, a nice savage. Are you listening to a word I'm saying?

—Goethe the football player.

—It's in the hour and a half of the game that I know myself, you understand? I have to face all over again that I'm short of wind, that I let the ball get away from me, that I can't kick straight half the time. I also know that I'm in a concentration of awesome power, a power that's an electricity or the gift of a *daimon,* the mystery of *form.* It isn't constant, it comes and goes, without reason or rule. My legs on the field scythe down all the hours of the rest of the day. I feel like a god, I feel reborn and new-made, and know all over again that the body has a soul of its own, independent of the other.

Lévy-Bruhl and Pastor Leenhardt came to the walk along the playing fields where they could see boys resting in groups as colorful as signal flags on a ship.

—The word is the thing, Pastor Leenhardt said, or the word and thing are so inextricably together that the thing is sacred, as the word is, too. A man's word, his yes or no, is the man. A liar is his lie.

—How we participate, Lévy-Bruhl said, stopping to thrust his hands into his pockets, *how* does not matter, for there are endless ways of participating. Surely the deepest participation is entirely symbolic, invisible, unmeasurable. I'm thinking of identity under differences, my Jewishness, your Protestant grounding. Neither of us ostensibly participates in French culture in my sense, and yet, keeping the remark between ourselves, we *are* French culture.

They could see boys straying from the fields, getting up from their bivouac, stretching tall, pulling up socks, shaking hands.

—You will find, I think, Pastor Leenhardt was saying, that all thought among primitives, and perhaps everywhere, begins with a perception of beauty.

—You mean form, symmetry, a coherence of pattern. The light is even lovelier after the rain.

—The past to the Kanaka is *old light.* The light in which the ancestors grew yams and made the villages into words.

—*How many autumns will an old man see?* asks a Japanese poet.

—Twilight in New Caledonia is only half an hour. Even so, it is understood to be in four movements. The first is when a dark blue appears in the grass, night's first step. The second is when field mice awake and begin to come out of their burrows. The third is when the shadows are dark and rich and the gods can move about in them unseen. The fourth is night itself, when one cannot see the boundaries of the sacred places and there is no blame for not knowing that your foot is on the grass of the sanctuaries.

A little girl, hustled into her pram by an officious nurse, discovered halfway home from the park that her doll Belinda had been left behind. The nurse had finished her gossip with the nurse who minced with one hand on her hip, and had had a good look at the grenadiers in creaking boots who strolled in the park to eye and give smiling nods to the nurses. She had posted a letter and sniffed at various people. Lizaveta had tried to talk to a little boy who spoke only a soft gibberish, had kissed and been kissed by a large dog.

And Belinda had been left behind. They went back and looked for her in all the places they had been. The nurse was in a state. Lizaveta howled. Her father and mother were at a loss to comfort her, as this was the first tragedy of her life and she was indulging all its possibilities. Her grief was the more terrible in that they had a guest to tea, Herr Doktor Kafka of the Assicurazioni Generali, Prague office.

—Dear Lizaveta! Herr Kafka said. You are so very unhappy that I am going to tell you something that was going to be a surprise. Belinda did not have time to tell you herself. While you were not looking, she met a little boy her own age, perhaps a doll, perhaps a little boy, I couldn't quite tell, who invited her to go with him around the world. But he was leaving immediately. There was no time to dally. She had to make up her mind then and there. Such things happen. Dolls, you know, are born in department stores, and have a more advanced knowledge than those of us who are brought to houses by storks. We have such a limited knowledge of things. Belinda did, in her haste, ask me to tell you that she would write, daily, and that she would have told you of her sudden plans if she had been able to find you in time.

Lizaveta stared.

But the very next day there was a postcard for her in the mail. She had never had a postcard before. On its picture side was London Bridge, and on the other lots of writing which her mother read to her, and her father, again, when he came home for dinner.

✳

Dear Lizaveta: We came to London by balloon. Oh, how exciting it is to float over mountains, rivers, and cities with my friend Rudolf, who had packed a lunch of cherries and jam. The English are very strange. Their clothes cover all of them, even their heads, where the buttons go right up into their hats, with button holes, so to speak, to look out of, and a kind of sleeve for their very large noses. They all carry umbrellas, as it rains constantly, and long poles to poke their way through the fog. They live on muffins and tea. I have seen the King in a carriage drawn by forty horses, stepping with precision to a drum. More later. Your loving doll, Belinda.

✳

Dear Lizaveta: We came to Scotland by train. It went through a tunnel all the way from London to Edinburgh, so dark that all the passengers were issued lanterns to read *The Times* by. The Scots all wear kilts, and dance to the bagpipe, and eat porridge which they cook in kettles the size of our bathtub. Rudolf and I have had a picnic in a meadow full of sheep. There are bandits everywhere. Most of the people in Edinburgh are lawyers, and their families live in apartments around the courtrooms. More later. Your loving friend, Belinda.

✳

Dear Lizaveta: From Scotland we have traveled by steam packet to the Faeroe Islands, in the North Sea. The people here are all fisherfolk and belong to a religion called The Plymouth Brothers, so that when they aren't out in boats hauling in nets full of herring, they are in church singing hymns. The whole island rings with music. Not a single tree grows here, and the houses have rocks on their roofs, to keep the wind from blowing them away. When we said we were from Prague, they had never heard of it, and asked if it were on the moon. Can you imagine! This card will be slow getting there, as the mail boat comes but once a month. Your loving companion, Belinda.

✳

Dear Lizaveta: Here we are in Copenhagen, staying with a nice gentleman named Hans Christian Andersen. He lives next door to another nice gentleman named Søren Kierkegaard. They take Rudolf and me to a park that's wholly for children and dolls, called Tivoli. You can see what it looks like by turning over this card. Every afternoon at 4 little boys dressed in red (and they are all blond and have big blue eyes) march through Tivoli, and around and around it, beating drums and playing fifes. The harbor is the home of several mermaids. They are very shy and you have to be very patient and stand still a long time to see them. The Danes are melancholy and drink lots of coffee and read only serious books. I saw a book in a shop with the title *How To Be Sure As To What Is And What Isn't*. And *The Doll's Guide To Existentialism; If This, Then What?* And *You Are More Miserable Than You Think You Are*. In haste, Belinda.

Dear Lizaveta: The church bells here in St. Petersburg ring all day and all night long. Rudolf fears that our hearing will be affected. It snows all year round. There's a samovar in every streetcar. They read serious books here, too. Their favorite author is Count Tolstoy, who is one of his own peasants (they say this distresses his wife), and who eats only beets, though he adds an onion at Passover. We can't read a word of the shop signs. Some of the letters are backwards. The men have bushy beards and look like bears. The women keep their hands in muffs. Your shivering friend, Belinda.

Dear Lizaveta: We have crossed Siberia in a sled over the snow, and now we are on Sakhalin Island, staying with a very nice and gentle man whose name is Anton Chekhov. He lives in Moscow, but is here writing a book about this strange northern place where the mosquitoes are the size of parrots and all the people are in jail for disobeying their parents and taking things that didn't belong to them. The Russians are very strict. Mr. Chekhov pointed out to us a man who is serving a thousand years for not saying *Gesundheit* when the Czar sneezed in his hearing. It is all very sad. Mr. Chekhov is going to do something about it all, he says. He has a cat name of Pussinka who is anxious to return to Moscow and doesn't like Sakhalin Island at all, at all. Your loving friend, Belinda.

Dear Lizaveta: Japan! Oh, Japan! Rudolf and I have bought kimonos and roll about in a rickshaw, delighting in views of Fujiyama (a blue mountain with snow on top) through wisteria blossoms and cherry orchards and bridges that make a hump rather than lie flat. The Japanese drink tea in tiny cups. The women have tall hairdos in which they have stuck yellow sticks. Everybody stops what they are doing ten times a day to write a poem. These poems, which are very short, are about crickets and seeing Fujiyama through the wash on the line and about feeling lonely when the moon is full. We are very popular, as the Japanese like novelty. Excitedly, Belinda.

✳

Dear Lizaveta: Here we are in China. That's the long wall on the other side of the card. The emperor is a little boy who wears a dress the color of paprika. He lives in a palace the size of Prague, with a thousand servants. To get from his nursery to his throne he has a chair between two poles, and is carried. Five doctors look at his poo-poo when he makes it. Sorry to be vulgar, but what's the point of travel if you don't learn how different people are outside Prague? Answer me that. The Chinese eat with two sticks and slurp their soup. Their hair is tied in pigtails. The whole country smells of ginger, and they say *plog* for Prague. All day long firecrackers, firecrackers, firecrackers! Your affectionate Belinda.

✳

Dear Lizaveta: We have sailed to Tahiti in a clipper ship. This island is all pink and green, and the people are brown and lazy. The women are very beautiful, with long black hair and pretty black eyes. The children scamper up palm trees like monkeys and wear not a stitch of clothes. We have met a Frenchman name of Gauguin, who paints pictures of the Tahitians, and another Frenchman named Pierre Loti, who wears a fez and reads the European newspapers in the café all day and says that Tahiti is Romantic. What Rudolf and I say is that it's very hot and decidedly uncivilized. Have I said that Rudolf is of the royal family? He's a good sport, but he has his limits. There are no *streets* here! Romantically, Belinda.

✳

Well! dear Lizaveta, San Francisco! Oh my! There are streets here, all uphill, and with gold prospectors and their donkeys on them. There are saloons with swinging doors, and Flora Dora girls dancing inside. Everybody plays *Oh Suzanna!* on their banjos (everybody has one) and everywhere you see Choctaws in blankets and cowboys with six-shooters and Chinese and Mexicans and Esquimaux and Mormons. All the houses are of wood, with fancy carved trimmings, and the gentry sit on their front porches and read political newspapers. Anybody in America can run for any public office whatever, so that the mayor of San Francisco is a Jewish tailor and his councilmen are a Red Indian, a Japanese gardener, a British earl, a Samoan cook, and a woman Presbyterian preacher. We have met a Scotsman name of Robert Louis Stevenson, who took us to see an Italian opera. Yours ever, Belinda.

❋

Dear Lizaveta: I'm writing this in a stagecoach crossing the Wild West. We have seen many Indian villages of teepees, and thousands of buffalo. It took hours to get down one side of the Grand Canyon, across its floor (the river is shallow and we rolled right across, splashing) and up the other side. The Indians wear colorful blankets and have a feather stuck in their hair. Earlier today we saw the United States Cavalry riding along with the American flag. They were singing "Yankee Doodle Dandy" and were all very handsome. It will make me seasick to write more, as we're going as fast as a train. Dizzily, Belinda.

❋

Dear Lizaveta: We have been to Chicago, which is on one of the Great Lakes, and crossed the Mississippi, which is so wide you can't see across it, only paddle-steamers in the middle, loaded with bales of cotton. We have seen utopias of Quakers and Shakers and Mennonites, who live just as they want to in this free country. There is no king, only a Congress which sits in Washington and couldn't care less what the people do. I have seen one of these Congressmen. He was fat (three chins, I assure you) and offered Rudolf and me a dollar each if we would vote for him. When we said we were from Prague, he said he hoped we'd start a war, as war is good for business. On to New York! In haste, your loving Belinda.

❋

Dear Lizaveta: How things turn out! Rudolf and I are married! Oh yes, at Niagara Falls, where you stand in line, couple after couple, and get married by a Protestant minister, a rabbi, or a priest, take your choice. Then you get in a barrel (what fun!) and ride over the falls—you bounce and bounce at the bottom—and rent a honeymoon cabin, of which there are hundreds around the falls, each with a happy husband and wife billing and cooing. I know from your parents that my sister in the department store has come to live with you and be your doll. Rudolf and I are going to the Argentine. You must come visit our ranch. I will remember you forever. Mrs. Rudolph Hapsburg und Porzelan (your Belinda).

THE MESSENGERS

His cabin at the Jungborn Spa in the Harz Mountains had large windows without curtains or shutters and a glass door so that sunlight fell in on all fours after its abrupt journey through space, home at last. Some pipe-smoking architect in knickerbockers who had seen English country cottages in *The Studio* had fused a *Mon Repos* with *Jugendstil* in its rectilinear and functional mode and come up with this many-windowed shoe box, perhaps with the help of an elf and a Marxist agronomist. He had never before had a house all to himself.

A naked idealist was already pushing a pamphlet under the door. An army of geese was making its way into the meadow.

His visions of *Naturheilkunde* were largely from *Náš Skautík,* the sun-gilded youth in which, awash with air and light, springing from rock to rock across streams, hatcheting saplings and roping them into structures with the genius of beavers, made him feel like Ivan Ilych envying rude health.

But the pamphleteer, whom he could see continuing along the dirt road, bowlegged, was bald and round-shouldered, and an elephant's tail would have fitted right in on his behind.

Would a household god set up shop in this cabin? Wouldn't its reek of sawn pine and shellac and the chemical aroma of the linoleum be uncongenial to a *lar* who for thousands of years was used to rising dough, peasants' stockings, and wine?

Outside, July. He could see the vast roof of the *pensione* over the trees. The cabins were set romantically along the leafy roads, or tucked into dells and glades.

The pamphlet was about vegetarianism and the diffusion of Mind throughout Nature. Just so.

Now for patience. It was impatience that got us thrown out of the Garden, and impatience keeps us from returning. Air and light and peace of soul were why he was here. Carrot juice and lectures. Presumably his effects were safe in his suitcase on the folding trestle at the foot of the bed. He laid out his toothbrush and comb beside the pitcher and basin. The household god, named Mildew or Jug Ears, must have noted him by this time, peeping from round the chamber pot or from inside the lamp. There was no key to the cabin.

Once, when there was a choice of being kings or messengers, we, being children, chose to be messengers, arms and legs flying as we romped from castle to castle. We got the messages wrong as like as not, or forgot them, or fell asleep in the forest while kings died of anxiety.

Bathing drawers. He would go out to the meadow, where he could see a man reading two books at once, in bathing drawers. Everybody else that he could see was nude.

And there, as he drew them on, watching him with an innocent smile, was the household god, its cap respectfully in its hands.

—My name is Beeswax, it said. I am going to sleep in your shoe. What is your name?

—My name? Why it's Amschel. I mean, Franz. By the world I am Franz Kafka.

—A *kavka* is a jackdaw.

—A grackle. *Graculus,* in Latin a blackbird.

—Yes.

Max was used to conversations between chairs in letters and would not challenge a household god in a cabin at a nudist health spa.

—Max Brod, my best friend, will like hearing about you. He and I have been travelling together. We visited Goethe's house. I dreamed that night of a rabbit in a Sicilian garden. I am here to breathe all the fresh air I can and to bathe in sunlight. So I'm going out now, to the meadow.

—Yes, I will look at your things. If you should chance upon a garden, I would like a turnip. The buttons on your shoes are particularly interesting.

From the people he met along the road he got sweet smiles or analytical stares. Walking and dawdling was apparently part of the therapy. Some were as white as he, some pink, some brown. On a path into the meadow a gentleman wearing only a pince-nez and a knotted handkerchief on his bald head referred to its narrowness as *these Dardanelles.* He heard talk of Steiner and rhythmic awakenings.

His bathing drawers were a mistake. The logic of nudism was to be nude, but nude and naked were different conditions. Michelangelo's David was nude and the lean scouts in *Náš Skautík* were nude in or out of their short khaki pants, but the old fart over there with wings of hair out from his ears and pregnant with a volley ball, with spindle legs and wrinkled knees, is naked.

They were twins, the boys who crossed the path in front of him, or cousins or brothers very close in age, two young Swedes who, God knows, may be Swedenborgians, more likely Lutherans, perhaps Baptists of some sect with pure morals, sonorous hymns sung to fiddles and concertinas, and sermons three hours long in a wooden church through the windows of which you could see birches and cedars and snow. But now they were Castor and Pollux in an Austrian meadow.

Later, when he was going to the lodge to mail his letter to Max, they crossed his way again, naked as ancient Greeks at Elis, healthy as dogs, honey brown from the sun, their hair the color of meal, their large eyes blue.

Next day, the pink evangelist lying in the meadow reading two bibles at once bade Kafka good day and asked his opinion of prophecy.

His books were under an umbrella stuck in the meadow. He himself, pink as coral, was undergoing heliotherapy on a Navajo blanket.

—Here in First Samuel, he said. A company of prophets coming down with a psaltery, a pipe, and a harp, an event itself prophesied.

—My opinion would be an ignorant one.

The two Swedish boys, Jonathan and David, came side by side from the path in the pine wood. They walked like people holding hands, shoulder to shoulder, in step.

A company of prophets from the bare rock of a high place came down, dancing stately forward, with a raised knee and a straight knee, with a gliding step and a stomp, in time to a tabret, exalted by the chime of a harp and the trill of a flute, prophesying. *Is Saul also among the prophets?*

—Everyone, Kafka smiled, seems to have a message for me, as if I'd fallen among prophets.

—A word to the wise, said the evangelist. The Lord knows his own.

The noises outside his cabin at night were probably messages, but not for him: field mice passing on to field mice the advance of the summer according to the stars and the latest news of the Balkan wars. He had gone out in the deep of night, to lean wholly naked against his door, for the liberty of it. He had never had a door, nor the freedom to stand like Adam in moonlight.

But moonlight, Dr. Schlaf said in his lecture, is bad for you, along with wearing modern clothes, eating fruit, and thinking pessimistically. He had been an officer, in what army he did not specify, and had the refined manners of an insane aristocrat, speaking delicately with his fingertips together, with moist eyes open wide. He had published several works, which Kafka as an educated man would find interesting.

—You will know how to weigh my words and draw your own conclusions.

The day began with calisthenics in a group, with a phonograph playing marches to keep time to. The exercises were from Etienne-Jules Marey's manual for the French army, as modified by Swedish gymnasts for civilian health and beauty.

Adolf Just, the director of the Jungborn Spa for Naturtherapie had invented the Nudist Crawl whereby they went on all fours in a wide circle. The Swedish boys moved like elegant greyhounds.

Here in the countryside, ankle-deep in nameless meadow flowers, metaphysics and jurisprudence were as outcast as Adam and Eve from their paradise in Eden. God did not destroy that garden. He put us out of it. It is still where it was, going to seed for lack of care, or flourishing under divine husbandry. Or waiting in the orange groves of Palestine for agronomists like Ottla.

Max found in a book that the American follower of Jakob Boehme Ralph Waldo Emerson had gone blind and lame in some theological yeshiva of the Protestants and sought to restore his health by becoming a common farm laborer, weeding turnips and hoeing rows of maize. On this farm he met a fellow worker named Tarbox, of the Methodist sect. Theology was their constant topic. Herr Emerson was wondering one day if indeed God ever pays the least attention to our prayers.

—Yes He does, said Farmer Tarbox, and our trouble is that He answers them all.

It was a strategy of the sacred to appear in disguise, like Tobias's angel, a prosperous kinsman. The most biblical thing they were doing at the spa was working on the model farm like Pastor Emerson. They pitched hay onto a wagon behind the angels with scythes. On ladders out of Flemish painting they picked cherries. The first evening after pitching hay he read the Book of Ruth. There was a bible in every cabin.

To read in an Austrian meadow texts written in the desert was a kind of miracle. The thirtieth year after Hilkiah the priest found the book of the law in the house of the sanctuary, at midnight, after the setting of the moon, in the days of Josiah the king.

—To care for the body, the evangelist said, wiping his brow with a blue handkerchief, to live cleanly here in this pure air, soaking in the vital influences of the sun, is to move toward an awakening of the soul from doubt and sloth. Here, take this pamphlet, *The Prodigal Son,* and this one, *Bought, or No longer Mine: For Unbelieving Believers.*

Kafka mentioned, quietly, the inner light, his conscience.

—And this one, *Why Can't the Educated Man Believe in the Bible?*

The Swedish godlings strolled up, stopping at a safe distance, to listen. Their long foreskins puckered at the tip. Their pubic hair was a tawny orange. Their rumps were dimpled just back of the hip, as if to indicate that their long legs were well socketed. They were as comely, slender, and graceful as deer. They were like Asahel in Samuel, as swift of foot as the wild gazelle. Like the young David they were ruddy and had beautiful eyes.

—There is no prospect of grace for me, Kafka said.

He could not match the evangelist's staring sincerity, and lowered his eyes.

A thin old man with white hair and a red nose joined them, offering a remark from time to time, perhaps in Chaldean.

—Are you a Mormon? The evangelist asked. A Theosophist? But as a lawyer from Prague you are a Darwinian, aren't you?

Again Kafka pleaded the inviolable inwardness of the heart.

—Is Darwin among the prophets?

The old man, after coughing and wiping his lips, made another remark in Chaldean.

Castor and Pollux smiled as sweetly as angels.

He dreamed that his fellow nudists all annihilated each other. It was a battle of the naked against the naked, as in Mantegna. They kicked and drove swift blows with their fists. It started when they formed into two groups, joking and then taunting. A stalwart fellow took command of his group and shouted at the other.

—Lustron and Kastron!

—Ach! Lustron and Kastron?

—Exactly!

And then the brawl began, like fanatics in Goya. When it was over, there was nothing of them left. The vast meadow was empty.

Kafka woke, wondering.

Could the household god see his dreams? What would Dr. Freud say? What in the world do *lustron* and *kastron* mean?

The habit he had fallen into of seeing the well-built Swedish boys as Castor and Pollux, disregarding that their minds were a vegetation of ignorance, superstition, folklore, archaic fears, provincial opinions, and Lutheran piety, and that any conversation he might have with them would be about automobiles and Jesus, had something to do with the dream.

Latin endings rather than Greek would make the words into *castrum,* a castle, and *lustrum,* a cleansing. Pollux, *pollutum,* a defiling. Clean and filthy: antitheses. When antithetical particles in the atomic theory collide, they annihilate each other.

Castor and Pollux could not exist simultaneously. One could live only when the other was dead, a swap made by loving brothers.

In the botanical garden at Jena by the elephant ear, in his charcoal coat with the blue collar, Friedrich Schlegel said that a fragment should be complete in itself, like a porcupine.

To Castor and Pollux, next they bowed to him in passing, and while they were smiling in their innocent nudity, *I am a lawyer,* he might remark, *and I have a sister who is an agronomist.* This would probably sound like *I am a judge but I have a little brother who spins tops.*

And Castor would inquire of Pollux, *What are an agronomist?* The sun-browned fingers of a classical hand would scratch around in hair the color of meal. Blue eyes would puzzle themselves closed. —She makes trees grow. She plans to emigrate to Palestine and grow oranges and apricots. Sinai apples. Golden green oranges.

Pollux would look at Castor, Castor at Pollux.

Opposites do not cooperate. They annihilate each other.

It was next day, while talking with Herr Guido von Gillshausen, the retired captain who writes poetry and music, that he learned that the beautiful Swedish boys were named Jeremias and Barnabas. They had bowed as they passed, and the captain had spoken to them by name. Fine specimens, were they not?

In the evening Kafka was invited to a rifle meet by Dr. Schlaf and a Berlin hairdresser. The broad plain sloping up to the Bugberg was bordered by very old lindens and cut across by a railroad. The shooting was from a platform. Peasants near the targets kept score in a ledger. While the shooting cracked, fifers with women's handkerchiefs down their backs played sprightly airs. They wore medieval smocks. The rifles were ancient muzzle-loaders.

A band arrived, playing a colorful march, and regimental banners from the time of Napoleon were paraded past, with excited applause from both the villagers and the patients at the spa. Then a drum-and-fife corps caused even greater excitement. Meanwhile, the firing went on, with shouts of bull's-eyes. In the awfullest bombardments in the American Civil War the bands had continued to play waltzes and polkas.

When the shooting was over, they all marched away to the band, at the dying of the day under banked storm clouds, the Champion Shot at the head of the procession in a top hat and with a scarlet sash wound around his frock coat.

Jeremias and Barnabas had not come to the rifle meet. Perhaps they were determined to remain mother-naked for their stay at the spa. At home in Sweden did they wear large-sleeved pleated shirts and tight knee-pants, flat Protestant black hats and tasseled hobnail shoes?

Had they a language other than Swedish? The spa was the lower slopes of the Tower of Babel. Herr Just did his best with nouns and their equivalents, along with a wild irresponsibility of verbs. A family all with crossed eyes could not understand *dinner* or *supper* or *evening meal* but, *ja ja,* they wanted something to eat. A woman in a large straw hat told him all about Prague, where she had never been. It was discovered that he, *the man in the bathing trunks,* bought strawberry sodas for girls, from serious six-year-olds to giggling and brazen sixteen-year-olds, none of whom had either conversation or gratitude.

One evening his matches could not be found when he returned to his cabin. He borrowed a match from the cabin down the lane and by its light looked under his table. He found his water glass there. The lamp was under the bed, and when he'd lit it he saw that his chamber pot was on a ledge over the closet door, his matches were on the windowsill, his sandals were tucked behind the mirror. His inkwell and wet washcloth were under the blanket on the bed. Austrian humor.

The household god was nowhere to be seen.

—Beeswax? He called. Come out, the pranksters are gone.

He put the lamp on the bedside table and opened his *Education sentimentale*. If he were at home his mother would say he was simultaneously ruining his eyes and wasting oil.

His cabin by lamplight was as congenial and private a place as he had ever longed for.

Light in a copse of small trees, softened by leaves, could not be suspected of having come from the raging furnace of the sun. And why is the hospitality of the one inhabited planet so consistently inadequate? The terror of God and his angels has grown remote over the years, but like the sun it is still there, raging.

At Goethe's house with Max he had remembered that when Eckermann paid his first visit he was thoroughly and silently inspected inside the door by the poet's pretty grandsons Walter and Wolfgang. Then they flew clattering and tumbling to tell Grossvater that a stranger had come in from the street. Messengers.

The white geese by the pond were the German soul.

The angels who came to Sodom were two. The message they brought is unrecorded. They only said that they preferred to spend the night in the street. They were antithetical beings annihilating a city. Like long-legged Jeremias and Barnabas they had perhaps forgotten the message they had so carefully memorized, or lost it on the way, having set out like children, elbows high and hair flopping in their eyes, feet flying, and come to a meadow where it would be jolly to pick flowers, or a river to skip pebbles on.

How long had the book of the law been lost when Hilkiah the priest found it in the house of the sanctuary, at midnight, after the setting of the moon, in the days of Josiah the king?

—Beeswax, where are you?

How peaceful, the night. He would learn next day, from sly comments he was meant to overhear, that it was the girls for whom he bought strawberry sodas who disarranged his cabin.

—I am here, Beeswax said, in your shoe.

—What are the crickets saying?

—Some are saying *yes* and some are saying *no*. Their language has only those two words.

From empty castle to empty castle the messengers are flying, backtracking to find a lost shoe, stopping to pick berries, asking cows and sparrows the way from here to there, happy and proud in their importance.

THE AEROPLANES AT BRESCIA

Kafka stood on the seawall at Riva under the early September sky. But for his high-button shoes and flaring coat, his easy stance had an athletic clarity. He walked with the limberness of a racing cyclist. Otto Brod, with whom he had spent the morning discussing moving pictures and strolling along the shore under the voluble pines and yellow villas of the Via Ponale, lit a cigar and suggested a light beer before lunch. A wash of sweet air from the lake rattled a circle of pigeons, who flapped up into a shuttle of gulls. A fisherman in a blue apron reclined on the harbor steps smoking a small pipe. On a staff over a perfectly square building rippled the Austrian flag with its black, two-headed eagle. An old man knotting cords in a net strung between poles watched them with the open concern of the Italians. A soft bell rang in the hills.

—Good idea, said Kafka. It will get the taste of Dallago out of our mouths.

His eyes, when they could be seen under the broad brim of a black fedora, seemed abnormally large. To the natural swarthiness of his square face, rough of bone, Italy had already added, Otto noticed, a rose tint.

The *ora,* the south wind blowing up from Sirmione, had begun to scuff the dark blue of the lake. The old Venetian fort between the Città Riva and the railway station seemed to Kafka to be an intrusion into the Euclidean plainness of the houses of Riva. It reminded him of the *schloss* at Meran that had disturbed him not only for being vacant and blind in its casements but also because of the suspicion that it would inevitably return in his most anxious dreams. Even without his intuition of the mute claim of this empty castle to stay in his mind as a presence neither welcome nor explicable, it was always terrifying to know that there were things in the world empty of all significance and yet persisted, like heavy books of the law which mankind in a stubborn reluctance would not destroy and yet would not obey. The castle at Riva, the *Rocca,* the Rock, was a barracks housing the new conscripts, but the castle at Meran, the Brunnenburg, was a great shell. Suddenly he heard a telephone ringing in its high rooms, and made himself think instead of the morning at the Bagni della Madonnina and of Otto's polite but equivocal replies to Dallago the poet who had apologized by rote man's oneness with nature. What a fool, Otto had said later, on their walk.

The cubes of Riva, white and exact, were an architecture, Kafka remarked, the opposite of the lobes and tendrils of Prague. And there was truth in the light of Riva that was, as a poet might say, the opposite of the half-truths of the cut-glass sunlight of Prague, which had no fire in it, no absolute transparency. Instead of tall slabs of squared light in just proportions, Prague had weather of a dark and glittering richness.

Otto replied that the light here was pure and empty, creating a freedom among objects. The very shadows were incised. It is an older world, he added, and yet one to which the new architecture is returning. Concrete is but the Mediterranean mud house again, and glass walls a new yearning to see light sliced as in the openness of the Aegean landscape. The newest style, he said, is always in love with the oldest of which we are aware. The next *Wiedergeburt* will come from the engineers.

Max Brod, whom they had left writing at the *pensione,* was already at the café, and was holding above his head a newspaper for them to see.

—They are going to fly at Brescia! he shouted, and a waiter who might have been bringing a selzer to the Tsar of Bulgaria, so grave was his progress, looked with uninterrupted dignity over his shoulder at Max, who to him was but a Czech and probably a Jew, stamping his feet and rattling *La Sentinella Bresciana* in the air.

—Aeroplanes! Blériot! Cobianchi! *Die Brüder Wright!*

—*Due bionde, piacere,* Otto said to the waiter, who was relieved that the Czech's friends did not flap their arms and dance on the terrace.

—Incredible, Otto said. Absolutely incredible luck.

Kafka laughed outright, for Max was as of the moment as he a brooding postponer, and their friendship had always been a contest between the impulses of Max and the circumspect deliberation of Franz. It was a comedy that popped up everywhere between them. They had been in Riva a day, Max had spent a month convincing Franz that he must come to Riva on his vacation, and here was Max dashing them off on the second morning. But, as he quickly said, he could not question the call of the flying machines, which none of them had seen. They were well worth giving up the sweet quiet of Riva.

Otto took the newspaper from Max and laid it out on the table.

—Brescia is just at the other end of the lake, Max explained. We can take the steamboat to Salò, and get a local from there. It's three days off, but we'll want to be there at least the day before, as Mitteleuropa will have arrived in droves, with their cousins and their aunts. I've written the Committee there in the second paragraph. Naturally there is a Committee.

—By all means, Franz said, a Committee.

At its head, in gilt chairs, sat Dottore Civetta, Dottore Corvo, and Mangiafoco himself.

—I told them that we are journalists from Prague, and that we require accommodations.

In the last analysis, Kafka sighed, all things are miracles.

There was a steamboat the next morning. They boarded it and marvelled at the antiquity of its machinery and the garishness of its paint.

Only six years ago, Max had told them the evening before at the café, under a sky much higher than the skies of Bohemia and with stars twice the size of those of Prague, two Americans had chosen the most plausible combination of elements from a confusion of theories and constructed a machine that flew. The flight lasted twelve seconds only, and scarely five people were there to see it.

By a fat wheatfield under the largest of skies an intricate geometry of wires and neat oblongs of stretched canvas sat like the death ship of a pharaoh. It looked like a loom mounted on a sled. It was as elegantly laced, strutted, and poised as the time machine of H. George Wells. Its motor popped, its two screw propellers whirred, bending the lush American weeds to the ground. Fieldmice scurried to their burrows in the corn. Coyotes' ears went up and their yellow eyes brightened.

Were they like the Goncourts, inseparable brothers, Orville and Wilbur Wright? Or were they like Otto and Max, twins in deference and simple brotherhood but essentially very different men? They were from Ohio, nimble as Indians, but whether Democrats, Socialists, or Republicans Otto could not say.

The editors of the American papers, taken up with duelling and oratory, paid no attention at all to their flight. The strange machine flew and flew before any word of it appeared. Icarus and Daedalus had flown above peasants who did not look up from their bowl of lentils and above fishermen who were looking the other way.

The Brothers Wright were the sons of a bishop, but, as Otto explained, the sons of an American bishop. His church was one of dissenters separated from dissenters, a congregation with a white wooden church on a knoll above a brown river, the Susquehanna perhaps. One could not imagine the dreams of Americans.

If one flew over this community in an aeroplane or drifted over it in a balloon, there would be school children below planting a tree. Buffalo and horses grazed in grass so green it was said to be blue. The earth itself was black. The houses, but one story high, were set in flower gardens. One might see the good Bishop Wright reading his Bible at a window, or a senator driving his automobile along a road.

The young Orville and Wilbur had constructed mechanical bats, Otto said, after the designs of Sir George Cayley and Penaud. For America was the land where the learning of Europe was so much speculation to be tested on an anvil. They read Octave Chanute's *Flying Machines;* they built kites. The kite was their beginning, not the bird. That was da Vinci's radical error. The kite had come from China centuries ago. It had passed through the hands of Benjamin Franklin, who caught electricity for the magician Edison, who, it was said, was soon to visit Prague. Men such as Otto Lilienthal had mounted kites and rode the wind and died like Icarus. The Wrights knew all these things. They read Samuel Pierpont Langley; they studied the photographs of Eadweard Muybridge. That was the way of Americans. They took theories as pelicans swallowed fish, pragmatically, and boldly made realities out of ideas.

But the morning's paper, which had come up to Riva on the steamboat, reported that the Wrights might fly in Berlin rather than at Brescia. It hinted of a rivalry between them and the American Curtiss, whose improvements on the flying machine were in many ways far in advance of theirs.

Villages on the lakeshore were stacked, house above house, as in a canvas of Cézanne, from the waterfront to the hilltops, where the church was the highest of all, ringing its bell. In the old city at Prague under the wall he had felt among the alchemists' kitchens and the tiny shops of the smiths in the old ghetto the alien wonderment he felt in Italy, as if an incantation had been recited and the charm had worked. Had not one of the gulls at Riva spoken a line of Latin?

The lake was as vast as the sea.

Otto, who wore a cap and belted jacket, did turns around the richly obstructed deck of the trembling steamboat. Max and Franz sat on a folded travelling rug by the wheelhouse. Otto and Max, it occurred to Kafka, might seem like two princes from an Art Nouveau poster for a Russian opera to those who did not know them. This was illusion, for they were modern men, wholly of the new age. Max was twenty-five, he had his degree, a position, and had published a novel last year, the *Schloss Nornepygge.* Was this why the desolate Castle Brunnenburg in the wild Camonica hills hung in his memory like a ghost?

They seemed not to feel the emptiness of the lake at noon. They had their inwardnesses, how deeply they had never let him see, inviolably private as they were, as all men were.

Otto had been born into the new world, conversant with numbers and their enviable harmonies and with the curiously hollow thought of Ernst Mach and Avenarius, whose minds were like those of the Milesians and

Ephesians of antiquity, bright as an ax, elemental as leaves, and as plain as a box. This new thought was naked and innocent; the world would wound it in time. And Max, too, had his visions in this wild innocence. A suburb of Jaffa had just a few months ago been named Tel Aviv, and Zionists were said to be speaking Hebrew there. Max dreamed of a Jewish state, irrigated, green, electrical, wise.

The destiny of our century was born in the lonely monotony of schoolrooms. Italian schoolrooms were doubtless the same as those of Prague and Amsterdam and Ohio. The late afternoon sun fell into them after the pupils had gone home, spinning tops and throwing jacks on the way. A map of Calabria and Sicily hung on a wall, as polychrome as Leoncavallo, as lyric in its citron gaiety as the chart of the elements which hung beside it was abstract and Russian. Sticks of yellow and white chalk lay in their troughs, and the geometry drawn by them was still on the blackboard, evident, tragic, and abandoned. The windows, against which a wasp rose and fell, testing all afternoon the hardness of their dusty lucidity, were as desolate and grandly melancholy as barn doors looking on the North Sea in October. Here Otto heard of the valence of carbon, here Max saw bright daggers drawn from a bleeding Caesar, here Franz dreamed of the Great Wall of China.

Did men know anything at all? Man was man's teacher. Anyone could see the circle in that.

Tolstoy was at Yásnaya Polyána, eighty and bearded and in peasant dress, out walking, no doubt, in those thin birch groves under a white sky where the sense of the north is a sharp and distant quiet, an intuition shared with the wolf and the owl of the emptiness of the earth.

Somewhere in the unimaginable vastness of America Mark Twain smoked a Havana cigar and cocked his head at the new automobiles three abreast on roads hacked through red forests of maple. His dog was asleep at his feet. Perhaps William Howard Taft called him on the telephone from time to time to tell a joke.

A sailboat passed, an ancient bearded hunter at its tiller.

Franz Kafka, jackdaw. Despair, like the crane's hunch on Kierkegaard's lilting back, went along on one's voyages. His degree in jurisprudence was scarcely three years old, he was rapidly, as Herr Canello assured him, becoming an expert in workingmen's compensation insurance, and the literary cafés of Prague to which he did not go were open to him, both the Expressionist and those devoted to the zithers and roses of Rilke.

Had not Uncle Alfred, who had been awarded so many medals, his mother's elder brother Alfred Löwy, risen to be manager general of the Spanish railways? The Spanish railways! And Uncle Joseph was in the Congo, bending over a ledger to be sure, but he could look up and there was the jungle. But then Uncle Rudolf was a bookkeeper at a brewery, and Uncle Siegfried a country doctor. And his cousin Bruno was editing Krasnopolski.

There were odysseys in which the Sirens are silent.

Without paper, he conceived stories the intricacy and strangeness of which might have earned a nod of approval from Dickens, the Pentateuch and Tolstoy of England. Before paper, his imagination withdrew like a snail whose horns had been touched. If the inward time of the mind could be externalized and lived in, its aqueducts and Samarkands and oxen within walls which the Roman legions had never found, he would be a teller of parables, graceless perhaps, especially at first, but he would learn from more experienced parablists and from experience. He would wear a shawl of archaic needlework, would know the law, the real law of unvitiated tradition, and herbs, and the histories of families and their migrations, to which stock of tales he might add his own, if fate hardened his sight. He would tell of mice, like Babrius, and of a man climbing a mountain, like Bunyan. He would tell of the ships of the dead, and of the Chinese, the Jews of the other half of the world, and of their wall.

—What silence! said Max.

—I was listening to the Sirens, said Franz.

From Salò they went by train, along with many hampers of garlic and a cock that crowed all the way, to Brescia.

The station was very night. Kafka wondered that the people milling outside didn't have lanterns. The train as it slid into Brescia was like a horse dashing through the poultry market in Prague, throwing cage after cage of chickens into a panic as it passed. Every passenger was out of his seat before the train hissed to a halt. An Austrian fell out of a window. A woman asked if anyone saw her brother-in-law outside, a gentleman and courier to the Papal court. A hat passed from hand to hand overhead. People getting off stuck in the doors with people getting on. They promised each other not to get lost, and suddenly they were outside the train. Otto emerged backwards, Kafka sideways, and Max frontwards, with his necktie across his face.

Panels of light carved in the blackness of the station disclosed vistas of Brescia the color of honey, almonds, and salmon. Red smokestacks rose above turreted palaces. There were green shutters everywhere.

Now that they were in Italy proper, Kafka's high-button shoes and black fedora which had been so smartly contemporary in Prague, his new frockcoat with its pinched waist and flaring skirts, seemed inappropriately sober, as if he had come to plead a case at law rather than to see the air show at Montechiari. The land of Pinocchio, he reminded himself, and, rubbing his hands together and blinking in the generous light of the street, he remarked to Otto and Max that here they were in the country of Leonardo da Vinci.

A hat sat on the sidewalk. A cane carried in the crook of an arm hooked a cane carried in the crook of a arm. Each pulled the other out and both fell together. Everything seemed to be the grand moment of an opera about the arrival of the barbarians in Rome.

Max through some quickness that was beyond Otto and Franz, who stood together more stunned than merely hesitant to decide the direction in which they ought to move, had already bought a newspaper. Under a headline in stout poster type the whole significance of their journey was proclaimed in prose which, as Max remarked, wore a waxed moustache. Papers in Italy were not read in coffee houses but on the sidewalks, the pages smacked with the backs of hands, the felicities of the paragraphs read aloud to total strangers.

—Here in Brescia, Max read to them once they had found a table at a *caffé* on the Corso Vittorio Emanuele, we have a multitude the likes of which we have never seen before, no, not even at the great automobile races. There are visitors from Venice, Liguria, the Piedmont, Tuscany, Rome, and even Naples. Our *piazze* swarm with distinguished men from France, England, and America. Our hotels are filled, as well as every available spare room and corner of private residences, for which the rates rise daily and magnificently. There are scarcely means enough to transport the hordes to the *circuito aero.* The restaurant at the aerodrome can easily offer superb fare to two thousand people, but more than two thousand must certainly bring disaster.

Here Franz whistled an air of Rossini.

—The militia, Max read on, has already been called to keep order at the lunch counters. At the humbler refreshment stands some fifty thousand people press daily all day long. Thus *La Sentinella Bresciana* for the ninth of September 1909.

They took a fiacre to the Committee, hoping that it would not fall to pieces under them before they arrived. The driver, who for some reason was radiantly happy, seemed to turn alternately left and right at every corner. Once they went up a street which they were certain they had seen before. The Committee was in a palace. Gendarmes in white gloves rattled their long swords and directed them to concierges in gray smocks who pointed to the heads of stairs where there were officials in celluloid collars who directed them to enormous rooms where other officials, bowing slightly, gave them frail sheets of paper on which they wrote their names and addresses and occupations. Max proudly listed himself as *novelist and critic,* Kafka wickedly wrote *journalist*, and Otto, humming to himself, *engineer.*

Pinocchio clattering down a hall with a gendarme hard on his heels was lost to sight when Kafka stuck his head around a door to see.

In a green room into which they were summoned their papers were spread out on a desk from which a bald official in a fuchsia tie welcomed them in the name of the Società Aerea d'Italia. He found the name of an *albergo* in a notebook and Max copied it down.

Pinocchio had just cleared a corner when they came outside, and a gendarme hopped awhile, and pulled his moustaches awhile, before giving full chase.

The landlord of the inn, when they got there, was a copy of the functionary of the Committee, except that he did not affect a tie. His fingers wiggled beside his face as he talked, spit flew from his lips. He rubbed his elbows, bowed from the waist, and put their money, which he knew that as men of the world and of affairs they wished to pay in advance, in some recess under his coat tails.

By asking each other in all seriousness they discovered that their room was the dirtiest that any of them had ever seen. Moreover, there was a large round hole in the middle of the floor, through which they could see card players in the room below, and through which, Max observed, Sparafucile would later climb.

Light lay flat and ancient upon the colonnade of the old forum. In the temple of Hercules, now green-shuttered and rusty with lichen, there was a winged Nike writing upon a shield.

The squares and streets of Brescia were pages from a book on perspective. One might write a novel in which every line met in a single room, an empty room in an empty building in an empty novel. Random figures could not be avoided. Perspective drawings placed gratuitous figures in empty *piazze* or mounting long steps, faceless men with canes, women with baskets, Gypsies with dogs.

What endurance there was in the long Italian afternoons! In Prague the city stirred about against the evening. Lamps came on in windows. Smoke rose from chimneys. Bells chimed. In Italy eyes hollowed in the faces of statues, windows darkened, shadows moved across squares and slid up the walls of buildings. The night was a mistake, it was fate, *sbaglio e fato antico la notte*. Da Vinci had put water in globes to magnify the light of his lamps, like Edison with his mirrors. And the Italians did not sleep at night. They slept in the afternoon, they were abed half the morning. At night they talked. They went up and down stairs. They ran in the street, like Pinocchio trying his legs.

The old Tarocchi lay on marble tables, the tray of cups beside a stone jug as Roman as a bust of Cinna. And the *Elementi Analitici* of Tully Levi-Città lay beside them with unquestionable propriety. Here was a country where Zeno's motion could be understood. Italy's monotonous sameness was like the frames of a film that moved with the slowness of sleep, so that accident and order were equally impossible. The shape of a glass and the speech of an anarchist were both decided upon millennia ago, and emerged daily, with all other Italic gestures, from a rhythm generated in the ovens and olive presses of Etruria.

In Vienna, in Berlin, the new smelled of frivolity and the old of decay, lacking the Italian continuity of things. A poster on a wall as old as the Gracchi announced in pepper greens and summer yellows a comedy with the curious title *Elettricità Sessuale,* and the old woman beside it in her black shawl and with a basket of onions might easily step into the gondola of the dirigible *Leonardo da Vinci,* which was expected to arrive at any moment from Milan, piloted by the engineer Enrico Forlanini, and sail off to market, gossiping about the priest's nephew Rinaldo, who, she had just learned at the baker's, was now the mayor of Nebraska.

A *galantuomo* in pomade and cream shoes cleaned his ears with the nail of his little finger while they dined across from him on sausages and peppers. After coffee and cigars they went to bed with a soldierly indifference. Max said that they must agree among them to remember the hole in the floor, through which they could now see a great red pizza being quartered with a knife that, as Kafka observed, was surely a gift of the Khan to Marco Polo, as each of them over the years would tend to doubt his sanity in remembering it. Before they went to sleep Otto had a laughing fit, which he refused to explain, and Pinocchio ran down the street with Mangiafoco after him and three gendarmes after them, and a woman narrated just under their window, as best they could understand her, the family affairs of one of the late emperors.

Kafka dreamed that night of Ionic columns in a field of flowers in Sicily, which was also Riva, as dreams are invariably double. There were brown rocks alive with lizards, a moth on a wall, a gyre of pigeons, a stitch of bees. The pines were Virgilian, shelved, and black. He was distressingly lonely and had the impression that he was supposed to see certain statues, possibly of statesmen and poets, wonderfully blotched by lichens and ravaged by the sun. But they were not there. Then Goethe came from behind a column and recited with infinite freedom and arbitrariness a poem he could not understand. There was a rabbit at his foot, eating a mullein.

The Committee had suggested that they take the train to the aerodrome, and they had agreed that, Italy being Italy, this was decidedly an order. What little gain over chaos they could find, Max laid it down as a principle, there they would scramble. The line to Montechiari was the local to Mantua and ran beside the road all the way, so that they had the illusion, once aboard, standing on the swaying and heaving platform between two cars, that the world in all its ingenuity was moving along with them. There were automobiles bouncing in their dust, trembling with speed, their goggled drivers keeping a strange dignity above the wild agitation of their machines.

There were carriages rocking behind horses that paced as if to the *bucca* and drum of the Praetorium, drawing Heliogabalus to the Circus Maximus. There were bicycles on which one could see characters out of Jules Verne,

Antinoos in a plaid cap, Heidelberg duellists, English mathematicians, Basques whose faces were perfect squares under their berets, and a priest whose dusty soutane flared as if he were Victory bringing in the fleet at Samothrace.

No aeroplanes were in the air when they arrived.

The way to the aerodrome was like a gathering of the Tartar tribes at an English garden party. Booths and tents, all topped with flags, rose above a crowd flowing in all directions, of people, carriages, horses, and automobiles.

A heron of a German flashed his monocle and pointed the way to the hangars. A Socialist with a wooden leg was selling *The Red Flag* to a priest whose purse was deeper than his fingers were long. From a bright yellow Lanchester descended a dwarf whose bosom protruded like the craw of a pigeon. His clothes were black and pearl, with many elaborately buttoned panels and facings.

Gypsies haughty as Mongol royalty stood in a line, watched by a gendarme whose very eyes seemed waxed.

Above the bumble of voices they could hear a band clashing its way through the overture to *I Vespri Siciliani,* and suddenly a clatter of cavalry parted its way through the crowds, a brave disarray of silken horses, tossing plumes, and scarlet coats.

An old woman with a milky eye offered them bouquets of tiny white flowers. Beside a French journalist in pointed shoes stood a peasant in a great coat that had seen Marshal Ney.

The hangars were like large puppet theatres, their stage curtains drawn, Otto explained, to keep all the inventions from prying eyes. Some aeroplanes were out, however, and they stood, rather guiltily, and allowed the strangeness of the insect machines to astonish them more than they had anticipated. They are too small, a Frenchman said from behind them.

The Brothers Wright were indeed not there. They were in Berlin, but here was their rival Curtiss sitting in a folding chair, his feet propped on a benzine tin. He was reading *The New York Herald Tribune.* They looked at him in utter awe. Kafka appreciated his professional nonchalance, which was like that of an acrobat who is soon to be before everybody's eyes, but who for the moment has nothing better to occupy him than a newspaper. He was satisfyingly an American.

Then they saw Blériot.

A man with calm, philosophical eyes stood with folded arms and legs spread. Twice he broke his meditative stance and strutted from the door of his hangar to the engine of an aeroplane on which two mechanics were working. The mechanic bending over the engine kept reaching back an empty hand, its fingers wiggling, and the other mechanic put into it a wrench or screwdriver or wire brush.

—That is most certainly Blériot, Otto said. Because that is his airship, the one in which he flew the Channel.

Max remembered later, at dinner, the anecdote of the father and son on horseback who came upon a painter at work in a field. *That is Cézanne,* said the son. *How in the world do you know?* the father asked. *Because,* the son replied, *he is painting a Cézanne.*

It was indeed Blériot. He wore a snug cap with ear flaps that tied under the chin, like the caps of the medieval popes. His nose was *cinquecento,* a beak befitting a bird man. He kept darting forward, standing on tiptoe, and watching the fingers of the mechanic.

The Bleriot XI was a yellow dragonfly of waxed wood, stretched canvas, and wires. Along its side ran its name in square letters of military gray: ANTOINETTE 25 CV. Otto offered the information that its motor had been built by Alessandro Anzani. Its power was clearly in its shoulders, where its wings, wheels, and propeller sprang at right angles from each other, each in a different plane. Yet for all its brave yellow and nautical wire-work, it was alarmingly small, scarcely more than a mosquito magnified to the size of a bicycle.

Near them a tall man with thick chestnut hair held his left wrist as if it might be in pain. It was the intensity of his eyes that caught Kafka's attention more than his tall leanness which, from the evidence about, marked the aeronaut and the mechanic. This was the age of the bird man and of the magician of the machine. Who knows but what one of these preoccupied faces might belong to Marinetti himself? This was a crane of a man. The very wildness of his curly brown hair and the tension in his long fingers seemed to speak of man's strange necessity to fly. He was talking to a short man in a mechanic's blue smock and with an eye-patch. From his mouth flew the words *Kite Flying Upper Air Station, Höhere Luftstazion zum Drachensteigenlassen.* Then the small man raised his square hands and cocked his head in a question. *Glossop,* was the answer, followed by the green word *Derbyshire.*

Further along another aeroplane was being rolled from its hangar. Before it an aviator walked backwards, directing every move with frantic gestures.

Otto squared his shoulders and approached a man who was obviously both an Italian and a reporter.

—*Informazione, per favore,* he said with a flamboyance Max and Franz had thought he used only upon the waiters of Prague. The reporter's eyes grew round and bright.

—*Per esempio?*

—*Chi è aviatore colà, prego?*

—*È Ruggiero. Francese.*

—Ask him, Franz said, if he knows who that tall man is with the deep eyes and chestnut hair.

—*E quest' uomo di occhi penetrante e capigliatura riccia?*

The reporter did not know.

Nothing seemed ready to fly. They wandered to the bales of hay which separated the flying field from the grandstand where society sat in tiers under a flag-hung canopy. It all looked like the world's most crowded Impressionist painting. In a wicker chair the heavy Countess Carlotta Primoli Bonaparte sat under a blue parasol. She was the center of a flock of young ladies veiled in blue and pink.

Were the three Bourbon princesses here, Massimilla, Anatolia, and Violante? To move from the long steps of the Villa Medici, now scattered with the first leaves of autumn, from the tall trees and noseless herms and termini of their walled Roman gardens to the hills of Brescia, was it simply an outing to which they were invited by male cousins all moustaches and sabres? Yet D'Annunzio was said to be here, who had published this year a *Fedra* and a *Contemplazione della Morte*, titles which reminded Kafka of mortuary wreathes, and had they not heard that he was taking flying lessons from Blériot?

They saw Puccini. He was leaning on the barricade of straw that protected the grandstand. His face was long and his nose a drunkard's.

The profile of a lady with a perfect chin and gentian eyes was blocked from Kafka's view by the top hat of a gentleman in bassets, and then, as Max was trying to show him a boy in a sailor suit walking on his hands, he discovered that all the while he had been thinking of the interior of high grass, the mouse's world.

Blériot was going to fly. Arms waved. Mechanics slapped their pockets. Blériot, with a nonchalant pivot in the swing up, was suddenly in his machine, holding the lever by which he was to guide, a kind of upright tiller. Mechanics were everywhere. One wondered if they knew what they were doing or if they were frantically preserving their dignity. Blériot looked toward the grandstand but obviously did not see it. He looked in all directions, as if to assure himself that the sky was still there, and that the cardinal directions still stretched away from him as they always had.

Kafka realized with a shiver somewhere deep under the lapels of his coat that nothing extraordinary was happening as far as Blériot was concerned. He had seen the wrinkling crawl of the Channel thousands of feet beneath him; he had seen farms and rivers and cities stream below him as casually as one watches fields from a train window. He had the athlete's sureness and the athlete's offhandedness. Perhaps only in the awful light of the extraordinary was there real calm in human action. Nothing he might do was superfluous or alien to the moment.

A mechanic was at the propeller, grasping it with both hands and standing on one leg for leverage. He pulled downward with a fierceness. The machine waggled its wings but the propeller didn't budge. Another mechanic took over, and this time it spun, kicked, and froze in another position. One after another they spun the propeller. The engine spit and whined, dying in its best efforts. They brought spanners and screwdrivers, a can of oil, and began work on the engine. One could feel the excitement in the grandstand wilt. Talk sprang up. Otto did not take his eyes off the beautifully trim yellow machine.

The propeller was stubborn, and worse than stubborn, for it stalled after a few hopeful whirrs as often as it refused to spin at all. Blériot's heroic indifference was wearing thin, though even the most comely Italian ladies could be made to understand that the fault was in the engine. A long-beaked oil can was brought from the hangar by a running mechanic. Another took it from him and poked it here and there in the engine. A mechanic brought what was probably a part for the engine. A part like it was unscrewed, taken out, and compared critically by three mechanics, who talked softly, as if in a dream. The Princess Laetitia Savoia Bonaparte watched them with purple eyes, as well bred as if she were at the opera.

Blériot climbed down. Leblanc swung up to replace him. Otto opened and closed his hands in sympathetic help. He remarked that Blériot had crashed some eighty times before he flew the Channel. He was not a man to be discouraged. In the Channel flight an English rain had all but swamped him just as he reached the coast.

The reporter who had identified Rougier for Otto was signalling them with his notebook. He opened it as he ran toward them, tearing out a page, which he handed Otto with a smile of ancient courtesy. Otto frowned over the page. The reporter took it back and frowned at it himself. Then with the air of a corporal delivering a dispatch to a field marshal, he gave the page back and hastened away, for something new was developing around Blériot's aeroplane.

Otto gave the page to Franz.

—There's the name of the man you asked about, he said. He wrote it down for the *giornalista*.

Kafka looked at the name. It read, in light pencil, the kind meticulous men used to jot down fractions and the abbreviated titles of learned journals, volume, number, and page, probably a thin silver pencil with fine lead, *Ludwig Wittgenstein*.

—Who? Max said.

Suddenly the propeller was spinning. Blériot ducked under a wing and vaulted into his seat. The mechanics grasped the aeroplane, for it was beginning to roll forward with trembling wings. Their clothes rippled. Blériot's moustache blew flat against his cheeks. The engine deepened its voice and the propeller whirred on a higher note. He was going to fly. Everyone exchanged glances and quickly looked back at Blériot. The aeroplane waddled forward.

It seemed to slide rather than roll, and darted one way and another like a goose on a frozen river. Kafka was appalled by its desperation and failure of grace before he reflected that the most agile birds are clownish on the ground. Surely there was danger that it would tear itself to pieces before it got into the air. Now it was making a long curve to the left, hopping and sliding. Then it wagged its wings and flew up, bouncing once in the air while no one breathed.

He flew out toward the sun. Then they realized that he was making a long turn and would fly over them. A slash of light flared on his wings when they dipped.

As he passed overhead he seemed to be a man busy at a desk, pulling now this lever, now that, and all with studied composure. Heroism, Kafka reflected, was the ability to pay attention to three things at once.

It was not after all a machine for the grave Leonardo, his white beard streaming over his shoulder, his mind on Pythagoras and on teaching Cesare Borgia to fly. It was rather the very contraption for Pinocchio to extend the scope of his mischief. A random wizard would have built it, an old Dottore Civetta of an artificer who had not been heard from by his friends since his graduation from Bologna. He would have built it as Gepetto carved Pinocchio, because the image was latent in the material, and would not have known what to do with it, being too arthritic to try it himself. The fox and the cat would have stolen it, being incapable of not stealing it, and enticed Pinocchio into it, to see what trouble would come of it.

Blériot hummed in circles around them like an enormous bee. There was obviously a rumor going through the crowd. They picked it up in German. Calderara had crashed on the way to the air show. There were distressed faces everywhere. He was flying his Wright. He was hurt when he crashed. He was not hurt when he crashed. The Wright was ruined. The Wright could be repaired in a matter of hours. He would still fly, if they all had patience. He was the only Italian who was to fly, and now the Italians must watch but foreigners fly at their own air show.

He would turn up, most certainly, with a gloriously bandaged head.

The band, which had been playing idle waltzes, struck up *La Marseillaise,* a tribute to Blériot, who was obviously going to fly over the grandstand. Women cowered and waved their kerchiefs. Officers threw him salutes. They could see him plainly. He did not look down.

He was going to land, they heard, only to go up again. The red windsock on its mast filled and rippled to the west. A man in a gray fedora remarked that the wind was just so, and that Curtiss was going to put down the *Herald Tribune* and fly. Blériot was flying for practise, they supposed, for the sheer fun of it. Now they were all to fly for the Grand Prix de Brescia. There was a stir on the grandstand. Officers and husbands were explaining it to the women.

Gabriele D'Annunzio, who was wearing a cream lounge suit striped in lime and a hot rose cravat, was paying his devoirs to Count Oldofredi, the chairman of the Committee. He twirled his poet's finger above his head. The Count grinned at him and nodded, and frequently looked over his shoulder. D'Annunzio waved his arms, spread his open hand on his chest, and talked like a herald in Sophocles. Kafka noticed how thin and short he was, and how accurately he resembled a rat.

Everyone was looking up. From nowhere at all the dirigible *Zodiac* had appeared, and was drifting majestically toward the grandstand. The band began a confused national anthem. Dignified Germans leaned backwards and stared, their mouths open. Two boys leapt up and down as if on springs.

Ladies and gentlemen hastened to the bales of hay. Photographers went under their black cloths. The violent, Republican flag of the *Vereinigten Staaten von Amerika* ran up a staff and as soon as its red stripes and blue reticulation of stars rippled out into the Lombard air there was a roar more sonorous than they had heard all day.

Curtiss's propeller had caught on the first kick. The man himself was standing beside the fuselage of his machine pulling on long-cuffed gauntlets. His throat was wrapped with a scarf which streamed over his shoulder in the wash of the spinning propeller. He mounted, settled himself, and with a toss of his head signalled the mechanics to stand away.

He was across the field before they realized that his preternatural composure was going to take him immediately into the air. The wheels cleared the ground with a dreamy laziness. The prospect which they had watched all afternoon was suddenly immense, and there was a wood on a knoll which they had not noticed either. Curtiss flew over the wood, lost to view. They watched the wood intently, and then they realized that he was now behind them. His machine had arisen from behind some farmhouses. Then he was above them. The underside of his wings looked peculiarly familiar and wildly strange all at once, like a ship in harbor. And while they watched his trim biplane it was already above the wood again, small and melancholy. This time everyone turned to watch the farmhouses. Because they were waiting, the trip seemed longer the second time, but there he was, as suddenly as before, up out of nowhere.

He made five flights over the wood and around a circuit they could not see, returning each time over the farmhouses. Before he was down, word went around that he had most certainly won the Prix de Brescia. He had flown fifty kilometres in forty-nine minutes and twenty-four seconds. He had won thirty thousand lire.

The bandstand stood and clapped as Curtiss climbed from his machine. His wife was standing with a group of men, who ushered her forward. The blood was draining back into her face, and she was trying to smile.

The man named Wittgenstein was again holding his left wrist, massaging it as if it were in pain.

They heard that Calderara was definitely injured, and that his Wright was a wreck.

Curtiss was scarcely down when three machines all started their engines. The evening was coming on, a brown haze with a touch of gold. Dust blew against dust.

The crowd became restless. Rougier was now in the air, between two great wings on a sled the runners of which curled up at both ends to bear smaller wings. He seemed to have more to do than he could manage, pulling and pushing levers. But apparently he was managing beautifully, like a man for whom writing with both hands at once is natural.

Blériot was in the air again, too. Leblanc's monoplane looked redder in the air than it had on the ground.

The crowd was moving away, to get seats on the train, which could obviously take only a small part of them. By running, they got to the train in time to pry themselves aboard.

Rougier was still in the air when the train began to move. *Ancora là!* His craft droned above them like a wasp at the end of a long afternoon at harvest time, drunk with its own existence and with the fat goodness of the world.

—Franz! Max said before he considered what he was saying, why are there tears in your eyes?

—I don't know, Kafka said. I don't know.

THE CHAIR

The Rebbe from Belz is taking his evening walk at Marienbad. Behind him, at a respectful distance, walks a courtier carrying a chair by its hind legs. This is for the Rebbe to sit on, should he want to sit.

The square seat of this upraised chair, its oval back upholstered with a sturdy cloth embroidered in a rich design of flowers and leaves, its carved, chastely bowed legs, and the tasteful scrollwork of its walnut frame, give it a French air. Like all furniture out of context it seems distressed in its displacement. It belongs in the company of capacious Russian teacups and deep saucers, string quartets by Schumann, polite conversations, and books with gilt leather bindings.

One of the Rebbe's disciples, a lanky young man with long sidelocks beautifully curled and oiled, hastens from the Hotel National. He has a bottle cradled in his arms. He is taking it to a mineral spring to have it filled. The Rebbe wants soda water. He hums as he walks, this disciple, the lively tune *Uforatzto*, a happy march that expresses his joy in being sent for a bottle of soda water for the Rebbe.

The Rebbe's carriage with its tasseled red velvet window curtains comes for him at half past seven every evening, when the shadows have gone blue. He drives to the forest. His court walks behind. One of them carries his silver cane, another an open umbrella, out to his side. It is not for him, but for the Rebbe, should it rain. Another carries a shawl folded on a cushion, in case the Rebbe feels a chill. And one carries the wellbred chair.

It is, by the common reckoning, the year 1916. The armies of the gentiles are slaughtering each other all over the world.

Somewhere along the leafy road the Rebbe will stop the carriage and get out. His court will assemble behind him. He is going to observe, and meditate

129

upon, the beauty of nature, which, created by the Master of the Universe and Lord of All, is full of instruction.

On this particular July evening a fellow guest at the Hotel National has asked and been given permission to walk in the Rebbe's following. He is a young lawyer in the insurance business in Prague, Herr Doktor Franz Kafka. Like all the rest, he must keep his distance, and always be behind the Rebbe. Should the Rebbe suddenly turn and face them, they must quickly run around so as to be behind him. And back around again should he turn again.

The Rebbe, a man of great learning, is neither short nor tall, neither fat nor thin. Wide in the hips, he yet moves with a liquid grace, like a seal in water. He will overflow the slender chair if with a vague ripple of fingers he commands it to be placed so that he can sit on it. Then his followers will range themselves behind him, the secretary leaning a little to catch his every word, the shawl bearer at the ready, should the Rebbe raise his hands toward his shoulders. The secretary takes down what he says in a ledger. These remarks will be studied, later. They will question him about them. The Rebbe means great things by remarks which seem at first to be casual. He asks questions which are traps for their ignorance. The entourage does not always read his gestures correctly. If he has to put into words what he means by an open hand, or raised eyes, or an abrupt halt, he will add a reprimand. *Hasidim is it you call yourselves?* he will say. *Or is it oafs maybe? For brains I'm thinking it's noodles you have.*

If he asks for the soda water, they've had it. The one chosen to fetch it had gone to the Rudolph Spring. It was the opinion of everyone he asked that it was further along this road, that road, another road. And it never was. He'd passed it, or it was another three minutes just around to the left. Around to the right. The Rudolph Spring, the Rudolph Spring, could that be its name? Some answers as to its whereabouts were in foreign languages and a waste of time. Some, sad to say, paid no attention at all to the frantic disciple of the Rebbe from Belz, hard to believe, but true. Moreover, it began to rain. Finally, a man told the disciple that all the mineral springs close at seven. How could a spring be closed? he asked, running off in the direction pointed out. The Rudolph Spring was indeed closed, as he could see long before he got there. The green latticed doors were shut, and a sign reading CLOSED hung on them. *Oi veh!* He rattled the doors, and knocked, and shouted that the Rebbe from Belz had sent him for soda water. All they had to do was fill his bottle and take his money, the work of a moment. All of life, it occurred to him, is one disappointment after another, and he was about to weep when a stroller suggested that he make haste and run to the Ambrosius Spring, which closed a little later than the others. This he did. The Ambrosius was open, by the mercy of God. There were women inside washing glasses. But when he asked them to fill his bottle, the women said that they were through with their work for the day. They should stay open for everybody who can't remember the long hours they were there filling bottles yet? Is the Rebbe from Belz different already? He should learn better how business is conducted in Marienbad. Who will write the history of despair?

Dr. Kafka waits at the steps of the Hotel National for the Rebbe and his following. In Prague Dr. Kafka was famous among his friends for the oxlike patience with which he waited. Once, waiting in the street outside a small Parisian theatre Dr. Kafka and a donkey had made friends. He was waiting to buy a ticket to *Carmen,* the donkey was waiting to go on in Act II. They both had big ears, Dr. Kafka and the donkey. They were both patient by nature, both shy. Waiting is an act of great purity. Something is being accomplished, in a regular and steady way, by doing nothing at all.

First the Rebbe arrived, and then the carriage. So the Rebbe had to wait a little, too. He had a long beard, beautifully white, and very long sidelocks. These are symbols of sound doctrine and piety. The longer your locks, it is said, the greater respect you get from the Rebbe. All boys with long sidelocks he called handsome and smart. One of his eyes, blind, was as blank as if it had been of glass. One side of his mouth was paralyzed, so that at his most solemn he seemed to be smiling ironically, with a witty and forgiving understanding of the world. His silk kaftan was worn open, held in place by a broad oriental belt. His hat was tall, and of fur. His stockings and knee britches were white, like his beard.

The Rebbe, walking at a plump pace, savors nature in the woods. So Chinese dukes must walk of an evening, stopping to smell an hibiscus, casually reciting a couplet that sounds like notes on a zither, about another hibiscus centuries before, an hibiscus in a classical poem which had made the poet think of a noble woman, a jade owl, and a warrior's ghost on the frontiers maintained against the barbarian hordes.

One of the Rebbe's legs is gimp, perhaps only sore from sitting all day at the Torah. When he gets down from his carriage he has a good cough. Then he sets out, looking. When he stops, the entourage stops, and Dr. Kafka behind them. If he turns, they swing with him, like a school of fish behind their pilot. He points out things, such as details of buildings in the woods, which they all strain to see. Is that a tile roof? he asks. They consult. Yes, one says, we think you are right, O Rebbe. It is a tile roof. Where does that path go? No one knows. What kind of tree is that? One thinks that it is a pine, another a fir, another a spruce.

They come to the Zander Institute high on a stone embankment and with a garden in front of it, and an iron fence around it. The Rebbe is interested in the Institute, and in its garden. What kind of garden, he asks, is it? One of the entourage, whose name Dr. Kafka catches as Schlesinger, runs up to the fence, elbows out, head thrown back. He really does not look at the garden, but turns as soon as he has reached its gate, and runs down again, knees high, feet plopping. It is, he says breathlessly, the garden of the Zander Institute. Just so, says the Rebbe. Is it a private garden? They consult in whispers. Yes, says their spokesman, it is a private garden. The Rebbe stares at the garden, rocking on his heels. It is, he says, an attractive garden, and the secretary takes this remark down in his ledger.

Their walk brings them to the New Bath House. The Rebbe has someone read the name of it. He strolls behind it, and finds a ditch into which the water from the bathhouse drains. He traces the pipes with his silver cane. The water must come from there, he says, pointing high, and run down to here, and then into here. They all follow his gestures, nodding. They try to make sense of pipes which connect with other pipes. The New Bath House is in a modern style of architecture, and obviously looks strange to the Rebbe. He notices that the ground floor has its windows in the arches of an arcade. At the top of each arch is an animal's head in painted porcelain. What, he asks, is the meaning of that? No one knows. It is, one ventures, a custom. Why? asks the Rebbe. It is the opinion that the animal heads are a whim of the designer, and have no meaning. Mere ornament. This makes the Rebbe say, *Ah!* He walks from window to window along the arcade, giving each his full attention. He comes around to the front of the building. Looking up at the golden lettering in an Art Nouveau alphabet, he reads again *New Bath House.* Why, he asks, is it so named? Because, someone says, it is a new bathhouse. The Rebbe pays no attention to this remark. It is, he says instead, a handsome, a fine, an admirable building. Good lines it has, and well-pondered proportions. The secretary writes this down. Look! he cries. When the rain falls on the roof, it flows into the gutter along the edge there, do you see, and then into the pipes that come down the corners of the building, and then into this stone gutter all around, from which it goes to the same ditch in back where all the pipes are from the baths. They walk around the building, discovering the complete system of the drainpipes. The Rebbe is delighted, he rubs his hands together. He makes one of the entourage repeat the plan of the pipes, as if he were examining him. He gets it right, with some correction along the way, and the Rebbe gives him a kind of blessing with his hands. Wonderful! he says. These pipes are wonderful.

Who will write the history of affection?

They come to an apple orchard, which the Rebbe admires, and to a pear orchard, which he also admires. O the goodness of the Master of the Universe, he says, to have created apples and pears.

The chair held aloft by its bearer, Dr. Kafka notices, has now defined what art is as distinct from nature, for its pattern of flowers and leaves looks tawdry and artificial and seriously out of place against the green and rustling leaves of apple and pear trees. He is tempted to put this into words, as a casual remark which one of the entourage just might pass on to the Rebbe, but he reconsiders how whimsical and perhaps mad it would sound. Besides, no word must be spoken except at the command of the Rebbe.

Instead, he prays. Have mercy on me, O God. I am sinful in every corner of my being. The gifts thou has given me are not contemptible. My talent is a small one, and even that I have wasted. It is precisely when a work is about to mature, to fulfill its promise, that we mortals realize that we have thrown our time away, have squandered our energies. It is absurd, I know, for one insignificant creature to cry that it is alive, and does not want to be hurled into the dark along with the lost. It is the life in me that speaks, not me, though I speak with it, selfishly, in its ridiculous longing to stay alive, and partake of its presumptuous joy in being.

Wide as the Waters: The Story of the English Bible and
the Revolution It Inspired, by Benson Bobrick.

Benson Bobrick (an accomplished independent scholar and the author of a
history of stuttering, among other books) begins this admirably clear and
abundantly informative history of the Bible in English by telling us that the
first question you were asked when you had fallen into the hands of the
Inquisition was, Do you know any part of Scripture in your own language?
If your answer was yes, there were no further questions: the stake is through
that door. As the flames crawled upward, a cross was held before your eyes,
to inspire last-second repentance, while angelic choirboys sang the dread
"Dies Irae." William Tyndale, the translator who, more than anyone, gave us
the King James Version of the Bible, was burned at the stake on October 6,
1536, though legend has it that he was strangled before the kindling was lit.
　　Tyndale's translation, the first into English from the original Hebrew and
Greek, was the basis for the Authorized Version of 1611 that is still *the* Bible
for most English-speaking Christians today and was the official Bible of the
Church of England for 350 years. The task of the fifty-four translators chosen
by King James lay mostly in tidying up Tyndale's work, the beauty and power
of which they accepted as what the Bible in English ought to be. "Suffer the
children to come unto me," Tyndale wrote. The committee added "little."
(Bobrick gives us an appendix of comparative passages, like Dr. Johnson in
his preface to the dictionary.) It was not until the 1960s that a New English
Bible was introduced, making room for contemporary idiom and the evidence of more ancient Greek manuscripts (though there had been various
revisions, called "Revised Standard Versions," from Victorian times onward,
to bring up to date Tudor locutions that had changed their meaning in spoken

English: "prevent," for instance, meant to precede or to anticipate; and "let" meant its opposite, to hinder). English is not so much a language as a family of languages. Once the tongue of Bronze Age tribes called Angles and Saxons, it early began to swap words and phrases with the Vikings, who were also colonizing the British Isles. The Saxon fought with an "edge," the Dane with a "sword." "Edge" became merely a detail of "sword." The evolutionary tactic was always to keep both words. In 1066, Normans invaded, and the same process went on: the "pig" in the sty became "pork" on the table; "cow" became "beef." It is as if English were an impressionable husband who had a Danish wife and talked like her; and then a French wife and talked like her. And when the King James translators took up their task, English had begun to add two rich vocabularies from Latin and Greek. Anglo-Saxon "dog" sported the Latin adjective "canine," and people who snarled like dogs were cynics (a Greek word).

Tyndale and his revisers were keenly aware that an authentic, archaic English to which they ought always to defer was the bedrock of the language available to them. They used only 8,000 words, 90 percent of which are Anglo-Saxon-Danish. From this *word hoard* they could invent words for practically all of the Bible. The Old Testament is inordinately concerned with *praeputii,* for which Tyndale invented "foreskynne." He combined a Norman and a Saxon word and gave us "beautyfull."

The very first English Bible was that of John Wycliffe (1328-84), from the Latin of Jerome, whose "Vulgate" translation from Hebrew and Greek was completed in 405. Wycliffe died before he could be tied to the stake. So the Church dug up his remains and burned his bones. (They got his disciple Jan Hus, however, and burned him as one infected by Wycliffe.) Wycliffe's postmortem burning in 1428 took place on a bridge over the River Swift, a tributary of the Avon. Bobrick takes his title from an anonymous hymn (taken in turn from a paragraph in Thomas Fuller's *Church History* of 1655):

The Avon to the Severn runs,
The Severn to the sea,
And Wickliffe's dust shall spread abroad,
Wide as the waters be.

Wycliffe's Bible was dispersed by itinerant preachers called Lollards. They were first-wave Protestants, outlawed and persecuted (Sir John Oldcastle, the model for Falstaff, led a Lollard uprising against his friend Henry V in 1414, and was simultaneously hanged and burned for it). The Reformation bloomed from many such seeds, broadcast all over Western Europe. Erasmus published his Greek New Testament in 1516, a scholarly rectification of age-old copyists' errors and variant readings, and one year later the German monk Martin Luther demanded that the Church quit selling time off from purgatory.

The Reformation in full spate depended on printing. The first book to be printed with movable type, by Johannes Gutenberg, was the Bible, in Latin. The way was then open for Bibles in German, Danish, and English. Bobrick gives a lucid and orderly account of the many translations (so many they're hard to keep straight), providing us a sense of how they were genetically born from one another: Miles Coverdale's following hard on Tyndale's (and completing Tyndale's work on the Old Testament), a Geneva Bible (the one Shakespeare read), a "Bishop's Bible," on up to the one commissioned by James I and achieved by a committee of Hebrew and Greek scholars at Oxford and Cambridge. These worthies were anonymous until 1958, when thirty-nine pages of their working notes were found in Oxford's Bodleian Library. Bobrick tells us as much as can be known about them at this late date.

Their average age was fifty. They were all clergymen except for Sir Henry Savile. Revealed after 350 years from their self-effacing, "deliberately cultivated" anonymity, they are a wonderfully interesting group of very human beings, and Bobrick gives us charming portraits of them all. Here he is on Lancelot Andrewes, head of the committee that revised Tyndale's translation of Genesis through 2 Kings (and the only reviser with a recognizable name, thanks to T.S. Eliot):

[He was] an immensely learned man who, it was said, "might have been interpreter general at Babel . . . the world wanted . . . learning to know how learned he was." The son of a master mariner, Andrewes had studied at the Merchant Taylors' School under Richard Mulcaster, a classical and Hebrew scholar of note, and as "a great long lad of 16," went up to Pembroke College, Cambridge on scholarship, where one of his companions was Edmund Spenser. . . . From a very tender age, Andrewes was "addicted to the study of good letters," avoided "games of ordinary recreation" such as cards, dice, chess, or croquet, and preferred long solitary walks in the company of earnest students like himself.

Bobrick's description of the long-lost notes offers a glimpse of scholars who were working to forge, in a very real sense, the language that we call our own. "[I]t is intriguing to see what might have been," Bobrick writes. Indeed. Anyone who has been to a Christian wedding in the last twenty years is roughly familiar with the King James version of I Corinthians 13:11: "When I was a child, I spake as a child, I understood as a child, I thought as a child."

The notes record that the scholar John Bois, a former child prodigy who was reading the Old Testament in Hebrew by the age of six, offered the following variant: "I understood, I cared as a child, I had a child's mind, I imagined as a child, I was affected as a child."

Translation is a metaphysical act: an incomprehensible set of words becomes comprehensible, or nearly so. In Sunday school I thought John the Baptist ate the succulent pods of *Robinia pseudoacacia* (black locust), which I and my friends fancied. What he ate was grasshoppers. My one contribution to biblical scholarship is to have convinced Reynolds Price to translate *akridas* as "grasshoppers" in his *A Palpable God* (the New English Bible still has "locusts"). But translation is also, strictly speaking, impossible. Ancient Hebrew is rich in untranslatable puns on the order of Homer's—Helen in the *Odyssey* refuses to say Troy *(Ilion,* in Greek); she calls it that *kakoilion* city, "dreadful." T.E. Lawrence managed to get around this by having Helen say "that destroyed city." The Prophets were similarly skillful with this kind of pun, as was Jesus when he changed Simon's name to Peter—"Rock" in Greek—and told the assembled that "upon this rock" He would build His church (the pun also works in Aramaic, which Jesus may have been speaking).

There are other difficulties. In its original text as well as in translations, the Bible is the most evolved of books. Scholars tell us that the Hebrew text is basically two texts intertwined, giving us, in the final result, two variant Ten Commandments handed down on two different mountains, two deaths of King Saul. Moses gets two fathers, and stories repeat themselves in "doublets." David gets to re-kill a giant who isn't Goliath. Scholars have teased these interwoven texts apart. In one, God is called Yahweh; in the other, El. Scholars have further identified two other strands woven into the fabric: a priestly addition of rituals and a "deuteronomical" one of laws. Even if every one of these theories is wrong, the Bible remains a collection of books, rather than a book. The word "bible" is from the Greek *biblia,* plural of *biblion,* "a little book." It is an archive of a thousand years of writing.

For most American Christians, however, the Bible is a book written by God, in English. The text is prophetic, instructional, and devotional. Baptists believe that it is "inerrant" (a nice tit-for-tat response by Protestants to papal infallibility). A logical mind can find itself in a bog. Why are we not told about the *other* creation of humankind (the one that Cain married into)? If Noah sacrificed two of all the animals, and had taken on two of each (Genesis 6:19), how were there any left? But in the very next chapter, God specifies that Noah take with him seven pairs, male and female, of the clean animals, with the unclean ones (non-cud-chewers) still two. So Mr. and Mrs. Pig were on board but escaped the holocaust on Mount Ararat. Still, how do you slaughter and burn two elephants? Two Tyrannosaurus rex?

King James's translators were working at a time when unicorns were believable. They understood allegory, fable, and myth. The text they were translating was from a different epoch. Only John Layfield had traveled (to Puerto Rico); beyond the mullioned windows of their Oxford and Cambridge rooms the Nile and Jordan, Jericho and Jerusalem, lay in an unimaginably distant past in which shepherd kings talked with God, the shadows of sundials moved backward at a prophet's command, and Solomon sat between golden walls with a thousand wives.

Seven hundred years before, the Anglo-Saxon Chronicle had dutifully recorded dragons swimming through the air in Northumbria. The Renaissance in England was as superstitious as it was religious: the Irish had tails, Jews poisoned wells, the king's touch cured scrofula. Miracles and impossibilities in the English Bible enhanced its credibility.

Tyndale was burned alive for translating *ekklesia* as "congregation" (rather than "church") and *presbyteros* as "elder" (rather than "priest")—throwing open the way for Baptists to worship God in cellars and for Presbyterians to sing hymns in darkest Scotland. The hierarchy in Rome feared that placing the Bible in the hands of weavers and grocers would fragment the Church into a chaos of amateur theologians, wild enthusiasts, and illiterate exegetes. They were right: Protestant sects have chosen a menu of virtues, vices, and fixations from the Bible. (I know of a congregation in South Carolina that does not wear neckties, citing Isaiah's putdown of gaudy apparel that the King James Version calls "tyres," archaic English for "attire." "Tyre" and "tie" sound the same on a South Carolina tongue.)

What Bobrick shows in his careful narrative of the Bible's slow and turbulent translation into English is the heroic, bloody, and awesome progress of the Reformation that ironically begot even more terribly oppressive societies (Calvin burned heretics, Puritans hanged witches, Anglicans drowned Baptists) while leading to deism and republican government. "One could almost say," he writes, "that the modern democratic state owed its origins in part to a defiance of Catholic dogma, but ended by adopting one of its fundamental tenets in the secular sphere"—that is, we have given to law, with its traditions and precedents, the authority once enjoyed by the Church. A cynic can remark that we have returned to the Old Testament, with its proscriptions and prescriptions, its judges and councils of elders.

What we know is that, at the beginning of the third millennium after the birth of a baby named Joshua ("Yeshua" in Hebrew, spelled "Iesous" in Greek, "Jesus" in Latin), the Bible continues to be printed in millions of copies. An article in the February 2001 issue of *Bible Review* cites a recent Gallup poll: 65 percent of American readers believe that the Bible answers "all or most of the basic questions of life" (though a third of this 65 percent admit that they've never read it). This article also revealed that a number of Bible readers consider "the Book of Joseph" to be their favorite, and that 12 percent think Joan of Arc was Noah's wife.

Walt Whitman and Henry Mencken, agnostics both, wore out several copies. English and American literature from Chaucer onward assumes that its readers know the Bible. We all quote it, constantly, unknowingly. It is like the flag: a sacred totem. There are many accounts by Civil War and First World War veterans of "lucky" pocket copies stopping bullets. It occupies a strangely awkward place in our culture: an unread book that many pious people believe is too hard to understand, an oracle (the belief that passages chosen at random have prophetic power lasts into our time), a text necessary for getting into heaven. Our presidents are sworn into office by placing their left hand on it, though it forbids oath-taking. George Washington, at his inauguration, kissed it, and it was noted that the pages he happened to kiss are those in which Joseph reminds the Israelites that God will bring them "unto the land which he swore to Abraham, to Isaac, and to Jacob." Parts of it may be older than the *Iliad* and the *Odyssey,* both of which it rivals in narrative.

GUNNAR AND NIKOLAI

I

And, yes, the sailboat on a tack for Tisvilde under a tall blue sky piled high with summer clouds was, oh my, slotting through the Baltic at a speed which the calm day and rigged mainsail and jib could in no wise account for.

At the tiller, it was soon easy to see, sat a boy named Nikolai, fetching and trim. He took a beeline for the beach, into the rocky sand of which he crunched his prow, to the amazement of a hundred staring sunbathers. Deftly lowering his sails with nonchalant ease, he folded them into smaller and smaller triangles, until they were no bigger than handkerchiefs. Then, with a snap here and a snap there, as if he were closing the sections of a folding ruler, whistling a melody by Luigi Boccherini as he worked, he collapsed the boat, mast, rigging, hull, keel, rudder and all, into a handful of sticks and cords. These he doubled over again and again, tucked them in with a napkin's worth of sails, and stuffed the lot into the zippered pocket of his windbreaker. His chart and compass he shoved into the pocket of his smitch of white pants. He rolled and squared his shoulders.

Indifferent to the astonished bathers, one of whom was having some species of fit, and to jumping and hooting children begging him to do it again, he strode with all the aplomb of his twelve years up the beach and across the road into the dark cool of the Troll Wood.

Søren Kierkegaard, most melancholy of Danes, used to walk here, a gnome among gnomes. An eagle in a spruce gazed at Nikolai with golden feral eyes, in acknowledgment of which he put both hands against a mountain pine, the tree friendly to spruce. Without one near, it would not grow. The eagle rolled a hunch into its shoulders, and Nikolai hugged the mountain pine.

A glance at the interplanetary mariner's chronometer on his left wrist alerted him to his appointment somewhere near Gray Brothers. So, with meadows and farms flickering past, he ran fifty kilometres in three seconds, slowing to a walk along Strøget.

A shoal of skateboarders flowed around him from the back as he passed a Peruvian gourd band, three games of chess that had been going on since the fourteenth century, and four fresh babies in a pram, each with a cone of ice cream.

The address was in an alley, once a very old street. The number was repeated on a wooden gate, which opened onto the place, one of the places, he'd been looking for all of his life.

Another was a cabin in Norway, deep in spruce and mountain pine near a steep fjord, where he could live like Robinson Crusoe, exactly as he pleased. A room of his very own, in Gray Brothers, free to come and go, to have friends in to spend the night and share hamburgers and polsers in the middle of the floor. A coffee plantation in Kenya. A lighthouse on a rock in the Orkneys, gulls blown past his windows, bleak dawns over a black sea, secure by a neat fire.

But this was just as good, a courtyard with a tree and rows and beds of flowers, a sculptor's studio with a pitched glass roof.

Along a pomp of dahlias in a line, rust mustard brick and yellow, he walked with a steady casualness to the blue door. A wicker basket beside it, for the mail. A stone jug with sweet williams. His mother was keen on botany, so he knew the names of flowers, weeds, and trees. And maybe an angel with nothing better to do would see him through this.

A card fixed to the door with a drawing pin: Gunnar Rung, the name Mama had said. He was about to push the doorbell when the door opened, wrecking his cool.

—Hello, he said in as deep a voice as he could manage, I'm Nikolai Bjerg.

The man who opened the door was tall, in jeans with a true fit and an Icelandic sweater, and was much younger than Nikolai had expected. His eyes were as friendly as those of a large dog.

—You're on time, he said. Gunnar Rung here. Come in and let's see you.

Books, drawings on the walls, tables, an unfamiliar kind of furniture. And beyond, through wide double doors slid open, under a glass roof, a tall block of squared rock that must have been hauled in from an alley in back. Nikolai looked at as much as he could, all of it wonderfully strange and likable, with quick glances at Gunnar, who was goodlooking and had wads of rich brown curls, almost not Danish, and hands as big as a sailor's.

—It's an Ariel I have a commission for, Gunnar said walking around Nikolai, looking at him through framing hands. Your mother thought you might do, and would like posing. Have you ever posed before? It's not easy, and can be tedious and boring. There's also a King Matt I'm to do, a boy who's king of an unimaginable Poland, and you might also be him. We'll have to see how you and I get along. What about some coffee? Do you drink it?

—Sometimes. I mean, yes.

Coffee! Gunnar was treating him like a grown-up, so don't trash it.

—You can undress while I'm putting the coffee on. Won't take a minute.

—Everything? Nikolai asked, instantly regretting the question, unbuckling a scout's belt of green webbing, offering his charmingest and toothiest smile.

—That's the way the stone is to be, without a stitch.

Eyebrows bravely up, Nikolai backed out of his short denim pants and knelt to untie his gym shoes. Briefs and thick white socks he pulled off together. Then his jersey over his head.

—Two sugars? There's real cream. You'll get over blushing. Good knees, good toes.

—Sorry. Didn't think I'd blush. The statue will be the same size as me? Hey! Good coffee, you know.

—Life size, oh yes. Keep turning around. Raise your free hand and stretch. Do you think you can keep to a schedule for posing?

—Sure. Why not? I really didn't think I'd go shy. Being naked's fun. My grandma and grandpa, Mama's mama and daddy, are Kropotkinites, and I'm boss in my own pants. My folks are as broad-minded green as they come, no barbed wire anywhere, good Danish liberals, to the point of being fussy. You know what I mean?

A mischievously knowing smile from Gunnar.

—Park your cup, there, and stand on your toes, arms over your head. Legs out more, each side. We can't do a Thorvaldsen nor yet an Eric Gill. I'm what they call a neoclassicist, a realist, and out of it. What's being boss in your own pants mean?

—A licensed devil, according to Mama. Liberal points for what boys do anyway, says Papa. Who's King Matt?

—Another character in a book, by a Polish doctor. Actually the work will be of a boy carrying Matt's flag. At an awful moment. I'll tell you all about it while we're working. You can read the book.

Eyes askew, Nikolai ran his tongue across the plump tilt of his upper lip. While *we're* working.

—You have kids? I guess they're too little to pose.

—No, and no wife, either, just Samantha, whom you'll meet. Arms out. Twist around to the right. You're going to do, you know? You're Ariel, all right.

2

Nikolai sat on his clothes piled in a chair. Coffee break.

—Why was Ariel naked?

—He was a spirit of the air. Like an angel.

Nikolai thought about this, guppying his coffee and sprucing the fit of his foreskin.

—Angels wear lots of clothes. Bible clothes. Steen and Stoffer are neat today, did you see? I'll bet this Ariel you're copying me for had pure thoughts and never a hard on, right? There was a Steen and Stoffer where Steen sees monkeys in the zoo jacking off and he says *O gross!* And his mom and pop are suddenly interested in showing him the cockatoos and toucans. Parents.

—What a face, Gunnar said, running his fingers over his cast of Bourdelle's study of Herakles. The model was Doyen-Parigot, military bloke. Physical fitness enthusiast. Used to arrive on his horse at Bourdelle's in full soldierly fig.

—Looks like an opossum, wouldn't you say?

Punktum punktum,
komma, streg!
Sådan tegnes
Nikolaj!

Arme, ben,
og mave stor.
Sådan kom han
til vor jord.

—Killed at Verdun. You make Edith glance heavenward when you twitch your piddler. Christian Brother from the Faeroes she is, you know. Though I once had a girl model who played with herself as liberally as you, and as unconcerned for convention, and Edith rather took to leaning around the door to see, in passing.

—What's Verdun? You know Mikkel, the redhead kid, my pal, with terminal freckles and chipmunk teeth? His dad is all for his doing it every day. Says it keeps him happy.

—Verdun was a terrible battle in the First World War. It Mikkel's daddy Ulf Tidselfnug? Break's over: back at it.

—Do you know him? He prints books. It's fun to go to Mikkel's, where, if we stay in his room, we can do anything we want to, and Mikkel's always answering the door in nothing but a T-shirt and wrunkled socks. His mom says that if he turns himself into an idiot how would you notice?

—O pure innocent Danish youth!

Questioning eyes.

—Teasing the model, Samantha said, is Gunnar's way of relating. You'll get used to it. Besides, you can tease him back. Gunnar's jealous, anyway.

TREE HOUSE

—How old is this Gunnar?

—He's had a rabbit, a Belgian hare I think it is, in a show, and a naked girl holding one leg by the ankle in another. He did those at the Academy, and then he was in Paris for a year. He was seventeen when he went to the Academy, that's four years, and Paris was just a couple of years back, so he's like twenty-four, yuss? Outsized whacker in his jeans.

—The bint's there all the time?

—Oh no, very busy girl, Samantha. She comes and goes. Spends the night a lot, too, I think.

4

—Brancusi's *Torso of a Boy,* there. My Ariel is to be as pure as that, but with all of you there, representational, as the critics say, thugs, the lot of them.

Nikolai tugged his foreskin into a snugger fit.

—It leks, and it doesn't, you know?

—The thighs make it a boy, and the hips the same girth as the chest. But further than that, in style, you can't go. Gaudier, here, had the genius of the age. Killed in the First World War, only 24. That's his bust of the poet Pound, and that's his *Red Dancer.*

—Real brainy is what I'm getting a reputation for, even at home. Would Brancusi have used a model, some French soccer player? He could at least have put in a navel. I'll have my pecker and toms, won't I, as Ariel?

—Shakespeare would insist. He liked well-designed boys and approved of nature.

—I'll bet. Did Brancusi?

—Brancusi's private life in unknown. I think he simply worked, sawing and polishing and chiselling. He did his own cooking. There was a white dog named Polar.

—What would an Ariel by him have looked like?

5

Commandant Nikolai Doyen-Parigot rode his white charger Washington among Peugeots and Citroëns to Antoine Bourdelle's studio. Tying Washington to a parking meter, he strode inside. Bourdelle was in his smock. A boy was mixing modelling clay in a tub. Amidst life-size casts of Greek statues Nikolai Doyen-Parigot took off his uniform, handing it piece by piece, epauletted coat and sword and spurred boots and snowy white shirt and suspenders and wool socks slightly redolent of horse and long underwear, to a respectful but blushing concierge.

Herakles with the head of Apollo.

Thick curly hair matted his chest. His dick was as big as his charger's and his balls were like two oranges in a cloth sack. His wife went around in a happy daze because of them, as did several lucky young actresses and dancers. Restocking the regiment for the next generation he called it.

He took the long bow that Bourdelle handed him and assumed the pose of Herakles killing the Stymphalian birds.

Later he would play soccer, and wrestle with Calixte Delmas. He would march his regiment up and down the street behind a military band.

—What are Stymphalian birds, Gunnar?

—Something Greek. Quit wiggling your head. One of the labors of Herakles.

6

—Sculpture should be a verb not a noun. The *David* is Jack the Giant Killer, handy with strings, so that he can play the harp and have his dark fate in hair, but in his eyes he is the friend of Jonathan, *that sweet rascal from crabstock*, as Grundtvig said. Where Rodin kept going wrong was in sculpting not only nouns but abstract nouns. Nikolai!

—Jo!

—Imagine you can walk on the wind just under the speed of light. There's a magic cunning in your fingers and toes. Fatigue is as unknown to you as to a bee. You have been commanded by the magus Prospero to dart all over an enchanted island to do things impossible for others but easy for you. You have just been given your instructions. The reward of your compliance is freedom. You're about to nip off.

Listening to Prospero, elbows back, chin over shoulder, eyes and mouth wide open, a jump into action, wheeling on toes, and a collision with Samantha who had walked into the studio. A laughing, staggering hug.

—Ariel digging off to execute Prospero's orders.

—Do it again. This time I'll be ready for the hug.

TREE HOUSE

The Korczak group will be this Polish doctor who had an orphanage in the Warsaw ghetto way back when the shitty Germans were burning up all the Jews and there was a day when the Germans took all the kids and Korczak and a woman named Stefa to die at Treblinka, and they all marched through the streets to the cattle cars. I'm to be the boy that carried their flag, the flag of their republic, the orphanage. Gunnar wants you and me to be two pals in the group, arms around each other's shoulders. You'll like Gunnar. He's real. For balls he has a brace of Grade A large goose eggs and a gooseneck of a cock, which his girl Samantha pretends she doesn't go goofy over. I mean all the time he isn't fucking her into fits. She's real, too, and gives me a hard time.

Winks at me when I'm posing, and hugs me when we're having a break and stretch. She writes poems and draws posters, and wears badges about Women's Lib. Knows the names of all the butterflies. On his big bulletin board in the studio Gunnar has this list of things Korczak talked to the orphans about every Saturday, or had them swot up, by way of learning about things, famous people like Gregor Mendel and Fabre the bug man, and good and evil, and doing one's duty, and the environment, and how to deal with loneliness, and what sex is, and Samantha has me writing what she calls my responses and ideas, also Gunnar has to write them too, and these go on the bulletin board.

THE YELLOW OF TIME

In his Roman garden Bertel Thorvaldsen sat reading Anacreon. A basket of Balkan melons, squash, and runner beans sat under the cool of the fig tree, delivered by a girl out of Shakespeare, soon to be carried into the kitchen by Serafina the cook. He had drunk a gourd of well water brought in a stone jug from the country. It tasted of gourd and stone, and of the depths of the earth. Johan Thomas Lundbye's landscape of a Danish meadow hung in his sitting room. There were letters from Copenhagen, Paris, Edinburgh. On his cabinet of Greek, Roman, and Byzantine coins stood branches of oleander in a yellow jug.

9

—Morning, halfling. You look tumbled and slept in. It's good you can come early on Saturdays.

—Is there more of that coffee? It was time to get up as soon as I got to sleep.

—Am I to ask intelligent questions or leave your private life private?

Thoughtful grin.

—You probably don't want to know. Mikkel is a maniac and I'm his understudy.

—What about we sit in the sun awhile, with our coffee, in the courtyard. You can skinny down to briefs. Cool air and warm sun, with roses and hollyhocks, lavender and sage, to unsnarl cobwebs from the brain.

—O wow.

—An orange juice and a Vienna bread too?

—Better and better. Gunnar, you're a grown-up Lutheran and all that, but you're a pal, too, aren't you, because the briefs I'm wearing are Mikkel's, or mine and Mikkel's swapped back and forth. Mama makes me wear snow-white underwears here, like I was going to the doctor's, but as I spent the night at Mikkel's, if you're following this.

—Are you embarrassed or bragging? Sounds wonderfully imaginative and comradely to my evil ears.

—Fun. Make Samantha hold her nose. Why evil?

—Evil's a vacuum, they say, where good might be. Nature abhors a vacuum. Therefor nature abhors, and excludes, evil. Grundtviggian logic, wouldn't you say? Being friendly with Mikkel is good sound nature.

—You think?

—I know.

Long silence.

—Nature's good.

—What else could she be?

10

A time machine, H.G. Wells's as modified by Alfred Jarry, made of brass, walnut, and chromium, with manufacturer's plate in enamel on tin. Levers, dials, a gyroscope, all real. Nikolai, older, in bronze as the pilot. Trim Edwardian clothes, scarf and backward cycling cap.

11

The girl Samantha was like the Modigliani on the big push-pin cork board where forty-eleven postcards, notes, letters, Parisian metro tickets, photographs made a collage for Nikolai to study while he doffed and donned his clothes.

—His mama had, yes, he answered Samantha's question, put it to him, in her arch voice moreover.

—I know mamas, Samantha said with her fetching smile.

—That Gunnar who was at somebody's house where she was, bald brainy people from the university, needed a handsome boy to pose for a statue without a stitch the Georg Brandes Society had commissioned, Ariel he's called, in a play by Vilhelm Shakespeare, and she said she had a rascally son.

—A sensitive son, I imagine she said.

An understanding grin from a crush of soccer jersey pulled up and off.

—Who's just going from cute to goodlooking.

—To adolescent beauty, and who at an astute guess instantly saw in a model's fee skateboards backpacks naughty comic-books and revolting phonograph records.

On one knee, undoing shoes.

—Ha. What about the score of the first Bach partita, and new fiddle strings, and these new briefs, see.

Gunnar with sharpened chisels.

—I'm getting acquainted, Samantha said, with this Danish angel with the unangelic plumbing fixtures.

—Do angels pee? Are they even oxygen breathers?

—They're all male in Scripture, I believe. But they don't fuck, as each is the only member of a unique species, and species don't crossbreed.

—What a dreary place, heaven.

—I'm not a species, Nikolai said. Gunnar, did you do this man in handcuffs here in the photograph?

—That's Martin Luther King. It's in a church garden over in Jylland, out from Aarhus.

PONIES ON THE FYN

Riding a pony naked through a meadow red with poppies on a sweet day in June, like Carl Nielsen at Østerport (commented on by mallards and green-shanked moorhens as *O a big one with six legs*), Nikolai drank the spring air like a Pawnee and looked for buffalo in the hollows and eagles in the clouds.

—Steady, said Gunnar. You need a break?

—He's miles away, Samantha said. I can see it in his eyes.

—What? Nikolai asked.

—Nikolai's rarely here. He turns up most business-like, sheds his britches, takes his pose, and goes away like Steen to fight the Nazis with the Churchill Gang or in his space pod through phosphorescent interplanetary dust to galaxies with forests of celery and creeping red slime.

13

A session of drawing, Gunnar intent, Nikolai bored, tolerant, behaved.

—Why are grown-ups so dumb?

—Those who are in your words dumb, friend Nikolai, have always been like that. They were dumb children.

Nikolai thought about this. The silence contained bees, a violin passage of lazy intricacies, a dense stillness.

—On the other hand you have a kind of point. Bright children do grow up to be dull. I wish I knew why. The century's mystery is that intelligent children become teen-age louts, who grow up to be pompous dullards. I'd like to know why.

—Is this a trick question?

—Brancusi at thirty-four had the liveliness to begin to be Brancusi.

—You talk to me as if I were grown up.

—You want me to talk to you as if you were half-witted?

—Only some grown-ups are morons. Most of 'em. You're OK, Gunnar.

—Thanks.

—Tell me more about Korczak, the republic of children, Poland.

14

—It's a meadow that shades off into a marsh with reeds and then does sand banks into the cold wet Baltic, out from Hellerup, we can take the train, want to go? You'll turn honey brown.

—Now?

—Just thought of it, so let's do it.

Their locomotive was the Niels Bohr.

—If you thought of this friendly outing, as you call it, when I turned up to pose, how come Edith had a thermos and snack ready in that satchel?

—Those pants, Nikolai. With the obliging fit.

Imp's grin, musing eyes.

—They're this short from the store, and then Mama took in the crotch at the inseam. Packages my mouse neater. If your look means was it her idea, well no. She's so good at sewing that it took her only a minute to do it, and she whistled in a meaningful way while she was clicking it through the sewing machine. A dry cough in the handing over, but never a word. So how come Edith knew you were going to these marshes?

—A meadow all greenest grass and one million wild flowers with a white strand at its foot. A marsh, too, with grebes and mallards.

—How come Edith knew you were going to this midge heaven?

—Second sight. They have it in the Faeroes.

Imp's grin, silly eyes.

Hellerup, a back street, a lane, a field, the meadow sloping down to the strand.

—Drawing block, pencils, sammidges, sunglasses, said Nikolai of the canvas satchel's contents. What's in the thermos?

—A nice couple I know, can't keep their hands off each other, live in that house we passed, in a maze of box hedges. They're now, poor dears, in the United States, at some conference on the economics of cows. This is their property, so we can make ourselves at home.

Curious gaze at Gunnar, a twitched nose, speculative crimping of the corners of the mouth.

—The meadow is a recurring image in Rimbaud. It's his image of the world after the flood. The world anew after being drowned. Shakespeare grew up in meadows, a country boy.

—Rimbaud.

—He called them a harpsichord. The harpsichord of the meadow.

—I like it when you babble, Gunnar. Go back to Rimbaud.

—No underwear.

—And one problem, learn from experience, with abridged and minimized pants is that you can't get them off over your sneakers.

—If you didn't have sneakers the size of boats and socks as thick as towels, you'd have a chance.

—Grownups are so fucking tiresome, you know? Who tied these laces? Not me. Blue toes and heels to these socks, see.

—Grown-ups know that you take your shoes off before your pants. Rimbaud was a French poet, probably the greatest of our time. He quit writing at 18, became a vagabond.

—I can't wait to have hair all over the top of my feet and toes, like yours. Drives Samantha crazy, I imagine.

Upper lip lifted, Thorvaldsen, eyes dimmed.

—Paisley underwears, what there is of them. Recite me a poem by this Rimbaud.

—Samantha's gift. One has to wear gifts.

O saisons, ô chateaux,
Quelle âme est sans défauts?
O saisons, ô châteaux,
J'ai fait la magique étude
Du bonheur, que nul n'élude.

—Hey! You're beautiful Gunnar. You've always been big shoulders under a sweater, and raunchy jeans, and forty-four shoes, and underneath you're an Olympic diver.

I see apples,
I see pears,
I see Gunnar's
Underwears.

Oh seasons, right? Oh chateaux. And something about magic happiness, yuss? This sun's great. I can feel myself turning honey brown.

—What soul is without its faults? I've made a magic study of happiness, or a study of the magic of happiness. Let's look at the marsh.

—Swap dicks with you. Now I see why Samantha drools when she looks at you. Why didn't you bring her, too?

—Two males dressed like Adam are free of the electricity that charges the air when Eve's along.

—I'd be an idiot if I were hung like you.

—It will grow if you drink your buttermilk, eat your spinach, and play with it diligently.

O vive lui, chaque fois
Que chante le coq gaulois.

—There are nests in the marsh grass, grebe or mallard. Every time the French rooster crows cockadoodle, cockadoodle, cockadoodledo!

—Let happiness thrive every time the cock crows. How many times they painted you in the last century, a naked boy on the ocean's edge, Peder Krøyer, Carl Larsson, Anna Ancher, all those masters of tone. The Finn Magnus Enckell. Hammershøi was their Vermeer. There's a charming story of Nexø's about naked spadgers on the beach, somewhere around here.

Devil dance on shining sand flat.

—How come?

—Symbolism, idealism, Walt Whitman, the Mediterranean past, hope, the beauty of the subject, Thorvaldsen, the Danish heart.

—Did Edith pack any peapods?

Fingers flipping at mosquitoes, midges, gnats.

—Nietzsche and Georg Brandes. We could go see.

—Hey!

—Walk up.

—I'm too big to ride piggyback, wouldn't you say?

—On my shoulders.

—Ho!

—Ho!

—What's in the thermos is cold milk. Edith thought it the only tipple for a growing Danish boy.

Fingers wrecking Gunnar's hair.

—I figured you'd go silly.

Legs out straight, Gunnar holding his shins, Nikolai leaned forward to stare eye to eye upside down.

—Catch! said Nikolai, doubling and pitching forward into Gunnar's arms, deadweight limp, laughing.

—Dig into the satchel and see what Edith calls a picnic. Should I make any remark, however friendly, about the incumbent of the diminished short pants pointing to the sky?

Downward stare, mock surprise.

—I guess I get a hard on when I'm happy. Sammidges in wax paper. Bananas. Eggs, Vienna breads with raisins and walnuts.

Brownish pink, stalk and bulb, scrotum round and tight.

Silly grin, happy eyes.

—It lifts and waggles when you're posing. At your age, it has a mind of its own.

—Yours doesn't? It has my mind, too, sometimes.

—The foreskin slides back, I hope? Some don't.

Foreskin withdrawn from palest violet glans by a ready fist.

—Why don't some don't?

—Why do some people have webbed toes and six fingers? Nature has an awful lot to do in designing a body. She did very well with you.

—This sammidge is country pâte, smells like gym socks worn for two summer weeks, and Gruyère. This one's ham, mayonnaise, and olives.

—One of each. Faeroe Islanders disapprove of choice, on religious principle, I think.

Nikolai among meadow flowers, eating his Vienna bread first.

—Banana next, then sammidges.

—It's a free country.

—Up there, blued out contrary to all you'd think, are the stars, too many to count, in boundless space, and the air that belongs to our planet only, and here at the bottom of the air, us, in a meadow in Denmark, full of wildflowers, ants, microbes, worms, and grass, and under us layers of chalk and clay and solid rock down to we don't know what, but whatever it is, it gets to a center, and starts the other half of a symmetry on out to the other side of the world opposite to where we are now, which is halfway between New Zealand and King Edward VII Land in Antarctica, pods of mooing whales and icebergs with penguins standing around on them gabbling with each other, the *Nautilus* with Kaptajn Nemo playing Buxtehude on his organ, great C-Minor chords thrilling through jellyfish, and then back to us and the mayflies and the grasshoppers, and here we are, Gunnar Rung, playing hookey from chiselling an Ariel out of stone, and Nikolai Bjerg, twelve-year-old Lutheran with his richard stiff.

—You're going to be a poet.

—You did hug me, you know. When Mikkel masturbates, and comes, it's like the white of an egg all over his tummy, maybe two eggs.

—Mikkel's how old?

—Thirteen, but advanced. He says he could come at eleven. This is fun, Gunnar, I should have brought a kite, the breeze is just about perfect. Ouch! Ant on my balls.

—Bring Mikkel around sometimes. Your best friend, is he?

Talking while chewing, eyes closed to think, thumb and fingertips wobbling glans.

—Because.

—When I start the Korczak group, I'll need several kids, girls and boys. You and Mikkel as friends, holding hands, or arms around each other, or somesuch. I want something Korczak would like. He loved his children. I ask you if Mikkel is your best friend, and you answer *because,* which probably isn't bright.

—Good eats, especially as consumed backwards. Actually, these are Mikkel's pants.

15

—The interleaving high outward stretch of the tall oak, Samantha said. That's how this Greek poem begins, by Antiphilos. A good shadower, *euskion,* for *phylassomenois,* people looking for shade, from the ungiving heat of the sun. Its leaves are thicker together than tiles on a roof. And is home to the ringdove, and home to the cricket. And then it says: let me be at home here, too, at perpendicular noon. That's all the poet says, with a hint at the end that he's going to have a nap in the cool shade under the oak.

—There's Holberg's oak over by the old library, Nikolai said, and that sacred oak out in the Hills.

—Don't wiggle, Gunnar said. It's a short poem?

—Six lines, and amounts to a big oak, green and enormous, with pigeons and crickets in it, and an ancient Greek, or Greeks, sitting or lying under it. It makes a lovely poem.

—What's its title? When was it written?

—Greek poems don't have titles. First century, in Byzantium. The ringdove is a *phatta,* and may be a wood pigeon or the cushat. In the Bible you get ringdoves in terebinth trees.

Nikolai cooed like a dove and chirped like a cricket.

—You're translating? Gunnar asked.

—Trying to. It seems to be so pure and innocent, yet the oak was Zeus's tree, and had a dryad in it, a kind of girl Ariel, and the dove belongs to Aphrodite, and the cricket's squeak and cluck is a symbol for shepherds letching after each other, or for the milkmaid with the sunburnt nose and slim bare feet in the daisies. So what looks like Wordsworth or Boratynski is actually Sicilian and pastoral, a long time after Theokritos. But it's looking ahead to nature poetry, if we want to see it that way, of the kind we begin to get in Ausonius.

—Have I ever heard anyone talk like Samantha? Nikolai asked the ceiling, crossing his eyes and rounding his tongue like the bowl of a spoon in his surmising mouth. No, I have never heard anyone talk like Samantha.

—Break! said Gunnar. Bumpkin has decided to play the village idiot.

—Let me, Nikolai said pulling on a sweater, see that Greek poem. What's that word?

—*Branches.*

—And and.

—*Hanging out over spreading oak good shadow high.*

—In Mikkel's tree house there's leaves all around us, even below, and the light's as green as a salad, and it's cool and private. Show me the house of the ringdove and cricket.

—*Oikia phatton, oikia tettigon.* House of the ringdove, house of the cricket. A *tettix* is a cricket.

—Named itself, didn't it?

—*Dendroikia paidon,* tree house for boys.

Golden smile with silver dots for eyes.

—My friend Birgit and I, Samantha said, used to climb out her bedroom window, in our shimmy tails, into a big tree, I think it was a very old apple, and sit on limbs, like owls. We thought it a very important thing to do.

BOY WITH GEESE

In the park, with lakes, in Malmö. Life-size Swedish boy in small britches, three geese, by Thomas Qvarsebo, 1977. Gunnar, Samantha, and Nikolai went over on the boat from Nyhavn to look at it. Nikolai liked the geese, Gunnar the candid modelling, Samantha the big-eared, honest-eyed frankness of the boy.

—And the obviousness, there in the britches, of his being male.

—Wait till you see my and Nikolai's Ariel.

—Sweden, Nikolai said, is Denmark's Lutheran uncle.

—Lutheran aunt, said Samantha.

BULLETIN BOARD

Red and brown poultry foraging in the high street, and dogs, grass between rocks once squared stone but there is no squared stone in these late days in antiquity, the autumn of an autumn, when portrait statues of the emperors had drilled pucks for eyes, all exactitude lost in swollen bulk, when discernible value was draining from things into money and into a frightened spirituality that hated the body.

—L'Orange, Gunnar said when Samantha asked, *Fra Principat til Dominat.* It happened again in Picasso's sculpture.

GOLDEN DOVES WITH SILVER DOTS

In the advanced light of a long afternoon, Samantha reading, Gunnar rolling his shoulders, Nikolai rubbing his knees.

—When each of us relates to an idea, separately, essentially, and with passion, we are together in the idea, joined by our differences.

—Kierkegaard, Gunnar said.

Nikolai butted and pushed his way into Gunnar's Icelandic sweater.

—In which, Gunnar remarked to the ceiling, he can pet his mouse, and those of us who are unobservant are none the wiser.

—He's among friends, Samantha said. Each is himself in himself, different. In our separate inwardnesses we keep a chaste bashfulness between person and person that stops a barbarian interference into another's inwardness. Thus individuals never come too close to each other, like animals, precisely because they are united in ideal distance. This unity of differentiation is an accomplished music, as with the instruments in an orchestra.

Nikolai, whistling, came to sit by Samantha and look at the page. She hugged him closer and wrecked his hair.

—He wears your sweater because it's yours.

—Isn't that barbarian, as you've just read us? Not as barbarian as grubbing around down in under the sweater, but then the two would go together, wouldn't they?

—I hope so, Samantha said.

—I don't know what anybody's talking about, Nikolai said.

—Love, I think, Gunnar said. Your namesake Grundtvig wanted everybody to hug and kiss. Kierkegaard, however, saw people in love as two alien worlds circling each other. Grundtvigians went at it along the hedgerow, watched by placid sheep, and in the Lutheran bed, and in the hayloft, but shy Søren was one for guddling down in under a sweater three sizes too large for him, without, I should think, the shameless grin.

—Quit twitting Nikolai, who's looking like the most innocent cherub in God's nursery. Kierkegaard looked like a frog with a sorrow.

—Nikolai Frederik Severin Grundtvig, Nikolai said. Could be I was named for him, do you think?

—You can say you are. We all live in our imagination, don't we? If we don't make ourselves up, others will make up a self for us, and get us to believe it.

Sweet puzzlement in Nikolai's eyes.

—I wonder, Gunnar said, if we don't make everything up? Man, I mean, is a damned strange animal. He lives in his mind. Of course we don't know how animals think, what their opinions are. What does a horse think about all day?

—Maybe, Nikolai said, they just are. Horses and ducks. But, you know, they have lots to pay attention to.

—What you're sculpting, you know, Samantha said over *L'Equipe,* which she had abandoned Kierkegaard for in her nest of cushions by the window, is not really Ariel at all, but Eros, Shakespeare's junior senior giant dwarf Don Cupid.

19

—It can't be done, Nikolai said, but Mikkel brought me piggyback on his skateboard.

—Hello, said Mikkel.

Blond and pink, with awesome blue eyes, Mikkel was dressed in spatter jeans and a sweater from the Faeroes. Fifteen, at a guess. Why did Nikolai say thirteen?

—See, Nikolai said of the stone Ariel, it's me, or will be when it's finished.

—Hey! You're good! Mikkel said to Gunnar, who was edging chisels at the grindstone. I mean, it's tremendous, you know?

—I get paid for posing. It's like a job. Are you ready, Gunnar boss man? Is it OK if Mikkel watches? He knows he's to stay out of the way.

20

On Saturdays at the Children's Republic, after their newspaper had been read and the weekly court had tried and fined those charged with bullying, disrespect, hair pulling, disobedience, fibbing, and other high crimes of their little world, Korczak would give a talk. The subject was chosen by the orphans, from a list on the bulletin board, frequently revised.

—So we have put one of those lists on our bulletin board, Gunnar said, compiled by Samantha from several sources. That's why The Emancipation of Women leads all other topics.

—I have not, Samantha said, sticking out her tongue, fiddled with the order.

21

Fox bark, gruff. Nikolai monkeyed from the bed to the sill, replying with a cub's whimper. Coupled hand and wrist, Nikolai pulled and Mikkel climbed until he had a kneehold, swinging his other bare brown leg into the room. They crept like panthers, on fingers and toes to the bed. Nikolai, naked under the blanket, watched Mikkel tug off his jersey, the tuck of his navel, a dab of shadow on his moonlit front.

In their shy and democratic privacy under the sheets Nikolai speculated on the interestingly different warm and cool places of the body, flinching from cold fingers and toes, the climate of a bed, the frankness of hands. Mikkel whispered that they should suppress talk, as parents can hear better than dogs, and, as Nikolai understood, words are scary and inadequate, things named being compromised thereby, and changed. In the tree house one took off one's pants if the other did, with no more than the complicity of a grin. The gossip of boys is largely fiction, anyway: they enjoyed each other's lies.

POLIXENES

We were as twin lambs that did frisk in the sun
And bleat the one at the other.

23

Nikolai had just returned from the red plains of Mars. He had parked his space cruiser in a meadow in Iceland, and had a leg-stretching walk through wildflowers and sheep. Then he transmitted himself through a hyperspace cavity with a swimming roll like that of the bubble in a spirit level, to Copenhagen, where he changed from his mylar-and-platinum antigravity overall into comfortable jeans and jersey. On Strøget he bought an ice cream and a sack of peapods. As usual, interplanetary travel and ice cream made him amorous, tightened his balls, and made him importantly happy.

At Gunnar's he entered without knocking, though he shouted in a breaking treble that he was there.

Silence, but one that had just gone silent.

—Hey! It's me. Ariel, Nikolai.

Thicker silence.

Whispers upstairs.

—O shit, Nikolai said. Look, I'll go away. When should I come back, huh?

More whispering.

—Come on up, Samantha said. You're friends.

—Better than friends, Gunnar said. You're family.

—I don't want to butt in, Nikolai said with plaintive honesty, imitating grown-up speech. I can come back.

—You can also come up. We're dressed like Adam and Eve before they found the apple tree, but then so are you most of the time you're here.

Nikolai peeked around the bedroom door and lost his voice.

—The fun's over, Samantha said. Over twice, to brag on Gunnar. We were fiddling around with afterplay and mumbling in each other's ear.

Gunnar rolled over onto his back, his hands under his head, the silliest of grins and closed eyes for an expression. Samantha gathered the eiderdown around her shoulders.

—An American sociologist, she said, would make lots of notes if I were to say that we have to get dressed so that Nikolai can take off his clothes to pose.

—Figure and ground, said Gunnar. Or is it context? Maybe just manners?

He sat up with a yawn and stretch, swinging his legs off the bed.

—A game, he said. I put on my shirt, Nikolai takes his off. I button my top button, you unbutton yours.

—It won't work, Samantha said. You can't put on a sock, or your underbritches, while he takes his off, as there's a shoe intervening, jeans intervening.

—OK, then. Off a shoe and I'll put on a sock.

—Still won't work, Samantha said. Nikolai can't take his jeans off over his shoes.

—Got to pee, said Gunnar.

—Undress, quick, quick, Samantha said. Get in the bed.

He untied his shoelaces as if he'd never seen a shoelace before, and his fingers on buttons, belt buckle, and zipper were as strengthless as a baby's. He had just dived under the coverlet Samantha was lifting, in his socks and briefs, heart beating like a chased rabbit's, when Gunnar returned.

—Oh, ho! The American sociologist has now walked into a wall.

He took off his shirt, raised the eiderdown, and pulled Nikolai into a hug.
—We still have on our briefs and socks, Samantha said, which I'm now peeling down and off.

A whistle of surprise and compliance from Nikolai.

The only strategy he could think of was to lie on his back with one arm under Samantha's shoulders, the other under Gunnar's. Out of the corners of his eyes he looked in turn at each, for instruction, for a clue. Could they hear his heart thumping? Samantha's breast was cool and warm at once against his ribs. Gunnar's hard freckled shoulder fitted awkwardly under his arm, making it tingle. He kissed Samantha on the cheek, and was kissed back.
—No fair, said Gunnar.

So he kissed Gunnar and was kissed back.

Samantha reached across him to Gunnar, and Gunnar across to Samantha, in some conspiracy of communication, as if words were no longer of any use.
—One big nuzzling rolling hug from each of us, Gunnar said, and we get on with the day. Samantha and Nikolai first, Samantha and me second, Nikolai and me third.

24

—Friendly trees, Mikkel said. When Colonel Delgar was turning the dunes and heaths of Jylland back into forests, he found that if you plant a mountain pine beside a spruce, the two will grow into big healthy trees. Spruce alone wouldn't grow at all. Mycorrhiza in the mountain pine's roots squirt nitrogen and make the spruce happy and tall.

Thick, ribbed, white knee socks, Mikkel's, banded blue and mustard at the top. Shoving them down, his back against Nikolai's shoulder. Flex of pullover hem over pod of his white briefs, hamp of hair tickling the nib of his nose, eyes meeting Nikolai's.
—By 1500 Jylland was a waste heath. Trees are masts. Can you get at the fig newtons? Down in under all the ziplocks they are.
—Friendly trees, Nikolai said, squirming around to work off his shorts. The space, lack of it, in this tree house is friendly. Why are you talking about friendly trees, huh?

Mikkel rocking on his back, wiggling out of his briefs. A smart pubic clump the color of marmalade.
—Fig newtons in one hand, Nikolai said, cock in the other. There are too many legs in this tree house.

Mikkel pulling down Nikolai's briefs.

The two small square windows in Mikkel's tree house looked onto roofs and the skylight onto leaves and branches.
—Gunnar's not *in* this world, Nikolai said. Well, he is and he isn't. To be a sculptor he says you have to read poetry and philosophy and know anatomy

like a surgeon and listen to music and go off and be by yourself to make peace with yourself in your soul, and he likes both boys and girls, that's for sure, and is trying to make up his mind which. But he's a good person. Good sculptor. His landlady, the Plymouth Brother from the Faeroes, gets a thrill out of imagining he's a devil, but you can see she likes him, and fusses over him. The looks she gives me when I'm posing.

25
The dove in Gunnar's dream flew upside down, carrying a sparrow in its claws.

HERAKLEITOS IN THE RIVER
Conventional psychology is misled by a primitive gnostic theory to the effect that things ought normally to appear to sense in their full and exact nature. Nothing could be further from the fact, or more incongruous with animal life and sensibility.

27
Gunnar drawing Nikolai's hand.
—King Matt. Tell me more about him.
—In good time. There's a play by Korczak in which children sit in judgment on God and history. Their indictment is almost too terrible to hear. His orphans were for the most children abandoned by their parents and at the mercy of Poland, which is like being a sparrow at the mercy of a hawk.

28
Splendid stare of blue eyes.
—Mikkel Angelo made a big buncher statues, yuss, and when was he? I'm so fuckering dumb.
—Last quarter of the 1400s, and sixty-four years into the 1500s.
  Fingers.
—Eighty fuckering nine years old.
—He was an architect, too, and a painter and a poet.
—David the giant killer.
—Moses with horns.
—The ceiling of the Catholic church in Rome, Italy. Horns?
—Beams of light from his forehead. You shine when you've talked with God. But they look like horns.
—What do you know about sand?
—Sand?
—We're doing sand in school. Geography. It drifts around like oceans. Sloshes. Sand is rock turned to grit by wind and water. Then it packs down again, over a million or so years, and turns back into rock. Crazy.

29

Samantha in a baggy jersey, Gunnar's, looking at drawings of herself. Arrival of Nikolai, pitching his book satchel into a corner.

—Let me see. Hello, Samantha, hello.

—You wore those pants to school?

—Where's Gunnar? Oh, yes. Truly short pants make your legs look longer, you know.

—Having a pee and putting himself back together. We rather got carried away.

—And with these there's no underwear on under, so your nuts and dink can nest in what there is of a pants leg, though they're apt to look out when you're sit, if you're not careful. Tuck back in easy enough.

—Gunnar! Samantha shouted. Come save me, or Nikolai, whichever you think needs protecting from the other.

Edith looked around the door. Pursed lips.

—Ho! said Gunnar bounding downstairs, zipping up. Flopping wet hair.

—Drawing, drawing! Some days you can, some days you can't. Degas was here, wasn't he? Are you're teasing innocent Nikolai, or is Nikolai trying to see what his charm will get him? A studio's a friendly place.

30

A giant land iguana in his silken brown and green network mail, *Conolophus suberistatus* Gray, safe in a convoluted viridity of pisonia, fish fuddle, and guava, trained his red eyes on his cousin amblyrynchus, changing from voluptuous pink to leaden lava, where red rock crabs grow. And with his eyes on the iguana, Caliban, who has also seen, after the thunder-strokes and howling winds of the tempest, drowned sailors, dropped from the moon, when time was. Their strange clothes are wet and black, rilled in the way of vines about their bony legs and arms, their feet buckled in sodden leather.

31

Nikolai danced, a puppet on jerked strings, an eel wiggling, a lunatic hopping, a farmer at Whitsuntide drunk and happy, a Pawnee stomping through the ghost dance, a Christy minstrel balling the jack, a new-hatched devil chasing Lutheran virgins.

Samantha joined him for a Mutt-and-Jeff foxtrot with something Mexican in it. The music was outside, in Gray Brothers. Gunnar and Edith were spreading a board for supper in the courtyard.

—The Lord makes allowances for the young, Edith said. It's a blessing he has on clothes.

32

Feeling friendly toward the bobble of red dahlias outside the windows, where the afternoon stood as a tall box of solid and perpendicular light, Nikolai began with a dip to undress. It was a remote out-in-the-country farmyard light, between kitchen and barn, with chickens, a well, old bricks with a felt of moss in corners and under trees. Butterflies, bees, midges.

—Your courtyard is a farm on Fyn, you know? Pushing down his jeans, he mouthed to the empty air *I am Batman.*

A new book lay on the coffee table, essays on Wittgenstein edited by Jaakko Hintikka.

—Who in private life is a reindeer. It's Wittgenstein you've done a bust of, right? Tall neck and gaze. In a leather jacket with zipper.

Briefs down, he tickled the neb of his penis, a baby's innocence in his smile. The drawing block, colored pencils.

—Today we're drawing. Pull your briefs up, leave your socks on, shirt off. Your hair's a nice muss today. Light's splendid, as you've said. And for reasons I probably oughtn't to pry into, you're sweetly happy, pleased with yourself.

—Happy with just being here, Gunnar. Can I say that? There are lots of good places, the Troll Wood, my room at home, Mikkel's room, the Ny Carlsberg Glyptotek and whichwhat, but this is my best place.

33

—We sculptors have no interest in time, and therefore have no language. What we and the critics say about sculpture is usually pig swill.

—Potato peels, mash, and buttermilk, Nikolai said. I've seen it. Tasted it. Oh a dare from my cousin on the farm. Pigs are delicate eaters, you know.

—Beautiful beasts they are, too.

—Part dog, part hippo.

KORCZAK TO JOSEF ARNON

Don't you think I look like an old tree filled with children playing like birds in my branches? I'm trying to exclude everything temporal from my thoughts, to relive all that I've ever experienced through the silence within silence.

35

Samantha throwing off a shawl and kicking off her shoes.

—Whatever will we do when the Ariel's finished and there's no Nikolai to do his fetching striptease and be beautiful and talk nasty?

—I can still drop in, can't I?

—There's the Korczak group, Gunnar said over the whirr of his grindstone.

I have other ideas, too. And then, if I wanted to, I could be jealous.
Samantha kissing Nikolai on the mouth.

—I saw that, said Gunnar.

—I'm in love, Nikolai said.

36

Having peed shoulder to shoulder at a urinal off The Greening toward the Fortress, Mikkel and Nikolai grinned at each other in purest idiocy.

—Some days, Mikkel said, I'm only half horny, you know? As if I were grown up or there's a hormone short out, but most days I wake up to a prosperous stiff cock that's going to butt my fly all day, and hums to itself, and plumps my balls up tight. Are you like that?

—Worse, I hope.

—Today's a hormone overload. Why do ducks come in threes? Two drakes and a hen. Is one her spare? Or is one drake the other's friend?

They walked, bumping shoulders, up the path behind the regimental chapel to the ramparts.

—Kierkegaard used to walk here, Nikolai said, round and around. Gunnar told me that the other afternoon. He said he only knew me as a kid who turned up on time, posed in the altogether, jabbered polite and awful nonsense, and went away. A walk is how you get to know people, he said, and we came up here. Said he liked the light and the trees and the quiet.

—And Nikolai.

—This is where Niels Bohr's father explained to him how a tree works, photosynthesis and water through the roots and all, and little Niels said, *But, Papa, if it weren't like that it wouldn't be a tree.* Gunnar likes me? Mna. I look like what he thinks Ariel looked like.

37

—The Korczak group will be bronze. With rock you have to know exactly what you're shaping, where Nikolai Ariel is inside, which I do, and which I need to get to all at a go.

Gunnar wore sneakers and an American baseball cap only, his naked body powdered over with marble dust.

Industrial yellow-and-blue work gloves, mallet, chisel.

—So your posing is for the finding you in the stone, that's behind us, and for the finishing and smoothing, which begins tomorrow. By tonight it will be here. I got up this morning with it in my eye, in my hands, all the thousand decisions made.

—Golly.

—Golly exactly.

—You want me around? Can I stay and watch?

—Hand me those goggles over there on the shelf. There's going to be dust when I bite into this fucker with the power saw. Samantha's bringing gauze masks, and sandwiches. Edith's away at her sister's. Said something about idols as she left. What she was thinking is that when I'm bringing a work up to the finish line I get raving horny.

—O wow.

—Probably make a little Dane as well as an Ariel, all in a day's work. Get the broom and dustpan and start sacking up the rubble. Into those paper bags it goes, and the bags you put in a neat line in the alley. First, find the wire brush.

Diligence of Nikolai, with stares at Gunnar.

—When did you start, Gunnar? Yesterday the block was my head and shoulders and the outside of my arms and legs, and you were working down the back to my butt. Now about half the rock I was in is on the floor and there're spaces between my arms and body and between my legs, and I can see how the legs are going to be.

—Six this morning. Shooed Edith away around half eight, quoting Scripture. Samantha turned up around nine, made coffee, and got fucked.

—Want me to make more coffee? I get horny, too, posing.

—We can imagine that Shakespeare writing the play, and rehearsing it, and probably acting in it, was not a Lutheran Swede in his great heart.

—First time I was here I went away with balls as tight as a green apple and my handbrother throbbing.

—Goggles. I hear Samantha at the door. And you jacked off twice, panting and mooing.

—Four times. I'm not a baby. Ho, Samantha.

Samantha with her jacket over her head, wet.

—It's raining cats, dogs, and Swedes. The streets are rivers. Nikolai! You count, of course. Gunnar's not in the world when a work fit's on him. When he went full throttle on the Georg Brandes I had to feed him for two days and remind him to pee. Charming reversal: Nikolai practically unrecognizable in clothes, with Gunnar pretty much the way he was born. Reminds me of a horse I saw the other day in the paddock at Rungsted Kyst. He was the only gentleman among mares, and he'd slid out half a metre of pizzle, and was frolicking back and forth, ready for the party, in case anybody invited him.

Ear-to-ear fun, Nikolai's face.

—One foot's here, said Gunnar to himself. The other one's there. Nikolai's going to grit his big square teeth and lay out the sandwiches and make coffee while there's an urgent party upstairs, if some of us take off our knickers.

—Don't have any on.

A sudden hug for Nikolai, and a kiss on the mouth.

—Don't get your feelings hurt. Be brave. Understand. We'll owe you a big favor.

Rain light. The coffee-maker was sort of like the one at home, with cannister and paper filter, reservoir in its back. Should he bolt? He would play it cool. That's how Mikkel would see it through, pants poked out in front and all. Bedspring music from upstairs, and grunts. A sweet laugh. Swarm of honey in his testicles. We're breathing through our mouth, aren't we, Nikolai, and feeling reckless? We're pouring sugar all over the table, everywhere but in the sugar-bowl. We're rattling cups and saucers.

He put the bag of sandwiches on the coffee table. He sat, looking as if he had a folded fish in his pants. He stuck his fingers in his ears, instantly taking them out. This was a learning experience. In Gunnar and Samantha he had people even more understanding than his tolerant, sweet, fussily liberal parents.

He listened to the rain. He composed his account of what was happening, for telling in the tree house.

He was just unbuttoning his pants and easing down the zipper when he heard Gunnar padding downstairs.

—There's beer, he said. I see the coffee making. You're family, I hope you know. Leastways, you are now. O Lord, I didn't even take off my sneakers. There'll be comments made.

—You didn't take off your sneakers. Samantha said coming in wrapped in Gunnar's dressing gown. I'll take over. You've done it all for me, though, sweet Nikolai. I hope you grow up to be a billy goat like Gunnar. It's lots of fun.

—Didn't know I was so hungry, Gunnar said through a mouthful of sandwich. See how the back of the legs echo the whole figure? Nikolai stands as if he were ready to fight the world anyway, but here it's Ariel realizing that if he does what Prospero's ordering, he's free.

Samantha mussed her hand around in Nikolai's hair while reaching for Gunnar's beer to have a sip from.

—Is anybody ever free?

—Only if they want to be. Nikolai's free. How else could he have posed for Ariel?

—Yes, but children don't know they're free, and think of grown-ups as free.

—Am I free? Nikolai asked, munching.

—If you aren't, *lille djævel*, nobody is.

—Two glups of coffee, Gunnar said. Goggles, mallet, chisel.

Nikolai cleaned up, and went back to sweeping dust and marble chips into paper bags. Samantha was curled up in the dressing gown on the couch, having a nap.

Gunnar chiselled, whistled, chiselled. Nikolai watched as intently as if he were doing it himself. The stallion ran around his paddock at Rungsted Kyst, half a metre of pizzle dangling and wagging.

—There is no reality to time at all, you know? None.

Samantha woke with a vague smile.

—I had a wet dream, she said.

—Girls don't *have* wet dreams.

—A lot you know. Complete with orgasm, sweet as jam.

—In that case, Gunnar said, I'll follow you upstairs.

—There's something maybe I ought to tell you, Nikolai said.

—What?

   Sigh, bitten lip, silence.

—Nothing, he said.

THURSDAY

Samantha was on Fyn, visiting her aunt. Gunnar had spent the evening with Hjalmar Johanssen the art critic, who had come to see the finished Ariel. The morning had gone to photographers, the afternoon to Samantha and to seeing her off. And here was Nikolai's knock on the door.

—I've come to spend the night, so you'd better not let me in if you don't want me to. Don't look at me like that.

—Come in, Nikolai. It's late, you know.

—What's that supposed to mean?

—That your parents will be worried you're not home, for one thing.

—Call the Bjergs, if you want to. They'll tell you that Nikolai is in his jammies and fast asleep. Or reading, or watching TV, or whatever he's doing.

—How have you rigged that?

—I haven't. Nikolai has.

—Let me sniff your breath. You're not drunk. Breath's as sweet as a cow's. But obviously I've lost my mind.

—I'm Mikkel. We're best friends, me and Nikolai, tight as ticks. You have only seen Nikolai the one time I brought him around and told you he was Mikkel.

   Gunnar sat down and crossed his eyes.

—Go on, he said.

—When Nikolai's mummy asked him if he'd pose for you, the plan fell into place. Nikolai has a girl who has the run of her house every afternoon, and she and Nikolai had already started fucking their brains out when this posing business dropped out of the sky. So I agreed to be him. As I have been. So every afternoon I've been here, he's been coming like a water pistol in the hands of a four-year-old.

—So, hello, Mikkel.

—Hi.

—Now that you've jolted me out of a year's growth, tell me again why you're here. Gently.

—Nikolai wants to pose for the Korczak. As my buddy, arms around each

other, on the death march. That will even it all out, right? He got jealous
when I told him about how close you and I have become, and about
Samantha. The Korczak got through to him. He thought the Ariel old hat.
He's the brainy one of us, you know. I've had to pass his parents off as mine.
I was sure I'd slip up there. Did I?

—No. Not even with Samantha talking to your, that is, to Nikolai Bjerg's
mother fairly often. And I talked with her several times on the phone. Good
God! What a talent for the criminal you two little buggers have. You have a
career in espionage.

—So here I am.

—And where do your parents think you are?

—I don't have any. I stay with an uncle, who's sort of not all there. The
clothes I've worn here were all Nikolai's. I have some of my own now, from
my pay from you for posing.

Gunnar speechless for an uncomfortably long time. He went to the front
door and locked it.

—Could I have something to eat? Mikkel asked. I can fix it myself.

—Let's fix something together. Ham and eggs, toast and jelly. Tall cold
glasses of milk. But come upstairs first. Let's make you feel at home.

—Gunnar.

—Right here, Mikkel. I'll have to practise. Mikkel, Mikkel.

—Are we friends?

—Friends.

Big crushing hug.

—Sit on the bed. I've watched you undressing so many times, and now I'm
going to do it, starting with these knotted laces which surely Nikolai tied, not
you. Socks that smell of dough. Stand up. Now we unbutton one shirt with a
whiff of vinegar underarm. Scout belt. Slides right through, right? Zipper.
And by the God of the Lutherans, you're liking this. Pants and nice briefs
down and off. Now you're in Nikolai's work clothes, but you've changed
from Nikolai to Mikkel, with Shakespeare grinning down from heaven,
don't you imagine? So I'm seeing Mikkel stitchless for the first time. But as
it's chilly, let's, if I can find it, here we go, put this on you.

—Sweat shirt. Royal Academy of Art. Golly.

—Sort of covers your butt halfway to the back of the knees and swallows your
hands. Here, let's add the American baseball cap and have our eats.

—Gunnar.

—Mikkel.

39

The high fields of Olympos. Yellow sedge in a meadow. Sharp blue peaks beyond, seamed with snow. The eagle sank out of the cold sky and set him in the field of yellow sedge.

But there was no eagle when he turned, heart still thumping so hard that he had to breathe through his mouth, only a man.

—So, said the man, in a splendid Greek that was neither of the farm or the city, we are here.

—Where be the eagle, Mister Person? It clutched onto me and grabbed me up away from my sheep, and carried me through the air. Closed my eyes, peed and prayed. Where be we?

—On Olympos, that great place. We walk over that knoll yonder and into the palace that rules the world, save for some infringements by fate and necessity, love and time, which are tyrants over us all. Everything that's evil comes from the north. But in the south of time I am king.

—Never been so mixed up in all my life. How do I git home from here, Mister Person? 'Cause that's all I aim to do: git home, and fast.

—You will not age here, and when you go home your sheep will not have noticed you've been gone. I can splice time onto time, with a bolt or two of eternity.

—Shit!

—You need not even imagine that you are here, now. Because on Olympos there is neither here nor now. You are so many words written by a polished writer named Loukianos, of Samosata in Kommagene, who will live two millennia from now. Look you, here before the gate, these are friendly trees. The one will not grow without the other.

The curving street inside the gate (it opened of itself) was paved with stones laid down when Ilion was a forest. They walked along narrow paths among trees which the boy Ganymed could not name until they arrived at a building with cyclopean rock fitted together in irregular hexagons.

—It sure is foreign here, Mister.

—A sweet soul, Loukianos. There was a time when he was an Aethiopian named Aisopos, who understood the speech of animals.

—I can talk sheep. *Baa, baa.*

Later, when Zeus had shown Ganymed to some very strange people, a nice lady who only looked at him briefly from her loom, a fat lady who sniffed, a handsome gentleman writing music and couldn't be bothered to look, an amiable red-faced blacksmith who squeezed his arm, and lots of others. At a long family table with buzzing talk, Zeus lifted him onto his lap and said that after so exciting a day they were going to bed, together.

—Don't recommend it, said Ganymed. I sleep with Papa at home, and he says that I twist and turn all night, and talk in my sleep, and that my knees and elbows are as sharp as stakes.

—I will not mind.

—Besides, I want to sleep with that fellow down there, name of Eros, your grandson. He's neat.

Whereupon the fat lady laughed so hard that she had to be helped from the table.

40

Sunlight through sheets. Twenty toes. The phone.

—Accept a call from the Fyn? Oh yes. Hello, hello! Yes, I'm probably awake. Nikolai's here in bed with me. Well, he spent the night. Listen carefully. He's not Nikolai and never has been. He stood in for Nikolai, who was having some kind of torrid affair with a bint, while his adoring trusting parents thought he was being an Ariel for Denmark's most promising young sculptor. He's Mikkel, the friend Nikolai talked about so much, I mean of course the Mikkel Mikkel talked about so much. Don't scream into the phone: it bites my ear. No, I'm not drunk and I haven't lost my mind. You should see him. Mikkel, that is. We've only seen him charmingly nude. Now he's decidedly naked, and his hair looks like a cassowary. Oh yes, you know what boys are like. Disgraceful, yes, and frowned on by psychologists and the police, but lots of fun. The clergy are of two minds about it, I believe. Actually, he went to sleep while we were talking about how friendly it was sharing a bed. I'm putting him on the thread.

A good cough, first.

—'lo, Samantha. I'm not as awake as Gunnar. Congrats on being pregnant. Gunnar told me last night. You must show me how to change diapers and dust on baby powder. None of last night happened, you know? Yes, I'm Mikkel.

Listening, head cocked, tongue over lips.

—And I'll give you a big hug, too, when you get back. Tuesday? OK, here's Gunnar again.

By way of good manners, Mikkel rolled out of bed. Downstairs he started coffee and poured orange juice into burgundy glasses, for style. The studio seemed strange, and he looked at the rosy marble of the Ariel as if he'd never seen it before.

MR. CHURCHYARD AND THE TROLL

When the chessboard in the coffeehouse seemed an idle ruse to beguile away the hours, and the battlements around Kastellet with their hawthorn and green-shanked moorhens and pacing soldiers ran thin on charm, and his writing balked at being written, and books tasted stale, and his thoughts became a snarl rather than a woven flow, Mr. Churchyard, the philosopher, hired a carriage to the Troll Wood for a long speculative walk.

The lout on the box was eating peasecods from his hat.

—To the Troll Wood, Mr. Churchyard said, tightening the fit of his gloves.

The sky was Baltic, with North German clouds.

Copenhagen was a thunder of rolling barrels, squeaking cart wheels, hooting packetboats, Lutheran brass bands, fish hawkers, a racket of bells.

And impudent imps of boys crying after him *Either! Or!* while their sisters warned *'E'll turn and gitcha!*

If it were a lucky afternoon, the troll would be in the wood. Mr. Churchyard knew that this troll, so strangely beautiful in a mushroomy sort of way, was a figment entirely in his mind, the creature of overwork, indigestion, or bile, perhaps even original sin, still it was a troll.

Socrates, that honest man, had his daimon, why not Mr. Churchyard his troll? Its eyes looked at him from among leaves, above. Its hair was Danish, like thistledown, and was neatly cut and finished, the shape of a porridge bowl. He did not come when called. You had to sit on a log, and wait.

The wood was of mountain ash and beech which had grown thick and dark among flocks of boulders silver with lichen and green with moss. Underfoot, spongy and deep, lay a century's mulch of fallen leaves, through which the odd wildflower pushed, convolute and colorless of blossom, from the morning of time. We are welcome in meadows, where the carpet is laid down, with grass to eat, if we are cows or field mice, and the yellows and blues are those of the Greek poets and Italian painters.

But here, in the wood, we intrude. Across the sound, in Sweden, there are forests with tall cone-bearing trees, and wolves. Nature has her orders. A wood is as different from a forest as a meadow from a marsh. Owls and trolls live here. And philosophers.

In Plato's grove you heard the snick of shears all morning long, and rakes combing gravel. Epicurus spoke of necessity and fate while watching his grass lawn being rolled smooth. Aristotle and Theophrastus picked flowers in Mytilenian meadows, under parasols. And there was the Swede Linnaeus, as he called himself, who studied nature in Dutch gardens, yawned at by fat English cats.

The troll was somewhere over there, where the leaves shifted.

If Nikolai Grundtvig were here, or Mr. Churchyard's brother, Peter, the bishop, they would invite the troll to join them in a jolly folk dance.

Was that a foot in the ferns, with cunning toes? If there was one troll, there were two. It would have a wife. Nature would have it so. And young. Why should one doubt trolls when the god has kept himself hidden all this time?

When Amos talked with the god, was Amos talking to himself? For the god is hidden in light, in full view, and we cannot see him.

Curled, small fingers in the beech leaves. Fate must drop like a ripe apple. He was not especially eager to see the troll. He was not, despairingly, eager to see the god, even if he could. He had, twice now, seen the troll. It was its singularity that was important. Beyond that he could not think. There was the pure goodness of the god, all but unimaginable, and there was the pure sensuality of Don Giovanni, imaginable with the cooperation of the flesh, and there was the pure intellect of Socrates, easily imaginable, as the mind, that trollish ganglion, like Don Giovanni's mutinous testicles, was a gift from the god.

Hegel's brain in a jar of formaldehyde on the moon.

The troll was another purity, that much was certain, but of what? Your coachman, Mr. Churchyard, is sitting out there, beyond the copse, picking his nose and waiting.

The troll had said its name was Hitch. Was it of an order, upward from the mushroom (which, he could not see, it was munching) as angels are an order downward from the god? He did not see it as one finds Napoleon in the drawing of two trees, where you find his figure delineated by the branches, but as an image soaking through the fabric of vision, leaf-and-berry eyes, peanut toes, sapling legs. An acorn for sex.

—There are interstices, Mr. Churchyard said, taking off his tall hat and setting it on the log, through which things fall. In one of the spurious gospels, for instance, there is Jesus choosing Simon from among the fishers drawing up their net. And with Jesus is his dog. Or a dog.

—Yes, Lord, Simon says, coming willingly.

—And when he calls you again, says the dog, you are to answer to the name Peter.

This has been edited out of the gospels as we have them, by some high-minded copyist who did not notice that an animal whose whole soul is composed of loyalty and whose faith in his master cannot be shaken by any force, neither by death nor by distance, is given a voice, like Balaam's ass centuries before, to remind us that our perception of the otherworldly is blind.

And then in a fanciful *Acts of the Apostles* there's a talking lion who works as a pitch for Paul and Barnabas.

—Hello folks! Though I am only a numble beast, and have no theology, I'm here to get your attention and invite you to rally around and listen to my dear friends C. Paulus, a Roman citizen, and Joseph Consolation Barnabas, who have a message for you.

A blue-eyed lion, washed and fluffed for his public appearance, paws as big as plates.

Was that the troll, there, peeping from behind a tree?

—We met last autumn, Mr. Churchyard said in a voice he used for children, when the sky was packed with clouds like hills of dirty wool, and a mist smoked along the ground. You would not, you know, tell me your name, and so I named you Hitch, by your leave, taking silence for assent. How have you fared since then?

There was a flicker of leaves, a deepening of the wood's silence.

—You are not afraid, are you, of my walking stick leaning here against the log? It is just a length of wood with a silver knob which gentlemen in Copenhagen carry about with them. It goes with my hat here, and my gloves. They make a set of things to indicate to the world that we have money and that we pretend to morals approved of by the police and the clergy. Come out into the open.

In a shared fish, said Demokritos, there are no bones.

—So let me tell you a story that may shed light on our predicament. There was once a highwayman in England who disguised himself with a great bag-wig, such as the noted Samuel Johnson was the last to wear in polite society. When a wayfarer came along the road he worked, so to speak, he emerged from behind a bush, giving the wayfarer the choice of giving up his money or his life. The frightened wayfarer quailed at his pistol, and probably at his wig, and turned over to him his horse and purse.

The highwayman, riding away, threw the wig by the side of the road, where a pedestrian later found it, and put it on as windfall finery.

Meanwhile, the wayfarer who had been robbed came to a town where the pedestrian with his newfound wig had also just arrived. The wayfarer, seeing him, called out for the bailiff and had him charged before the magistrate with highway robbery. He would, he testified, know that wig anywhere.

The magistrate sentenced the pedestrian to be hanged.

Now this was a small town, and the assizes drew a large crowd, among whom was the highwayman.

—Fool! he cried out to the magistrate. You are sending an innocent man to the gallows. Look, give me the wig, and I will put it on and say, *Your money or your life,* and this false accuser will see his mistake. *Yes, yes!* the accuser said. That is the voice I heard from under the great wig.

The magistrate, however, ruled that the first identification was made under oath, before God, and that the sentence, pronounced through the majesty of the law, had been passed. And must stand.

Surely there was a shifting of shadows over there, between the Norway pine and the larch, upward and sideways, where the troll must be.

It would be charming if the troll looked like a Danish child, if it upended itself and stood on its head, pedalling its feet in the air and turning pink in the face. Or stand on its right leg with its left foot hooked around its neck, like the Gypsy acrobats on market day.

—The law, you see, is unbending. We made the law after the manner of the god, so it has nothing human in it. Let me tell you about the god. When he brought his people out of bondage in Aegypt, he led them to Kanaan, but for forty years they wandered in the desert, where the god fed them with a white fluffy bread, manna it was called, of which they became tired. So they asked for something different, something savory. Like quails, quails roasted brown on a spit over a fire, basted in their own juice, salted and rubbed with sage. So the god, who was in a proper snit about their ingratitude and greed, with their placing the sensuality of taste before a just appreciation of his grandeur and might, said:

—Ye shall eat until it comes out of your nose!

And a hail of dead quail fell from the sky, and his people dressed and cooked them, and (here I quote Scripture) even as the meat was yet in their teeth, the god caused a deadly plague to kill them who had eaten of the quail.

—What do you think of that? It was a prayer he was answering.

The troll's eyes were those of a happy child and therefore unreadable, for a child's happiness is something we have all had to forget. It is a happiness that comes from wrenching the hands off the clock, of pitching Grandpa's false teeth in the fire, of stealing, of lying, of pulling the cat's tail, of shattering the china vase, of hiding from one's parents to make them sick with worry, of hitting one's best friend's toes with the hammer. Of a child with beautiful hair, as if of spun and curled gold, and with big blue eyes, culture says *behold an angel!* and nature says *here is your own personal devil.*

A bird in those branches, or the troll?

—Listen! he said. You see me here in my great coat of German cut (in which

I have heard Schelling lecture, for German auditoria are as cold as Greenland), gloves, stovepipe trews, cane, and handkerchief up my sleeve, but you cannot see from any of this, from my large nose or the face that my brother Peter is a bishop, that I live in a city of merchants who imagine themselves to be Christians. You might as well say that a banjo player from Louisiana is Mozart.

You cannot guess from any of this that my father once shook his fist at the god on a hill in Jylland, and cursed him to his face.

The troll, the troll! But no: a hare or fox whose home this wood is.

Trolls belonged, Mr. Churchyard imagined, to the genera of toadstools, in the same way that trees were kin to angels. Mr. Churchyard's century was looking into nature, and the Germans were scrutinizing Scripture. Why have the god, after all, when they have Hegel?

Were not there passages in Scripture where the scribes wrote the opposite of what mercy and fear suggested that they suppress? Abraham most certainly sacrificed Isaac.

His father had cursed the god and moved to Copenhagen and prospered as a merchant, money begetting money in his coffers. He died in the arms of angels bearing him to heaven.

The corollary, is it not, is that if we pray we are answered with death while the meat of the quail is yet in our teeth. But the world is here, and to despair is sin. Even in their churches the tall light, the ungiving hard January light in the high windows bespeaks that worldliness of the world which no Hegelianism can pretend isn't there, isn't here.

Mr. Churchyard lifted his specs onto his forehead, ran his little finger along an eyebrow, massaged his nose, closed his eyes, licked the corners of his mouth, and coughed softly.

The irony of it.

A horse was as alive as he, and a cow had exactly as much being. A midge.

It would be some comfort if he could know that he was precisely as ugly as Socrates. He was, like all Danes, beautiful in his youth. Then his nose had grown and grown, and his back had warped, and his digestion gone to hell.

Perhaps the troll was not the size he thought it was, and was wrapped in a leaf.

Whatever we say of the god that he isn't, he is.

—*Absconditus* we say he is, seeing him everywhere. What's with us, O Troll, that we have faith in the unseen, unheard, and untouched, while rejecting what's before our eyes? In the mists of despair I see that we prefer what isn't to what is. We place our enthusiasm in scriptures we don't read, or read with fanciful misunderstanding, taking our unknowing for knowing. Our religion's a gaudy superstition and unlicensed magic.

Mr. Churchyard knew that the troll was behind one of the trees before him. He felt it as a certainty. He would have, when seen, a flat nose, round green eyes, a frog's mouth, and large ears.

—Listen! This Sunday past, in the palace church, the court chaplain, who is very popular and who in his bishop's robes looks like a Byzantine emperor, preached a sermon to a select congregation of fat merchants, lawyers, bankers, and virgins. He preached with eloquence and resonating solemnity. His text was *Christ chose the lowly and despised.* Nobody laughed.

The afternoon was getting on and the sky was graying over with clouds. Mr. Churchyard decided to make a bargain with himself, a leap of faith. He would believe the troll was there, and not bother whether it was or not. An event is real insofar as we have the desire to believe it. Bishop Mynster preached his eloquent sermon because Mr. Churchyard's father had admired him, not because Mr. Churchyard was sitting between an outlaw dressed as a merchant banker and a lady whose bonnet was made in London. He heard Bishop Mynster for his father's sake. He would converse with the troll for his own sake.

And so, the troll. He was not prepared for it to be naked. Its Danish, when it spoke, was old.

An urchin from up around Swan's Mill. It put out an arm for balance, standing on one leg, swinging the other back and forth.

—Be you a frog? it asked.

—I am a human being.

—Could have fooled me. What way comest ye, through or under?

It was amused by the consternation on Mr. Churchyard's face and crimped the corners of its mouth.

—If through color, that be the one way, to butt through yellow into blue, through red to green. T'other way's to back up a little, find a place to get through, and wiggle in. Through the curve, at the tide. Even's one, odd the other.

The troll came closer. Mr. Churchyard could see a spatter of freckles on its cheeks and nose. It cautiously touched his walking stick.

—Ash, it said. I did not know the tree. Always on this side, one moon with another, bayn't ye?

—This side of what? Mr. Churchyard asked quietly.

—Ye've never been inside the mullein, have ye? Never in the horehound, the milkweed, the spurge? What be you?

—I am a Dane. What if I were to ask you what you are? You are to my eye a boy, with all the accessories, well fed and healthy. Are you not cold, wearing nothing?

The troll raised a leg, holding its foot in its hand, so that its shin was parallel to the forest floor. It grinned, with or without irony Mr. Churchyard could not say. Its thin eyebrows went up under its hair.

—Let me say, Mr. Churchyard said, that I am certain you are in my imagination, not there at all, though you smell of sage or borage, and that you are a creature for which our science cannot account. When we think, we bind. I have not yet caught you. I don't even know what or who you are. Now where does that get us?

—But I am, the troll said.

—I believe you. I want to believe you. But this is the nineteenth century. We know everything. There is no order of beings to which you could belong. Do you know the god?

The troll thought, a finger to its cheek.

—Be it a riddle? What have ye for me if I answer right?

—How could it be a riddle if I ask you if you know the god? You do, or you don't.

—Be you looking hereabouts for him?

—I am.

—What be his smell? What trees be his kinfolk?

—I've never seen him. No description of him exists.

—How wouldst ye know did you find him?

—I would know him. There would be a feeling.

—Badger, squirrel, fox, weasel, hopfrog, deer, owl, grebe, goose, one of them? Or pine, oak, elderberry, willow, one of them? Elf, kobold, nisse, one of us? Spider, midge, ant, moth?

The troll then arranged itself, as if it had clothes to tidy the fit of, as if it were a child in front of a class about to recite. It sang. Its voice had something of the bee in it, a recurring hum and buzz, like the *Barockfagott* in Monteverdi's *Orfeo,* and something of the ringdove's hollow treble. The rhythm was a country dance's, a jig. But what were the words?

Mr. Churchyard made out *the horse sick of the moon* and *the owl who had numbers.* The refrain sounded Lappish. *One fish, and another, and a basket of grass.*

When the song was over, Mr. Churchyard bent forward in an appreciative bow. Where had he heard the melody, at some concert of folk music? At the Roskilde market? And had he not seen the troll itself, astoundingly dirty, in patched clothes and blue cap, on the wharf at Nyhavn?

And then there was no troll, only the forest floor and the damp green smell of the wood, and the ticking of his watch.

That the god existed Socrates held to be true with an honest uncertainty and deep feeling. We, too, believe at the same risk, caught in the same contradiction of an uncertain certainty. But now the uncertainty is different, for it is absurd, and to believe with deep feeling in the absurd is faith. Socrates's knowing that he did not know is high humor when compared to something as serious as the absurd, and Socrates's deep feeling for the existential is cool Greek wit when compared to the will to believe.

A papyrus fragment of a gospel written in the first century shows us Jesus on the bank of the Jordan with people around him. The fragment is torn and hard to read.

In the first line Jesus is talking but we cannot make out what he's saying: too many letters are missing from too many words to conjecture a restoration. It's as if we were too far back to hear well.

We catch some words. He is saying something about putting things in a dark and secret place. He says something about weighing things that are weightless.

The people who can hear him are puzzled and look to each other, some with apologetic smiles, for help in understanding.

Then Jesus, also smiling, steps to the very edge of the river, as if to show them something. He leans over the river, one arm reaching out. His cupped hand is full of seeds. They had not noticed a handful of seeds before.

He throws the seeds into the river.

Trees, first as sprouts, then as seedlings, then as trees fully grown, grew in the river as quickly as one heartbeat follows another. And as soon as they were there they began to move downstream with the current, and were suddenly hung with fruit, quinces, figs, apples, and pears.

That is all that's on the fragment.

We follow awhile in our imagination: the people running to keep up with the trees, as in a dream. Did the trees sink into the river? Did they flow out of sight, around a bend?

DINNER AT THE BANK OF ENGLAND

—Bank of England, guvnor? Bank of England'll be closed this time of day. Jermyn Street, gaslit and foggy on this rainy evening in 1901, pleased Mr Santayana in its resemblance to a John Atkinson Grimshaw, correct and gratifyingly English, the redbrick church across from his boarding house at No. 87 serenely *there,* like all of St. James, on civilization's firmest rock.

—Nevertheless, the Bank of England.

—Climb in, then, the cabman said. Slipped his keeper, he said to his horse. Threadneedle Street, old girl, and then what?

Quadrupedente sonitu they clopped through the rain until, with a knowing sigh, the cabman reined up at the Bank of England. Mr Santayana, having emerged brolly first, popping it open, paid the driver, tipping him with American generosity.

—I'll wait, guvnor. You'll never get in, you know.

But a bobby had already come forward, saluting.

—This way, sir.

—I'll be buggered, the cabman said.

The inner court, where light from open doors reflected from puddles, polished brass, and sabres, was full of guards in scarlet coats with white belts, a livelier and more colorful *Night Watch* by a more Hellenistic Rembrandt.

The room where he had been invited to dinner by Captain Geoffrey Stewart was Dickensian, with a congenial coal fire in the grate under a walnut mantelpiece.

Captain Stewart, as fresh and youthful as he had been when they met the year before in Boston, was out of his scarlet coat, which hung by its shoulders on the back of a chair in which sat his bearskin helmet. A stately and superbly British butler took Santayana's brolly, derby, and coat with the hint of an indulgent, approving smile. Whether he had been told that the guest was a professor from Harvard or whether he read his clothes, shoes, and face as gentry of some species, he clearly accepted him as a gentleman proper enough to dine with his captain.

—You mean Victorian fug when you say *Dickensian,* the captain laughed. I have to do an inspection round at eleven, but as I believe I said, you're a lawful guest until then. The bylaws of the Bank of England allow the captain of the guard to have one guest, male. The fare is thought to be suitable for soldiers, and here's Horrocks with the soup, mock turtle, and boiled halibut with egg sauce will be along, mutton, gooseberry tart with cream, and anchovies on toast, to be washed down with these cold bottles, for you I'm afraid, I've been taken off wine. Not, I imagine, your idea of a meal. Horrocks knows it's just right for his young gentlemen in scarlet.

—Philosophers, Santayana said, eat what's put before them.

—High table at Harvard will be amused. I'm awfully pleased you could come.

A handsome young barbarian out of Kipling, the captain's manners were derived from a nanny and from a public school and modified by an officer's mess. The British are charming among equals and superiors, fair to underlings, and pleasantly artificial to all except family and closest friends.

—But you can't, you know, saddle yourself with being a foreigner. I gather your family is Spanish but that you are a colonial, growing up in Boston and all that. Most colonials are more English than the English. You see that in Canadians. Your George Washington Irving, we were told at school, is as pukka British as any of our authors. Longfellow also. Same language, I mean to say.

—My native tongue is Spanish.

—Not a trace of accent. Of course you don't *look* English, I mean American, but then you can't go by that, can you? Most of the Danes I've seen look more English than we do, when they don't look like Scots. You look South American. It's the moustache and the small bones, what? I know a Spanish naval officer with absolutely the frame of a girl. Probably cut my throat if I were to say so, devilish touchy, your Spaniard. Doesn't Shakespeare say so somewhere?

—I'm various kinds of hybrid. Bostonians are a breed apart in the United States. I can lay claim to being an aristocrat, but only through intermarriages. As a Catholic I'm an outcast, and as a Catholic atheist I am a kind of unique pariah.

—That's jolly!

—I am, I think, the only materialist alive. But a Platonic materialist.

—I haven't a clue what that could mean. Sounds a bit mad.

—Doubtless it is. This wine is excellent.

—No offence, my dear fellow, you understand? Our fire needs a lump or two of coal. Horrocks!

—The unexamined life is eminently worth living, were anyone so fortunate. It would be the life of an animal, brave and alert, with instincts instead of opinions and decisions, loyalty to mate and cubs, to the pack. It might, for all we know, be a life of richest interest and happiness. Dogs dream. The quickened spirit of the eagle circling in high cold air is beyond our imagination. The placidity of cattle shames the Stoic, and what critic has the acumen of a cat? We have used the majesty of the lion as a symbol of royalty, the wide-eyed stare of owls for wisdom, the mild beauty of the dove for the spirit of God.

—You talk like a book, what? One second, here's somebody coming. Sorry to interrupt.

Horrocks opened the door to admit a seven-foot corporal, who saluted and stamped his feet.

—Sir, Collin's taken ill, sir. Come all over queasy like, sir, and shivering something pitiful, sir.

Captain Stewart stood, found a note case in his jacket on the back of a chair, and ordered the corporal to pop Collins into a cab and take him to the dispensary.

—Here's a quid. Bring back a supernumerary. Watkins will sub for you.

—Sir, good as done, sir.

—Thank you, corporal.

And to Santayana, picking a walnut from the bowl and cracking it expertly:

—Hate chits. Rather pay from my own pocket than fill up a form. I suppose I have an education. Latin and Greek are cheerful little games, if you have the brains for them, and most boys do. Batty generals in Thucydides, Caesar in Gaul throwing up palisades and trenching fosses. Never figured out Horace at all.

—There are more books in the British Museum about Horace than any other writer.

—My God!

—Civilization is diverse. You can omit Horace without serious diminishment. I look on the world as a place we have made more or less hospitable, and at some few moments magnificent. When would you have liked to live, had you the choice, and where?

—Lord knows. Do drink up. Horrocks will think you don't appreciate the Bank of England's port. Eighteenth century? On the Plains of Abraham. The drums, the pipers, the Union Jack in the morning light. Wolfe reciting Gray's *Elegy* before the attack, to calm his nerves. Wouldn't have thought that there was a nerve in his body. Absolute surprise to the French, as if the army had appeared from nowhere. I would have liked to have been there.

—That plangent name, both biblical and Shakespearean, the Plains of Abraham. It was simply Farmer Abraham's cow pasture.

—Is it, now? Well, Bannockburn's a trout stream and Hastings a quiet village.

—And Lepanto the empty sea.

Horrocks permitted himself a brightened eye and sly smile. He was serving qualify, after all.

—English mustard is one of the delights of your pleasant country. My friends the Russells would be appalled to know that one of my early discoveries here was cold meat pie with mustard and beer. I like to think that Chaucer and Ben Jonson wrote with them at their elbow.

—There's a half-batty Colonel Herbert-Kenny, in Madras I believe, who writes cookbooks under the name Wyvern. These address themselves to supplying a British mess with local vegetables, condiments, and meat. Simplicity is his word. All the world's problems come from a lack of simplicity in anything you might think of, food, dress, manners. The bee in his bonnet is that food is character and that to eat Indian is to whore after strange gods. That's scripture, isn't it?

—He's right. Spinoza and Epicurus were Spartan eaters.

—I thought Epicurus was a gourmet, or gourmand, banquets and puking?

—He has that reputation, a traditional misunderstanding. He ate simply. He did insist on exquisite taste, but the fare was basic and elementary.

—Herbert-Kenny must have read his books.

—Cheese and bread, olives and cold water. He and Thoreau would have got along.

—Not familiar with this Thoreau, a Frenchman?

—A New Englander, hermit and mystic. Americans run to originality.

—Examined his soul, did he? I heard a lot of that in America.

Horrocks poked up the fire, removed plates, replenished Santayana's glass, silently, almost invisibly.

The dormitory and the barracks had shaped his world. He was probably far more ignorant of sensual skills than an Italian ten-year-old, a virgin who would be awkward with his county wife, and would become a domestic tyrant and brute, but a good father to daughters and a just but not affectionate one to sons.

Their friendship was a sweet mystery. The British explain nothing, and do not like to have things explained. The captain had doubtless told his friends that he'd met this American who was dashedly friendly when he was in Boston, had even given him a book about Harvard College, where he was a professor wallah. Followed sports, the kind of rugger they call football in America. Keen on wrestling and track. Speaks real French and German to waiters, and once remarked, as a curiosity, that he always dreams in Spanish. Says we English are the Romans of our time, but Romans crossbred with

Protestantism and an inch from being fanatics except that good Roman horse sense, which we take from the classics, and a native decency and love of animals keep us from being Germans. Talks like a book, but no airs about him at all.

—I like this room, Santayana said. It is England. The butler, fireplace, and mantel out of Cruikshank, the walnut chairs, the sporting prints, the polished brass candlesticks. You yourself, if a foreigner who reads may make the observation, are someone to be encountered in Thackeray or Kipling.

—Oh, I say! That's altogether too fanciful. No servants in America?

—Only Irish girls who drop the soup.

—Back to your being a materialist, Captain Stewart said. I'm interested.

—Your Samuel Butler was a materialist, the Englishman of Englishmen in our time. He was a sane Voltaire who was wholly disillusioned intellectually while being in bondage to his comfort and his heart, a character Dickens might have invented if he hadn't his readers to consider. The nonconformist is an English type, a paradox the English themselves fail to appreciate, for they have long forgotten that exceptions might be a threat to the community. An American Butler, even if he sounded like Emerson, would find himself too often in hot water.

—Don't know this Butler. Is *materialist* a technical term?

—The world is evident. Begin there.

The captain laughed.

—The substantiality and even the presence of the world have been called into doubt by serious minds, by Hindus, by Chinese poets, by Bishop Berkeley and German idealists.

—Extraordinary! Hindus! I daresay. And your being a materialist is your firm belief that the world is, as you put it, evident? Does all this have anything to do with anything?

Santayana laughed.

—No. What interests me is that all thought and therefore all action stands on a quicksand of tacit assumptions. What we believe is what we are and what we expect of others, and of fate.

—Here's my corporal again.

—Sir, Collins is taken care of, sir.

—Carry on, corporal.

—Sir! Yes sir!

—Spirit lives in matter, which gives rise to it. We are integral with matter. We eat, we breathe, we generate, we ache. Existence is painful.

—Do try the walnuts. They're excellent. Do you think we live in good times or bad? I mean, do you want us all to be materialists?

—I am content to let every man and woman be themselves. I am not them. When man is at last defeated and his mind bound with ungiving chains, it will be through a cooperation of science and what now passes for liberalism. That is, through his intellect and his concept of the good, just, and useful life. This is, of course, a cruel paradox, but it is real and inevitable. Science is interested only in cause and effect, in naked demonstrable truth. It will eventually tell us that consciousness is chemical and the self a congeries of responses to stimuli. Liberalism is on a course of analyzing culture into a system of political allegiances which can be explained by science, and controlled by sanctions, all with the best of intentions. All of life's surprises will be prevented, all spontaneity strangled by proscriptions, all variety canceled. White light conceals all its colors, which appear only through refractions, that is, through irregularity and pervasive differences. Liberalism in its triumphant maturity will be its opposite, an opaque tyranny and a repression through benevolence which no tyrant however violent has ever achieved.

—Here here! You're talking for effect, as at the Union.

—There is no fanaticism like sweet reason. You are as yet free, being wonderfully young, and having the advantage of the liberty of the army.

—Liberty, you say?

—The most freedom anyone can enjoy is in constraint that looks the other way from time to time. You know that from childhood and from school.

—The army is school right on. And one does and doesn't long to be out. I can't see myself as a major in India, parboiled by the climate and becoming more conservative and apoplectic by the hour.

—Youth does not have as much of childhood in it as early maturity has youth. There is an abrupt demarcation between child and adolescent, a true metamorphosis.

—Something like, yes.

—The English fireside is as congenial an institution as your culture has to offer. We Americans find your bedrooms arctic and your rain a trial, but the saloon of the King's Arms in Oxford, after freezing in the Bodleian or walking in the meadows, is my idea of comfort. As is this room, as well. And as a philosopher who speaks his mind, I delight in your receiving and feeding me in your picturesque undress, those terribly uncomfortable-looking galluses, do you call them? Over your plain Spartan undyed shirt. I might be the guest of a young Viking in his house clothes.

—You should hear the major on the subject of gravy on a tunic. And you decline to convert me to materialism. What, then, to believe? Horrocks and I ought to have something to benefit us from a Harvard professor's coming to dine.

—We seem to need belief, don't we? Skepticism is more than likely unintelligent. It is certainly uncomfortable and lonely. Well, let's see. Believe that everything, including spirit and mind, is composed of earth, air, fire, and water.

—That is probably what I have always believed. But, look here, my dear fellow, it's coming up eleven, when I must be on parade in the dead of night, with drums and fifes. All civilians must be home in their beds. Look, Horrocks will give you to the corporal, who will give you to the bobby outside, and you're on your own. This has been awfully jolly.

—It has, indeed, said Santayana, shaking hands.

—Good night, sir, Horrocks offered.

—Good night, and thank you, Santayana said, tending him a shilling.

The rain had let up. He would walk to Jermyn Street, keeping the image of Captain Stewart in his martial undress lively in his imagination, as Socrates must have mused on Lysis's perfect body, or on Alcibiades whose face Plutarch wrote was the handsomest in all of Greece. The world is a spectacle, and a gift.

The perfect body is itself the soul.

If he was a guest at the Bank of England, he was equally a guest at his boarding house on Jermyn Street, the world his host. Emerson said that the joy of an occasion was in the beholder not in the occasion. He is wrong. Geoffrey Stewart is real, his beauty real, his spirit real. I have not imagined him, or his fireside, or his butler, or his wide shoulders or the tuft of ginger hair showing where the top button was left unbuttoned on his clean Spartan undervest.

Suppose that in a Spanish town I came upon an apparently blind old beggar sitting against a wall, thrumming his feeble guitar, and uttering an occasional hoarse wail by way of singing. It is a sight which I have passed a hundred times unnoticed; but now suddenly I am arrested and seized with a voluminous unreasoning sentiment—call it pity for want of a better name. An analytical psychologist (I myself, perhaps, in that capacity) might regard my absurd feeling as a compound of the sordid aspect of this beggar and of some obscure bodily sensation in myself, due to lassitude or bile, to a disturbing letter received in the morning, or to the general habit of expecting too little and remembering too much.

CHRIST PREACHING AT THE HENLEY REGATTA

Isn't it lovely, the river, with its flags and barges and laughter and music carrying so far over the water? How curiously the tuba, bouncing like the Bessy in a Morris dance, comes through the windwash, while all the other instruments fade in and out of a deafness.

Henley on such a day has touches of Deauville and of Copenhagen, and the Thames through Oxfordshire gleams as if Canaletto, Dufy, and Cézanne had got at it. Flags of Oxford and Cambridge, Sweden and France, Eton and the United States, of Leander and Thames, Harrow and Bordeaux, rill and snap in our skittish English breeze.

Mrs. Damer's sculpted heads of Thames and Isis look from the posts of the High Street Bridge at Scandinavians smiling and gathering to a clapping of hands before the chantry house and at a file of gypsies of the Petulengro clan moved along by the admonitions of a constable.

Above the noise of automobiles and motorcycles there are pipes and drums playing *Leaving Rhu Vaternish* as they swing with Celtic pluck over the bridge. A county fair at Olympia! And English bells above it all, a course of changes joyously in the air.

—*Sex quattuor tris, quinque duo,* Berkshire calls.

—*Duo tris, quattuor, quinque sex,* the answer falls.

—*Twa threo fower fif six, six fower, threo fif twa,* reply the bells of Oxfordshire.

Through a window, beyond the geraniums on the sill, you can see a photograph of the Duke of Connaught in a silver frame, wearing a leopard skin, head and all. Its jaws fit the duke's head in a yawning bite. The skin of its forelegs drape his shoulders, its tail hangs between his legs, and its hind feet dangle at the duke's tasseled kilt.

—Commander of a bicycle regiment, says Reggie to Cynthia after they have squeezed each other gazing at the duke's photograph. He was returning a salute while wheeling along in review when he wobbled and crashed, engaging himself so intricately in the ruin of his machine that a boffin from the medics had to come and extricate him, don't you know.

—Reggie old thing! screamed Cynthia. Sausage and mashed!

She was as shy and obvious as a rose, but she could stand on one leg, touch her heel to her butt, flip her scarf and laugh like a gasping halibut.

—Cynthia old darling! Pip pip, what?

Her scarf is in the colors of the London Rowing club. Curls crisp as leaves flourish around her neat tam. Having laughed, she skips and hums, and chucks Reggie under his chin.

They throw themselves into each other's arms. The interested eyes observing them are those of the painter Raoul Dufy, who has come to sketch the Regatta. He wiggles his fingers and smooths his hand along the air to see English brick, the tricolor against ash and yew, panamas and blazers, the insignia of barges carved in oak argent and d'or, taupe and cinnamon. Not he but Seurat should be here. And Eakins and Whitman. And Rousseau.

regardez Georges Seurat ces verts
et ces azurs ces outriggers
si étroites et si légères

cette rivière plus bleue
que les yeux saxons
regardez cet homme si mystèrieux

He jumps nimbly, Raoul Dufy, out of the way of a Jaguar XKE nosing toward the bridge and gives it a manual sign of French contempt.

les coups des avirons les étincelles d'eau
ces épaules puma ou il y a en marche
des souris sous le peau

ô filles minces ô garces oiseaux en vol
mères truitées autruches milords et morses
ô gigue des parasols

rameurs grands insouciants et blonds
et delà en maillot rouge
près de la rive un brave garçon

les mains en conque et florentines
les joues gonflés et romanesques
un triton gosse au chapeau mandarine

qui trompete à travers
la lumière nordique des après-midis immobiles
un son peut-être imaginaire

que l'oreille soit la preuve
un air moiré et grec et dur
et musclé comme la fleuve

Isambard Kingdom Brunel, spanner of rivers and oceans, pray for us now and at the hour of our death.

A man in an ulster and cloth hat searches the pavements and edges of gardens for the droppings of dogs, which, if the way is clear, he puts in his pockets, for later inspection in his room above the Swan and Maiden. He is, as Raoul Dufy does not know, Stanley Spencer.

A nanny across the street asks herself whatever is that man doing, and her charge, a boy in a sailor suit, reads her eyes and answers.

—Picking up dog shit and squirreling it away on his person.

—God save the poor sod, says the nurse.

—Now he's pulling his pudding.

—Charles Francis!

An old woman in a plaid shawl has caught Stanley Spencer's attention. She wears gaiters and a fisherman's hat. The crop of white whiskers on her chin pleases Spencer. He imagines her as a girl, as a bride, as a woman getting fleshy about the hips, a woman who would cast her eyes upwards when she laughs. If only he could see her feet.

Dancing angels know a fire
makes this river wind and air
seem an iron snarl of wire

The pipe band returns over the bridge, playing *The Hen Scratches in the Midden*. The melody perplexes a poet who has been dreaming with open eyes. Was it the green of the girl's eyes who was talking with British toothiness to a grenadier in mufti, or the gorgeous quiet of the gardens beyond these ancient walls that loosed his mind into revery? Louis Jean Lumière, pray for us now and at the hour of our death.

Girlish, vivacious, and brash afternoon
That lifts with the wine of its wings
From the haunted seasons of yet to be
Summer's blond and Illyrian winters.

Flat light shimmers on the Thames. An airplane drags a streamer through the air, advertising Bovril. A dowager aims her ear trumpet so that a constable can direct her electric wheelchair.

—If Mum will turn left at the pillar box just there at the chemist's and then turn sharp left at the Bird and Baby, you will find yourself right at the royal enclosure. Can't miss it, I shouldn't think.

—Left and left?

Off and away, Spencer's eyes on her Princess Marie Louise hat, she buzzes past tall oarsmen in a row, their fluent sunblenched windblent hair embellished in swirls by limber gusts, Danes in singlets and shorts, with long brown legs and eighteen blue eyes. Louis Jacques Mandé Daguerre, pray for us now and at the hour of our death. Swans ride downstream midriver aloof and alone.

Spencer fixes the old lady and her wheelchair in his memory, the velvet glove at the tiller, the hat that might have been Jacobean, the lace collar spiked out from the back of her neck.

She steers between French oarsmen naked as snakes save for brief white pants and whistles on a string around the neck.

Bugles: a rill and snap of flags. Picnickers look up from their baskets. A couple with loosened clothes behind a hedge look out.

The poet from France adjusts his spectacles.

Launch the antique swan whose silence began
Under Babylon where the wisteria hung,
When he should have sung in the red pavilions
Passacaglia, toccata, and fugue.

He inspected shingles, brick, and windows. Bees stitched along the bells of a file of hollyhocks. *Greatly comforted in God at Westchester,* a voice came through a parasol. And *ever so nice, ame shaw.* And from a clutch of gaitered clergy, *nothing but my duty and my sin.*

There milled and trod and eddied a flock of little girls with the faces of eager mice, a family from Guernsey all in yellow hats, Mr. C.S. Lewis of Belfast in belling, baggy, blown trousers and flexuous flopping jacket, his chins working like a bullfrog's, tars from H.M.S. *Dogfish* with rolling shoulders and saucy eyes, pickpockets, top-hatted Etonians chatting each other in blipped English, a bishop in gaiters regarding with unbelieving mouth a Florentine philosopher peeing against a wall, Mallarmé wrapped in his plaid shawl rapt.

The inward white of radiant space,
Cygnus and Betelgeuse and the Wanderers,
And swam instead but swan, exile and island and
Is now in this utter reality a brilliant ghost,
An archangelical, proud, fat bird,
Ignorant of what the stars intend by Swan.

River light wiggles on the ceiling of the Royal Danish Rowing Club locker room. Oarsmen trig of girth and long of shoulder suit up in the red and white toggery of their *roningteam*. The illapse of a Jute foot into a blue canvas shoe, the junt of hale chests under jerseys, bolled *skridtbinder,* Dorian knees remember, so transparent is time, a tanling foot into a sandal, lynx grace of athletes at The Shining Dog beyond the harness makers, potters, and wine shops on the angled and shady street that crooked from behind the Agora over to the Sacred Way those summers Diogenes made his progress in a wash of curs to the market along the porch.

How foreign and sudden these spare athletes seemed to old men who remembered William Gilbert Grace and Captain Matthew Webb. Longlegged rowers file to their boats, carrying oars like the lances at Breda in Velazquez's painting. Signal flags rise on a mast frivolling. A trumpet, a pistol shot.

By Stanley Spencer tall oarsmen in shorts and singlets bear their boat above their windblent vandal hair. He is preoccupied with another, inward grace.

Wild Sicilian parsley
and wasps upon the pane!

Old Man Cézanne, he tells himself, was all very well for the French temperament, going at things logically, vibrating with a passion for the École Polytechnique, for ratios and microscopes, precisions and a constant polishing of everything with critical sandpaper. He was a Poussin run by electricity. But that woman there shaped like a bottle and her daughter shaped like a churn, they want to be seen by Cimabue, by Polish buttermold carvers, by eyes begot of the happy misalliance of stiff northern barbaric chopped wood sculpture, polychrome embroidery, and beaten gold with autumnal Roman giant stone: roundly ungainly, stubborn as barrels, solid as brick kilns.

A coxswain light as a jockey clacking the knockers swung around his neck whistles with Jacobean trills and sweetenings that some talk of Alexander and some of Hercules, of Hector and Lysander, and such great names as these. To Spencer he is a conceited ass from the continent, the pampered son of a Belgian manufacturer, but he excites the Petulengros who in a fatter time would steal him as merchandise negotiable on the docks.

*There has not a minute been
in one thousand nine hundred years
twenty months or seventeen*

*But that one Christian or another
kissed his image in the mirror
standing on his slaughtered brother*

A cousin of Vice Admiral Sir Reginald Aylmer Ranfurly Plunkett Ernle Erle Drax snubs a cousin of Commander Sir George Louis Victor Henry Sergius Mountbatten Lord Milford Haven. Lord Peter Wimsey and Bunter bow in passing to Bertie Wooster and Jeeves. The aging Baron James Ensor of Ostend sweeps the horizon with his ear trumpet picking up the piston click of oars, the barking of coxes, and inflorescence of Scandinavian band music, Romany cheek, an indecent proposal in French to a vicar's sister and her reply in the French of Stratford at Bow as to the pellucidity of the day's air, the freshness of all the foreign young folk, and the silvery azure of the Thames.

Stanley Spencer pockets a nice yellow bit of dog shit and lifts off into a revery to the awful knees of Mont Sainte Victoire and the quarries at Bibémus, green wind awash in Cézanne's trees, fiercely mean old man who orders God about, and shakes his mahlstick at Him, *Seigneur, vous m'avez fait puissant et solitaire: laissez-moi m'endormir du sommeil de la terre.* A shaken fist, a plaintive cry. *I have not painted all of this, and until I do I refuse to die.*

It is the *Grande Jatte,* is it not? There is a lady with a whippet on a leash that will stand for the monkey, and clerks from banks, and little girls in tulle and ribbons, and people picknicking and gazing at the river and lolling on the banks. And those fat women over there with parasols from Camberwell, they make a touch of *The Feast of the Sardine,* do they not? The touts in their candy-stripe trousers and panamas, how they contrast with Sir Charles Parsons on the arm of the Very Reverend Dean Inge, with Margaret Jourdain and Ivy Compton-Burnett in such an inexplicable mixture of purples and greys, toques thirty years out of date.

189

Giacomo Antonio Domenico Michele Secondo Maria Puccini, pray for us now and at the hour of our death.

Stanley Spencer anticipates with relish the droppings in all his pockets, the scorched stink of wheat bunt, the dark odor of blight, mealy mildew, the reek of fomes and juniper conk, of black punk rot, potato scald, bruised galls, and scurf.

What gnathion and gullet to the Finns! They sound like foxes talking, and they laugh with their eyes. The American rowers breathe through their mouths and keep their arms crossed, and walk on the balls of their feet.

Pablo Diego José Francisco de Paula Juan Nepomuceno Maria de los Remedios Cipriano de la Santissima Trinidad Ruiz y Picasso, pray for us now and at the hour of our death.

A roopy laugh and: I can't help it I tell you, Alfie, *whoops! Whoops!* it's the little pants they have on, you can see everything they have a plain as cups under a tea towel, *I'll die!* And: Look it, he's vomited all down his front, the poor sod, gorgonzola and beer it smells like. And: Dear chap, these noonings and intermealiary lunchings in air this electric brace me for excesses unknown at the parsonage. Would you believe that I got to pee next to one of those *matelots* with the pom-poms? His caution was, shall I say, ironic. Democracy is so exciting, wouldn't you say?

Auguste Lumière, pray for us now and at the hour of our death.

Spencer pulled his wool bell hat lower over his thatch, getting now onto fat women's elbows, the wrinkles of the tuck, and the sway of loose biceps rolling. What silly treasure of heart and head I would come and steal, soft as the field mouse's white-foot tread. Like the blind bone in Beethoven's ear, I spoke, she spoke, and the drum spoke that could and could not hear. Under Mrs. Damer's eyes of Cotswold stone the Cherwell marries the Thames.

India and Turkey were in her smile,
Madras her breasts, Izmir her hips,
That cross-eyed lady of Carlisle.

Cambridge, and Bob's your uncle! A boy with a bloody nose stands defiantly by a lamp post, answering *no* to every question a policeman puts to him. A woman stung by a wasp is being helped into a pub by a Jamaican and a Hindu. A member of Parliament who has just exhibited his shrivelled penis to three Girl Guides has sunk to the sidewalk, dead.

The crew of the Club Sporting de Marseilles climbs from its boat, victors gasping, sweating, smiling. Cameras whirr and flash as they toss their coxswain in the river. A toothy official shakes their large hands and acknowledges their Mediterranean smiles with a rabbity scrunch of his lips.

—Good show! he says.

—Sink you! they reply.

Afternoon's long shadowfall across the grass and the garden walls is like music at the end of a day of self-indulgence.

As the crowds milled to the banks for the last race, which was rowed in late level golden light, a peal of Stedmans rang out from churches round-about.

—*Sex quattuor tris, quinque duo,* Berkshire calls.

—*Duo tris quattuor, quinque sex,* the answer falls.

—*Two threo fower fif six, six fower, threo fif twa,* reply the bells of Oxfordshire.

PERGOLESI'S DOG

Some dozen years ago, in the middle of one of those conversations which are apt one minute to be about Proust's asthma and the next about the size of chocolate bars in these depraved times, Stan Brakhage, the most advanced guard of filmmakers, asked me if I knew anything about Pergolesi's dog.

Not a thing, I answered confidently, adding that I didn't know he had one. What was there about Pergolesi's dog to know? There, he replied, is the mystery. Just before this conversation, Brakhage had been shooting a film under the direction of Joseph Cornell, the eccentric artist who assembled choice objects in shallow box frames to achieve a hauntingly wonderful, partly surrealistic, partly homemade American kind of art. He lived all his adult life, more or less a recluse, on Utopia Parkway in Flushing, New York, sifting through his boxes of clippings and oddments to find the magic combination of things—a celluloid parrot from Woolworth's, a star map, a clay pipe, a Greek postage stamp—to arrange in a shadow box.

He also made collages and what you could call sculpture, such as dolls in a bed of twigs; and films. For the films he needed a cameraman: thus Brakhage's presence on Utopia Parkway. The two got along beautifully, two geniuses inventing a strange poetry of images (Victorian gingerbread fretwork, fan lights, somber rooms with melancholy windows). Brakhage was fascinated by the shy, erudite Cornell whose hobbies ran to vast dossiers on French ballerinas of the last century, the teachings of Mary Baker Eddy, and the bric-a-brac of all ages and continents.

In one of their talks Pergolesi's dog came up. Brakhage asked what the significance might be of the Italian composer's pet. Cornell bristled. He threw up his hands in profound shock. What! Not know Pergolesi's dog! He had assumed, he said with some frost and disappointment, that he was conversing with a man of culture and sophistication. If Mr. Brakhage could not command an allusion like Pergolesi's dog, would he have the goodness to leave forthwith, and not come back?

Brakhage left. So ended the collaboration of the Republic's most poetic filmmaker and one of its most imaginative artists. The loss is enormous, and it was Pergolesi's dog who caused the rift.

I did the best I could to help Brakhage find this elusive and important dog. He himself had asked everybody in the country who he thought might know. I asked. The people we asked, they in turn asked others. Biographies and histories were of no help. No one knew anything about a dog belonging to, or in the society of, Giovanni Battista Pergolesi. For ten years I asked likely people, and when my path crossed Brakhage's I would shake my head, and he would shake his: no d. of P. yet found.

We never considered that Cornell was as ignorant of Pergolesi's dog as we. In Samuel Butler II's *Notebooks* there is this instructive entry: "Zeffirino Carestia, a sculptor, told me we had a great sculptor in England named Simpson. I demurred, and asked about his work. It seemed he had made a monument to Nelson in Westminster Abbey. Of course I saw he meant Stevens, who made a monument to Wellington in St. Paul's. I cross-questioned him and found I was right."

We are never so certain of our knowledge as when we're dead wrong. The assurance with which Chaucer included Alcibiades in a list of beautiful women and with which Keats embedded the wrong discoverer of the Pacific in an immortal sonnet should be a lesson to us all.

Ignorance achieves wonders. The current *Encyclopaedia Britannica* informs us that Edmund Wilson's *Axel's Castle* is a novel (it is a book of essays), that Eudora Welty wrote *Clock without Hands* (by Carson McCullers), and that the photograph of Jules Verne accompanying the entry about him is of a Yellow-Headed Titmouse (*Auriparus flaviceps*). The *New York Review of Books* once referred to *The Petrarch Papers* of Dickens and a nodding proofreader for the *TLS* once let Margery Allingham create a detective named Albert Camus.

Vagueness has vernacular charm. A footnote in a Shaker hymnal identifies George Washington as "one of our first presidents."

Cornell when he had his tizzy about Pergolesi's dog was beyond vagueness and into the certainty of the dead wrong. Sooner or later I was bound to luck onto the right person, who, as it turned out, was wise to Cornell's waywardness with bits of trivia. This was John Bernard Myers, art critic and dealer. What Cornell meant, he felt sure, was Borgese's dog. I looked as blank as Brakhage had on the previous, fatal occasion. What! Not know Borgese's dog!

Elisabeth Mann Borgese, daughter of Thomas, professor of political science at Dalhousie University, the distinguished ecologist and conservationist, had trained a dog in the 1940s to type answers to questions on a special machine that fitted its paws. The success of this undertaking is still dubious in scientific circles, but the spectacle it made at the keyboard of its machine stuck in Joseph Cornell's mind as one of the events of the century, and he supposed that all well-informed people were familiar with it. La Borgese's accomplished beast's habit of typing BAD DOG when it had flubbed a right answer had brought tears to his eyes. He had a dossier of clippings about all this, and despite its sea-change in his transforming imagination, had no qualms about dismissing people tediously ignorant of such wonderful things.

HORACE AND WALT IN CAMDEN

Intimate with Walt: Selections from Whitman's Conversations with Horace Traubel, 1888-1892, edited by Gary Schmidgall.

On Wednesday the twenty-eighth of March 1888, the twenty-nine-year-old Horace Traubel began taking down in shorthand what Walt Whitman had to say in the poet's upstairs bedroom on Mickle Street in Camden, New Jersey. "At Walt's this evening. Called my attention to an old letter in the Philadelphia Press describing a visit to Emerson with Louisa Alcott, and Emerson's senility." Whitman was sixty-nine, not yet wholly housebound. Traubel wrote up his visit within an hour of leaving the house. He kept to this routine until March 26, 1892, on which day Whitman died at sunset. His last word was "shift," a request to be turned on his water bed. An inflammation of the pleural membrane made it too painful for him to lie in one position for more than a few minutes.

Horace Traubel published the first volume of these daily conversations as *With Walt Whitman in Camden* in 1906. A second volume came out, with a different publisher, in 1908; a third, with yet another, in 1914. Traubel died in 1919 (an even one hundred years after Whitman's birth—his last words: "Walt says come on, come on"). It took thirty-four years for the fourth volume to be published, in a preposterously small number of copies, by the University of Pennsylvania Press. This is an all but unobtainable book, and very expensive. Volume 5, edited by Horace's daughter, Gertrude, was published in 1964 by Southern Illinois University Press. Over the next thirty years, the same press brought out Volumes 6 and 7. Only within the last five years have Volumes 8 and 9 (the last two) been published by W. L. Bentley Rare Books. (This undertaking was financed by the Fellowship of Friends, a California "cultural organization" whose leader has been lively enough in his pursuit of Whitman's ideals to provoke a lawsuit.) Ninety years and six different publishers for the conversation of our greatest poet to get into print!

Each volume runs to around 600 pages; that's 5,400 pages for the nine volumes. Thoreau's journals—fourteen volumes—were published only forty-four years after his death, though his *The Dispersion of Seeds* had to wait 130 years. Montaigne's travel journal lay in a trunk for several centuries.

The old Tolstoy was a great talker; people came from all over to hear him. "Yes," said his son to one of them, "but you don't have to hear him every day." We know Blake through Crabb Robinson, and Tennyson (who liked to read all of "Maud" to his captive visitors) through a generation of young writers. Goethe's Johann Peter Eckermann, Samuel Johnson's Boswell, Ben Jonson's Laird of Hawthornden: to all of these interlocutors we are grateful for leaving a record. There are people remembered only for their talk: the infinitely witty Sydney Smith, the champion gossip Samuel "Breakfast" Rogers; and, to a substantial degree, Coleridge and Oscar Wilde.

But four years of Walt Whitman, 1,458 evenings by the stove at 328 Mickle Street? I acquired the first three volumes of Traubel in 1961 and found that they made good reading. When Volume 5 came out in 1964, I decided to read Traubel right through—but needed Volume 4, which I hadn't known existed. Finding it took a while. In fact, 6 through 9 were published before I tracked down 4 (and paid and arm and a leg for it—the motherly bookseller in Santa Monica who sold it to me said, "You and the Library of Congress are now the only people who have all nine volumes"). So the elusive 4 ended up being the last that I read. A long book must become a habit, a kind of ritual (and reward) away from the day's other demands. A bedtime book, as it turned out: as many pages an evening as kept my attention.

Whitman's room became a little theater for two actors. The house is small. The windows remain closed (there is a fertilizer factory close by). Walt's old bones love heat: the potbellied iron stove is kept glowing. Walt is in his rocking chair with a wolf hide for a cushion. What catches the eye is the floor—ankle-deep in letters, manuscripts, newspapers, and books. Mice, too. Beside the rocker is Walt's "medicine," a bottle of bourbon regularly replenished by Thomas Biggs Harned, one of Walt's extended family of friends. This littered floor, which always gave first-time visitors, especially women, a jolt, is a rare kind of housekeeping that psychology has no word for, as far as I know. My bachelor uncle, Broadus Dewey Davenport, kept house so (and was furious when a niece and I cleaned it up when he was in the hospital for a week). I have seen it in Charlie Mingus's New York apartment: a thousand opened Campbell's soup cans covering the whole living-room floor, with a space cleared for three chairs and Charlie's collection of Debussy recordings. And, for history's sake, in an undergraduate's room in Adams House at Harvard.

Whitman's midden contained wonderful things, and Horace was always finding letters from Emerson and Tennyson in it, from the pre-Raphaelite William Michael Rossetti or the poet and early proponent of gay-acceptance Edward Carpenter. Walt claimed to be able to find letters and manuscripts in it, but this was an idle boast. Twice sparks from the stove set fire to it. Yet Whitman himself bathed daily and was finicky about clean linen. Many remarked on how sweet he smelled. He neither smoked nor chewed tobacco. His patriarchal beard was always clean and neatly fluffed.

Horace usually found him reading Walter Scott or George Sand, both favorites, or newspapers. Following a comradely kiss, Walt swapped news. A good day would be one with a letter from Maurice Bucke, the London, Ontario, doctor whose insane asylum Whitman had visited. (There's an interesting film about this visit, *Beautiful Dreamers,* with Rip Torn as Walt.) There were visitors to be told about: total strangers who disapproved of *Leaves of Grass* (at whom Walt would smile placidly, saying nothing), autograph seekers, old friends, neighbors, and, once, a "beautiful boy" who stared for a while and left in silence.

Horace and Walt met when Horace, fifteen, was carrying home a stack of library books. Walt, who knew no strangers, wondered aloud to Horace if a boy his age ought to read *quite* so many books, or to carry such a load *that* way. Their paths kept crossing. On the Camden ferry, a passenger asked the adolescent Horace, "Say, bubby, is that Walt Whitman the man who writes the dirty novels?"

"Yep!" said Horace happily. "That's him."

Once the evenings began, Horace gradually slipped into being Whitman's liaison with the world. He knew where to buy the broad steel-nibbed pens Whitman fancied. In the war you "wrote big" and clearly, to be read by lantern light in a tent.

Walt's Quaker clothes and hat were made—reluctantly—by a Philadelphia tailor; his stationery was cut to specifications. Horace learned how to handle such details. There were proofs to be fetched and returned (when Walt could be persuaded to correct them). Horace's father, a German lithographer in Camden, translated the letters Walt received in German and French. Horace fell into correspondence with Walt's English admirers. Being Whitman's confidant, secretary, and errand boy was obviously gratifying to a thirty-year-old autodidact, school dropout, and ardent Socialist. After the Whitman years he became a newspaper editor and third-rate poet.

A biographer of Whitman, Gary Schmidgall, has now made a digest of Traubel: *Intimate with Walt: Selections from Whitman's Conversations with Horace Traubel, 1888-1892.* He does not lift out excerpts, as one might expect, but tells us what Traubel said, what Walt said, with his own narrative and commentary. The large part of this condensation, however, is Walt *verbatim*. Schmidgall has categorized his selection: "Peeves," "Famous Authors," and so on. The decision is an odd one: between reading Traubel whole and savoring choice excerpts there's scant middle ground. One could, of course, make an anthology of whole evenings, with concise narrative bridges. The texture would be different all three ways.

Now that we have, after almost a century, Traubel's complete conversations with Whitman in Camden, and Schmidgall's selections arranged topically, is there any point in comparing them? Their difference is grandly obvious. For two hundred years people have exchanged in conversation their favorite ripostes of Samuel Johnson as recorded by Boswell. But reading Boswell's *Journal of a Tour to the Hebrides, with Samuel Johnson, LL.D.* (1785) and the *Life* (1791) is an *experience*. Reading Schmidgall's book is entertaining and informing, but it lacks (again, obviously) the tone and texture of the original.

There is a kind of plot, thoroughly Proustian (or Sternesque), to Traubel whole. On fourteen nights Walt promised to divulge a "great secret," deferring it to "some day—the right day." He never does. When Traubel presses him, he is "not in the mood to talk." Was the secret Walt's imaginary children—some black, some white—the number of which changed every time the subject came up?

"No boys, no *Leaves of Grass*." That Whitman was aesthetically and erotically pleased by young males is no longer disputed. Academic snoops looking for "the real Whitman" beyond the poetry have been thwarted at every turn. The word "homosexual" was coined, illiterately, by a German psychologist and introduced into English the year Whitman died. Whitman's word would have been "pathic." He repeatedly insisted to British enthusiasts for pederasty (John Addington Symonds, Edward Carpenter, the "college" of boy-fanciers at Bolton, others) that he was thoroughly heterosexual and polyphiloprogenitive. That males should be democratically "adhesive" and "amative" was a dimension of his vision of the new civilization he longed for America to have.

Edith Wharton wrote a brilliant story about Whitman's love of boys as the generator of his nursing the wounded in the Civil War, as well as of his poetry: "The Spark" in *Old New York*. A veteran of the war comes across *Leaves of Grass* on a library table. He remembers Whitman from the field hospitals—the kind Quaker nurse who wrote letters home for the incapacitated, who brought bouquets of dandelions and violets, tobacco, candy, pencils, writing paper and envelopes. Having forgotten his name, the veteran recognizes Walt from the frontispiece. The narrator of the story tells him. "Yes; that's it. Old Walt—that was what all the fellows used to call him. He was a great chap; I'll never forget him. —I rather wish, though . . . you hadn't told me that he wrote all that rubbish."

The Traubel volumes are full of statements Whitman's biographers have a hard time knowing what to do with. David S. Reynolds alone, in his superb *Walt Whitman's America,* has really tried to come to grips with the poet's ideas about race and slavery, which were multitudinous and contradictory. "The nigger, like the Injun, will be eliminated: it is the law of races, history, whatnot," Whitman told Traubel one evening. As an opinion, this is appalling. The question becomes, how important is it? Idle and relaxed conversation is not a diplomatic telegram. The "scholars" who read authors' private mail— who hold up "the real Larkin," for instance, as disgraced and exposed—disgrace only themselves. Walt's standing as a prophet of democracy cannot be diminished by an old man's obiter dicta on evenings by the stove.

Knowing Whitman is knowing his poetry, and it's a rare reader who knows *Leaves of Grass,* a ninety-five-page book that came out in 1855, on the Fourth of July—price, two dollars—and that grew over the years, revision after revision, into a 574-page "deathbed edition." A "book of fragments," he told Traubel. It is, in baldest definition, Whitman's *Collected Poems.* Harold W. Blodgett and Sculley Bradley's comprehensive edition (Norton, 1965) adds sixty-five pages of uncollected poems and manuscript drafts. Every edition in Whitman's lifetime subtracted and added. It is a book that was worked on for forty-five years, beginning as notes when Whitman was editor of *The Brooklyn Daily Eagle.*

Leaves of Grass begins with the pre-Socratic (Heraclitean) observation that we're all made of identical atoms and are therefore materially the same. "Song of *One's* Self" the title should be. Whitman is not peddling a boastful confession; he is writing a script for readers to recite. We are each of us a self, unique and individual. It was this sense of "Song of Myself" that caused Sojourner Truth to exclaim at a recital, "Who wrote that? Never mind the man's name—it was God who wrote it!"

"Grass nowhere out of place," Ezra Pound quotes a Chinese philosopher as saying. Grass goes way back, and ranges in size from lawn grass to bamboo. At some unknown time millennia ago mankind discovered that the seeds of certain grasses could be ground into flour to make bread: "civilization" began. Nomadic hunters settled in villages. The oldest breakfast is porridge. Ancient Greeks understood grain to be the gift of a goddess (Demeter, the Roman Ceres). The primitive cook kept a batch of dough going. If you had a squirrel or rabbit to stew up, fine. Pizza remains *das Uressen,* the primordial meal: bread with topping according to the day's catch.

In naming his book, Whitman chose the most universal object imaginable, one synonymous with both nature and civilization. Critics complained that grass has *blades.* But apart from the double meaning the poet intended (the leaves were also the pages of his book) he was botanically correct: grass has leaves, which we call "blades." There may even be a bit of etymological protest in Whitman's choice. Our "blade" of grass most likely does not come from *blatt,* German for "leaf," since Old English already has "léaf" as the primary word. "It would almost seem then," the OED tells us, "that the modern 'blade' of grass or corn is a later re-transfer from 'sword-blade.'" By taking the object away from metaphor and returning it to its original name, Whitman made a title worthy of his great book, a line of which is, "Haply the swords I know may there indeed be turn'd to reaping-tools."

World poetry has nothing to place beside "When Lilacs Last in the Dooryard Bloom'd" or "Out of the Cradle Endlessly Rocking" (Whitman's reply to Poe's "The Raven") and no analogue at all for "Song of Myself." A selected, culled, and exclusive *Leaves of Grass* makes more sense than a selected Traubel. Perhaps only Proust's latter days were as absorbed in his novel as Whitman's were by the "deathbed edition" of *Leaves.* Typography, paper, balance of poems, binding, cost, punctuation (at which Traubel was a whiz and a pedant). Walt kept a big dictionary beside the rocker, constantly curious about words.

There is comedy too, in Traubel: the elaborate preparations for getting Walt into his wheelchair for an afternoon's outing to see boys "playing base" down the street, the visitors that the housekeeper Mary Davis screened downstairs (no reporters, no preachers), and Whitman's curiosity about the technological revolution in which he lived. "Horace, this telephone thing, can you really hear the fellow on the other end?" He never wholly understood half-tone engravings of photographs in magazines and newspapers. He could be foul-mouthed about politicians. Horace was a Marxist; Whitman "liked rich people."

Traubel and newspapers were Walt's only contacts with the world beyond Mickle Street. And the mail. Should one invite Grover Cleveland *and* Leo Tolstoy to the seventieth birthday party? Tom Eakins? Andrew Carnegie?

This birthday party is like one of the great *salon* pieces in Proust, or the wide-screen deployment of a hundred characters in *War and Peace.* Traubel engineers it all: getting Walt by carriage over to Morgan's Hall, in Quaker gray and black. Policemen lift Walt and carry him upstairs to the hall. The crowd stands as his male nurse wheels him to the center table (a brass band playing "The Battle Hymn of the Republic"). But halfway to his table, a black woman, a cook from the kitchen, appears. Walt (understood to be an invalid wheelchair-bound) stands. The cook mentions her husband's name: Walt had nursed him in one of the unimaginably horrible hospitals of amputees and the dying.

It is a grand evening. There are eight speakers, all of them now forgotten. (Whitman himself declines to speak, referring "any one who may be curious" to *Leaves of Grass,* and spends the evening lapping up every word from behind a vase of lilacs.) Letters from William Dean Howells and John Addington Symonds are read, and one from Mark Twain congratulating the poet on having lived long enough to witness so many "great births," including "the amazing, infinitely varied and innumerable products of coal-tar."

I prefer to imagine Horace Traubel, quietly watching. He must have known that all his devotion and surreptitious shorthand on Mickle Street were repaid by the spectacle of a frail old man painfully getting out of his wheelchair to embrace a soldier's widow.

WE OFTEN THINK OF LENIN AT THE
CLOTHESPIN FACTORY

A city, not Paris. NOTCH, *an old woman in a chair made from a barrel, beside a tall porcelain stove, a basket of potatoes in her lap. Kerchief, shawl, ample skirts, boots.* POLDEN, *a young soldier with lots of brown curly hair, Mongol cheekbones, green uniform with scarlet shoulder tabs.*

NOTCH

There was once an Englishman named Vernon.
He was hunting hyenas near Carthage.
This was back in the nineteenth century.
He stumbled and fell into an abyss.
He was surprised, however, going down,
That it seemed indeed to have no bottom
And when one came, it was as if he'd dropped
Down into a great goosefeather mattress.
What's more, he was coming back up again,
Rising on a steady and busy heave
Which by degrees brought him to the pit's edge
And rolled him out onto *terra firma.*
He had fallen into a mass of bats
Which, disturbed from their slumber, had risen
All together out of the deep abyss
And brought the English hunter up with them.

POLDEN

Is that true?

NOTCH

Every beautiful word.
My husband Osip read it in a book.
He was a poet. They took him away.
I have all of his poems off by heart.

POLDEN

Are they published in a book?

NOTCH

No, never.
One of them is about the Old Cockroach
Seeing his face in the shine of his boots.

POLDEN

Did he write a poem about Lenin
Taking a walk in his automobile?

NOTCH

The square. Barracks of the Guard to the north.
Flagpole with flag. Blue sentries pacing there,
Scarlet facings with the odd number nine
In gold threadwork on their tunic collars.
They pace, cold, along the top of the wall,
Pace from the turrets to the tower gate
Where they meet, and about-face with a stomp,
And then tread back to the turrets again.
Below, along the blank wall, another
Pair of cold guards make the same cold movements.

POLDEN

The square, west. Friedrich Engels Institute.
Iron doors. Allegory of Labor.
Classical columns. Red bunting banners
Across the front on anniversaries.
Sometimes, a delegation with roses
From the People's Republic of China.
The committee from Shqiperija
No longer visits, nor its football team.
The windows are lit at night twice a year
And then you can hear Rimsky-Korsakov.

NOTCH

But not Stravinsky or Francis Poulenc.
The square, south. The Ministry of Culture.
Bicyclists from Czechoslovakia.
Paintings by Aleksandr Deineka.
Sevastopol Dynamo Aquasports
Workers' Summer Vacation Swimming Pool.
And *Lenin Taking a Walk in His Car.*

POLDEN

Peasant embroidery from Hungary.
Lenin teaching history to children.

NOTCH

The square, east. Ministry of Peace. The Dom.
Though it is understood that modern men
Do not light candles in Sankt Pavl's Dom,
They still wear garlic against the Devil
And say nine novenas under their breath
When they have heard an owl hoot at night
Or by evil luck a bootlace has snapped
Or the mirror has fallen from the wall.
Women and children slip into the Dom
Before they have to go and wait in lines.

POLDEN

Old women do talk.

NOTCH

              Puppies make doodoo.
Another tale, already. Herr Schriftbild,
A publisher, as soon as he had found
The apartment building specified in
Robert Walser a Swiss writer's letter,
In a court off a square, both with children
And dogs, also found Walser's door inside,
And, drawing the pull, heard a bell jangle
On a bouncing coil of wire deep within.
An interval, and the door was opened
By a butler in a swallowtail coat.

POLDEN

Capitalism.

NOTCH

With large liquid eyes,
Military moustache, hair brushed back
With such parallel regularity
That you suspected a pigtail in back.

POLDEN

Imperialism, English navy.

NOTCH

Was this, Herr Schriftbild asked, the apartment
Where Herr Robert Walser the writer lived?
Exactly, Sir, said the butler, taking
Herr Schriftbild's card.

POLDEN

Decadent plutocrats.

NOTCH

If the Herr Schriftbild would wait a moment,
Herr Walser would be told of his presence,
Which, in very fact, he was expecting.

POLDEN

What a prick.

NOTCH

Herr Schriftbild sat. He took in,
By way of passing the time, the carpet,
Old furniture, strange pictures on the walls,
Probably German, certainly modern,
Some meadow flowers in a blue pitcher,
A paper parrot on a bamboo perch,
A chromolithograph of Palmyra,
A plaster bust of Gottfried von Leibniz,
One of whose eyes had been outlined in red.
A blank brick wall, the view from the window.
Clearly, he thought, it pleases this Walser
To let visitors cool their heels awhile.

Perhaps he was ending a paragraph,
Seeing another visitor, female,
Down the back stairs? Then again, you never
Knew what these writers might not be doing.
Paring their toenails, sitting in a trance,
Reading right through the French dictionary.
And this one, now could afford a butler.

POLDEN

A pampered bourgeois.

NOTCH

The carpet had lived
At many addresses before this one,
The chairs had ridden through the streets in carts
Pulled by elderly horses. Herr Schriftbild
Avoided the paper parrot's yellow
And Liebniz's red eye and gazed instead
At the flyspecked ruins of Palmyra,
And was wondering if that city is
In the Bible or profane history
When the door through which the butler had gone
Opened just enough to admit a man
In rumpled corduroy and blue flannel
Shirt as fancied by British Socialists.
Large liquid eyes, military moustache.
If his bohemian hair were brushed back
With a parallel regularity,
You would suspect a pigtail tied behind.

POLDEN

Imperialism, English navy.

NOTCH

God help us, Herr Schriftbild said to himself,
This is the butler wanting me to think
He's Walser, who has some frump on his lap,
Or is reading the French dictionary.
The voice, however, greeting Schriftbild
With a familiar and bright nonchalance,
Was wholly different from the butler's.

POLDEN

Karl Marx brooding with folded arms, his head
Massive in bronze, Lenin raising his fist,
Exhorting the people.

NOTCH

Walser, you see,
Was his own butler. He could do voices.
A poet. After a while, he gave up
And lived in a lunatic asylum.
Our poets all went into prisons.

POLDEN

His own butler?

NOTCH

The world was like that, then.
Variety. Versatility. O!
The century before ours, the nineteenth,
It was a kind of earthly paradise.
Avenues of lindens and of poplars.
Men, women, and children, horses and dogs.
And now it's only old women sweeping.
News of tomatoes at a market
Over near Tramstop 6 on the Prospekt.
As soon, ha! Believe the clowns at the Cyrk.
They would be gone, anyway, when you came.

POLDEN

In America gangs roam the cities,
Taking the workers' money at knife point.
The rich, without conscience or character,
Are addicted to narcotics and die
Drunk in hideous automobile wrecks.
Imagine fifty thousand wrecks a year.
The sole policy of the government
Is to suppress freedom and to finance
Fascism all over the world.

NOTCH

Heigh ho.

POLDEN

At Sankt Boris some poets and workers
Staged a protest last Tuesday in the street.
They had a 1917 banner
And some modern paintings done on cardboard.
The Ideal of Life they called one of them
And *What Does It All Mean?* was the other.
Very ugly, the paintings. Daubs, in fact.
One of the poets was wearing blue jeans
Made in Pinsk, hammer-and-sickle label.
They did not fit and did not have the look
Of Western jeans, and the blue was purple.
The poet shouted a pukey poem
Before the Guard came and took them away.

NOTCH

The Old Cockroach.

POLDEN

And the gypsies are back.
They have made a camp where the synagogue
Used to be. With beautiful white horses.
Why was he his own butler?

NOTCH

For the joke.
People used to do such things. It was fun.

POLDEN

Silver thunder. That was in the poem.

NOTCH

A bust of Pomona, and a cabbage.
A copy of *The Red Dawn* beside her.
The goods train, when it passed, rattled the cups
And made Pomona shake. The window shook.
And a shiver of light opened her eyes.
That was long ago. In old poetry
She is the spirit of apples and pears,
A tall woman dressed in flowers and leaves.
The clock on the tower no longer works.

Still, it is a fragment of Italy
Here in the gray, in the sameness, the drab.

POLDEN

You live in the past.

NOTCH

I live in my mind.

POLDEN

Her mind.

NOTCH

Where dreams appear in old colors.
Come, shadow, come, and take this shadow up,
Scarlet in the shadow of an orange.
Words.
    This oak, this owl, this moon.
                        There is a
Death in this wind the owl cannot find.
Death in the thistle, white loaf of the moon,
Death in snow, the cricket and wildflowers.
You do not know, Polden Wolf Eyes, what things
There used to be. The thousand-branched oak tree,
With a thousand leaves a branch, red red leaves,
The red oak of Velimir Khlebnikov.
That was red.
            Now there are no more cities,
Only distances of stone. Verona
Was yellow, Venice was red. And we had
Urbs et fanum, city and cathedral,
Gorod I khram, and bell sound in the air.
Being's the gift. It's difficult to be.

POLDEN

But I am, and you are. What is so hard?

NOTCH

The stitch of things. He had a mind that was
Part centaur and part streets of Megara.
That was a lecture I once heard in school,
About Theognis, ancient Greek poet.

Silver-rooted waters of Tartessos!
You wouldn't know. He wrote of oiled athletes,
Laws of property, and of irony
And rhythm in behavior, of archers,
Real wealth and vain wealth, loving friends, good talk.
He was critical of democracy,
Muttering that horses were better bred
Than sons and daughters. He fancied the studs
Of both genera, a wide-minded man.

POLDEN

That's against nature.

NOTCH

Lenin was a prig.
Theognis lived through a revolution
That cost him his books, olive groves and house,
His racehorses.

POLDEN

Good.

NOTCH

And another war
That cost him his Spartan control of self.
He moved from city to city, always Greek,
Writing in a geometry of words
A poem that was to Homer's beauty
And the verve of Hesiod what later
Apollos modelled on gymnastic slaves
Were to the stiff archaic *kouroi*.

POLDEN

You remember all this?

NOTCH

Shakespeare and Petrarch.
It keeps coming back. Lensky and Pushkin.
Willows and stars.

POLDEN

Before the *Aurora*

Flew the red flag. A moment of glory.

NOTCH

There is a woman sweeping the crossing.
You see her: over there.

POLDEN

I see her, yes.

NOTCH

The clock tower and the barracks. Do you
See how they make a perspective for her,
As in a painting by Canaletto?

POLDEN

Italian landscapist. Hermitage.

NOTCH

And the sky above her, dull as a ditch.
What is she thinking of?

POLDEN

Nothing. Lenin.

NOTCH

Save the hectic red, the bilious yellow
Of the flag over the barracks, there is
No color anywhere.

POLDEN

None. Patch of red,
Smitch of yellow. All of the rest is gray.
You are going to make something of it,
As if she could help being a figure
Alone in the square. She is a picture
In your imagination.

NOTCH

Old woman
Is what she is. Events happen again
In memory, knowing, or narrative.

Time rolls up as it goes along, bringing
The past with it. Nothing is left behind.

POLDEN

That old woman with the besom gets paid
Ahead of the commissars in the line.

NOTCH

Rilke and Lou Andreas Salome
Visited at Yasnaya Polyana.
They talked about Harriet Beecher Stowe.
Ah! The music, string quartets. Poetry.
You could meet someone who had seen Monet
At Giverny, beside the lily pond.
Proust. If you knocked on his door his servant
Had the same set speech for everybody:
Monsieur Proust wants you to know that there is
No waking hour when he is not thinking
Of you, but right now he is too busy
To see visitors. The Boratinskies,
Khlebnikov, Tatlin, Osip Mandelstam.
People who had been to Gertrude Stein's house.
Who recommended that you come? Was what
She asked at the door. What a time that was,
Back then.

POLDEN

Parasites.

NOTCH

Venice, Rome, London.
Every shop had potatoes for sale,
Heaps and hampers of potatoes for sale.
Oranges, grapes, editions of Homer.
And Lenin had the cleanest bicycle
In Zürich. And he did Indian clubs.
One two three, one two three. At the window.

POLDEN

If there had been no Lenin, there would have
Been a Lenin.

NOTCH

And a sealed German train.
Red flags on the locomotive, a crowd
To welcome him at the Finland Station.
Committee of peasants wanting to learn
Hegelian dialectic.

POLDEN

A worker's brass
Band playing the Internationale.

NOTCH

Springtimes were sweeter, summers were greener.
The apple trees, the singing, and the gold.
There is no kindness now in the years.

POLDEN

But there are years.

NOTCH

Oh yes, the promised years,
Right on time.

THE ANTHROPOLOGY OF TABLE MANNERS

A businessman now risen to a vice-presidency tells me that in his apprentice days he used to cross deepest Arkansas as a mere traveling salesman, and that there were certain farms at which men from his company put up overnight, meals being included. Once, on a new route, he appeared at breakfast after a refreshing sleep in a feather bed to face a hardy array of buttery eggs, biscuits, apple pie, coffee, and fatback.

This latter item was unfamiliar to him and from the looks of it he was damned if he would eat it. He knew his manners, however, and in passing over the fatback chatted with the lady of the house about how eating habits tend to be local, individual, and a matter of how one has been raised. He hoped she wouldn't take it wrong that he, unused to consuming fatback, left it untouched on his place.

The genial Arkansas matron nodded to this politely, agreeing that food is different all over the world.

She then excused herself, flapped her copious apron, and retired from the kitchen. She returned with a double-barreled shotgun which she trained on the traveling salesman, with the grim remark, "Eat hit."

And eat hit he did.

Our traveler's offense was to reject what he had been served, an insult in practically every code of table manners. Snug in an igloo, the Eskimo scrapes gunk from between his toes and politely offers it as garnish for your blubber. Among the Penan of the upper Baram in Sarawak you eat your friend's snot as a sign of your esteem. There are dinner parties in Africa where the butter for your stewed calabash will be milked from your hostess's hair. And you dare not refuse.

Eating is always at least two activities: consuming food and obeying a code of manners. And in the manners is concealed a program of taboos as rigid as

Deuteronomy. We rational, advanced, and liberated Americans may not, as in the Amazon, serve the bride's mother as the wedding feast; we may not, as in Japan, burp our appreciation, or as in Arabia, eat with our fingers. Every child has suffered initiation into the mysteries of table manners: keep your elbows off the table, ask for things to be passed rather than reach, don't cut your bread with a knife, keep your mouth closed while chewing, don't talk with food in your mouth, and on and on, and all of it witchcraft and another notch upward in the rise of the middle class.

Our escapes from civilization are symptomatic: the first rule we break is that of table manners. Liberty wears her reddest cap; all is permitted. I remember a weekend away from paratrooper barracks when we dined on eggs scrambled in Jack Daniel's, potato chips and peanut brittle, while the Sergeant Major, a family man of bankerish decorum in ordinary times, sang falsetto "There Will be Peace in the Valley" stark naked except for cowboy boots and hat.

But to children, hardest pressed by gentility at the table, a little bending of the rules is Cockayne itself. One of my great culinary moments was being taken as a tot to my black nurse's house to eat clay. "What this child needs," she had muttered one day while we were out, "is a bait of clay." Everybody in South Carolina knew that blacks, for reasons unknown, fancied clay. Not until I came to read Toynbee's *A Study of History* years later did I learn that eating clay, or geophagy, is a prehistoric habit (it fills the stomach until you can bring down another aurochs) surviving only in West Africa and South Carolina. I even had the opportunity, when I met Toynbee at a scholarly do, to say that I had been in my day geophagous. He gave me a strange, British look.

The eating took place in a bedroom, for the galvanized bucket of clay was kept under the bed, for the cool. It was blue clay from a creek, the consistency of slightly gritty ice cream. It lay smooth and delicious-looking in its pail of clear water. You scooped it out and ate it from your hand. The taste was wholesome, mineral, and emphatic. I have since eaten many things in respect-able restaurants with far more trepidation.

The technical names have yet to be invented for some of the submissions to courtly behavior laid upon me by table manners. At dinners cooked by brides in the early days of their apprenticeship I have forced down boiled potatoes as crunchy as water chestnuts, bleeding pork, gravy in which you could have picked a kettle of herring, and a *purée* of raw chicken livers.

I have had reports of women with skimpy attention to labels who have made biscuits with plaster of Paris and chicken feed that had to be downed by timid husbands and polite guests; and my venturesome Aunt Mae once prepared a salad with witch hazel, and once, in a moment of abandoned creativity, served a banana pudding that had hard-boiled eggs hidden in it here and there.

Raphael Pumpelly tells in his memoirs of the West in the good old days about a two-gunned, bearded type who rolled into a Colorado hotel with a viand wrapped in a bandana. This he requested the cook to prepare, and seated at a table, napkined, wielding knife and fork with manners passably Eastern, consulting the salt and pepper shakers with a nicety, gave a fair imitation of a gentleman eating. And then, with a gleam in his eye and a great burp, he sang out at the end. "Thar, by God, I swore I'd eat that man's liver and I've done it!"

The meaning of this account for those of us who are great scientists is that this hero of the West chose to eat his enemy's liver in the dining room of a hotel, with manners. Eating as mere consumption went out thousands of years ago; we have forgotten what it is. Chaplin boning the nails from his stewed shoe in *The Gold Rush* is thus an incomparable moment of satire, epitomizing all that we have heard of British gentlemen dressing for dinner in the Congo (like Livingstone, who made Stanley wait before the famous encounter until he could dig his formal wear out of his kit).

Ruskin and Turner never dined together, though an invitation was once sent. Turner knew that his manners weren't up to those of the refined Ruskins, and said so, explaining graphically that, being toothless, he sucked his meat. Propriety being propriety, there was nothing to be done, and the great painter and his great explicator and defender were damned to dine apart.

Nor could Wittgenstein eat with his fellow dons at a Cambridge high table. One wishes that the reason were more straightforward than it is. Wittgenstein, for one thing, wore a leather jacket, with zipper, and dons at high table must wear academic gowns and a tie. For another, Wittgenstein thought it undemocratic to eat on a level fourteen inches higher than the students (at, does one say, low table?).

The code of Cambridge manners could not insist that the philosopher change his leather jacket for more formal gear, nor could it interfere with his conscience. At the same time it could in no wise permit him to dine at high table improperly dressed. The compromise was that the dons sat at high table, the students at their humbler tables, and Wittgenstein ate between, at a card table, separate but equal, and with English decorum unfractured.

Maxim's declined to serve a meal to Lyndon Baines Johnson, at the time President of the United States, on the grounds that its staff did not have a recipe for Texas barbecue, though what they meant was that they did not know how to serve it or how to criticize *Monsieur le Président's* manners in eating it.

The best display of manners on the part of a restaurant I have witnessed was at the Imperial Ramada Inn in Lexington, Kentucky, into the Middle Lawrence Welk Baroque dining room of which I once went with the photographer Ralph Eugene Meatyard (disguised as a businessman), the Trappist Thomas Merton (in mufti, dressed as a tobacco farmer with a tonsure), and an editor of *Fortune* who had wrecked his Hertz car coming from the airport and was covered in spattered blood from head to toe. Hollywood is used to such things (Linda Darnell having a milk shake with Frankenstein's monster between takes), and Rome and New York, but not Lexington, Kentucky. Our meal was served with no comment whatever from the waitresses, despite Merton's downing six martinis and the *Fortune* editor stanching his wounds with all the napkins.

Posterity is always grateful for notes on the table manners of the famous, if only because this information is wholly gratuitous and unenlightening. What does it tell us that Montaigne glupped his food? I have eaten with Allen Tate, whose sole gesture toward the meal was to stub out his cigarette in an otherwise untouched chef's salad, with Isak Dinesen when she toyed with but did not eat an oyster, with Louis Zukofsky who was dining on a half piece of toast, crumb by crumb.

Manners survive the test of adversity. Gertrude Ely, the Philadelphia hostess and patron of the arts, was once inspired on the spur of the moment to invite home Leopold Stokowski and his orchestra, together with a few friends. Hailing her butler, she said breezily that here were some people for pot luck.

"Madam," said the butler with considerable frost, "I was given to understand that you were dining alone this evening; please accept my resignation. Good night to you all."

"Quite," said Miss Ely, who then, with a graciousness unflummoxed and absolute, set every table in the house and distributed splinters of the one baked hen at her disposal, pinches of lettuce, and drops of mayonnaise, not quite with the success of the loaves and fishes of scripture, but at least a speck of something for everybody.

I, who live almost exclusively off fried baloney, Campbell's soup, and Snickers bars, would not find table manners of any particular interest if they had not, even in a life as reclusive and uneventful as mine, involved so many brushes with death. That great woman Katherine Gilbert, the philosopher and aesthetician, once insisted that I eat some Florentine butter that Benedetto Croce had given her. I had downed several portions of muffins smeared with this important butter before I gathered from her ongoing conversation that the butter had been given her months before, somewhere in the Tuscan hills in the month of August, and that it had crossed the Atlantic, by boat, packed with her books, Italian wild flowers, prosciutto, and other mementos of Italian culture.

Fever and double vision set in some hours later, together with a delirium in which I remembered Pico della Mirandola's last meal, served him by

Lucrezia and Cesare Borgia. I have been *in extremis* in Crete (octopus and what tasted like shellacked rice, with P. Adams Sitney), in Yugoslavia (a most innocent-looking melon), Genoa (calf's brains), England (a blackish stew that seemed to have been cooked in kerosene), France (an *andouillette,* Maigret's favorite feed, the point being, as I now understand, that you have to be born in Auvergne to stomach it).

Are there no counter-manners to save one's life in these unfair martyrdoms to politeness? I have heard that Edward Dahlberg had the manliness to refuse dishes at table, but he lost his friends thereby and became a misanthrope. Lord Byron once refused every course of a meal served him by Breakfast Rogers. Manet, who found Spanish food revolting but was determined to study the paintings in the Prado, spent two weeks in Madrid without eating anything at all. Some *Privatdozent* with time on his hands should compile a eulogy to those culinary stoics who, like Marc Antony, drank from yellow pools men did die to look upon. Not the starving and destitute who in wars and sieges have eaten the glue in bookbindings and corn that had passed through horses, wallpaper, bark, and animals in the zoo; but prisoners of civilization who have swallowed gristle on the twentieth attempt while keeping up a brave chitchat with the author of a novel about three generations of a passionately alive family.

Who has manners anymore, anyhow? Nobody, to be sure; everybody, if you have the scientific eye. Even the most oafish teen-ager who mainly eats from the refrigerator at home and at the Burger King in society will eventually find himself at a table where he is under the eye of his father-in-law to be, or his coach, and will make the effort to wolf his roll in two bites rather than one, and even to leave some for the next person when he is passed a bowl of potatoes. He will, naturally, still charge his whole plate with six glops of catsup, knock over his water, and eat his cake from the palm of his hand; but a wife, the country club, and the Rotarians will get him, and before he's twenty-five he'll be eating fruit salad with extended pinky, tapping his lips with the napkin before sipping his sauterne Almaden, and talking woks and fondues with the boys at the office.

Archaeologists have recently decided that we can designate the beginning of civilization in the concept of sharing the same kill, in which simple idea we can see the inception of the family, the community, the state. Of disintegrating marriages we note that Jack and Jill are no longer sleeping together when the real break is when they are no longer eating together. The table is the last unassailed rite. No culture has worn the *bonnet rouge* there, always excepting the Germans, who have never had any manners at all, of any sort.

The tyranny of manners may therefore be the pressure placed on us of surviving in hostile territories. Eating is the most intimate and at the same time the most public of biological functions. Going from dinner table to dinner table is the equivalent of going from one culture to another, even within the same family. One of my grandmothers served butter and molasses with her biscuits, the other would have fainted to see molasses on any table. One gave you coffee with the meal, the other after. One cooked greens with fatback, the other with hamhock. One put ice cubes in your tea, the other ice from the ice house. My father used to complain that he hadn't had any cold iced tea since the invention of the refrigerator. He was right.

Could either of my grandmothers, the one with English country manners, the other with French, have eaten on an airplane? What would the Roi Soleil have done with that square foot of space? My family, always shy, did not venture into restaurants until well after the Second World War. Aunt Mae drank back the tiny juglet of milk which they used to give you for coffee, and commented to Uncle Buzzie that the portions of things in these cafés are certainly stingy.

I was raised to believe that eating other people's cooking was a major accomplishment, like learning a language or how to pilot a plane. I thought for the longest time that Greeks lived exclusively off garlic and dandelions, and that Jews were so picky about their food that they seldom ate at all. Uncles who had been to France with the AEF reported that the French existed on roast rat and snails. The Chinese, I learned from a book, begin their meals with dessert. Happy people!

Manners, like any set of signals, constitute a language. It is possible to learn to speak Italian; to eat Italian, never. In times of good breeding, the rebel against custom always has table manners to violate. Diogenes assumed the polish of Daniel Boone, while Plato ate with a correctness Emily Post could have studied with profit. Thoreau, Tolstoy, and Gandhi all ate with pointed reservation, sparely, and in elemental simplicity. Calvin dined but once a day, on plain fare, and doubtless imagined the pope gorging himself on pheasant, nightingale, and minced boar in macaroni.

Honest John Adams, eating in France for the first time, found the food delicious if unidentifiable, but blushed at the conversation (a lady asked him if his family had invented sex); and Emerson once had to rap the water glass at his table when two guests, Thoreau and Agassiz, introduced the mating of turtles into the talk. Much Greek philosophy, Dr. Johnson's best one-liners, and the inauguration of the Christian religion happened at supper tables. Hitler's table-talk was so boring that Eva Braun and a field marshal once fell asleep in his face. He was in a snit for a month. Generalissimo Franco fell asleep while Nixon was talking to him at dinner. It may be that conversation over a shared haunch of emu is indeed the beginning of civilization.

To eat in silence, like the Egyptians, seems peculiarly dreadful, and stiff.

Sir Walter Scott ate with a bagpipe droning in his ear and all his animals around him, and yards of babbling guests. Only the truly mad eat alone, like Howard Hughes and Stalin.

Eccentricity in table manners—one has heard of rich uncles who wear oil-cloth aviator caps at table—lingers in the memory longer than other foibles. My spine tingles anew whenever I remember going into a Toddle House to find all the tables and the counter set; not only set, but served. One seat only was occupied, and that by a very eccentric man, easily a millionaire. He was, the waitress explained some days later, giving a dinner party there, but no one came. He waited and waited. He had done it several times before; no one had ever come. It was the waitress's opinion that he always forgot to send the invitations; it was mine that his guests could not bring themselves to believe them.

And there was the professor at Oxford who liked to sit under his tea table, hidden by the tablecloth, and hand up cups of tea and slices of cake from beneath. He carried on a lively conversation all the while, and most of his friends were used to this. There was always the occasional student who came to tea unaware, sat goggling the whole time, and tended to break into cold sweats and fits of stammering.

I was telling about this professor one summer evening in South Carolina, to amuse my audience with English manners. A remote cousin, a girl in her teens, who hailed from the country and had rarely considered the ways of foreigners, listened to my anecdote in grave horror, went home and had a fit.

"It took us half the night to quiet down Effie Mae," we were told sometime later. "She screamed for hours that all she could see was that buggerman under that table, with just his arm risin' up with a cup and saucer. She says she never expects to get over it."

VERANDA HUNG WITH WISTERIA

The adoration of mountains, Mr. Poe read in Alexander von Humboldt's *Cosmos,* and the contemplation of flowers distinguish Chinese poetry from that of Greece and Rome. Ssu-ma Kuang, statesman and poet, described in his *Garden,* written around the time of the Norman invasion of England, his wide view of the river Kiang crowded with junks and sampans, the black green of the pines beyond his terrace of peonies and chrysanthemums, the blue green of the shrubbery, the red gold of the persimmons, while he expected with contentment the arrival of friends who would read their verses to him and listen to his.

THE JULES VERNE STEAM BALLOON

KING OF PRUSSIA I IN D MAJOR, K.575

Summer morning, awake a tick before the clock's ring, the work of bird-charm and circadian wheels, Hugo Tvemunding, assistant Classics master and gym instructor at NFS Grundtvig, Troop Commander of Spejderkorps 235, and doctoral candidate in Theology, sat bolt upright in bed to yawn and stretch.

—The Great Walrus, said Mariana beside him, her eyes still closed, is on the loose, grumping all rivals away from his rocks. His walruser is reared up like a gander trying to see over the hedge, but first we must say our prayers.

Hugo recited the prayer to the creator of being that he'd said every morning since he was a very little boy, a prayer composed by his pastor father.

—Amen, said Mariana. Franklin has slept through it all.

—Have not, Franklin said. Amen too. Tickle me and I'll bite.

—My rocks, said Hugo. Franklin for all his contribution to the dialogue is still asleep.

—Long hairy feet on the floor, said Mariana, who wore a shirt of Hugo's for a nightgown, square pink-toed feet on the floor, shapely girl's feet on the floor, plop, slap, and gracefully silent. Who lost a Band-Aid in the bed? Your T-shirt fits Franklin like a potato sack on a weasel.

HOLLYHOCKS

Hugo's run before breakfast was along a macadam road through pinewoods with an undergrowth of fern and laurel. He freed himself with every stride of the residue of dreams, of warm lethargies that had nested in his muscles, of anxieties that had made trash in his mind. He spoke to rabbits hopping across the road, to a cheeky fox doing a little dance in a clearing. The light was silver, early, cold. He had dreamed of his mother standing beside hollyhocks and coleus. Idiotically, he had said, *They're dead, aren't they?* She'd said, with her usual placid composure, *Why no, dear, they're not dead.* And indeed nothing could have been more alive than these dream hollyhocks and coleus, so crisply beautiful in the accurate light of the dream. And his mother's kindly ghost was like a blessing. She wore her apron, as for housework, and her voice was as sweet as springwater. White latticework of the back porch door behind her. A perfectly temperate summer day. *Why no, dear, they're not dead at all.*

CABIN WITH SKYLIGHT
Stables once, Hugo's room was designed and appointed by a drawing master who, having made it into a Danish Modern oblong of continuous space with a skylight, left to take a position elsewhere. Bed and worktable under the skylight, bookcases, chairs beyond, toward the kitchen area, which had a small barn window over the sink and cabinets. On the walls were a large photograph of Bourdelle's *Herakles the Archer*, a Mondriaan of the severest geometric period, a Paul Klee angel grinning about some sacred mischief, a photograph of Brancusi's *Torso d'un jeune homme*, and three paintings by Hugo: Mariana naked, slouched reading in a chair, a still life of meadow flowers in a coffee mug, and a large painting that had once been of the Bicycle Rider, repainted with Tom Agernkop as model.

GARDEN
The colors in the dream where his mother stood placidly in her coverall, print cotton polka-dot gloves, and straw hat were those of photographs in *The Country Garden* and *House and Family*: early greens, soft browns, reticent blues in sharp silvery focus.

WATER
—This is Franklin the Rabbit Who Invented Electricity, Hugo said to Rutger, Kim, Asgar, Tom, and Anders in the showers.

—We've run six kilometres, Franklin said. Oof! These wolfcub mystery knots you did my laces in, Hugo, won't come loose.

Hugo! Knowing eyes found laughing eyes.

—Let me, Rutger said kneeling.

Franklin, looking hard at Kim and Anders under a shower together, soaping each other, wiggled his fingers at his ears and ruckled like a dove.

—They like each other, Skipper, Hugo said.

WHEAT
—He wasn't out to set himself up through signs and wonders, Hugo said to his Sunday School class. He was not concerned about who he was. That showed in everything he did. And from moment to moment he was the peo-

ple he suffered with, whom he could comfort or cure or free. Most of these were people estranged from themselves by pain or deformity. People who are out of their minds are no good to anybody else, and Yeshua's idea of us is that first of all we are someone who can help another.

EYES BLUE WITH FATE

—A nipper, Mariana sighed, locked herself in the laundry room and no amount of cajoling or instructions about the latch did anything but make her howl the louder, so I had to climb onto the roof and jimmy open a window the size of a handkerchief and plead with the little demon to listen while I showed her how to let herself out, and another nipper stuck modelling clay up his nose and turned blue, and another had hiccups for an hour, and another was passing around color Polaroids of her big brother doing it with his girl on the sunroom floor, and another barfed on the vocabulary cards. So I've had it and want love, sympathy, and sour cream pineapple pancakes for supper.

She was holding an ice cube to Franklin's knee, which was skinned bloody. His silkflop thatch had leaftrash and twigs in it. A smutch of mud saddled his nose. The seat of his pants was piped with clay. They had all converged at the bus stop, Franklin from the soccer field, Mariana off the bus, and Hugo from class, going home.

While Mariana set up a field hospital to deal with Franklin, Hugo, out of his jeans, exiguous briefs taxed by a randy flex, said that he would provide love, Franklin sympathy, and Mariana sour cream pineapple pancakes.

—Iodine, Mariana ordered, and fill the sink with hot soapy water, skin Franklin of his pants and underpants and put the one in the other.

—The two in the other, Franklin said. Hugo is hanging out like the donkey in the zoo.

—Better still, Mariana said, strip the lout and stand him in the sink, soap him up, and pour potfuls of water over his head.

—Family life is wonderfully exciting, Hugo said lifting Franklin into the sink.

—You know Pascal? Franklin asked.

—I know Pascal, Hugo said. He is the apple of Holger Sigurjonsson's eye, as everybody from the kitchen staff to the headmaster knows.

—He, Franklin said around the washcloth, lost one of his shoes. So I told him to throw the other away. What good is one shoe? They tease him real pitiful about hr. Sigurjonsson, so we beat up Otto with the weasel eyes. He was picking on Pascal. I heard him.

—I didn't know, Hugo said, that you were friends with Pascal.

—I am now, Franklin said. After we beat up Otto.

—Well yes, Hugo said, let's hear about that.

—I booted him in the butt, Franklin said, hard. He called Pascal a name, and

Pascal just took it. I was behind them both, you see, and here was Otto's butt for the kicking. That's when he tried to pin me, and I did my knee there.

—I'm not listening, Mariana said, I'm not hearing a word of this.

—So, Franklin said, Pascal got in it then. He pushed Otto on his shoulder while hooking his ankle: laid him flat. Then we both jumped on him. Hr. Sigurjonsson's showed Pascal how to defend himself.

YESHUA IN THE WHEAT

—Goose grass, Hugo said, found with knotweed in hard poor soil cinder paths. Old meadows are thick with it, an archaic wheat from which the horse-riding plunderers made bread and foddered their shaggy Shetlands. It came to Eleusis, Joseph Gaertner thought, by way of India. That's why he named it *Eleusine indica.* Crabgrass and crowfoot are of the same family. The florets are ashlared thick along the spikes, see? And there's no awn.

—Grass, Franklin said, is just grass.

—Here, said Mariana, is where we get Hugo's handsome blond cross-eyed stare. Meaning I hear it but I don't believe it. The pathfinders never get it, only us, and the occasional Grundtvigger.

Franklin calm and unheeding. What Mariana says is what Mariana says. Nothing to do with him until she starts shouting.

—Emmer of the prophets embedded in the clay of Ugaritic pots under the botanist's microscope is like implicit information in a text. It came along, like Franklin underfoot, of itself.

—Now I'm grass, Franklin said.

ACORN IN ITS CUP

To get to the bus stop where Mariana with shining eyes and bright smile arrived at afternoon's end, Hugo damp from his second gym class, his book bag charged with Latin and Greek exercises to correct, had but to cross the soccer field and amble along two blocks of guardedly prosperous houses with colorful gardens behind low front walls. If he let the class go ten minutes early and skipped a shower, he had time to walk to the bus stop by way of the meadow beyond the wood where he could sit under a favorite oak, elbows on knees, and have a rich moment of calm and anticipation. The river shone at the other side of the meadow, if the light was right. Here passages of the thesis on Yeshua took form and texture, the day disclosed patterns, abrasions healed, letters were opened and read.

Papa's hollyhocks. Papa's reading, the lectures and concerts he had been to. A note on a Hebrew word.

Aakjaer Minor had begun a cataleptic syndrome that was as yet more comic than serious. He hugged people and wouldn't, or couldn't, let go. In the locker room he'd seen Golo Hansen embarrassed and helpless in Alexander

Aakjaer's grasp. I don't want to hurt him, Golo had wailed to Hugo. He grabs people like this, his eyes go blank, and he won't turn loose. Hugo had said, quit trying to pull him loose. Just stand cool. He got me the other day, Asgar said, and two people couldn't pry him off. It's mental. He doesn't know what you're talking about when it's over. Hugo had studied the unfocussed eyes, the sweaty back of the neck, cold wrists, locked knees and elbows. Gently he'd guided Golo out of Alexander's gripping arms, hoisted the suddenly slack Alexander onto his shoulders and carried him to the infirmary where he said to Nurse that Aakjaer Minor had had a dizzy spell in gym and only needed to lie still for a while. Nurse nevertheless stuck a thermometer in Alexander's mouth and took his pulse, seeing nothing interesting in either.

JONAS

The pompion or million creeps upon the ground if nothing be by it whereon it may take hold and climb with very great ribbed rough and prickly branches whereon are set large rough leaves cut in on the edges with deep gashes and dented besides, with many claspers also, which wind about everything they meet. The flowers are great and large, hollow and yellow, divided at the brim into five parts, at the bottom of which grows the fruit sometimes of the bigness of a man's body and oftentimes less, in some ribbed or bunched, in others plain and either long or round, green or yellow. The seed is great flat and white, lying in the middle of the watery pulp. The root is of the bigness of a man's thumb, dispersed underground with many small fibers. They are boiled in fair water and salt, or in powdered beef broth, sometimes in milk, and so eaten, or else buttered. The seed, as well as of cowcumbers and melons, are cooling, and serve for emulsions in the like manner as almond milks, for those troubled with the stone.

BLUE PUP TENT

In the ferns beyond birches, Hugo slowed, running in place, and hollered *ho!*
—Whoever you are, he sang in stentorian *buffo*, I come in peace.
Silence. Brilliant early morning light.
—*Ho!* from the pup tent.
—I'll go away, Hugo said, if you want me to. This is school property. Grundtviggers are you? Tvemunding here, having a run before breakfast.
A head, bare shoulders, an ironic sleepy grin. Anders. Out of the tent on knuckles and toes, mother naked.
—Morning, he said.
Through the birches, behind Anders, Quark on a silver wolf loping.
—Kim and I, Anders said.
Kim looked out, blond hair over eyes. He crawled out monkey-nimble. A hug from Anders.

RIVER

The divestment of Franklin in the meadow by the river. Mariana flourished an imaginary trumpet.

—The grasses, Hugo said, go from Tolland Man's gruel of flaxseed and goosegrass to Roman porridge, which was linseed roasted with barley and coriander, pounded in a mortar, salted, boiled, and served in a bowl to Horace dining with Virgil. Columella fancied it, and Pliny mentions the toothsomeness of rustic Tuscan porridge on a winter morning. Meadow with goats to gaze at as he ate.

—Like us, Mariana said, bleating and folding Franklin's togs.

—There were Iron Age grape pips at Donja Dolina.

—Bet they ate frogs too, Mariana said, and green lizards.

—People upstream in a boat, Franklin said. Voices carry over water. It's Master Sigurjonsson and Pascal without a stitch.

—Ho, said Mariana.

—Pascal I mean, Franklin said, climbing Hugo to stand on his shoulders. Hr. Ess has on a cap, wristwatch, and little triangle underpants like Hugo's.

—Swim out, Hugo said, and climb aboard.

OLD MIRRORS FLECKED AND TARNISHED

On a long walk that took him near the Nordkalsten seawall and warehouses, Hugo had seen the Bicycle Rider hefting his bike up the stone steps, swinging onto it in the road. Their eyes met, with no recognition in the Rider's, though he was already a day student at NFS Grundtvig but not yet someone Hugo had tried to be friendly toward. His jeans were unzipped, the pod of his dingy briefs pouching through. His eyes had been dead, as when Hugo had last seen them in the police morgue.

ASTERS AND ZINNIAS

Papa in a folding hammock chair by his hollyhocks, straw boater over his eyes.

—Hugo's theology, he said, is of course his need to undo me. Not by cracking my head on a dusty road in Greece, but as an intelligent child takes its toys apart to see what makes them go. Ridiculous, but there you are.

—Papa, Hugo said, I know what makes you go. And the machinery is too fine for my fingers. I hope I'm something like.

—Peas in a pod, Mariana said, if you know what to look for. You have the same sense of house, of space, of time. You eat alike. I didn't know how to take a walk until Hugo annexed me. Or how a room can be the whole world.

—It's awful, Franklin said, but it's fun.

—Tell me, Pastor Tvemunding said from under his hat, holding out an arm to invite Franklin over.

Franklin came, got hugged, and climbed astride.

—Papa, Hugo said, keeps his hat over his eyes so as not to look at Franklin snake naked.

—How modern I'm willing to be, Pastor Tvemunding said, is, I see, still a matter for doubt.

—Notice everything, Franklin said. Know where everything comes from, a hundred years back.

ANEMONE

—Matter, the physicists seem to be saying, was not stuff before creation: critical tensions in nothingness, the universal emptiness, became so energetic that they blew up.

—Critical tensions? Papa asked.

—Force, Hugo said. The only thing the physicists can reach back to is a great force present in all matter and space.

—Well then, Papa said, scattering leaves with his stick, there's God. As they see Him.

—If, Hugo said, man in God's image was Adam, God in man's image was Yeshua. If matter was not stuff before creation, then God can be a pattern of energy rather than an oxygen breather and processor of carbohydrates. That we are in His image then means that He is and we are animations of the same energy system. Except, perhaps, His anima occupies the whole sea of neutrinos that's boundless but limited, and we each occupy bodies only, energy systems that are limited but boundless, exchanging love and conversation, procreating both bodies and minds. God's procreation is continuous, ours occasional. Yeshua is an occasional aspect of a continuity.

BREAKFAST

Franklin. Hair carrot and brass. Irides seagreen, pupils hyacinth. Pathfinder brogans, collapsed socks. Lots of practical irony and cautious reticence, the hippety-hop who invented electricity. Love me some geography, he says to the mush bowl, because a map is a jigsaw puzzle. What I like is where the driblet islands make a trail at the south poke of things, left behind, all on a drift to the west. And to the north, crumbly islands. Love islands. Show him the inland island in France, bounded by four rivers. Plains islands bounded by mountains. A country, then, he opines, is a lot of people pretending they're an island, because they all speak the same language. Well, sometimes. Or because they have a common interest, like the Swiss. There is no place without time, no time without place. So, says Franklin, knuckling his nose, you can't say where without saying when. The Mediterranean when it had seals in it. Holland before tulips. Everything wanders, he says. Land, people, animals, trees.

OUT FROM JOPPA

Two ways, Hugo said, and Papa cocked his head to listen. Like John, as in eleven Matthaeus, neither eating nor drinking, and the opinion of the public is that you are owned and operated by a devil, or like Yeshua, eating and drinking, and the people say here's a glutton and a drunkard, the friend of tax collectors and sinners. And, Papa said, that's yet another logion where the sign of Jonas is the pivot. The vine is to be judged by its gourd.

DOVE

By wholeness of being.

FIG

Neutrino here, Hugo said, our Franklin, is as yet all luck. Whenever the angel rings the silver run in a sound of trumpets, he thrusts his sickle in, the wheat topples in a golden rush, the chaff dances in the air, and the harvest song is the only one his red tongue knows morning noon and night. Whereas those of us who shave and pay taxes always seem to get in line at the post office behind an Oriental trying to mail a live chicken to Sri Lanka. Look at McTaggart the English master. He loses his car habitually in the parking lot. That his disciples in Transcendental Meditation and Buddhist raising of the consciousness are all feebleminded hankerers who will clot around any mountebank he does not notice. He walks across flower beds puffing the beauties of nature to one of his morons. He was the only one of the faculty the Bicycle Rider esteemed and thought a bright teacher. To blow like a dead leaf in the wind, irresponsible, irresponsive. Which beautiful teaching, Mariana said, laid the Bicycle Rider out on the slab at the police morgue.

MONKEYS AND PARROTS

If, Mariana read to Franklin lying on the carpet and rolling a soccer ball inchmeal from crotch to chin, the forest were darker it did not seem to be more silent. They could hear a kind of buzzing in the treetops, a vague noise coming from the branches. Looking upwards, the three men could see indistinctly something like a great platform stretched out some forty meters above the ground. There must be at that height a tremendous entanglement of branches without any cranny through which the daylight could pierce. A thatched roof would not have been more lightproof. This explained the darkness that prevailed beneath the trees. Where they had camped that night the nature of the ground had changed greatly. No more intermingled branches or brambles, no more of those thorns that had kept them from leaving the footpath. A scanty grass, like a prairie that neither rain nor spring ever watered. The trees, at intervals from seven to ten meters, resembled pillars supporting some colossal edifice, and their branches must cover an area of several thousand hectares. There were masses of African sycamores whose trunks were formed of a number of stems firmly united toward the ground, bob bobs.

—Baobabs, Hugo said from his desk, a majestic great graygreen tree that huddles its trunks like celery.

—Bob bobs, read Mariana, recognizable by the gourdlike shape of their bole, with a circumference of seven to ten metres and surmounted by an enormous mass of hanging branches. There were silk cotton trees with their trunks opening into a series of hollows big enough for a man to hide in. Mahogany trees with trunks a metre and a half in diameter from which might have been excavated dugout canoes from five to seven metres long.

—Ho, Hugo said, Zuntz on the centurion with Jules Verne from across the room has filled me with lovingkindness, expecially as Monsieur Verne's expositor has had her hand in her knickers from the beginning of the chapter.

—Can I help it if I'm a sweet person? she said.

—When, Franklin said twirling the soccer ball on his chin, I get to my peter, it jumps. See? Chin to peter, peter to chin.

—Phenomenal! Hugo said. I'll bet if you went to the baker's, by way of the kiosk for an evening paper, you might find a half dozen strawberry-jam cakes with custard topping that we can have with coffee, which I'll make, as Mariana is not going to be able to walk or see straight after our expression, or expressions, of mutual esteem.

BLUE SUMMER SKY

Hugo under his oak at the meadow's edge saw the oval shadow of the hot-air balloon sliding toward him before he looked up and saw the balloon itself, a gaudy upside-down pear shape the oiled silk of which was zoned in bands: the equatorial one was a rusty persimmon, a Mongol color, and around it were the figures of the zodiac copied from the mosaic floor of Bet Alpha Synagogue in Byzantine Israel, archaic but supple of line. The band above was bells and pomegranates in orange and blue, the one below was egg-and-dart Hellenistic. The basket was of wicker and belonged to the protomachine age, for a propeller that seemed to be made of four cricket bats was turned by a fanbelt connected to a brass cylinder leaking steam vapor. There was a wooden rudder, and levers at the taffrail. Three ten-year-old boys were the crew, as happy as grigs at their work bringing the balloon down right in front of Hugo, who stood and gaped, at a loss to account for anything he was seeing. The boys were dressed in nautical Scandinavian togs, with long scarves around their necks, as if the air from which they'd descended was very cold. One boy manipulated a lever that seemed to bring the balloon down, another braked the propeller, which stopped spinning and rolled to a lazy halt. Puffs of vapor smoked from the cylinder. The boys' bright grins were for the joy of surprising Hugo, for the joy of being aeronauts in a balloon on a fine summer day, and for the joy of being messengers, which they said they were, talking all at once.

—Who in the name of God are you? Hugo asked. Where have you come from, hey?

—My name is Tumble, and my friends are Quark and Buckeye. Where we've come from we're not to say, and we're messengers.

—Bringing a message, Quark said helpfully.

—The coordinates are right, Buckeye said consulting a length of paper scrolled between two rollers. Oak tree, meadow, Sjaelland, Denmark. Hugo Tvemunding by the world for name. Shapes alphabet into words about the Company. *Yeryuzu kendi kendine bir toprak.*

—Buckeye! Tumble said sweetly, you've slipped off band. That's Turkish.

—Sorry! said Buckeye. I was about to blush anyway, this part of the printout about shepherd to the young, a good son, and superb lover in both flesh and spirit, *tam avidus quam taurus* in a different hand in the margin, the dispatcher I suppose. *Nesuprantamas disonansas tarp*, oops! Sor-ree. Anyway, you're the right soul.

—Yes, said Tumble, and here's the message. *Road auspicious. Though young, act like a man. Be steadfast, patient, and silent.*

—About what? Hugo asked. And Why?

—That, smiled Quark, we are not free to say.

BOUNDARY

There is only one sense: touch. The sun, by way of caroming off a mellow brick wall with lonely afternoon light on it, firm plump pair of breasts with delectable nipples, a page of Homer, touches the eyes. Eating is touch carried to the utmost. Vibrant air touches the ear. Smell is so many particles from aromatic things. The world is a mush of matter rather than the separateness we ascribe to things. Franklin in his Wolf Cub cricket cap, blue shirt with yellow kerchief, little blue pants, tall ribbed socks, and red sneakers listened to Hugo in Eagle Scout khakis with solemn attention. Boys named Abel and Bruno had got out of him, moments before the powwow, that he has no father, that his sister Mariana is the bedmate of Scoutmaster Tvemunding, that he has only been camping with Hugo and Mariana, that he is poor, that Hugo makes love to Mariana lots and lots, and that his uniform is so new it has little squares of paper in all the pockets with an inspector's number, to accompany complaint of manufacturing defect. As to other questions, Franklin had offered to bloody Bruno's nose for him. Knots, naming of tent parts and tools, cards with animal tracks, cards with flowers and weeds, and here was Scoutmaster Tvemunding, who taught Latin, Greek, and gym at NFS Grundtvig and Sunday School at Treenigheden, talking about everything being touch.

—Eugenius, he said, front and forward. Face each other, tall and straight, shoulders back. Theodor, cup your hands. Eugenius is going to give you something, out of his wild imagination, and you are going to feel it, in your wild imagination, and describe it, how it feels.

—A frog! Eugenius said.

—Well, said Theodor, I had a frog in my hands just the other day, and a snake, and a hedgehog, so I'm not up a creek. A frog looks damp but is dry, looks flabby but is hard. It twitches, trying to jump away, but can be still, probably because it's scared. I'd be scared. It's cool. Its throat pulses.

ZUM ZIELE FUHRT DICH DIESE BAHN

—Theodor, Hugo said, didn't know the dative of accommodation from a rat's ass, and has been stricken with amnesia in the matter of ablative absolutes, Frits and Asgar bloodied themselves in a fight back of the gym, nasty little beasts, and the grounds trolls ran a power mower outside the windows for half of Greek, and around three Ulrich gave me a frantic signal to come quick. Golo and Abel were, for reasons best known to themselves, having a little conviviality outside study hall, playing push and pull with each other's pizzles while gazing into each other's big soulful eyes. Fine by me, though they have rooms and showers and woods and meadows in which to welcome puberty cross-eyed and breathless, but why waste the ten minutes before study hall, and then Aakjaer Minor, who grabs people and goes cataleptic, happens along and pins them both. Ulrich was the first to notice this predicament, and knowing that McTaggart had study hall and would be stomping along crabwise at any moment, and would bore everybody for days with the psychology of it all, had the diplomatic genius to push all three into the broom closet and sprint for the gym. We nipped back. McTaggart was bleating about combining study with transcendental meditation, so we could craftily open the broom closet and walk the interlocked three down the hall, one walking backward and zipping himself up, the other sideways, and both carrying the clinging Aakjaer with my and Ulrich's help, God laughing at us all fit to kill. We disentangled the mass in my office. Abel, who had not managed to get his britches up with his arms pinned to his sides, stood there in pretty outrage. What in hell does it mean? he begged of me.

Mariana, listening with wide eyes, had deshoed and unsocked Hugo as he talked in the chair where he had flopped and sagged, tugged his trousers off, and was unbuttoning his shirt when a banging on the door announced Franklin in full Cub Scout fig.

—O Lord, Hugo sighed, I was forgetting that tonight's the little bastards in yellow and blue, with beanies.

—Hi, said Franklin. Things look real interesting.

—Hugo, Mariana said, has had a trying day, and has taken a whole ten minutes to get over it.

ZWECK

In pipestem trews snug of cleft, flat Dutch cap, thickwove jersey, Norfolk jacket, hobnailed brogues, and Finnish scarf with an archaic pattern of reindeer and runes worked into its weave, Tumble climbed from the basket of the steam balloon, bounced from his jump, and cued Quark and Buckeye, poised with flute and glockenspiel, to give him a tune. *Master Erastus*, he sang, stomping with seesawing shoulders and chiming smile, *Equuleus quagga!* Likes, said Quark in recitative over the catch, clover bluegrass dill, spring onions oats and hay. Kin to, said Buckeye, lowering his flute, Eohippus Five Toes, silver wolves, red deer on Rum, dandelions, and Ertha when she's broody. Maybe, said Quark, depressing the declinator, which seeped vapor, but the mykla puts them in with asses burros zebras and horses of the good old Hwang Ho Valley, don't it? Yuss, said Tumble, but Buckeye means chord. Spartan spadgers, springbokker, leapers and runners. So hold fast, wait long, and don't speak. No, not to anybody.

ARCHAIC TORSO OF APOLLO

Even though we can never see the head that sang, with its deer's eyes staring at infinity, we have the strong torso from whose animal grace we can imagine the hot summer clarity of its gaze. If the gone head is still not there, in light, why then does the proud chest disturb your looking, or the sweet shift of the hips, slight as a smile, that takes our eyes down the cunning body, to its cluster of seeds? Otherwise this stone would stand senseless under the polished slope of its shoulders, without its wild balance, and would not be as rich with light as the sky with stars. The world sees you, too. You must change your life.

AN EVENT ALSO HAPPENS WHERE IT IS KNOWN

Out past the warehouses and quays on Nordkalksten is a seawall of gray stone. A catwalk at its base, a bicycle path along the top, with iron rail. Harbor, river, barges. Here one could see old men fishing, sailors sleeping off a terrible drunk, and sunbathers spread against the slant of the wall. Boys in dingy bargain-basement briefs, boys impudently naked.

UNDER

We distinguish this seventh stratum by stringers of the stone that readily melts in fire of the second order. Beneath this is another ashy rock, light in weight and five foot thick. Next comes a lighter stratum the colors of ash and a foot thick. Beneath this lies the eleventh stratum, dark and like the seventh, two foot through. Below the last is a twelfth stratum, soft and of a whitish color, two foot thick. The weight of this sits on the thirteenth stratum, ashy and a foot thick, whose weight in turn is supported by a fourteenth stratum of black color. There follows this another black stratum half a foot thick, which is again followed by a sixteenth stratum still blacker in color, whose thickness is also the same. Beneath this, and last of all, lies the cupriferous stratum, black colored and schistose, in which there sometimes glitter scales of gold-colored pyrites in very thin sheets, which, as I have said elsewhere, often take the forms of various living things.

HOLLYHOCKS ALONG A GARDEN WALL

—I'm wonderfully delighted, Pastor Tvemunding said to Mariana, that you and Hugo are friends. He has always been a friendly boy. He used to toddle off behind the postman, and grieve that he could not stay longer than to hand over the mail and exchange comments on the weather. He made friends with the girl who delivered butter and eggs. He fell in love with all his schoolmates.

—He's a loving person, Mariana said, that's for sure.

—His loving nature causes him grief from time to time. You know about the student he calls the Bicycle Rider?

—Who's dead, Mariana said. I know what you mean. He hurt Hugo.

—Because, Pastor Tvemunding said, Hugo had never really before encountered evil face to face. He doesn't want to admit that evil cannot be dealt with. He cannot believe that there are wholly selfish people drowned in themselves, beyond the reach of love or understanding. That there are people who, impotent to create, destroy. That there are people whose self-loathing is so deep they know nothing of generosity and invariably do the mean thing even when they might as easily do the generous one. The young man was on drugs, and had been for years, but I'm not one to blame drugs for human evil: the evil is there before the drugs, which are part of the meanness and not its cause.

—You couldn't be righter, Mariana said.

—All this theological work, which will not take him into the ministry, began with a remark I made years ago, that God will remain inscrutable and uncertain forever, but that Jesus (Hugo's Yeshua, for the Aramaic name is of the essence for him) had an intuitive idea of God that put goodness in our hands. He is light, of which we are free to partake, or be in darkness. We can be transparent to our fellow man, or opaque.

BUCKEYE

Possum ate a lightning bug and now he shines inside.

RED AND YELLOW ZINNIAS

—I want to be up-to-date, Pastor Tvemunding said at tea, reaching over to wipe whipped cream from the corners of Franklin's mouth with his napkin. There's Hugo's room, and the guest room that's so jolly with the apple tree at the window.

—Mariana and I, Hugo said, will sleep together, and I'll rig out my old scout cot for Franklin.

—But, said the pastor, there's the guest room he can have all to himself.

—Oh, no, Hugo said, travellers stay together.

MEADOW WITH GOLDFLOWERS AND POPPIES

Buckeye in a Portuguese sailor's shirt, abrupt white denim pants, beret, and espadrilles climbed backward down the rope ladder of the balloon, singing *onward under over through!*

Quark tossed the anchor onto the meadow. The balloon tilted its drift, exhaled vapor from its cylinders, bounced and swayed as Tumble pumped the declinators. Quark swung himself over the wicker taffrail with a deft scissors kick and landed springing.

Tumble closed valves, cinched a line, made an entry in the log and vaulted out, rolling forward in a somersault.

—*Hejsa!* said Buckeye.

—Hi! said Quark.

—Hup! said Tumble.

For adoration beyond match

sang Tumble pulling his sailor's middy over his blond rick of wind scrumpled hair,

The scholar bulfinch aims to catch.

The soft flute's ivory touch

sang Quark sopranino, his gray American sweatshirt halfway over his head.

And, careless on the hazel spray,

Buckeye sang as he snatched off his Portuguese sailor's blouse,

The daring redbreast keeps at bay

The damsel's greedy clutch.

Shoeless, sockless, Tumble backed out of his sailor's pants singing

While Israel sits beneath his fig.

With coral root and amber spring

Quark sang with trills and a cadenza as he wriggled off his Sears Roebuck blue jeans.

The weaned adventurer sports

Buckeye sang tossing his short white pants into the gondola of the balloon.

Tumble, pretending to blush, thumbed down his drawers, Quark and Buckeye their pindling briefs, and the three in the pink-brown slender ribby nakedness sang in chiming Mozartian harmony

Where to the palm the jasmin cleaves

For adoration mongst the leaves
The gale his peace reports.
—*Now labor*, they sang making a triangle of arms on one another's shoulders,
his reward receives.
For adoration counts his sheaves,
To peace, her bounteous prince.

The nectarine his strong tint imbibes,
And apples of ten thousand tribes,
And quick peculiar quince.

TROLLFLÖJTEN

Ring-tailed kinkajous trotting on the logging road, bouncing and siffling, squeaking and hopping, in pairs and trios, alone and in quartets. Yellow parrots above them, monkeys and kingfishers. Franklin's world, Mariana said. Years ago he was a rat in the Pied Piper festival, he and scads of littles in brown and gray rat suits with rope tails, creeping along behind the Piper playing Mozart. I remember a rat who lost his way and had to be carried by a woman and restored to the pack. Wasn't me, Franklin said. I crept good.

GOLDEN SAMPHIRE

Buckeye in the meadow, where the balloon was tethered. Tumble and Quark were leapfrogging by the river. He held out his hand for a meadowlark to fly to him and stand on his palm. She spoke to him. He answered in quail. Silly! she said. Do I look like a quail hen? He spoke goat. She laughed. Frog. Giggle.

AURIGA. BETELGEUSE. BARNARD'S STAR.

In spite of their intangibility, neutrinos enjoy a status unmatched by any other known particle, for they are actually the most common objects in the universe, outnumbering electrons by a thousand million to one. In fact, the universe is really a sea of neutrinos, punctuated only rarely by impurities such as atoms. It is even possible that neutrinos collectively outweigh the stars, and therefore dominate the gravity of the cosmos.

RIGHT THE SECOND TIME

—Tom'll be here in a bit, Hugo said to Mariana nose to nose.
—I think I can walk, Mariana said, though my brains are all gone. Melted into a jelly. Who's at the door?
  Franklin.
—O wow! he said looking squiggle-eyed and pretending to barf.
—Who, said Mariana, pulled his piddler until his eyes rolled back in his head

the whole week we were at Papa Tvemunding's, while we had to make do with teenage smooching?

—You *said* Augustus would spoil me, Franklin said solemnly. I like Augustus.

—I imagine so, Hugo said. Nasty little spy. Papa with a dry cough to introduce the subject, which amused him tremendously, said that you confided in him that we were not making love, but only kissing a lot and whispering before we went to sleep. You thought Papa wouldn't want us to, not knowing that he says that people are close to God when they make love. And being Franklin, you got Papa to say a good word for rabbity-nosed boys jacking off, in moderation, of course.

—It's nature, Franklin said. And fun. Once in the morning, and once in the afternoon. Augustus said I was to. And at night *you* said I was to.

—I suppose, Mariana said to the skylight, if a third party had assured Franklin of the naturalness of the kinship between monkeys and boys, he would have had no time to eat, sleep, or those long talks with Papa Tvemunding.

—Who spoiled him rotten, Hugo said.

—I promised to write him a letter, Franklin said.

—Tom's here, Mariana said.

Hugo, who had pulled on long sweat pants and a singlet and was howling for coffee, set the painting of the Bicycle Rider on the easel. He had whited out the lazily handsome blond face and dead blue eyes. The right arm, on the fist of which the head had leaned, was also overpainted.

—Dark background's going too, Hugo mused. It wants to be white.

Mariana, her breasts loose under a rich blue pullover, was zipping herself into snug coral shorts when big Tom, tossing his floppy hair out of his eyes, shifted from foot to foot. He crossed his hands on his behind, nudging a lampshade with his elbow. He then cupped them over his crotch, seeing instantly that, expand or contract, he was equally awkward. He tried sliding his fingers into his pockets, hitting the lampshade again, and settled for knuckling his nose and scratching a convenient itch on his thigh. Shown the painting, he stared at it.

—That, Hugo said, was the dopey kid who was a day student, the one who floated around on lysergic acid and managed the ultimate trendy distance by killing himself with an overdose of God knows what. I tried getting his head out of his ass. I failed.

—No, Mariana said. He failed you.

—Anyway, Hugo said, I'm going to repaint.

—Tom hates coffee, Mariana said brightly. Every time he's been here, he has suffered and squirmed. Beer, milk, fizz water, which?

—Beer, Tom said, his voice rasping at his audacity.

—Head turned slightly, Hugo said, so that you're looking at me out of the side of your eyes. Right elbow on the chair arm. Everything else the same, except that your body is much harder and better muscled than the Rider's. I have all sorts of changes to make. Take off your pants.

This sloshed Tom's beer.

—Leave your briefs on. They're nicely stinted and stressed.

The balloon, Hugo could see through the skylight, was just outside. He had learned on a walk with Mariana that she could not see Buckeye, Quark, and Tumble. They had come and stood gravely interested while they sat under the oak, Mariana's head in Hugo's lap.

—Burnt sienna, Hugo said, raw sienna, titanium white.

Franklin made a great show of finding the tubes and laying them on the little table that served as a palette.

Buckeye was on the skylight, peering in. Short khaki pants, gray white and ochre striped soccer jersey, and not till he came into the room, in less time than an eyeblink, could you see his dinky blue cap.

—Calabash! he said to Hugo, straked gourd pumpkin vine!

—If I had some paper and pencil and an envelope and a stamp, Franklin said, I could write Augustus a letter.

—And, Mariana said, if you could spell and write so that anybody but God could read it.

—Put in your letter, Hugo said, that while we visited I saw what I needed to see. Say that the casting out of demons is the hub on which everything else turns. He'll know what I mean. The self is the demon. Demon out, daimon in.

—O wow! Franklin said. Start spelling.

Hugo painted. Tom, with only his good nature to get him through this ordeal, took courage from the fact that it was his good looks that got him into this, and thought of seducing Franklin without breaking Lemuel's heart, share him perhaps, and Mariana, and even Hugo, and the green-eyed sailor with silver eyelashes at the recruiting station, the one with the sleepy friendly smile and crammed trews.

Mariana spelled, Franklin wrote and erased and wrote again. Hugo painted.

Tumble was at the skylight, Quark looking over his shoulder.

—Why do you keep looking up? Mariana asked idly.

—The light, Hugo said. It's what I paint by.

Buckeye was inspecting Tom, closely, with doggish curiosity. His eyes met Hugo's. *Under all's a fire so fine it is and isn't in and out of time, a pulse of is, a pulse of isn't.*

—But, Buckeye mouthed inaudibly, with a shrug of his boney shoulders and a crinkle of dimples in his smile, that isn't worth knowing, is it? Over all's the nothing that's something because of the curving tides of the is and the isn't.

No matter that, either.

He stood behind Tom and put his arms around his neck and rested his chin in Tom's hair.

Quark read Franklin's letter. Tumble sniffed Mariana.

—What matters, Buckeye said, is that there are so many who don't know their right hand from their left.

THE BICYCLE RIDER

I

They could see through the grime of the barnloft windows, Anders and Kim, how far the field of sunflowers they'd walked across stretched down to where the sawgrass begins back of the beach, sunflowers higher than their heads, bitter green and dusty to smell. They could see yellow finches working the panniers, butterflies dipping and fluttering, the glitter and lilac blue of the sea where they'd been horsing around on the sand. They'd filed along the narrow path like Mohawks, Kim brown lean and naked except for the skimpy neat pouch, cinched by string around his hips and down the cleft of his butt, in which his sprouting peter and spongy scrotum made a snippy jut, Anders behind him, a head taller and with a livider tan, his bathing slip a pellucid Danish blue. Jellyfish bit me once, Kim said, his hair like maize silk flopping in a spin as he smiled over his shoulder, and did it ever sting but I didn't cry, brave me, and once I cut my toe on a shell, and got sunburned once real piti-ful. Glowed in the dark. They were pals in a Greek goatherd-and-shepherd poem, *idyllisk*. Boldly sneaky, Anders, but with Kim you didn't sneak very far. His blue eyes saw all.

2

Macadam road through pines, early morning, a red fox slinking through grass bent with dew, rabbit into bramble. Happiness is a sensual totality of being, Hugo Tvemunding, assistant classics master at NFS Grundtvig, wrote in his journal after his run. *Le bonheur* was the better word. *Lyksalighed* had northern sharpnesses of light and dark. Luck has nothing to do with happi-ness, which comes from rhythms, order, clarity. A card from Papa in the mail, and *Der Eisbrecher*. Greek torso, Apollo, third century. *I do hope, dear Hugo, that you're getting this hurt of the unfortunate young man you call the Bicycle*

Rider behind you. Hurts that cry out to Heaven do not go unheard. The hollyhocks are more beautiful than ever. Come see them, why don't you?

3

Pastor Tvemunding, who was reading H.G. Wells's *The Passionate Friends* in his garden time about with a detective Penguin by Michael Gilbert, after leafing through the *Church Times*, said to his cat Bobine Pellicule, Well, old girl, the letter from Hugo (yes, he's coming to scritch you under the chin) with its question about an aorist in the gospel of Markus made you yawn, though you found the bit about latching onto a young lady of great interest, *jo?* We remember others, do we not? Do we not, indeed.

4

I didn't think, Kim said, you'd even notice that I exist, much less make friends. The barn had a grand smell of oats cows chickenfeed old wood and time. They could hear only their steps up the steep ladder to the loft, the nattering of finches in the sunflowers, the white noise of wind and sea. Chinks of blue, Kim's eyes, after he'd said that the yellow light paced along the smooth wide floor in rectangles was beautiful and that the silence was sweet and the barn snug and private. *O jo!* Anders said, cozy secret bright, stepping from window to window. Our place, all our own. Kim turned on a heel, stomped, and took off his cache-sexe, hanging it around his neck. His penis cantered out over a round and compact scrotum, its longish foreskin pursed at the tip. He scrunched his eyes, feeling naughty and in love. Anders, mouth dry, swallowing hard, shoved down his bathing slip, snapped it inside out, and hung it on a peg. Earlybird sharp, eyes rounding, Kim whistled to admire Ander's lifting penis nudging its glans free. *Ih du store!* Skin yours back, Anders said. It's a thumper for twelve. You think? Kim asked.

5

This golden flower of Peru, or sunflower, being of many sorts, both higher and lower, with one stalk, without branches, or with many branches, with a black or with a white seed, yet not differing in form of flowers or leaves one from another, but in size only, rises up at the first like a pompion with two leaves, and after two, or four, more leaves are come forth, it rises up into a tall stalk, bearing leaves at several distances on all sides, one above another to the very top, being sometimes seven, eight, or ten foot high with leaves which standing out from the stalk are very large, broad below and pointed at the end, round hard rough, of a sad green, and bending downwards: at the top of the stalk stands one great large and broad flower bowing down its head to the sun, and breaking forth from a great head made of scaly green leaves like a great single marigold having a border of many long yellow leaves, set about a great round yellow thrum in the middle, which are very like short heads of flowers, under every one of which is a seed larger than any seed of the this-tles, yet somewhat like, and lesser and rounder than any gourd seed, set in so close and curious a manner that when the seed is taken out, the head with its hollow cells seems very like a honeycomb.

6

Rutger, he said, and Rutger he was. Anders invented for his bunched brown curls an adoring mommy, pederast of a barber, and Narcissus complex. We're stuck with each other, Johannes Calvin having laid it on us in his pep talk that getting along with your roommate is character itself. You don't look pukey. Rutger here, and you're? Anders. He wore American jeans, perfect fit, an English plaid cotton shirt, rotten sneakers, germless white wool socks, a French undershirt with skinny straps, and a smidgin of briefs, Hom style micro, with the little triple-flame trademark on the left below the spandex waistband. Out of these he flopped an outsized dick. Lucky you, said Anders. It serves, said Rutger, and stays in tone by coming without let or cease, spurt spout splat. Scrounging in a canvas bag of silver scissors, combs, shampoo, nail clippers, dental floss, toothbrush, orange sticks, he located a green tube of Panalog from which he squeezed gunk that he smeared on his glans. Vaginitis, he explained. From his girl Meg, the second time the sweet slut had given it to him. You've never caught it? An infection that itches like fire and parches the foreskin. He was going to get laid around four, and give it back to Meg, and she back to him. Crazy.

7

Nu vel, Anders said, we'd got into our *sammenslynget* when, with sandpipers nittering and pecking and the edge of the sea was sliding the plies of its bor-der back and forth, and that's all the universe was doing in our part of it, except that the sky was being bright summer blue over our heads, and I sweetened my gaze at you and wriggled my toes, you said, you little rascal, Keep looking at me like that and my peter will stand bolt upright and whim-per, and I kept looking at you like that, and here's your peter, *herre Jemini!* rose-petal pink, standing bolt upright. So why are you blushing? Robin-eggs in gelatin, Kim's balls to Ander's feel. For answer Kim curled his fingers around Ander's rigid haft, squeezing gently, tentatively. It's beautiful, he said. So's yours, Anders said. Do you come yet? I think so, Kim said. I'm not near-ly as brave as I want you to think I am. Why do you like me? Because, Anders said, there's a poem by Rimbaud that begins *Aussitôt que l'idée du Déluge se fut rassise, un lièvre s'arrêta dans les sainfoins et les clochettes mouvantes, et dit sa prière à l'arc-en-ciel à travers la toile de l'araignée.* And the dove came back with an olive branch in its foot.

8

Here, said Mariana, I've brought you a rose. And I've brought you a weed, Franklin said. Thought it was a flower, but Sissy says it's a weed. Girls are like that, Hugo said, hard to please and never satisfied. *Hejsa!* I'll put them together in the one vase here, to show that I like them both.

9

Franklin standing under Hugo's metre-square photograph of Emile-Antoine Bourdelle's *Héraklès archer* (1910) in a thin silver frame was like all the children in the world in museums, their innocence and alert attention virginal before a Mondriaan, a broken Hera, a case of paleolithic axes, a Cubist harmony. A convincing Greek, Hugo said, the cunning of Odysseus, or of a mountain lion, in that muzzle. I think he looks like a possum, Franklin said. What's he shooting? Monsters, said Hugo. All terrible things.

10

A glass jar of acorns. A nautilus shell. Shale slab with a fossil gingko leaf. A Greek coin from Metaponton in Sicily. A snail shell. Greek text of Marcus, dictionary, coffee cup, running shorts drying on a hanger hooked to the skylight latch. Boy Scout Handbook, with markers. Mariana, said Franklin, says she likes this place better than any she's ever been in, and I do too. Sure glad we met you on the beach.

11

The greatest of these beautiful thistles has at the first many large and long leaves lying on the ground, very much cut in and divided in many places, even to the middle rib, set with small sharp (but not very strong) thorns or prickles at every corner of the edges, green on the upper side, and whitish underneath: from the middle of these leaves rises up a round stiff stalk, three foot and a half high, set without order with suchlike leaves, bearing at the top of every branch a round hard great head consisting of a number of sharp bearded husks, compact or set close together, of a bluish green color, out of every one of which husks start small whitish blue flowers, with white threads in the middle of them, and rising above them, so that the heads when they are in full flower make a fine show, much delighting those who look at them: after the flowers are past, a seed grows in every one, or the most part of the bearded husks, which still hold their roundness until, being ripe, it opens of itself, and the husks easily fall away one from another, having in them a long white kernel: the root is great and long, blackish on the outside, and dies every year after it has borne seed.

12

Kim, home, strayed into his father's study. Before Henricus Hondio's *Nova Totius Terrarum Orbis Geographics ac Hydrographica Tabula*, he smiled at the lion and ox reclined by a pumpkin in the border. Gerardus Mercator Flander. Grapes peaches cucumbers. Like Papa to have so narrow neat and black a frame. Then he stared at the engraving of Holberg to the left of the map and reset the nudge of his penis in his pants. The view through the French windows was a Bonnard. He read all the dull mail on the desk while fitching his crotch with meditative fingerings. At the harpsichord he played a gavotte by Bach, to keep from thinking of Anders just then. Midnote a repeat he froze, swivelled around, and turned a cartwheel. The view through the French windows was Bonnard because of the greens and mauves, the rusty pink of the brick wall. Anders, talking or strolling, liked to roll the ball of his thumb against his dick through his pants, and laugh like a dog about it, no sound, only a happy look and slitty eyes. Kim slid his pants down and off. Whether anybody was home he didn't know. His briefs caught on his shoe and had to be hopped free. He yawned grandly, and stretched. He finished the gavotte at the harpsichord, did another cartwheel, and sauntered upstairs, britchesless. On the bed he allowed himself to think about Anders, happily, wondering if he were wicked, silly, or simply lucky.

13

How, Mariana said, did you talk a horse out of it? And with accessories to match. I thought only sailors were so gifted. I haven't blushed since I was ten, Hugo said. Are you always so uninhibited, and so generous? Born so, Mariana beamed. Judging character at a glance is my best talent. They were sitting on the free beach, friends of half an hour, Mariana combing her black hair dry, keeping a lookout for Franklin in the shallows. He'd picked up spadger friends and they were idiotically scooping water into each other's faces, squealing, stomping, kicking. Mariana, naked, was on her knees undressing Franklin when Hugo strolled up on the momentum of an impulse he dared not let flag. Hi! he said, Hugo, scoutmaster, schoolteacher, adept at small fry and making friends with beautiful strangers. What do you teach, Mariana asked, weight lifting? She hauled Franklin's jersey over his head, unpantsed and debriefed him, and combed his hair with her fingers. Little brother Franklin, she said. Our day at the beach. Mariana Landarbejder. Work in a kindergarten, with brats. So I get to sunbathe with one. Maybe he'll drown. Hi, brat, Hugo said. Isn't it exciting to have so sweet and good-looking a big sister? Hugo undressed, making a neat stack of his clothes beside Mariana's. You're gorgeous, she said as they trotted into the waves. You're beautiful, he replied. Life can be very simple, Hugo said after their swim. I have a room over the old stables at the school where I teach, wonderfully private, which you're going to like. And I won't ever know if I do or not if I don't come and see, will I?

14

Papa? Kim in stubby blue pants all but occulted by a jersey with the collar flicked up cockily in back, fists at thighs, head down. Yes, dear Kim? You're as brown as an Etruscan and as fetching as Ganymede. Who's that? Charming chap your age in Greek legend filched by Zeus to do God knows what with. Speaking of which, scamp, an hysterical mother, dash it, called to say that you've been exciting the school with jabber about sex. Something she said you said about the rights of children to it in great heaps and doses as a revolution against stuffy middleclass oppression. O my yes, and the red flag down the village road followed by troops of naked youngsters. All of this, and more. My ear was ringing, rather, before she finished. All I ask, Kim my boy, is that you take the persuasions and fiercely guarded decencies of others into consideration. Eh, what? Don't look so damnably glum. I'm only talking reason. And you're not listening. Papa, Kim said, looking up bravely, I'm in love with my friend Anders. We want to sleep together. We've got to. Every night, I mean. In his bed in the dorm, or in my bed. Anders Hammel. He's fifteen. There are other boys here who love each other. They're just like anybody else. Anders is not a sissy or anything. Mama won't even notice.

15

Rhinopithecus, a permanent inhabitant of the cold high forests of Moupin, has a very thick fur, like the Macacus. Aeluropus, the most remarkable mammal discovered by Père David and kin to the singular panda (*Aelurus fulgens*) of Nepal, is as large as a bear, the body wholly white, with the feet, ears, and tip of the tail black. It inhabits the highest forests, and is therefore a true Palaearctic animal, as most likely is the Aelurus. Nyctereutes, a curious racoon-like dog, ranges from Canton to North China, the Amoor and Japan. Hydropotes and Lophotragus are small hornless deer confined to North China. A few additional forms occur in Japan: Urotrichus, a peculiar mole, which is also found in Northwest America; Enhydra, the sea otter of California; and the dormouse (*Myoxus*). Pallas's sandgrouse (*Syrrhaptes paradoxus*), whose native country seems to be the high plains of Northern Asia, but which often abounds near Pekin, astonished European ornithologists in 1863 by appearing in considerable numbers in Central and Western Europe, in every part of Great Britain, and even in Ireland.

16

I'm a little drunk with you, Hugo said to Mariana. We began with busting the mattress, which is fun, and now I hear your voice when you aren't here, and smell you in my nostrils, your girl smell and your vanilla panties and that cucumber taste of your breath, milk and cucumber, and see your China-blue eyes when I'm working. Sounds awful, Mariana said. By drunk, Hugo said, I mean I lose my balance a little when, coming from class, I tell myself that I'll see you soon, and kiss and fuck you, and hug you a nice long time afterwards, and then we'll talk, and I'll learn that you've never heard of Ibykos or Li Po or Braque. Greek poet, way back, quinces in one of his poems, and a black wind from. From. Thrace, he said. Thrace, she said. Chinese poet, green rivers, plum blossoms. Braque is a painter. Blobbed mandolins, skinny little clay pipes, anemones in a bowl. Just like Picasso but different. Read Greek, look at Braque, and then go teach Scouts how to tie knots, sheepshank clove hitch stoppers trumpet shoestring and square. Life is very simple, Hugo said, when you know what you're doing. Yes, said Mariana, but I'll bet you don't.

17

At Elseus Sophus Bugge they swam naked, boys and girls together, showered together, and learned where babies come from. Good enough, Anders said. And, Kim went on, they learned that *masturbere* is good in moderation, and it was Kim who asked how many times a day is moderate, and why in moderation anyway? Girls had giggled and Kim's friend Karl put his hands over his face and peeked through his fingers. And here, freckles, foxred hair, beaver teeth, and snatchy glances, was *unge hr* Karl in person, brought by Kim to be shown Ander's dick. He comes a handful, Kim said, and it's white and thick. Scrounge it out, Anders, so Karl can see how crazy big it is. Kim's, Anders said, obliging, is going to be a whopper if he keeps it in condition with steady exercise and long workouts. *Aldrig i livet!* said Kim. Karl asked to feel. Sure, Anders said. Kim's friend's my friend, and friends can snug anyway they want, *jo?* Karl swallowed a frog, and said, he'd like to see Anders shoot off. No problem, Anders said. Back of the boathouse, under the willows, there Kim says he used to whack off before we imprinted on each other. Gee whillikers, said Karl. It jumps when he comes, Kim said, and bounces. At Grundtvig they walk around in the dorm in their underpants, some in nothing, and everybody whacks off whenever they want to.

18

Who's Grey Eyes here in his birthday suit? Mariana asked of a canvas. That, said Hugo, is the Bicycle Rider. He never came again for me to finish the picture. He was a student here, bone lazy, a day student who lived out on Nordkalksten where, as you know, there are dens of louts mainly American and German, and where the Gospel has not been preached. Pretty nasty place, Mariana said. Creepy. I've seen him about I think. Tall, blond, very pretty face, clothes from the Salvation Army? He was in my Greek Myth class,

Hugo said, and by the third day it began to get through to me that he was quite simply the handsomest boy I'd ever seen in my life. But with arrogantly messy hippy hair, and as you say, oil rags for clothes. A young prince in peasant disguise, I said to myself. And then he had very little to do with anybody, except some students who envied his revolutionary costume and easy cynicism. He was quick to point out to his admirers the particular stupidities of all the faculty, whom he pitied for their stodginess. He was alert in class, though, and could fake the most sincere interest in myths and Greek culture.

19

Reindeer across golden moss in a cloud of their own breath, Sibelius. The forest, Kim said lying face down on the bed, talking into the pillow. Snow down the steep sides of fjords. Wolves with silver eyes. A dust of frost in the air that gets up your nose and stings, and tickles the corners of your mouth. He reached under his hips to undo his jeans, buckle, brad, and zipper. Fucking the bed, he worried and wiggled his jeans down to his knees. Bach, he said, dances. Mozart dances. But Sibelius flies. He tried getting his jeans off with a squirm of toe work, hobbling his ankles. Keeping the cadence of his humping steady, he thumbed down his underpants and fidgeted them, wriggle by twitch, as far as the wadded jeans. My wizzle, he croodled, is up so loving touchy stiff that it's got a crick in it. He freed a foot and pushed jeans and briefs off the end of the bed. Imp, Anders said. One deplorable imp. See how long you can keep it up. I hear Rutger down the hall. O wow, Kim said. Rutger. Does he josh you about me? Wait and see, Anders said. Sibelius, Rutger said, and *for guds skyld*, Ven Anders, take Nipper here up on whatever he's pushing.

20

The white Mountain Daffodill with Ears rises up with three or four broad leaves, somewhat long, of a whitish green color, among which rises up a stalk a foot and a half high, whereon stands one large flower, and sometimes two, consisting of six white leaves apiece, not very broad, and without any show of yellowness in them, three whereof have usually each of them on the back part, at the bottom upon the one side of them, and not on both, a little small white piece of a leaf like an ear, the other three having none at all: the cup is almost as large, or not much less than the small Nompareille, small at the bottom, and very large, open at the brim, of a fir-yellow color, and sometimes the brims or edges of the cup will have a deeper yellow, as if it were discolored by saffron: the flower is very sweet, the root is great and white, covered with a pale coat or skin, not very black, and is not very apt to increase, seldom giving offsets: neither have I ever gathered seeds, because it passes without bearing any with me.

21

Anders husking down his briefs, fighting out of his jersey, stripping loose his shoelaces, said that the black stripe on the neck and feet of archaic horses and asses is called in Greek the *mykla*. From the plains of Poland, Kim said, grasslands from this horizon to the other, the last herds of wild horses in Europe, rounded up like a hundred years ago, *jo?* Lovely big horses, iron grey, nickering and whinnying, up to their knees in Russian pink and Ukrainian blue meadow flowers, frolicking foals and dignified mares. *Hej!* So last night, reading in my sockfeet across from Papa in his fog of burnt applejuice pipesmoke and telling me bits from the paper, what assholes politicians are, my dick began to burrow in my jeans like a perky little mouse. So I nudged it along, by way of petting it, until it was hard as a rib, and throbbing. *Den er mægtig!* We sluddered three jumping slurps out of it over the afternoon, with that crazy bird saying *Well I never! I think so!* in the tree above us, and here he was randy again. And Papa looked funny over the top of his glasses and then up to heaven, and then paid me a wink. O boy. *Lille djævel,* Anders said. You're going to have little nubbly horns growing. One here and one here.

22

Six or so, I suppose it was, Hugo said, when an agemate and I, Ole Vinsson, all freckles and towhead, made a scientific study of sexual differentiation, with his sister, who was ten and had a mind both forthright and level. We simply took off our togs and satisfied our curiosity. It was his sister Julie's opinion that whereas God gave babies, people had to love each other to show that they wanted them, and that parents fucked all night long, all day long too, right after they're married, with ineffable pleasure, until God was convinced, and supplied the baby. We found out about her *kildrer*, and she gave us a demonstration of tickling it. She had friends who could tickle themselves into hysterics, passing out with the pleasure of it. Real boys, she gave us to understand, had stiff peters all the time, like the satyrs of old. Surely, Mariana said, you were older, eight or nine? By then, said Hugo, Ole and I had learned from a rangy teenager the fly of whose jeans always seemed to be cordially distended that jacking off makes one's peter grow. Doesn't it? Mariana said. Don't tell Franklin if it doesn't.

23

Squeamish, me? Rutger hooted, towelling down. Meg'll not blink a lash, and like all women is nosey about you and your gamy sweetmeat nipper. Give her a hot crotch maybe even. Anders, well balanced in the articulately inflected fit of his jeans and smug about the sidesway wrench of his fly that gapped the top teeth of his zipper and canted out its tab, was in a whickering good humor, hard balls, he said. Cock growing a bone inside. But, said Rutger, you milked that rowdy last night, and grunted a lot doing it. Twice, said Anders, and got pulled off twice in the dingle, by untuckering boypower, a tongue in overdrive, and an everloving will. Does he pant, Rutger said, when he sees your dick rearing up, like Meg? Says her heart lurches. What if I'm turned on by your pukey kid and his pink little sprig of a weewee? Every man his specialty, as you say. Whereupon Kim stomped in, hair tousled, and got hugged by Anders and, wickedly, by Rutger. I think I'm scared, Kim said, judging by one cold shiver or another I keep getting. Makes it spicier, said Rutger. Meg's setting out about now. We meet her at the bend and head for the boathouse. Then we all fuck and whatever it is you do until we pass out with coming. And then go at it again, gasping and weak, squish squish. Crazy, said Kim.

24

Through the hornbeam and beech forests of Transylvania and the Djerdap Gorge, the Danube over seething rapids, white shoals, falls, foaming sluices, comes to the whirlpool of Lepenski Vir. Here, on a ledge above it, lived an epipaleolithic people whose vestiges Dragoslav Srejović found in 1960. Their community sat on a horseshoe shelf above the great spiral of water, with the steep cliffs of the Koršo Mountains at its back. Among apron-shaped houses laid out like steps stood monumental Erewhonian statues whose faces groan with the agony of birth, or with awe before some wonder or terror. The endemic plants were lilac smokewood manna ash slow buckthorn Dalmatian toadflax cypress spurge oxeye camomile. Bone bracelets needles awls. The dead were buried as if giving birth, the skull of a stag over the shoulders. A frieze of geese on a pot, deer in a thicket. Ovens altars hearths were decorated with wave patterns. Elk and salmon, and the navel of the river below. Owl in the hornbeam was father's sister's daughter, redcombed quail mother's brother's son, celt hook lilac, lilac circle spinning water. Night rain, noon rain. Salmon river, bear wood.

25

He was a pleasant interest, Hugo said. I like people. He was moreover poor, taking courses at NFS Grundtvig as a day student on tuition from a government grant, parents divorced, making him eligible for a stipend for the disadvantaged. He had the one pair of ratty jeans, a few secondhand shirts, and perhaps not enough to eat. So the first time I invited him over, ostensibly for a drawing, I laid in sausages, beer, cold ham, a potato salad, a melon. He was charming. It was his second time over that I learned he slept in a large box in a hallway. This he rented from a hack freelance artist, gay, unfortunate personality. By the third visit I'd decided to move him in with me. There's room. So I said, Bring your traps. He said that the idea of sharing quarters with me was like a dream. He would have all these books to read. Engines in the switching yard would not wake him before dawn. No hideous fights among toughs in the street outside one's window. No cockroaches. He was to move in on the Wednesday. I waited in a nice excitement. I like new things, new turns. I knew it would be difficult having him here. What did I know about him, really? Pretty much nothing, except that he needed taking in. I waited and waited. He never came.

26

Six Ryvitas, Mariana gasped. And came like a brass band passing the royal box on Liberation Day. Franklin at his lookout was chinning on a limb, up and down like a puppet on elastic strings. *Det hele?* he called. *Forbi.* The river's not the ocean, Hugo had said. Drop in, holding your nose, bob up, and I've got you. Hang on around my neck and I'll swim you out to the sandbar. Your own island. Here he danced out some intricate fantasy, crouching, springing, kicking water, falling down shot, rebounding to repulse ten insectoid invaders from another galaxy with laser spurts. *Zonk, zink, zonk.* Ferried back twice now to stand guard while they fucked, jeans rolled to pillow Mariana's bottom. At Skordbærbjerg, experimental school for brats and trendies, Mariana said, run you know by worldsavers and psychologists, there was this little nipper of a girl, all of ten, going up and down the hall holding her twat, naked as a newt, and in her free hand two Ryvitas and a krone, which she was offering to whoever for a fuck. Fun was, the look on a face of some government functionary inspecting the school that day, who had already seen two teenagers doing it in the library and half the kids naked in the pool, and had been propositioned by a boy with a twinge of pubic hair if you looked close.

27

Bunce, Hugo said. Five kilometers, ten lengths of the pool, and I find a girl looking hopeful on my doorstep and her little brother, The Rabbit Who Invented Electricity, looking bored. He wants to go to the beach, Mariana said. Does his big sister? Hugo proposed the river instead. Is it textile? Oh no, they're boys there from school naked as they came into the world, and as innocent, and as loud. Lay out croissants and jam while I shower, Hugo said, and explain why I'm happily lecherous so early on a Saturday. Crazy, I guess, Mariana said. It is standing sort of straight out, isn't it? And slipping its big pink head out of its hood. A cold shower? Mariana suggested. Pure thoughts? Shower with you, Franklin said, untying his shoes. Two cold showers, Mariana said, and shall I make coffee, and why do I have a monkey for a brother? Is that him there, under the suds? Grit your teeth, Hugo said, cold rinse, needle spray. They both howled, falsetto and baritone. Nobody,

Franklin said, has dried me in ages. Lean over and I'll dry you next. Not only did your dick not wilt in the shower, Mariana said, but now the little shaver has his up, too. Lovely, said Hugo. Let's bounce the bedsprings, eat, and go to the river. I'll eat all the breakfast, Franklin said, and hide my eyes and think pure thoughts if my pizzle will let me.

28

I'll understand it, Mariana said. You too, but not him. Yes, said Hugo, but you have given me the bow of Hercules. Didn't need to give you his balls, Mariana said.

29

So Muggins came over here the first time to be sketched, Mariana said, and radiated charm from wall to wall? He was two hours late, Hugo said. I didn't recognize the sign at the time. He explained, when I asked him to, that he met somebody on the way he wanted to talk to. I'm listening, Mariana said. I'd made supper, which he picked at. He posed well enough, and I got two good drawings. We talked about all sorts of things over beer afterwards. He recited a poem, rather awful, but with expression.

30

In moments of sweet clarity, Hugo said, I doubt if we can communicate at all. You mean one thing, I hear another, benignly in banter, violently in an argument. But, said Mariana, we've never had an argument. Of course not, Hugo said, and don't intend to. I mean that human beings probably can't make each other understand what they mean. We have to get our meaning from art, from writing. That's awful, Mariana said.

31

Rutger barefoot on his shoulders, Anders stood, all the way to tiptoe. A fingerhold on the sill and Rutger monkeyed up the wall. A heave, and he was in Meg's room. He blew a kiss to Anders in the dark. Hours later he shinnied through his own window at NFS Grundtvig, feet wet with dew, in briefs only, hair tangled. Anders, Kim asleep in his arms cheek to cheek, woke and whispered *hi!* Rutger wrapped himself in a blanket and sat beside the bed. Came three juicy everlastingly sweet ballcramping times, on a pallet, as the bed sounds like a tin wheelbarrow loaded with kettles over cobbles, Meg's roommate obligingly away. Then, just as they were in the heaves and wild thumping of the third fuck, there was some species of Gorgon stalking the hall and opening doors. He'd just had time to pull on briefs and drop from the window. Passed a rabbit, he said, but I turned an ankle somewhere along the way and hopped the last fifteen or so meters. My feet are ruined forever.

Isn't it time for Nipper there to be decanted from your bed and sent home?
You look wonderful, Anders said, with your hair all a charming mess.

32

Meadows, Anders said. If I could write a poem it would be about a meadow.
A symphony, Kim said. Only music could get the feel of a meadow, I think.
Monet, Rutger said, painted lots of meadows, and Pissarro. Lots of painters.
Russians, Norwegians, they're good at meadows. So what do I say? Kim
asked, who had to write an essay on meadows. Sunday afternoon, Meg visiting her parents, they were walking in the long meadow that flowed speckled
with wildflowers and butterflies down from the knoll back of the wood to the
river. Us and those cows yonder, Anders said, we have the world to ourselves.
I love quiet. Be inventive: say the *long* quiet of a meadow, the green minty
grassy smell. They sat. Kim took off his shoes and socks. Kim's brown as a nut
all over, Anders said, the brownest he's ever been. Anders pulled off Kim's
jersey, standing over him and hauling it up inside out over rolling bony shoulders. Bare feet in clover and daisies, he said, I'll put that in. Wild strawber-
ries, chickweed, darnel, cowflop. He stood by caprice and doffed his britches.
Baby in his nappies, Rutger said. A sight, said Anders. Baby out of his nappies, Kim said, tossing his briefs in the air. See, Anders said, nutbrown all
over. You're going to have a cock, Rutger said. Why do we wear clothes, Kim
asked, when it feels so good to have air all over you? To keep people from
going crazy looking at you, Anders said.

33

I like my sandbar, Franklin said, like my river. Also Hugo's house all one
room and a big window in the roof. Sand on your dick and balls, Mariana
said, brushing. And, said Franklin, you and Hugo have come three times and
I've only come once. *Hejsa!* that feels yummy. This isn't icky? Hope not,
Hugo answered for her. But, said Franklin, his eyes squeezing closed, acute
pleasure making his fingers spread and his mouth a muzzle, when she lollies
your dick you're kissing her between the legs, and then you fuck. *Oh ho,*
Hugo said, sweet and slow. Hunch in, and you'll get a flutter of tongue-tip on
the backdrag. Warm and wet, Franklin said, and good. Me next, Hugo said.
Mariana shooed him away, smoothing hands up Franklin's thighs to his col-
larbones. Faunulus on the mossbank, Pastorella on her knees. The blithering
phone. *Hallo, jo.* Not really: an afternoon with friends. Love to, but can't.
Later, then, or another time. Bore's delight, the telephone. Going to come,
Franklin said. Coming! he sang. Figmilk, said Mariana, a nice skeet and a
fribble. What a blush! Hugo hefted him out of the chair and crushed him in
a hug. Bet you, he said, you can't come again, two handrunning, and then
we'll all be even, and start over.

34

His top lip jibbed out and tucked at the corners by baby fat, lively eyes speculative and fluttery by spells, Kim laughed at Anders's bashfulness. He was at the bus stop, as they'd agreed, in, as Anders said, the world's shortest pants, book satchel foolishly balanced on his head, coquettish looks out of the sides of his eyes. Anders slid his bike sideways right to his toes, radiant, breathless. Eyes met, but they said nothing. Kim on the seat holding him by the waist, Anders biked off down the macadam road that went through the woods. Only when they'd reached the beech copse with high ferns and moss clearing did Anders say, And how was school? Just school, Kim said. We're going to have sensitivity classes, so we'll be aware of our bodies, and our space, this teacher, she's a woman, said, I think her name is Miss Pumpkin or Squash or Beanvine. Girls have boney hips, do you know? I'm going to like geography and in Danish we have to learn some kind of dumb poem about Iceland. Are we going to take our pants off? I guess I was feeling my peter through my pants when we were standing around, because teacher frowned and shook her head. Did you jack off last night? But yes, Anders said, and yesterday afternoon, and a long time at both. It's out here somewhere that Rutger fucks Meg into fits. Have you fucked girls? Kim asked.

35

Well, she said, you're crazy. Some crazies are a misery to themselves, and some a nuisance to the world, but you've figured out a shipshape Calvinist glitch-free craziness in absolute kilter, so that your eyes fly open at six, you hit the floor like an Olympic champion, hard-on and all, jump into a dinky pair of shorts, jog three kilometers, swim ten lengths of the gym pool, nip back here for wheatgerm carrot smush while reading Greek, communing with your charming freckle-nosed *kammerat* Jesus, shower with unreasonable thoroughness while singing hymns, dress in a French shirt and American tie, English jacket and experienced jeans that show how horsily you're hung, teach your classes, Latin, gym, and Greek, meet me, pretend you're interested in what I've done while eating me with your eyes, bring me here for wiggling sixtynine on the bed, tongue like an eel, melt my brain, fuck me simpleminded, race off and instruct your Boy Scouts in virtue, knots, and nutritive weeds, sprint back here, fuck me into a fit, teach me English while fixing supper, show me slides of Monet and Montaigne, fuck me again, walk me home, make eyes at Franklin, come back and read two books at once, say your prayers, jack off for an hour, and sleep like a lambkin. It isn't bright, you know.

36

Gustav, said Mariana on her back in clover and daisies, chewing a leaf of mint, big brown eyes, thatch of hair always washed and feathery. Handful of balls and a stout stubby dick. And Jorgen his buddy, blond as a duckling, long all over, long chin, long forehead, long legs, long peter, big feet. Stammered something horrendous. Gustav finished his sentences for him. We had a rabbit hole of a place, cozy inside under brambles. Crawled in on hands and knees. A snuggery of great privacy, though a bit crowded with the three of us. And from the military academy across the way, Hjalmar, who rammed and grunted and was fitted out like the assistant classics master at NFS Grundtvig, or a horse.

37

In Argentina, Anders said, they arrest people who have read Einstein, torture them with electric shocks through the dick or cunt, and drop them while they're still alive from a helicopter into a marsh outside Buenos Aires. They're doing this *now*, forty years after Buchenwald. A Russian truck driver has just been arrested for owning a copy of the poet Mandelstam printed in the west, and given seven years lard labor in Siberia. Einstein! He was a Jew, you see, and the church tells the fat-necked military that his physics threatens to undermine belief. The USA has enough atomic bombs to blow the planet into orbiting rubble. And all these bullies want to idiotize us into thinking of all affection except that decreed by the state as immoral. Pigs, Kim said. Anders said: Don't insult pigs.

38

Tom Agernkop, strand of hair across an eye, signaled Anders with a look and confirming nod. So Anders followed him to the far edge of the soccer field. You saw us, Tom said, picking a blade of grass and chewing it, Lemuel and me, hugging in the shower. Anders shrugged. Your business entirely, he said. Who've you told? Nobody. What's to tell? Rutger my roommate, maybe. A mouthbreather, Tom. Meaty upper lip, Greek nose, honest eyes. Look, it's fine by me, Anders said. Nothing scary about it. You love each other. Tom grunted, squeezed his crotch, flipped his hair out of his eyes, talked. It just happened, he signed. It's very good, tender, exciting. It's terrific to be so close to him. We're each other, you know? And he's so fucking good-looking and good-natured. We were real dimwits, at first, hot blushes and cold feet. That was dumb. Now, though, we're out to love each other into feeblemindedness, like maybe they'll have to carry us limp to a home, with permanent smiles on our faces. You're giving me ideas, Anders said, and also a hard-on. *Gud!* Can I tell Lemuel? Who is it? Let me ask him before I tell you, OK? But absolutely, Tom said. Lucky, whoever he is.

39

The housemaster Holger Sigurjonsson with Pascal in tow looked in by way of bedcheck, Rutger towelling his hair, Anders writing in his journal. Pascal, seven-eighths naked and slender as a greyhound, grubbing at the pod of his briefs, broke off his discourse on trilobites and the planet Mars to inspect the girls on Rutger's wall. How goes it, you two? the housemaster said to give Pascal his fill of the pictures. *Tosset!* Anders said, standing to thumb down his briefs. Rimbaud in French, Mimnermos in Greek, and gametophytes in botany. What's this girl doing? Pascal asked. O the infants around this place! Rutger said. She's whiffling her *kildrer* and coming like Beethoven's *niende.* What did you think she was doing? Got me, Pascal said, I'm cryptogonadal still. Iceland, Middelhavet, and Bornholm, he said of three maps on Anders's wall, and you, Anders, stark naked. Is that your blue grizzly tent? *Hej!* that's Kim Eglund with you. He's neat. Fellow baby, said Rutger. Who are these kids with their peepees standing out? Swedes, Anders said, riffling Pascal's hayrick hair. With it, the housemaster said. Come on, Pascal. OK, Boss, Pascal said, trying to read a bit of Anders's journal while being herded out by Rutger.

40

The disk of the Medusae is as truly an abactinal structure as the calyx of the Crinoids. As in all Discophorae, the substance of the disk is a gelatinous mass, consisting of immense cells, the caudate prolongations of which traverse it in different directions, assuming the appearance of flat muscular fibres. But this appearance is deceptive, and the substance of the disk does not, in reality, contain distinct muscles, though it is highly contractile, especially in the thinner part of the margin. Its movements are owing to the structure of the lower floor. The amount of water contained in the tissue of the disk is truly extraordinary. A specimen, weighing thirty-five pounds, exposed to evaporation, left a viscous mass, chiefly composed of common salt, showing the water to be common seawater. The salt having been washed out with fresh water, and the organic substance dried simply in the sun, weighed less than an ounce. For all its pellucid grace and unearthly subtlety of curtained tentacles and hyaline genitalia in radial clusters on a cincture, the Cyanea jellyfish is little more than organized water.

41

Owl call low and clear after bedcheck and lights out. Rutger said, There's your boyo. Quit looking like a calf that's lost its mama and haul him in through the window. Skinned a knee, Kim whispered after he'd been hugged hard and was shucking his briefs, but the rope works fine. He stripped in moonlight, Anders lifting the sheet for him to skittle into bed. Let's see the knee, Rutger said. I've got iodine. A hard-on already. That's the spirit. Yee-ouch! Like don't pour the whole bottle on, Rutger friend, huh? Keep the bedclothes over you, Rutger said, tucking them in and mussing Kim's hair, so that I don't get ideas or a skeet of sperm in my eye. Love good. Did you, Kim asked, do it with Meg this afternoon? Twice, Rutger said. With our jeans under her butt in the ferns, after the foreplay of the century, talk about fine tuning. I hear snurfling, I hear Kim sighing. We love you too, Rutger, Kim said.

42
So, said Hugo, Tom. Come in: timing's perfect. I've come at a bad time. Tom said with a robin's hop of blinks and rueful smile. Not a bit of it, Hugo said pulling on denim shorts and combing his hair with his fingers. My Mariana and I were just getting out of the sack when you knocked. Hi! said Mariana shoving her arms into Hugo's shirt, modern times and all that. You've seen scads of stitchless girls before, and maybe one or two in hr. Tvemunding's bed. I couldn't be the first. Tom, uneasy but boldly shy, sheep snarls in the silkfloss hanks of his rascal hair, his scruffy shirt parting at the shoulder seams, tail out in one side, shuffled, forced his big hands into the pockets of his jeans shorts, looked hacked, and sat with a bounce when Hugo pushed him into a chair. Here, said Mariana, *pariser* leftbank intellectual coffee with four sugarcubes in it, did I guess right? *Mange tak*, said Tom. So? Hugo said, you look demented. When, said Tom, can I come back? Right now, Hugo said. Frøken Landarbejder, besides being the soul of discretion, will probably understand you better than I. If that's the way you want it, hr. Tvemunding, Tom said, miffed. Tom! Hugo said, relax eh? We're all friends. Some of us, Lemuel and I and a few more, want to start a club for friends who love each other, and we need a faculty sponsor with balls and a very broad mind, Tom said. Our part in the Revolution, you know. Revolution, Hugo said, ah yes, the Revolution. Sounds wild, Mariana said. Explain it all.

43
Anders had sat cockminded through the dullest English class of the century, besotted with Kim's grubby sneakers that made his feet too big, like a puppy's outsized paws, socks, dinky short pants, net brief with their narrow mid-seamed cotton panel in front, his toes, legs, the celts of his knees, his springy supple peter growing like a weed. Gym, its perfunctions. Lunch, raisin pudding yet again. A wink from Tom. Kim, brash devil, scrunched the crotch of his snippety jeans shorts as Anders reached the bus stop on his bike. The high ferns, spackle light and green shadow through the beeches, Kim tumbling down his briefs and into Anders's hug, they breathed in the same measure, rubbing noses, grazing lips, touching tonguetips. You're crazy, you know,

Kim whispered, but you've got to stay crazy. I know, Anders said. Even before lights out last night, I began jacking off, to keep our afternoon yesterday in my head, some of which I told Rutger, and kept it up, and didn't see any point in quitting. So it rained sperm all night on my side of the room. I got a second wind toward sunrise, a fever in my dick, my balls sore, but your eyes looking sideways, like now, kept me going. Toes, smile, knees.

44
Quick, Rutger said, standing to slip off his briefs. Our keeper and Chipmunk. Check, said Anders, whippering his dick to a lolling halfminded erection. *Pok pok pok!* Pascal was saying as he spun in, turning on his heels, the explorer craft from outer space, *swoosh*, has come to bed check, where are we? Ah yes, Rutger and Anders. Commander Sigurjonsson! Hi boys, said the housemaster. O wow! said Pascal, new pictures. On Rutger's wall an athletic youngster fucking a deliciously shapely girl whose enthusiasm was unqualified, on Ander's a towheaded skyblue-eyed summerbronzed naked adolescent with a lucky penis and plump scrotum. Pascal flicking his fingers on his ribs, inspected both. The housemaster sighed. Rutger leaned in a long stretch from his chair, caught Pascal by the hips, turned him around, and yanked down his piffling underpants. Just looking, he said. I'm slow, Pascal said. You should help it along, Rutger said, forefinger and thumb. In moderation, the housemaster said, looking troubled. Show me, said Pascal. You have the highest IQ in all of NFS Grundtvig, Rutger said, and don't know how to play with your peter? It's retarded, Pascal said.

45
What I didn't know, *stor* Hugo, Mariana said, was what a hideaway from the world your place is. Freedom itself, Hugo said, nidge away, sweet girl. She'd turned up bushed, with Franklin, pitched her jeans across the room, flopped into the big reading chair, nudged down her flimsy underpants, and begun to quiddle her *kildrer*, to jolt off the kicker she'd been playing toward all day. Woke up horny, she said, worked it to a buzz, and then off and on, two minutes here and five there, a sweet shiver and a tickly ripple. Franklin, Hugo's scout hat over his ears and eyes, was trying to crack limbs for kindling over his knee like Hugo, who was laying a fire before which they were to eat. Sitting on the floor, Franklin said with approval, all beside each other, sandwiches and milk and pickles. But first, Spejder Franklin, I must hug and kiss Mariana awhile, and get hugged and kissed. Why don't you see how much more firewood you can pick up over beyond the soccer field? Can I wear your hat? Absolutely, Hugo said. Let me tighten the strap and tie your shoe.

46

OK, said Franklin, two armloads of firewood. Admirable spadger, Hugo said. Your smart generous pretty sexy sweet sister says we can fall upon our supper, soon as I light the fire and lay things out, or you can have your dink jiggled to your heart's content, so you won't feel left out, *jo?* Franklin, Mariana said, is the only little brother in the world who can fake a blush and say *honest?* with such innocence. What he means, Hugo said pulling on a sweater and hooking his briefs off the floor with a toe, is that he chooses to grub by the fire. Not really, Franklin said. O yes, but really, Mariana said, throwing cushions toward the hearth. Nothing like both, Hugo said. Fire's catching good. Mariana laying out plates and glasses, Hugo fetching eats. Franklin wriggled down his pants, which would not then go over his shoes. Hugo obligingly unlaced them, pried them off socks and all, and made a neat stack of shoes, socks, pants, and underpants beside Franklin. Nice pinkish-brown peter, he said. As soon as Franklin comes, Mariana said, he starts over. Mouth full of pressed veal and orange slices, Franklin grumped contentedly, stripped his foreskin back, and drank deep from his milk. Plop him between us, Mariana said, and we'll take time about. Did you fuck good? Franklin asked politely. Mariana leaned around and kissed him on the nose, which wrinkled.

47

This place, Meg said, could use a broom driven by a strong and busy elbow, and a mop, and all the windows open the whole of a breezy day. What it really needs, Rutger said, is two mattresses lifted in the old Danish manner from the supply room. My knees survived the sand last summer, and forest-floor grit, moss, sticks, and boulder rubble, but these pine planks are going to sandpaper them raw. They'd unfolded and laid out a sail, the area of which brought them chummily together, so that Meg, thoroughly fucked and wrung limp by a whalloping sweet orgasm, could reach over and muss Kim's hair and tickle the back of his neck. Modesty, she'd said when they were undressing, sort of has to be dispensed with, *jo?* Kim, pulling his jersey over his head with his back to her while Anders untied his sneakers and slid down his briefs, did a military about-face, with eyes shut and a broad smile. O what a charming pink blush! she said, pulling him into a hug. Timidly he hugged back, and then hugged warmly, with a kiss for her nose. She returned the kiss on his navel, and gave him up to Anders's claiming arms.

48

If you put it that way, Hugo said, then yes I was a fool. But it pleased me to be a fool. In the dark you learn by bumping into things. But, Mariana said, he knew what you would bump into. He knew what would hurt you. I taught him, all unknowing, Hugo said, how to hurt me. That turned out to be his style: to listen in silence and a mask of charming innocence, and lay in wait. Because that's all he had: the power to hurt. Don't ask me why. It's a gratuitous meanness that's everywhere nowadays. In people without character, it's a passive vindictiveness. They are too lazy and unmotivated to be evil actively, that's too much trouble for the drifting will. But if opportunity puts anything alive in their path, they kill it, for the idle sport of it. To care about anything is a threat to their slothful passivity, so carelessness becomes the only plan you can see in their liquid will. If you encounter a flower bed, trample it. It's the casualness of their hate that's so discouraging. No, Mariana said, it's the difference. What you say is true, but what makes you hurt inside is how different this trashy kid is from everything that's familiar to you. You give people things, and this kid smilingly accepted what you gave him and smashed it with his foot before your eyes.

49

What we have, Hugo said, is an unfinished room with good proportions and pleasant light once we wash these windows as clean and bright as Perrier water, no other NFS Grundtvig clubroom will be half so spiffy modern. We can sandpaper the floor to a plain Shakerish natural finish. Composition boards for walls. Let's paint everything white overhead except the rafters, which want to be Mondriaan Red, *jo?* on the uprights and Sailor Suit Blue on the beams. What else do we want? No chairs, Tom said, but maybe a table? A bookshelf, posters, slogans painted right onto the composition board. Danish Spartan it all needs to be. OK, Hugo said, let's see it with work, then. Lemuel'll be here in a bit, Tom said, and Kim and Anders later. Composition board to be delivered tomorrow. So let's sweep and scrub and haul junk out and cancel cobwebs. We want the outside stairs painted, too, and the door. Danish Blue. Light bulbs, a journal for minutes, paint, sandpaper, Windex, rags, detergent, a pail, hard brushes, hammers, nails, a roll of white gummed stripping. Ho, Anders! Ho, Kim! With brooms. And Rutger! I like cleaning things Rutger said. Don't get ideas. I'm here as an enemy of dust and a lover of straight lines and clean surfaces.

50

God knew exactly where he lived. In among all those warehouses and dockside pubs. The school had his mother's address only, and she had no phone. My feelings were hurt, I suppose: snubbed. But that was an afterthought. I was anxious, befuddled. What I discovered two days later was that he had simply forgotten. He'd run into an old friend that Wednesday afternoon that he was to move in, when I was to make the effort to do something about him, give him a home, feed him, make a close friend of him. When I finally saw him, he grinned nonchalantly. He was, he said, thinking about my offer to take him in. Why had he not called or signalled for two days? I said, Look. People don't act like this. O I'm a shit, he said. Besides, your kind of structured middleclass life is not mine. It's against my Buddhist principles to live on a schedule. Your Buddhist principles! These, it turned out, he'd acquired from McTaggart's Transcendental Meditation Group, which he'd twice attended. McTaggart is one of the English masters, and has his group. He talks a lot of bilge which, because of its gaseous vagueness, appeals to the feebleminded, ladies from town, slobs, prigs, and nonstarters of all sorts. A free spirit, said my Bicycle Rider, blows about like a leaf in the wind.

51

Tidsskriftet Hermes. Ih! Letters from Oskar and Papa. *Nature, Arkæologi,* Haydn's *Mass in Time of War,* hollyhocks, a sermon on responsiveness, a twinge of rheumatism, and some jolly good damson preserves. Oskar into the antinuke protests, a salt-free diet, and a Swedish girl's knickers. A cycling-capped blond *purk,* alert blue eyes, *pik* dangling through his open jeans, smiled a cocky grin from the cover of *Hermes. Meget vel!* Hugo said to himself of a *15årig* inside, *splitternøgen* and healthy as a horse, heel of right thumb along shaft of distended penis, ball of thumb on glans, fingers curled underneath and partly around, face faunish, nose pert, eyebrows arched, feathery eyelashes lowered in gaze at penis, at least 18 cm, foreskin rolled back of glans in a fat wet crumpled ruck, the thick stalk ridged with callopy wales branched over by a relief of veins, glans in snubby profile glossy with a slick of bulbourethral drool. On his bike, with a buddy. And, three pages along, wilted and content on a sleeping bag on a forest floor, he gazes amiably, with a nacreous splash beside his left nipple, a milky spatter across his midriff, and a puddle of cloudy egg white on his abdomen, with runnels into his scant crimp of pubic hair and into his navel.

52

If the Angraecum in its native forests secretes more nectar than did the vigorous plants sent me by Mr. Bateman, so that the nectary ever becomes filled, small moths might obtain their share, but they would not benefit the plant. The pollinia would not be withdrawn until some huge moth, and with a wonderfully long proboscis, tried to drain the last drop. If such great moths were to become extinct in Madagascar, assuredly the Angraecum would become extinct. On the other hand, as the nectar, at least in the lower part of the nectary, is stored safe from the depredation of other insects, the extinction of the Angraecum would probably be a serious loss to these moths. We can thus understand how the astonishing length of the nectary had been acquired by successive modifications. As certain moths of Madagascar became larger through natural selection in relation to their general conditions of life, either in the larval or mature state, or as the proboscis alone was lengthened to obtain honey from the Angraecum, those orchids which compelled the moths to insert their proboscides up to the very base would be best fertilized.

53

Kim, the blue bill of his red cycling cap turned up, and Tom, his amiably mussed hair brilliant under the steep pitch of Hugo's skylight, sat on the bed. Anders, hugging his knees, and Hugo, holding his elbows, head down, listening, agreeing with nods and doubting with his shoulders, sat on the floor. Lemuel, thumbs in the belt loops of his short pants, stood and talked. As I see it, he said, we'll be just another school club like Botany, Greenpeace, or Hiking. Hr. Tvemunding is, *Gud være lovet*, our faculty sponsor. Hugo, said Hugo. In class, in the gym, in the quad, hr. Tvemunding, but in the fellowship of the club, Hugo, please. And before we proceed, let's do what I have my scouts do, all of us hug each other. Us too! said Mariana, arriving with Franklin. Mariana and Hugo with tongues in each other's mouths, Mariana and Anders with an awkward squeeze, Mariana and Kim friendlily, Mariana and Lemuel warmly, Mariana and Tom sweetly, Mariana and Franklin with a kiss bravely consented to and wiped off. Hugo and Anders robustly, with a soldierly kiss on the cheek, Hugo and Kim timidly but repeated boldly, Hugo and Lemuel tightly, Hugo and Tom sexily, Hugo and Franklin (when caught) recklessly, with squeals.

54

Anders and Kim chastely, nubbling noses, until a *nej hør nu* from Tom, whereupon they kissed with closed eyes and roaming hands, Anders and Lemuel, spiritedly, Anders and Tom, brashly, Anders and Franklin audaciously. Kim and Lemuel confidently, Kim and Tom with madcap indiscretion, Kim and Franklin impishly, prodding each other's crotches. Lemuel and Tom with easy affection, Lemuel and Franklin outrageously, with hoots and promiscuous kisses and tickles and goosings and a roll across the floor. Tom joined in, capturing Franklin from Lemuel, who captured him back, with the loss of a sneaker. His jersey ruckled to his chin and his britches half off, Franklin, howling that he was being kissed to death, wrenched a gym shoe off Lemuel and tugged Tom's shirt over his face. *Oh ho!* Lemuel hooted, pinning Franklin in a hug while Tom deprived him of his britches, and on second thought, unzipped and hauled off Lemuel's, too. Us against him! said Lemuel to Franklin, and they threw Tom and debreeched and deshirted him.

55

Pentstemon Glaber, Pursh. Very glabrous, leaves usually glaucous, sessile, entire, the cauline lanceolate or ovate-lanceolate. Flowers large, in a thyrsoid panicle, sepals broadly ovate, submembranous upon the margin, obtuse or more or less pointed. Corolla bright purple, widely dilated above, the limb shortly two-lobed, with the lobes rounded and spreading equally. Anthers loosely hairy or glabrous, the divaricate cells dehiscent from the base nearly to the summit, but not expanded. Sterile filament short and hirsute towards the apex, or glabrous. Specimens accord nearly with Var. *Occidentalis* Gray (*P. speciosus*, Dougl.), having the numerous violet-purple flowers an inch or more in length. Washington Territory (Douglas) and Nevada (Beckwith, Stretch). Frequent in the valleys and foothills from the Trinity to the Havallah Mountains, Nevada, 5 to 7000 feet altitude, May-June. Var. *Utahensis*. Stems straight and slender, cauline leaves long, oblanceolate, tapering to the clasping base, sepals ovate-acuminate, not at all membranous, anthers and sterile filament hirsute.

56

Stitch of bronze midges over daisies, bees working wild hyacinths, butterflies yellow and white nuzzling clover at the meadow's edge, Kim and Anders glistening wet rolled their shoulders and stretched like limbering gymnasts to dry in the hot light and sweet air from the river. Lovely, hr. Sigurjonsson called from the spit, joining them with Pascal astride his shoulders, a skinny *basunengel* whose wet eyelashes gave a look of wild freshness to his teasing gaze. You're like the picture in your room, Anders, he said, you and Kim on that beach. That was last summer, Anders said, when we became friends. And, the housemaster said, you've been fast friends ever since. Jacobsen says, I believe in *Niels Lyhne*, that the tenderest and noblest affection is that of boys for each other. It is both warm and shy, not quite daring to show itself with a hug, a glance, or in words. It's all tacit, reluctant, anxious. Beautifully, it is a fusion of admiration, selfless generosity, loyalty, and a great quiet happiness. Got it in one, said Anders, sliding his arm across Kim's shoulders, Kim an arm across his. *Opkastig*, said Pascal. Do that again. Whereupon the housemaster lifted Pascal down and lay in the sun on the spit. *Sludder*, said Pascal, and bosh. Pascal, said the housemaster, don't be a snob.

57

Guess what, Mariana said. Mom was out for the night with her friend the toothbrush moustache and I was reading a bit before dropping off. *Unge hr*. Franklin was mucking around with the stamps and album you gave him, like a lamb in clover, and then here he was in nothing but his nightshirt and best cherub's grin, climbing into bed with me. So what the heck. A hug is a hug, and the essential differences in anatomy that he explored by hand come under the heading of education. The little devil, Hugo said. And then what did you do? Explored back, she said, and jacked him off thoroughly, but not so thoroughly that he didn't repeat the pleasure while I hugged him, with the odd kiss on the cheek or a nice puff in his hair. And then we fell asleep. He's comfortable to have in bed, and smells good. He acted grown-up this morning, and kept offering me things at breakfast, as polite as if feeling his sister's breasts had civilized him more than all the shouting at him I've done over the years. Perhaps we've discovered something? He also said, though it's not the first time, that he thinks you're great, and wonders if you like him as much as he likes you. Of course I like Franklin, Hugo said, he's our Cupid.

58

Meadow flowers, Kim said, hard yellow buttons, white stars, blue bells tight against stalks, pinks and purples. Nations of gnats, mists of midges sawing through the air. Are you enlisting nature to excite your dick? Rutger asked. He lay drowsy and shirtless beside Anders. *Mna*, Kim said, my hand strays when I'm bare-assed. It is, now that you mention it, feeling good. Anders beckoned him with a crooked finger. *Akja*, Rutger said, our *englebarn* is going to sprinkle the meadow with his own personal dribble, three whole drops. Kim crawled between them, flopped on his back, nestling his head on Anders's shoulder, sprawling his spread legs over theirs. He gawked at Rutger eye to eye, and at Anders, who licked the tip of his nose. Sunday afternoon in the middle of the meadow, he said to the sky. Rutger slid his hand down Kim's abdomen, nipped his penis between two fingers, and played it in a wobble. *Hejsa!* Anders said. Cool it, Rutger said, I'm only being friendly, though it's interesting that my prick seems to be making an unseemly display of its manly size. Woof! said Kim, you're good. I'm blushing, Anders said. Rutger sat up, for better purchase. When it's feeling really lovely, he said, Anders can take over. What a happy grin. Rutger, Kim said, is our best friend, isn't he, Anders?

59

The Bicycle Rider was as unresponsive as God. The young are in their own minds immortal, and assume Olympian indifference to their own deaths. They die drunk on dormitory floors, in automobile wrecks, hundreds a day, on futile battlefields, needles under their tongues, in their arms, in epileptic seizures for want of a fix, but this violent and pitiful mortality does not disturb their liquid minds any more than the screams of the dying at Waterloo caught the attention of the geese in the sky above them.

60

Neither *la poussière olympique* nor the waters of Galilee had touched him. He partook of nothing Hugo could eventually recognize. He had found a new way to be inhuman. His face, a harmony of Scandinavian lines and Slavic planes, gave no hint of his addiction to lysergic acid, from age twelve, or of his cold hatred of his family, of his delight to hurt.

61

He was thinking, he said out of the blue the last time he was here to pose, of laying off the acid for awhile. He'd had forty-one hits in the previous five weeks, thirty in the past three. Indulgence, yes, he said, but not indulgence carried to the extreme. Lysergic acid diethylamide, a wheat smut that corrodes synapses in the brain while binding with its tissues, causing the delusions of dementia praecox. Using it is deliberately simulating a senile deterioration of the mind. The pushers on Nordkalksten cut it with strychnine, and with speed. He was willing to endure stomach cramps that bit his guts for days to have these waking bad dreams that he called mind-expanding. *Shit* was what I said. What else, said Mariana, was there to say?

62

He would come home through the vicious traffic of Nordkalksten on his bicycle, carry it up back stairs in an alley. A hovel, when I saw it. Trash everywhere. Britchesless, for the acid was his sex, he would melt a tab of the acid under his tongue, whacking off, beginning to see the world through a tacky snow of purple and silver flakes, lines bending, volumes swelling and diminishing, all colors mixing with yellow. There was a feeling of grand euphoria, of well-being, of success, of being immensely clever and wise and at peace. Drunk, said Mariana. Drunk is drunk.

63

Pallets, said Tom. *Akjo*, pallets. Aren't they neat? Yes, said Hugo, but where did they come from? Well, said Tom, you know Asgar Thomsen, third year thickshock cornblond gymnast type? And you know Elsa, works in the kitchen, fifteen or sixteen, with the stickup breasts and sliding eyes? Well, those two fuck their brains out in the laundry room, never miss a day. Elsa knows where all sorts of things are, like a stash of gear from when NFS Grundtvig ran a nursery, and these pallets are from that, nippers' naptime pallets. They fold up Japanese tidy. Elsa, eh? *Jo*, Tom said. Asgar says she's great. She loves giving wee boys their first pussy, and is a good teacher, and likes five or six at a go, but her soft spot is for big Asgar. God knows what goes on at this school, Hugo said. Let's hand the Otto Meyer here, with the Hajo Ortil, what say? North and South. Swiss Boy Scouts in a summer meadow all daisies, lots of skinny brown legs, three bare butts, two thumb-sized dicks. Norwegian Scouts in Sicily, one of Ortil's expeditions of *teutonsk* youngsters big and little. Greek boy with hoop and rooster in the middle. Posters coming from Düsseldorf, Tom said. Anders's doing, that. Radical Left rights-of-kids' stuff. Wide-eyed German idealism.

64

Tjajkovskij, said Mariana, pulling off a tall sock. I can listen to him. Teach me English. And French. What's the good of getting laid by a teacher, never mind one with shoulders like the Stock Exchange and a peter like a pony, if I don't learn something. *Kiss*, he said, and demonstrated. *Kiss on the tit*. Plural, *tits*. You're slurpy wet, Hugo observed. Because, she said, I was playing with myself waiting for you. Passed out twice. It depraves Franklin, who wiggles out his grub and whisks it to a blur, great egg-beating technique.

65

He was, the Bicycle Rider, trying to feel. That's what makes your hair stand up on your head. Trying to feel. What began with some jaded old fools, Aldous Huxley, a giggling British neurotic, moral idiots like Burroughs and the poet Ginsberg, and the shit-for-brains Timothy Leary, what began for them as a desperate attempt to feel something, anything at all I suppose, became an initiation of the young into feeling. Young who had not yet felt love or wonder or surprise or the use of their minds learning math or Greek or history took their little trips on acid. Death, of course, is something that happens to other people. To talk crazy and act crazy is chic.

66

Nose like a buck hare, said Hugo. Square toes. Eyes slyly sweet and sweetly sly. Hugo, liking the world, was an accurate draughtsman. Franklin sat on a chair, elf naked. You see? said Mariana, there's nothing to it. If you get the giggles, you get the giggles. Hugo can wait. You can kick your heels when he's drawing your face, and roll your head like a moron when he's drawing your feet. I'll tell you what to keep still. What you going to do with the picture? Franklin asked. Look at it when I need to throw up, Hugo said. *O Gud!* Mariana said, the giggles. It's going to be a good painting.

67

This. He told me. One day in class, listening to me lecture on Greek myth, his mind was following but it was also anticipating jacking off while stoned later that afternoon. LSD, you know, binds with the brain and is a permanent chemical activity of it. It volunteers hits weeks after you've had any of it. It rarely volunteers the euphoria of good trips, preferring nightmares. So the satyr's leer in his gray eyes changed suddenly to cold fear. He was, while still hearing me on the bow of Herakles, facing a classmate who has hit him, cutting his lip, unsocketing a tooth that bleeds salty and hot. He must swallow the blood and try to focus his courage and twining eyesight, neither cooperating, and then a surge of desire drenches his balls and tingles in his lifting glans. He holds back a wave of nausea. The loose tooth bleeds freely. The taste of blood sickens him. He must jack off. He can't trust himself to stand and leave the classroom. His bowels seem to have a knife through them, cutting. He'll walk into the wall. The bully who hit him stands nose to nose whispering insults. Fairy, cocksucker, flit. His throat is full of blood. Sissy, morphadite, jerker off. If he could get to the hall, he could puke there, green phlegm that the acid makes. He could jack off in the hall, fuck who'd see him. With acid time is elastic. Class would last another four hours. Or two seconds. And all I saw was a handsome Scandinavian face with a charming vagueness in the eyes.

68

Something's in there hurting, Mariana said, pushing into Hugo's chest with both hands. Something that needs to be healed. You're doing it, Hugo said, holding her close. Let me tell you this, and we won't mention the Bicycle Rider again, *jo?* I made the one last attempt to make friends with him, to show him a world he could see and feel and live in once he'd got his head out of his ass. I found out where he lived, even went there twice, and I wrote him a letter offering to take him along on a visit I'd planned to Paris, my favorite city. I'd pay for everything. All he had to do was come along. No answer to my letter. I ran into him (he had no phone, naturally) one day a week later and asked him, with some annoyance, if he'd got my letter. O yeah, man, he said, airily. That's great. Paris, France! You're a good man, you know. Denmark was such a backward hole of a country. He'd always longed to see Paris. He would go with me, and split when we got there, and he'd meet me for coming back. I didn't believe my ears.

69

In our time Apollo is sound asleep.

70

You have been my best teacher, he said. I'd love to take your inhibitions away from you. My inhibitions! You're not free, man. We had a wild talk. He had made me mad, confused me. So I'm a shithead, he said. What's that got to do with anything? A good exchange of name-calling cleared the air. Generosity, I can see looking back, was simply not in him. He'd put the worst construction on all my friendliness, and now that I knew he was on dope I felt a kind of mission to save him. I insisted that he come to Paris. We would look, walk, see all the beautiful city. I would get him out of himself, his head out of his ass. He would see. I showed him slides, books. He agreed to go. I gave him a big hug, and he froze, saying that he wasn't used to affection. So what happened? Mariana asked. Nothing, said Hugo. We met a few times, always by accident, as he would never turn up when he would say he would, made plans. I was to meet him here and we'd go together to the train station. He never came.

71

I went over to his place after going to the train station to see if the white-trash slut might have decided to meet me there. These neosixties young imagine that you know what they're thinking, and can't be bothered to tell you. I found him eating cold mashed potatoes and rice in a dirty bowl. He was naked except for a hospital gown, the kind they put on you for surgery. Hi, he said. He was eating with his fingers. Where the hell were you! I shouted at him. Man, I feel good, he said. Don't shout at me. I had this cold clot in my brain but I'm melting it out, you know? All I know, I said, is that you were to meet me at nine. Why didn't you, where were you, what the fuck do you mean by all this? I'm unstructured, man, he said. I'll go to your crazy Paris with you, but not today. I've got to decide for myself when I want to go. I'll let you know. Do that, I said sweetly, and left.

72

Magnus, one of my Scouts, said Hugo of a boy whose hair, blond as a lamb, curled in swashes and scrolls over his forehead. Pectorals in robust definition, he was otherwise as lean as a whippet. Hi, Mariana said, you're pretty. Don't dress on my account. Micro undies are more than I usually see on Grundtviggers. Look, Magnus, Hugo said, even though you're blushing already and going miserable again, I'm going to lay your problem out for my Mariana, sweetest of women. It'll do you wonders. All ears, said Mariana, if there's a stray orange juice, coffee, and roll about. Greengage jam and fresh butter too, Hugo said. We've just been glupping it. Magnus here, stout chap, turned up last night in the grips of a crisis. Beat around the bush, he did, for the longest, and then scared me witless by pitching right out of his chair in a roll, onto the floor, where he bawled like a baby. Wow, said Mariana. Puberty, Hugo said strolling about and stretching, good old puberty. And, as more than likely, our balls charged with manly juices and our unruly cock made our heart tick *allegro* and hanker to hug somebody and be hugged. Oof! and sweet Magnus had tied himself into knots because it's his own gender he likes. I'm horrified, Mariana said, and think I'll faint. You see? Hugo said. She's going to barf.

73

So Magnus and I talked for hours. I called his folks and said it was too late for him to walk home and that I'd put him up for the night. Heard that one, Mariana said. Please, Hugo said. And *ho!* here's Tom. Mariana Sweety Pie, Tom said, giving her a kiss. What's all this about, Hugo? I got your note. Magnus Pennystykke, said Hugo, Tom Agernkop: be friends. Magnus is a Spartan, and a little confused. You and Lemuel might, good fellow that you are, show him how friendship works. Don't you have a buddy? Tom asked. We have a club. It's in pairs. What's fun, Mariana said, is two big rascals like Tom and Lemuel hugging like bears and kissing like puppies. Imprinting, it's called. Sex, said Tom. Love, said Hugo. All of the above, Mariana said.

74

For the clubhouse, two large photographs, gift of Hugo: Brancusi's *The Kiss*, which Tom named "The Smooching Boxes," and Picasso's *Tête d'une Femme* in the churchyard of St. Germain des Près, his tribute to Guillaume Apollinaire. He had bought them to flank his *Héraclès archer* but thought they belonged on the walls of the clubhouse, offering a prize for the best paper on why they were appropriate.

75

Tom's beautiful, said Lemuel. See how his neck fits into the muscles of the collarbone and shoulder triangle, and those dogleg lines from hip to dick, they're neat. What if Tvemunding likes boys? He's always talking about ancient Greek sentimental loyalties, as he calls them, and then there're his Scouts, but next he's off on Jesus and Sankt Paul, and he has that dark-haired girl he's most certainly fucking. So? said Anders, why can't he like both, love both? I like girls, but right now don't love one. I love hr. Kim here. If you don't love somebody, you end up loving yourself, or hating yourself because you're afraid to love, or because you're scared to. People are hysterical about sex, anyway.

76

This, O Bicycle Rider. That the acid, which binds itself with the fatty tissues of the brain, may have displaced you altogether. When you showed no interest in taking our trip to France, I was up the good part of a night trying to answer why a young man would prefer the roach kingdoms of Nordkalksten to the bright avenues and parks of Paris. What I arrived at is that you can no longer feel anything without this damnable LSD, and that what you've been reinforcing with it (cowardly evading God knows what)—sex, I suppose, as that's all you've told me about—has been wholly replaced by chemically induced neural hallucinations, so that what you think is sex (or reflection, or thought) is only LSD, or marijuana, or the cocaine you say you want to come by if only you can. That is, you limply decline so rich an experience as France because you know that you cannot feel it, cannot observe it: you can only take this diabolic acid along, and feel that. You have built a wall of concrete shit between yourself and reality. This you call sensory enhancement: it is sensory deprivation. You call it mind-expanding: it shrivels the mind to a nubbin. The mind, Sartre said, is not what it is, it is what it is not. With LSD you ask the mind to be itself only, not the world it can observe. You have your head up your ass, deep in shit. It hurts me to say these things, but I can't live with myself if I don't. When I see you I don't any longer know if it's you or the acid I'm talking to. You are coquettish about visits and conversations and meals and walks, the things we began with when I thought your problems were only loneliness and a proud poverty. Your time, I now know, is the acid's, not yours to share. What frightens and disgusts me is the sudden turn to a limp and feminine unresponsiveness. I'm concerned that you've lost all self-respect: a sane person would be ashamed of such lazy, characterless passivity. I scarcely have any hope anymore that I might be your friend, with exchanges of ideas, walks, trips abroad, letters, meals: all those things that sociable and happy people have always valued. A psychiatrist with whom I've talked about you says that you won't seek help, or respond to it, until much later, when this addiction becomes intolerable. By then you will have no feeling of experience to remember when you're detoxicated, and very likely no mind, either. I can forgive all your shitty, erratic behavior now that I know it was the acid and not you. It was you and not the acid who drew *The Apple that Ate the Serpant* on my terrace, and came and talked afterwards. The theme of your drawing was, of course, temptation, and you were trying to tell me (why me is something I can't answer) that temptation had got you into a bind where all is perverse (turned around the wrong way, is what that word means). Snakes offer apples in the myth, apples cannot eat serpents. There's a wonderful passage in the Bible, in *Acts*, where a devil speaks from inside a possessed person. For devil read Perverse Personality, if you want. It says, Paul I know, and Jesus I know, but who are you? Let's, if only as a figure of speech, say that the displacement of person that happens when you drop acid is a devil. It wasn't even in your *voice* that you said to me the morning we were to leave for Paris and you didn't show up, *I don't know you.* I'm glad the acid doesn't know me. But you know me. I have a strong suspicion that the acid won't allow you to know me, for it is jealous of its power to steal your capacity to feel. It doesn't want me to give you a friendly hug, for that implies comradeship and tenderness and understanding, and these human things it hates as furiously as the Devil hates all love and friendship and kindness and responsiveness. Your beloved acid is a master of seduction, and will have no rivals however innocent. It does not want you to feel French country roads. It wants you zonked out of your mind in that graveyard you say you like to go to when you've taken a hit. It wants you to be lonely and friendless. It is all the friend you need. Why sit in a Parisian café, with all the fun of talking and learning and seeing, when you can be puking frogspawn all of a night in a filthy toilet on Nordkalksten, and endure three days of unrelenting cramps from strychnine poisoning? Why respond to anybody's love when you have your acid for a friend? It understands you, doesn't it? You don't have to try to communicate with it all those tedious things friends like to talk about. You don't have to keep appointments, or have manners, or be generous, and most of all you don't have to respond. The acid is quite happy with your limp, feminine, lazy, self-indulgent unresponsiveness. It knows how to possess.

77

Oh but we had some lovely walks, Hugo said, when I thought we were beginning to be friends. I liked his company, his handsome presence, and the more I learned about him, the more a kind of paternal, or big brother's solicitude grew in me. He'd been expelled twice from schools, for fighting, though I now wonder if fighting is the truth. More like pushing, Mariana said. What you won't admit, Hugo, is that this kid was white trash. I don't mean that he started that way. I mean that he chose to be white trash. It's important to them, the student riffraff crowd, to be hateful. That's why they take dope. But, Hugo said, he was wonderfully sweet and sensitive. After our walks, he'd say Thanks for the comradeship. I'd say Tomorrow afternoon, around three? And of course he wouldn't turn up.

78

Emanzipation, to Anders in the mail. He thought it would never come. Düsseldorf postmark. Federal Republic stamp with house on it, blue envelope. Printed Matter: Educational. Two boys on cover, 10 and 12, mayhap, arms over each other's shoulders, 10 beaver-toothed, naked, full head of hair, foreskin down and puckered to a point, 12 in red billcap and undershirt, pubic hair beginning, foreskin back, smiling, *Emma für Kinder*. Inside, two teeners at summer camp holding each other's dicks, tents and naked boys in background, forest trees, green sunlight. Pinewoods, canoes, swallow-tailed flags on short poles. Norwegian boy with great suntan and lank blond hair having his big erect dick admired by a fetching nipper all taffy curls deer's eyes long legs and thumb's up of a peter sticking out of the blue briefs' fly. What, said Kim when it was shown him, does all this German say? Friendship and affection, bonded loyalties. Fun. I'm glad it says fun, Kim said. Full-page close-up penis, meaty head as big and smooth as an egg, olive gray pink. Something about a brother. Dieter and Axel, 13 and 15, looking as innocent as dogs in their jeans and University of Northwestern T-shirts.

Good stuff, Kim said. Who's this old man in the silver-rimmed specs and Nazi crewcut? And this supergerman fourth-former with a grub for a peter.

79
Which what's that? Mariana crossed her eyes and gave at the knees. Soccer shorts for little Franklin. Can he get in them? Chalk blue. Are you, she said, trying to curl up with the adorable monster, his dimples and dink, and kiss him all over? He'd like that, Hugo said, unbuttoning her blouse.

80
Friends, unlike your acid, do not possess. They possess things together, books, films, experiences, moments, fellowship, joys, triumphs, fun, talk, places. You cannot share the experience of the acid. Higher consciousness, you call it. Jesus! What could it add to a work of art, to a place of importance? I have, O Bicycle Rider, wept at the monument to the Deportation, a Kafkalike and grim and pitiful place in Paris where some sixty thousand Jews were loaded onto boats to be taken to their death at Drancy. There's a small light in a long-crypt for every Jew deported. I've sunk to my knees there and wept. What would you feel in this place? Would the stupid acid feel sympathy, terror, pity? Charity, as best I can guess, is not one of the acid's specialties. It can fake neural events like sex and euphoria, but of solicitude for others it knows nothing. It doesn't tolerate others. It would not have allowed you to weep for a hideous injustice. This is, shall we say, obscene. Higher consciousness, from McTaggart's phony Buddhism and transcendental meditation to hallucinatory drugs, is trendy Drug Culture Doublespeak for no consciousness at all. My psychiatrist friend says that an addiction as longstanding and ingrown as yours cannot be reached by persuasion or treatment. He says that when this preference for deadness rather than responsive liveliness has become a boring terror and aching intolerable misery to you, only then will you try to free yourself of its jealous possession. I know, and admit, that I'm talking from the outside, but it may be useful to you, if the acid will let you hear these words, to know what you look like. The acid has already made you schizoid: all science agrees that this is what it does. This word means split. I have no doubt that the acid allows you to feel that being schizoid is romantic, free-spirited, and privileged beyond dull clunks like me. I have only my Mariana, that delightful girl, and my classical scholarship, and my Boy Scouts, and my sober round of reading, gymnastics, my thesis for the Theological Faculty at the university, my painting, teaching, learning. I can share what I feel. Not always well, but the possibility is there. I believe what the Boy Scout Manual says: Forget Yourself. The important thing to me is to know, so that I can respond, how others experience being, love, lust, food, a film, a summer afternoon. I try to paint because I want to show others what I think is beautiful. I

know by now that the acid won't let you respond. I liked you, saw you as interesting and in need of a friend. I took the trouble to reach out. I still don't want to believe that these fucking hellish vegetable acids delta-9-tetrahydro-cannibinol and lysergic acid diethylamide have made you so stupid that you can't get your head out of your ass long enough to talk to another human being, and perhaps even to respond.

81

Hi Anders! Hi Kim! We're doing wildflowers, have seen a bunny, and a perfectly round ring of mushrooms. It was Pascal, with Housemaster Sigurjonsson. What are you doing? Mucking about, Anders said. Hello, hr Sigurjonsson. Fine afternoon, said the housemaster. Pascal and I were making our way to the sandspit for a dip: join us. Looks out of tails of eyes, and *Sure!* Our bikes are over there. We'll come around by the road and meet you, OK? Pascal had found a turtle when they reached the spit and the housemaster was doing breaststrokes and frog kicks in the river. The reason, Pascal said, you shouldn't make a pet of a turtle is that he can't digest his food if he's the wrong temperature. And, as with snakes, you can't tell from their eyes what they're thinking. Why are you undressing Kim, can't he do it himself? Don't splash me, I hate water, and it's cold.

82

Germans in their city parks, Anders said undressing on his pallet. There was this bare-chested boy, California tan, jeans with zipper maybe on the fritz, maybe just down, front of his briefs jutting through, like those little balls sacs back in history. Codpieces, said Tom. Had a barefoot friend in short pants of no matter, student cap, like 13, I'd say. Shot Zipper offed his jeans right in front of a line of girls naked as sardines all turning from hot pink to gingerbread brown right before your eyes. Student Cap dropped his little pants, Adam before the Fall beneath. And, being Germans, very serious about it all.

83

No absolute petrographical distinction is attached to the terms Berkshire schist and Rensselaer grit. The upper part of the east side of the plateau, its southeastern, western, and northern faces, and its top, consist of grit or graywacke, a dark green, exceedingly tough, and in some places calcareous, generally thick-bedded granular rock, in which the quartz grains are apparent, and, upon closer inspection, the feldspar grains. Numerous veins of quartz, and sometimes of epidote, traverse it. This rock is, however, interbedded with strata of purplish or greenish slate (phyllite), varying in thickness from a few inches to perhaps a hundred feet. A small section, measured south of Bowman Pond, in Sandlake, shows, beginning above, fine grit five feet, slate eight inches, coarse grit fifteen feet, slate one foot six inches, fine grit five feet, slate eight inches. About a mile north-northeast of Black Pond, in Stephentown, surrounded by grit, is a mass of slate six hundred feet in width which belongs either to the grit or the Berkshire schist. There is a considerable area of green phyllite at West Stephentown and of the purple northwest of Black Pond. The thin purple phyllite layers along the west edge of the plateau, in Poestenkill, contain minute branching annelid trails.

84
Forest light on bare butts. Kim smelled of mint between the toes.

85
Silver look from the hornbeam's Athena strix. Yellow eyes, Pan. Herds of boys, agemates, in Sparta, ate together on the floor of the mess, with their fingers, from the bare boards. They wore as their only clothing winter and summer an old shirt that left their legs bare from crotch to toe, handed down from elder brothers, the nastier snagged daubed patched and too small, the better. They learned together grammar, law, manners, and singing. Each herd had a Boymaster, who taught them to march in time to the flute and lyre. Each boy sooner or later was caught by an older lover, and carried away to the country. The boy's friends came along, too, for the fun of it. This outing lasted through three full moons, and thereafter the two were friends for life. The lover gave the beloved, as was required by Spartan law, a wine cup, shield, sword, soldier's cape, and an ox. With the ox he threw a banquet, and invited all of his herd, together with their lovers, and gave an account, in intimate detail, of how he had been loved for two months. After this, the beloved wore respectable clothes given him by his lover. They went hunting and dancing together, and ran together in races.

86
This was our discovery, Rutger said, Anders's and Kim's and Meg's and mine. I know, I know: your club is for superrevolutionary Kids' Rights underage snuggling and jacking off, but just because my pal happens to be a girl is no reason I can see for you to blackball us. Man, look at this red! Kim, a smudge of blue paint across his nose and his hair bound with a piratical bandana, said he voted for Meg and Rutger to be admitted. Meg taught me and Anders how to French kiss. She's done it with a girl, so she's like one of us, kind of, right?

87
Morale, said Tom. Openness, brashness, spirit. Boundaries of freedom moving outwards. Put that down in the minutes, Hugo said. What I think, Anders said, is that with all the rockets and megadeath bombs and poverty

and violence and fanaticism, Lebanon Ulster Nicaragua Honduras Afghanistan Poland Libya, whole bunches of us need to say there are better revolutions. Talk about simplistic, Lemuel said, O my. When we lose our sense of history, Hugo said, reasoning becomes a lucid madness. That's Piet Mondriaan, the painter. He sat at the feet of the mathematician Brunschvicg, who said, *The more a man imagines himself independent of history, the more, on the contrary, he makes himself its prisoner.* So let's learn some history.

88

Blue café awnings winter square Paris trees gray buildings green shutters and Rimbaud in a tightjeaned boy with curls and broad shoulders. Order is freedom, order is grace. The centurion's child (Günther Zuntz's essay, Stanley Spencer's painting). Cock upslant warped bell flare to glans. Deep slick. In the park Mariana leaned an ear for a whisper in birdy sibilances from Franklin, shifty of eye and grin. My word's my word, she said. He won't bat an eye. He's for gosh sakes a scoutmaster and knows all about boys, understands boys. He even likes them. Franklin, dubious, heel to toe, deepened his pockets.

89

Headmaster Eglund, Kim's father, a Latinist who had written about Cicero and Seneca, was an authority on classical weights and measures. Or, as Kim's mother the gardener always said, amounts. My dear husband studies Grecian amounts. He had welcomed young Tvemunding after choosing him from among many applicants, and bragged about him to colleagues at other schools. And here was a beautiful essay by Tvemunding on Virgil and St. Paul, their ideals of magnanimity and courage. He called him in. Do you, he said over tea, think there is enough rascal in my Kim? His sister, did Hugo know, was married and with children of her own, his brothers were an engineer in the navy, exec. officer on a submarine, and a graduate student in chemistry. Kim, our Eros, was an afterthought on a second honeymoon in Italy, begotten on a sunny afternoon in a village inn from the windows of which they could see a hill slope with shepherds and goats, an olive grove and a farm that seemed, as it might be, Horace's. Life does beautiful things once in a while, what? O decidedly, Hugo said. But, said Eglund, he's in love, as he calls it, with dear Anders, a gentle boy and a bright one. We know from psychology that this is all properly inevitable, and it has done wonders for Kim. He feels so good about it, and he has been so manly and honest. You work with Scouts and run a well-disciplined and effective classroom. What do you think? It's beautiful, Hugo said. Quite, what I say, said Eglund. I try not to be puritanical. They've started this club, and have put you down as faculty sponsor, and have renovated the old boathouse. Should I look in on it, give it my blessing, do you think? Not without announcing when you're coming, Hugo said, believe me. What would I see? Eglund asked. Come in, dear, he said to his wife pulling off gardening gloves. Classics Master Tvemunding, she said, how delightful.

90

Green world. They'd come through deep ferns from the country road, and then up to a ledge of flat rock velvety with moss, hefting their bikes on their shoulders. Lemuel's hair, as blond as Kim's, spiked out in warps from under his racing cap, which he still wore after putting every other stitch neatly rolled in his rucksack, its provender unpacked and lined just as neatly by his bicycle: thermos of cold milk, apples, blue cheese and onion sandwiches, chocolate bars, and a tin of oysters in their liquor. Oysters, Anders said. Oysters, said Tom. To make us hornier, so they say. You swallow them whole, very sexy, with some of the juice. Raw, said Kim. Raw. What an absolutely lovely place. Anders squatted to undo Kim's shoes and pants. You undress him? Lemuel said. Neat. *Hejsa!* the kid has no more public hair than an infant. I do too, Kim said, some. He comes, Anders said, and I love him. You're kissing, Kim said to Lemuel and Tom, like a boy and a girl.

91

Kim was a wolf, weight on four paws like a table, ears cupped and keen. A green frog, hopping. Anders, creeping up from behind, flopped on him, pinning his arms. His nose, a wolf's could savor the grassy suet odor of a rabbit's spoor, the hairy stink of a dog, the fermented turnip reek of a bear, all the mellow pollen green turpentine bitterbutter acorn smells of the woods, dark smells of punk lichen leafmold. In bed, sleep taking him, he could be a hedgehog, a badger.

92

Lizard, the Greeks called it, Hugo said, flipping Kim's penis with a nonchalant finger. We didn't think, Anders said, you'd come up when we weren't having a formal meeting. But Tom asked me, Hugo said. I've seen everything anyhow. I wanted, said Tom, to see if you'd come. I don't see anything but some bare boys such as I see thrice weekly with my Scouts, Hugo said. Officially I'm not here. And I must skedaddle in a bit, to meet my Mariana. Kim's the lucky one here, jumping the gun by several years. You met Anders last summer? His folks' summer place is near ours, Kim said. The first time we undressed together to swim, he asked if I knew how to jack off, and I said O yes! And did I? O yes! Lots? O yes! Then, Anders said, he did a stomp dance, snapped his fingers, and whistled, and flopped his hair about. He had seen me throwing my javelin and jogging and reading under a tree and had come over and said he was Kim, eleven, soon to be twelve. I think he thought

I was generous to notice him at all. Fifteen is pretty scary, Kim said. So after all the things you do to make friends, we found a sunny old barnloft across a field of sunflowers, where we proposed to do some serious jacking off. I remember that my dick was hard as a bone when I took off my swimslip and had a thrum of benevolence in it. Veins and knots all over it, Kim said. And juice beading out. Bulbourethral secretion, Hugo said, to be coolly pedantic. What an afternoon, Kim said. And all the ones since.

93

Rutger's slow eyes' sliding look at Meg makes her hold her breasts with squeezing fingers, red snicks in grass halms fusing their green with mauves and browns. Rutger's quick eyes' bolting look at Meg makes her caress her breasts with fingertips, blue glints in grass halms fusing their green with yellows and blues. Rutger's slitted eyes' satyr's look at Meg makes her knead her breasts with tight fingers, green tones on grass halms fusing their pale straw with tan and cream. Rutger's sly eyes' longing look at Meg makes her pinch her nipples, yellow bosses on grass halms fusing their cedar green with dusk and dew.

94

A slope of daffodils down to the river. Old trees. One of those days when Kim was full of himself. Spin and stomp! Spin on your left foot, stomp on your right. He was, he said, into imagination soak. He could be a rabbit, a fox, a mouflon, a cow. Rimbaud's rabbit, Anders said, looking through a spiderweb strung with dew in a meadow. Dürer's handsome Belgian hare, Peter Rabbit in his red jacket and blue slippers, and what's imagination soak? When you see what was always there for the first time, Kim said, you know? The way you see it is to imagine you're something else, like a dog. A dog sees up, and low, and when I'm dogminded I look at the ground, and at the undersides of things, bike seats, chairs, to see how a dog sees it. And, really hard, to do imagination soak and try to be, say, Master Tvemunding, who knows the history of everything, and would see people completely different. He must see me as a squirt with lots of blond hair, and his girlfriend Mariana looks at me and wonders if my diapers are wet. Do you know Mendelssohn's *Reformation Symphony*? When it's raining, but the sun's shining, and you see the sun through chestnut leaves, and you're walking along wet flagstones, doesn't a shiver tickle up your neck? Tell me about Sven Asgarsen again, huh? Anders a freshman at NFS Grundtvig had fallen in love with Sven Asgarsen a quiet muddleheaded sophomore who loved animals, spoke in riddles, and was out of it. Who are you? he said one day to Anders, who had hitherto studied Sven's good looks from afar and who answered with his name. No no! Names won't do. Science or books? City or farm? Anders said: Books, city, though

I've milked a cow and slopped pigs. So Anders learned how to talk with Sven. Pigs, their breeds and who raised them and how and why, flop or stand of ear, curl of tail, rake of trotters. Then goats, bantams, cows. You didn't do anything? Kim asked. I just worshipped, Anders said. And one day he went home. Folks came for him, just like that. I'd never been so lonely in my life.

95
Friend of mine from way back is on shore leave, Mariana said on the phone. I really ought to be nice to him. Will you understand? I'll try, Hugo said. The other thing, she said, is that Franklin needs a place to sleep tonight. He shouldn't be by himself. Mommy's off somewhere. Bring him over, Hugo said. Better still, I'll come get him. I won't be replaced? she said. Can't promise, Hugo said. If Franklin looks at me with those big eyes, I may kiss him black and blue. Wiggle his toes, she said, he likes that better.

96
Going to fetch Franklin, he remembered at the foot of the stairs the evening he'd come out for a breath of fresh air and found the rider drawing in colored chalk on the concrete terrace. An apple, a snake. He'd lettered around it, *The Apple that Ate the Serpant*. That, said Hugo, is not the way to spell *serpent*. The rider said, I was going to draw it and go away. For you to find. And, said Hugo, what does it mean? Don't you know? the rider asked, all charming smile and handsome eyes.

97
Hugo, having graded a set of Greek papers (conditionals, optatives) and a set of Latin (ablatives and datives), written his father (Schillebeeckx, a promise to visit with Mariana while the hollyhocks were at their best, Scouts), washed bowl plate glass and tableware, realizing that it was no effort to be generous toward Mariana, her generosity being enough for them both, set out to meet her and Franklin. No *Apple that Ate the Serpant* on the terrace at the foot of the outside steps, only clean concrete with a cricket in a corner, a beech leaf in the center. The friend from way back was a sailor with a neat wide box of a nose, flat cheeks, good looking, trim. Seems, he said in his handshake, I'm lucky to see Mariana without knowing six languages. Glad to know ya, fella. The same, said Hugo. Franklin and I are going to dare each other to eat a banana split on the way back, the *deluxe extraordinaire* with everything on it, topped with Chantilly and the Danish flag. Then we're going to have a wild evening of dissipation playing checkers. And we intend to have silly dreams.

98

Franklin, full of banana split, was going to be a Scout, both a Cub (*Dyb!
Dyb! Dyb!*) in a blue uniform with yellow neckerchief, and the mascot to
Hugo's troop going with them on all hikes and campings-out. Moreover, he
and Hugo were going to sleep together, like buddies, no pyjamas. In the
morning they were going to run four kilometers before breakfast. Hugo was
his big friend.

99

They were asleep, Franklin's head on Hugo's shoulder, arm across his chest,
when a steady tapping at the door woke Hugo. Mariana, would you believe.
O wow, she said, naked and all. O, I'm here because sacking out with Hjalmar all night seemed wrong. He has changed, people do. He's as good a lover
as always, proved it twice, to be friends. His feelings aren't hurt. Sailors are
tough. I belong here. The bed will be sort of crowded, Hugo said. Don't
mind, she said, he can be between us. The phone. Who in the name of God is
calling at this hour of the night?

100

He was chalk white from messy hair to toes, no pink anywhere, so that the
shallow definition of muscle in the chest, abdomen, and quadriceps seemed
sculptural, a young Hermes by a sentimental follower of Thorvaldsen working in alabaster. The eyes were open and blank, the mouth peaceful. Both
hands were curled as if in anxious preparation for catching some object about
to fall. A student of yours? the policeman asked. He had a letter from you in
his jeans pocket, wadded up. That's why we called you. Last session, Hugo
said, at NFS Grundtvig, day student, lived on the warehouse end of Kalksten.
He'd dropped out of school. Cocaine, the policeman said, OD. They're doing
it all over the world, and why? I don't know, Hugo said, needing to cry but
knowing that he couldn't. Do you?

WO ES WAR, SOLL ICH WERDEN

I

—See? Pascal said, handing Housemaster Sigurjonsson a bunch of chicory and red valerian, they're flowers, for you, because Franklin brings them to Hugo Tvemunding, who puts them in a jar of water and says he likes them. They're sort of from the edge of fru Eglund's garden.

—So will I put them in a vase, Holger said, if I have such an article. Which I absolutely don't.

—The marmalade, Pascal said, is down to just about enough to go on a slice of bread, with some butter, and then you'd have that to put the flowers in. Hugo keeps pencils in a marmalade jar.

—Ingenious solution, Holger said. And who do we know fossicking for tucker to finish off the marmalade with a cup of tea, perhaps?

—Milk, a big glass of cold milk. There's half a bottle and one not opened yet. You've been grading papers, all done, with the rollbook on top and a rubber band around the lot. And reading. Saw you at the gym.

—Danish grasses and wildflowers, the papers, Holger said. And what in the name of God is that?

Pascal, eyes as wide as kroner, was wiping marmalade out of the jar with his fingers.

—Sounds like somebody's mad at somebody, he said.

His sandwich built of wedges of butter and runnels of marmalade, Pascal took as large a bite as he could, for the comedy of it, accepting a tumbler of milk from Holger.

—One of 'em's Franklin, he said, cocking an ear.

His smile gilded with marmalade and wet with a chevron of milk, Pascal eased down the zipper of his fly: his accompanying Holger on bed-check rounds every evening was always in night attire, pert briefs with a snug pitch to the cup.

The ruckus down the hall became fiercer. What Holger saw when he whipped open his door and sprinted out was Franklin Landarbejder and Adam Hegn, whose tenor insults and shoulder punches had exploded into a locked scuffle, pounding each other in white hate. Falling in a flailing crash to the floor, they were rolling, kicking, caterwauling, elbowing and biting along the corridor floor like a bearcub attacked by a hive of bees, trying all at once to tuck itself into a ball while thrashing out at its stinging tormentors.

The first out of his room was Asgar with a yellow pencil between his teeth.

—Knee him in the balls, he said. Buggering Jesus, there's blood.

Tom, pulling on shorts that snagged on his erection, poked a bare foot into the grunting ferocity, trying to pry Franklin's elbow away from Adam's throat.

Edvard with a calculator, Olaf in a white sweatshirt with *ungdomsfrihedskæmper* in blue lettering vertical from waist to collar, Bo stark naked.

—Go it, Franklin, Bo said. Go it, Adam.

—Back! Holger shouted, straddling the fighters and pulling them apart. Pascal, from nowhere, got Adam in an armhold and rolled him smack against the wall. Holger had pinned Franklin's arms, walking him backward. Adam was promising Pascal that he would kick the shit out of him as soon as he got the chance. Franklin shouted that Adam was the lover of his mother. Adam bled from his nose, Franklin from a cut lip.

—Tom, Holger said, get Matron. Pascal, fetch Hugo Tvemunding. Edvard and Olaf, take these outlaws to the infirmary. Where's Rutger? Jos?

Matron, in a bathrobe suggestive of the last imperial court in Peking and with hair improbably crisp for the time of day, lifted Adam and Franklin onto the examining table, side by side, where they sat glaring straight ahead. Adam she gave an ice cube in a twist of gauze to hold under his nose. Franklin she dabbed on the lip with a swab of iodine, commanding him to keep his mouth well open. Then she stripped them, had a thorough prodding look at their mouths, ears, eyes.

—No loose teeth, she said. Lucky, that. There will be bruises. I want to see you both again tomorrow afternoon. Animals, she added under her breath.

—Animal, Adam said to Franklin.

—You'd better believe it, Franklin said.

Adam, green, said he was going to barf. And did, into the gleaming stainless-steel basin Matron held under his chin with a magic pass.

—What precisely the fuck is all this? Hugo asked. Beg pardon, Matron.

—Fine example, Matron said, I must say. Onto your elbows and knees, Adam. Yes, on the table. Move down, Franklin. Breathe deep, relax.

—These two, Holger said, were mixing it in the hall. No great matter.

—End of the world, Mariana said. Look at them. I'm the blond rat's big sister, first certificate in nursing, St. Olaf's Day Care.

Matron smiled viciously.

—Ever so pleased.

Pascal, peeping around the door, got the full blast of a stare from Matron and disintegrated.

—Gotcha! Jos shouted, blocking, scooping up, heaving over his head, and catching Pascal hammocked knees and nape in his arms.

—Hoo! Pascal said, scare me out of a year's growth, huh?

—So look where you're going. What's in the nursery, shrimp?

Jos, Apollo in dirty white sweatpants rolled low on his narrow hips, hefted Pascal onto his shoulders.

—Franklin, Adam. They had a fight. Nosebleed, cut lip. Boy, do you stink. Hugo and Mariana have come over. Matron shot me with one of her looks.

—Working out. Adam's never even seen somebody like Franklin. To be beautiful. Is that your peter poking the back of my neck?

—Hugo's barefoot, fly's open and no underpants, and his sweater's on backward.

—Canarying in the bed with frøken Landarbejder, wouldn't you say, weasel?

—Look neither left nor right, Hugo said. Holger's rooms are at the far end.

—But if you look straight ahead, Mariana said, you see Tarzan in sweatpants held up by faith alone and with Pascal on his shoulders.

—Girl in the hallway! Bo called out.

Hugo guiding Franklin, Holger Adam, Mariana sorting and inspecting their clothes, deployed themselves around Holger's sitting room.

—Pascal! Holger called.

Mariana introduced herself to Adam.

—And just because I'm his sister doesn't mean that I'll take his side.

Pascal, wet and hugging a towel, said that here he was.

—I'm having a shower with Jos.

—Go get your dressing gown, for Franklin, would you, and Adam's, and be slippy, back here before I count ten.

—The things I'm learning, Mariana said.

The phone rang: the Headmaster.

—Tempest in a kettle, Holger said. We have the combatants, Tvemunding and I, here now. I'll give you a report. And a good evening to you, sir.

Pascal's dressing gown, the first Franklin had ever worn, was plaid, Adam's, soft with many launderings, Norwegian blue.

—A room to live in, Mariana said, work in, read in. books by family and size, all these maps, good chairs, sheep in a pasture so nicely matted and framed.

—That's a Louisa Matthiasdottir, of an Icelandic meadow.

—Holger's an Icelander, Hugo said. I admire the Klee, glyphs of fruit and vegetables yellow and lavender on that blue ground. Two pears nuzzling. Apples, pears, cherries, and would that be a fig?

—Good botanist, Klee, accurate with structure.

—Where's Pascal's room? Mariana asked brightly.

While Holger was saying *really, I don't think you should,* she went out singing *Pascal!*

—Nosebleed would seem to have quit, Hugo said, but keep the ice under it a bit more, eh?

—Who cares? Franklin said.

—Enough out of you. And I don't want to hear an antiphony of *he started it.* Fights are things that happen. Gorbachev and Reagan do it with intercontinental ballistic missiles, you and Adam do it with fists and feet.

—He bit me.

—And teeth. It's ourselves we don't like when we think we don't like somebody. This unseemly fratch when you should have been doing your homework was Adam fighting Adam, Franklin fighting Franklin.

—He started it, Adam said.

Mariana came back peeping through her hands over her eyes.

—We'll take Franklin home with us, and Pascal too, for company. No war if the troops are restricted to barracks. Jos is very beautiful when he blushes from forehead to toes and everywhere in between.

—Here I am, Pascal said. Musette bag, see? Toothbrush comb jammies slippers and whichwhat. Had a shower. Jos says I look like a newt wet, an oiled elver. Uliginous eel I called him, ha!

—Wait till my parents hear about this, Adam said.

—Oh boy, Franklin said, searching the ceiling.

—You'll come over with us, Holger? Mariana asked.

—If I may. Let me set up a provisional government, with Jos in command, just in case this skirmish was the beginning of a revolution of sorts. Back in a sec.

—You look spiffy in Pascal's dressing gown, Beavertooth. We must get you one.

—I like it, Franklin said, solemn doubt in his voice.

—It's for the infirmary, Pascal said. You can have it.

Jos had followed Holger back, dressed in a towel knotted around his hips. A handsome smile for Mariana, a wink for Pascal, a sergeant's glare at Adam, a scout's salute for Hugo.

—Go on over, Hugo said, I'll be along. I want to hear Adam's side of this, just the two of us.

Adam said:

—We're not supposed to let outsiders in the dorm after six. I know he's a day student but that's an outsider 'sfar's the dorm is concerned. He gave me some sass, and, well, we got into it. I was following the rules. He doesn't belong here, anyway. He had no right to hit me.

—I couldn't agree more, Hugo said. And you were right to follow the rules. On the other hand, you knew perfectly well who Franklin is, and that he and Pascal are rather special friends. If I'd been in your place, I think I would have been less of a bufflehead, you know, and told Master Sigurjonsson (he was here) that Pascal had a visitor.

Stubborn silence, defiant eyes.

—So, Hugo said, this is really not my affair, it's Master Sigurjonsson's, and he's a good man, wouldn't you say? Jos is standing in for him for half an hour or so. Ho, Jos!

—*Adsum!*

He bounded down the hall and stood mother-naked at attention.

—All yours, lieutenant. I'm off. One wounded trooper here to cheer up.

With an easy hoist Jos heaved Adam butt up over his shoulder, about-faced with a military pivot and stomp, and strode along the hall.

—Node bleed! Adam squealed.

—What else? Hugo said. Carry on, corporal.

Mariana was making hot chocolate, Holger was looking the place over, holding his elbows, and Franklin was laying a fire, with a lecture for Pascal on how it's done.

—So this, Holger said, is Bourdelle's *Herakles the Archer.* I know everything here from Pascal's accounts. There's Tom Agernkop. What talent as a painter you have, Hugo. And the Muybridge.

—I like a bathrobe, Franklin said. It's like being in bed.

—World's coziest place, Mariana said. If ever I meet the art teacher who converted this over-the-old-stables upstairs into a studio apartment of such friendly privacy and then skedaddled precisely in time for Hugo to move into it, I'll give him a big hug and kiss.

—Continuous space, Holger said, and yet one can see that that's bedroom, this sitting room, and that kitchen, differences that are really distinctions in a sense of space. Whereas my rooms have walls and doors.

—Our bedroll goes here, Pascal said. Franklin calls it a pallet. In front of the fireplace. Camping out indoors: that's the fun of it.

—A bivouac of mice, Mariana said. Who wants marshmallows in their chocolate? Gerbils, maybe.

—No TV, but a radio, Franklin said.

A cork bulletin board to the right of the fireplace: a yellow-and-blue Cub Scout neckerchief, *museau de loup* and *fleur de lys* for insignia, a photograph of Pastor Tvemunding in a garden with Franklin polliwog naked by the hand, a map of NFS Grundtvig and its grounds, a dental appointment, a blue penny-weight *badebukser*, flimsy and nylon, lined housing of about a gill, a photograph of a frog and fieldmouse nose to nose, an embroidered shoulder patch for Wilderness Foraging (pine branch with cone), another for woodcraft (red hatchet on a buff ground), and one shoelace limp over a drawing pin.

—For having our chocolate on, Franklin said, lugging a sleeping bag from the closet, unrolling it along the hearth. I have Pascal's bathrobe, so he doesn't have one.

—Have Hugo's, Mariana said, fetching it. Woolly warm, modish slate gray with red piping and a red belt, only four sizes too large.

- –Oh wow.

—Get in it bare-assed, like me, Franklin said.

—End of the summer, month before last, Pascal explained to Holger, we all went nude, except Pastor Tvemunding, at Hugo's cabin. I was embarrassed at first, but got used to it.

—In about fifteen seconds, Mariana said.

—Pastor Tvemunding was naked, too, I ought to say, when we had a dip in the ice-water pool of the ice-water forest stream. We bathed with him, and then Hugo and Mariana bathed, though we could bathe with them, too, and once we all had a bath in the pool together, as Pastor Tvemunding said water that cold made impure thoughts sheer folly.

—What in the world is this? Holger asked.

He had gotten up to walk around the room while Pascal stripped.

—A harmonium, Hugo said. For hymns.

He brought it over to the fire, explaining its workings, and put it in Mariana's lap.

—Stanford in A, he said. OK, rats, sweet and high.

Mariana began an updown-updown dactylic ground, vibrant and rich.

—*The Owl and the Pussycat*, Franklin sang.

—*Went to sea*, Pascal joined.

And together:

—*In a beautiful pea-green boat!*

Holger stood in charmed surprise at the beauty of their voices.

—*They took some honey and plenty of money*
Wrapped up in a five-pun note.

Franklin, off key, signaled for a pause until the melody came round again.

—Somebody's voice is changing, Hugo said in a deep bass.

—Go on! Holger pleaded. Go on!

—*The Owl looked up to the stars above,*
And sang to a small guitar,
O lovely Pussy! O Pussy, my love,
What a beautiful Pussy you are!

—*You are!* Mariana sang.

—*You are!* Hugo joined.

In quartet:

—*What a beautiful pussy you are!*

Franklin, sipping chocolate, slid his free hand up Pascal's nape and mussed his hair with wriggling fingers, and began the second verse.

—*Pussy said to the Owl, you elegant fowl,*
How charmingly sweet you sing!
O let us be married, too long have we tarried:
But what shall we do for a ring?

Mariana and Hugo:

—*They sailed away for a year and a day,*
To the land where the Bong-tree grows
And there in a wood a Piggy-wig stood
With a ring at the end of his nose.

Franklin:

—*His nose!*

Pascal:

—*His nose!*

Mariana, Hugo, Franklin, Pascal, and, hesitantly, Holger:

—*With a ring at the end of his nose!*

—Oh wonderful, Holger said.

Franklin's trying for a saucy pursing of his lips while he ran a hand down Pascal's back inside Hugo's roomy bathrobe ended in a grimace.

—Poor split lip, Mariana said.

Franklin shrugged: heroes don't complain.

—Instant retribution for wandering hands, Hugo said.

—Friendly hand, Pascal said.

Mariana, as if to change the subject, pranced a jig of chords on the harmonium, and began the third verse.

—*Dear Pig!* she sang. *Are you willing to sell for one shilling*
Your ring? Said the Piggy, I will.

Franklin and Pascal took over:

—*So they took it away and were married next day*
By the Turkey who lives on the hill.
They dined on mince and slices of quince,
Which they ate with a runcible spoon.

Hugo and Mariana:

—*And hand in hand on the edge of the sand*
They danced by the light of the moon.

Pascal, wild mischief in his eyes:

—*The moon!*

All, with a sassy arpeggio from the harmonium:

—*They danced by the light of the moon!*

II

BLUE TENT IN A GROVE OF BIRCHES

Once, God Almighty came to visit Adam and Eve. They welcomed Him gladly and showed Him everything they had in their house, benches and table and bed, ample jugs for milk and wine, the loom and ax and saw and hammer, and they also showed Him their children, who all seemed to Him very promising. He asked Eve whether she had any other children besides the ones she was showing Him. She said no, but the truth of the matter was that Eve had not yet got around to washing some of her children, and was ashamed to let God see them, and had pushed them away somewhere out of sight. God knew this.

YELLOW VOLKSWAGEN

Holger Sigurjonsson liked to spend a night or two on weekends camping out alone, for the quiet, the peace of mind and soul, the integration of himself. He had said to Hugo that he was never busier than on these excursions, with nothing that had to be done except eating and sleeping. There was a keen excitement to the strategies of it all: packing precisely what was needed, choosing books to take along, discipline balanced to a nicety with freedom. He returned a much better person. I understand perfectly, Hugo said, and wish I had such talents. His camping out was with his scouts, or with Mariana and Franklin. Unity is at minimum two, and when Pascal had gone on an outing with Hugo and Franklin he came back radiant, less random in his conversation, which was famous in the school for moving without warning from the layered territories of a rain forest to the color theory implicit in choosing red socks to wear with a gray sweater. Hugo and Franklin, he reported, were friends of ever so interesting a psychology, for they were big brother and little brother without being kin, uncle and nephew, father and son (Pascal ticked these relationships off on his fingers), host and guest, and then there was something else which had to do with Franklin's being Mariana's brother.

4

Iceland is situated just south of the Arctic circle and considerably nearer Greenland than Europe, yet its plants and animals are almost wholly European. The only indigenous land mammalia are the Arctic fox (*Canis lagopus*) and the polar bear as an occasional visitor, with a mouse (*Mus islandicus*), said to be of a peculiar species. Four species of seals visit its shores. Ninety-five species of birds have been observed; but many of these are stragglers. There are twenty-three land, and seventy-two aquatic birds and waders. Four or five are peculiar species, though very closely related to others inhabiting Scandinavia or Greenland. Only two or three species are more related to Greenland birds than to those of Northern Europe, so that the Palaearctic character of the fauna is unmistakable. The Great Auk is now extinct.

ICELAND

Dingy sheep in a meadow. Tall sky, banked clouds, through which shafts of glare. A yellow house.

JUCK! SAID THE PARTRIDGE

Everything, Jos was saying to Pascal, Sebastian, and Franklin, can be done well. The art of eating an orange, watch. We want all the juice, *jo?* The long blade of your pocketknife, whetted truly sharp, with which we make a triangle of three neat jabs in the navel of this big golden orange picked by a Spanish girl with one breast jundying the other. Lift out the tetrahedral plug so sculpted. Suck. Mash carefully and suck again. Now we slice the orange into quarters, sawing sweetly with the blade, so there's no bleeding of juice. Like so, O puppy tails. One for each of us. Nibble and pull: a mouthful of tangy cool fleshy toothsome orange. And Sebastian has squirted his all down his jammies, the world being as yet imperfect. Eat a bit of the peel along with the pulp: not as great as tangerine peel, as preferred by God and several of the archangels, but still one of the best tastes in the world. Seeds and the stringier gristle into the trash basket. Swallow the seeds and they'll grow an orange tree out of your ear. People who don't know how to eat an orange, like people who don't have the patience and cunning to pick all the meat out of a walnut, who don't eat peaches and apples skin and all, do not have immortal souls.

HARRAT EL 'AUEYRID

We removed again, and when we encamped I looked round from a rising ground, and numbered forty crater hills within our horizon; I went out to visit the highest of them. To go a mile's way is weariness, over the sharp lava fields and beds of wild vulcanic blocks and stones. I passed in haste, before any friendly persons could recall me; so I came to a cone and crater of the smallest here seen, 300 feet in height, of erupted matter, pumice, and light rusty cinders, with many sharp ledges of lava. The hillside was guttered down by the few yearly showers in long ages. I climbed and entered the crater. Within were sharp walls of slaggy lava, the further part broken down—that was before the bore of outflowing lavas—and encrusted by the fiery blast of the eruption. Upon the flanks of that hill I found a block of red granite, cast up from the head of some Plutonic vein in the deep of the mountain.

8

—Oh, I take him everywhere with me, Holger had said to Hugo. I can be brave enough to say that. Is that what you mean by imagination?

—No, Hugo said, that's love. Imagination's how you see him when he's with you. Because the Pascal you see isn't there, you know. That is, where Holger and Pascal maintain, you create in your imagination first a Holger, then a Pascal. That's why you're nuts about him: you like the imaginary Holger the imaginary Pascal brings into being.

—Is this something you're making up to be clever, Holger had asked, or could it be the reality of the matter?

—The reality, Hugo had said, is what you build on, a sprite of a boy with big intelligent gray eyes, crowded butterteeth, all that. No need to stammer and blush.

PASCAL STUDYING HIS TOES

The hornbeam explains its leaves. Lays them out flat to the sun. Human honesty should do no less.

A COPPERISH YELLOW ROSE

In the summer of 1925, Mikhail Maikhailovich Bakhtin, the theorist of narrative, attended a lecture by A. A. Uxtomskii on the chronotope in biology. In the lecture questions of aesthetics were also touched upon.

CHICORY AND RED VALERIAN

The flowers Pascal had brought from the edge of fru Eglund's garden had been forgotten during the scuffle in the hall, and when Holger was leaving Hugo's, Pascal reminded him that the marmalade jar was to be washed and the flowers inserted.

—Put them, Franklin added, where they can eat some sunlight.

—A peculiar domestic event, Hugo said, cut flowers in a vase. Plutarch mentions the custom. A bouquet in among the dishes at dinner, and the diners wore garlands. I wonder if in a Greek house there were arrangements of flowers, on Plutarch's desk, for instance?

—Of course there were, Mariana said.

CORAL COMB DOMINICKER ROOSTER

The soldierly carriage Holger had seen in Pascal of late he could trace to Franklin Landarbejder, whose spine at port arms and calves braced well back of a plumbline from knee to toe, square shoulders and high chin, parallel feet boxed in gym shoes of outsized sturdiness and socks thick as blankets, were the scoutly model. Trousers once chastely kneelength were now cockily short.

13

Hugo says that liking is not to be nattered at, Pascal said as he and Holger were walking in the long wood between the grounds and the river. He says there are two civilizations, one of the human in us, table manners, science, and such, and one of the animal in us. He says none of us is as good a human being as a dog is a dog, and this is because we're not good animals. He says Franklin and I like each other as animals like each other, two friendly dogs, say, and that he and Mariana like, he said *love* I think, each other as male and female animals, and she kicked him for saying this, but so that it was funny, you know. Franklin laughed, and Mariana said she'd always been able to see Franklin's long ears and tail and another word I didn't understand. But Hugo meant, he said, that we live in lots of ways at once, as animals and humans, and whatever our work is. Also, as doors that open onto things. A math teacher is a door opening onto math, a Christian is a door opening onto God. Something for others, and when he said this he made horns of his fingers above his ears and wiggled them at Franklin. But he wasn't talking to anybody in particular, that's what I like about him. Hugo just talks, to everybody or anybody.

SAMOVAR WITH LEMON

The tall windows of the lecture room where Bakhtin heard Uxtomskii on the chronotope suffused a drab light upon rows of academic benches, the yellow oilcloth on rollers for diagrams and unfamiliar words, the lectern with kerosene lamp, water pitcher, and glass. One eye of Marx's bust was a pallid coin of light, the other a scoop of shadow. Holger was reading Bakhtin because he didn't understand narrative. Hugo had said that some French thinker held all understanding, especially self-knowledge, to be narrative in essence. A surprise, but there you were. A chronotope is the distinctive conflation of time and place fixing the Cartesian coordinates of an event or condition. Edward Ullman would have been interested, and Carl Sauer. The philosopher Samuel Alexander taught that finished time becomes a place. So every *where* needs a *when* in an account of it, and every event has a narrative past. Tvemunding, for all his dash, was up on everything, and Holger prided himself on following up. And here was a chronotope from ancient biology cropping up in a Russian book about narrative. The examples tended to be from Rabelais and Sterne, authors Holger had not read. Unlike the Russian lecture room remote in time and space, begrimed by poverty, political desperation, tedious idealism, his rooms at NFS Grundtvig were congenial and modern. The protocol was for the boys to knock and be invited in, or not, except for Pascal, who could enter when he pleased, always backing in with a double turn to close the door, a maneuver that maintained even if the door were open. One narrative might be to recall how it happened that Pascal fell into the habit of going with Holger on bed check, to ascertain room by room that everybody was in and accounted for. Pascal had once worn pyjamas on these rounds, as if to establish that he was ready for the evening, and Holger was sometimes in a dressing gown, sometimes in slacks, slippers, and tieless shirt. And as Pascal became accepted as Holger's familiar, as a teacher's pet whose transparent candor and chuckleheaded ignorance of privilege threatened no one, he began to imitate everybody else in the house by wearing briefs only, or a shirt only, for student by student God knew from day to day what, if anything, they would be wearing. Hugo was always in the know, and could answer why one style of undress had replaced another, or hairstyle, color of socks, brevity of underpants, snugness of jeans, the iconography of walls. Pascal's answers were unilluminating but current. Black socks were in, he would report. How did he know? Well, they just are. Papa's secretary is sending me some. So Mama will send me money for some. They duplicate everything.

15
There are no depths, Hugo had said, only distances.

16
—Rutger? Jos said.

He laid a protractor and compasses on graph paper nipped to a clipboard.

—He's on his knees and elbows out in the ferns jumping up Meg with sweet slick liquid shoves, and his tongue's down her throat, and his hot hands on her cool teats, having jittered her button until she was bucking. They're real friends, those two.

Holger, on bed check with Pascal in tow, sighed and smiled his patient smile. Asgar, reading on his bed, slid his hand inside his briefs.

—I know that problem, Pascal said, studying the clipboard.

—Psychologists and poets, Jos went on, are in the absolute dark about people like Meg and Rutger. They can be talking about Reagan and Gorbachev, Marilyn Horne and Pavarotti, Joyce and Kafka, and Meg's in there galvanizing his balls, mashing, petting, tickling, until she starts on his risen rosy pecker, giving little jumps, while he's groping in her panties until in the middle of Reagan and Gorbachev she's wagging her head like an idiot and Rutger's interspersing his remarks with whistles of appreciation, and they're both half in and half out of their clothes, a plump suntanned breast on view here for God and me to admire, a fine brace of balls there, a belly buckle, a healthy butt.

—You were there? Pascal asked.

—I'm not making this up, Jos said.

—Of course not, Holger said.

—And after they've made morons of each other, they resort to fucking as the only way back to sanity and this world, thumping like two rabbits.

—Ha! Pascal said, I've seen rabbits. The wife keeps chewing her lunch while the husband hunches her rear.

—Precisely, O infant friend, Jos said. And yes, I was not helplessly there, but there nevertheless. We were walking Meg back, I'd run into them and they insisted, so's I could walk back with Rutger, and we sprawled in the sun in the dell awhile. I'm used to their pawing each other, and they'd probably just screwed their brains sodden in Rutger's room after soccer practice. Anyway, once they've done Mr. and Mrs. Rabbit, they're themselves again, fresh as kittens after a nap. They give each other a silly look with deep eyes, find their underpants, brush off leaf trash, say hello to me, and start in on Reagan and Gorbachev again. One keeps one's cool with manly restraint. You hear that, Pascal? But exactly where Master Rutger is, I couldn't say.

17

The self, Hugo said, is the body. Our knowledge of what's other is a knowledge of our body. My seeing a Monet is a knowledge of my own eye, which is both an obstruction between me and the Monet and the medium by which I see it at all. If my eye is healthy and keen I can forget it. The self is invisible to itself when it goes economically about its real business. It is consumed in attention, and comes to being through attention. We do not watch our hand, nor yet the hammer, when driving a nail. We watch the nail. Reading, we see Robinson Crusoe with his parrot on his shoulder, yellow sands, green ocean, three goats on a knoll.

18

When Pascal and Franklin sang *The Owl and the Pussycat* to Mariana's accompaniment on the harmonium, Holger had blushed: thin wisps of tickling fire ran together deep inside him, surfacing on his cheeks and forehead, seeping back again, chill and stinging. Mariana gave him a merry look.

—Didn't half suck, did it? Franklin said.

—Did you like that? Pascal asked.

Holger's *Oh yes* was weak, and he blushed again. He took courage, and said that the old-timey tone of the harmonium made him remember hymns by lamplight in Iceland, his childhood.

—I must, he said, learn to read poetry.

—Join us, Mariana said. Hugo teaches me, and Franklin has to get yards of poems off by heart, Hugo's idea.

—Papa's, Hugo said. Once you know a poem, you have it for good.

VESUVIUS

Standing from the morning alone upon the top of the mountain, that day in 1872 on which the great outbreak began, I waded ankle-deep in flour of sulphur upon a burning hollow soil of lava: in the midst was a mammel-like chimney, not long formed, fuming with a light corrosive breath; which to those in the plain had appeared by night as a fiery beacon with trickling lavas. Beyond was a new seat of the weak daily eruption, a pool of molten lava and wherefrom issued all that strong dinning noise and uncouth travail of the mountain; from thence the black dust, was such that we could not see our hands nor the earth under our feet; we leant upon rocking walls, the mountain incessantly throbbed under us: at a mile's distance, in that huge loudness of the elemental strife, one almost could not hear his own or his neighbor's voice.

A BOWL OF ROSES

Yellow kerchief, short blue pants.

—Roses? Holger said. I don't think I've ever really looked at one.

—Nor I, Hugo said. They are Italian opera, Austrian churches, German pastry. A proper flower is an aster, a daisy, a sunflower, something with decisive color and architecture.

—Precisely, Holger said. But Rilke's poem you say is superb, beginning with boys fighting, like Adam and Franklin, nasty little savages baring their teeth and hammering away at each other and rolling together like a bearcub attacked by bees. And then the poem goes on to be a description of a bowl of roses?

—*Die Rosenschale*. Anger flashing, two boys rolled themselves up in a knot of naked hate, tumbling over and over like some animal beset by a beeswarm. An outrage of going the limit. A cataract of runaway horses. Lips raised as if about to be peeled away. Rilke says he saw that, and I daresay he did, at military school where his father sent him after his mother raised him as a girl. Saw it and forgot it, he said, but obviously didn't forget it. Then the poem turns coolly to a bowl of roses. Like the battering boys they too occupy space. They are, they bend and open. They drink and digest light. They are boy and girl, stamen and pistil. Cool and ripe, their order of being is wholly beyond us, but we watch them as a lover watches his mistress. Inedible, they yet seem to belong with vegetables and fruit. But they belong to nothing but themselves, are nothing but themselves. Which means that, like us, like the pure being in us, they can take the outside in: wind, rain, the surge of springtime, shuffling chance and the inevitable, night, clouds running across the moon, on out to the most distant stars, can take all this and make an inwardness of it.

—I think I see, Holger said, but would hate awfully to be put on the spot and made to explain it. Fighting boys, roses in a bowl. Yellow roses, at that.

—The roses, Hugo said, are the boys. Where boys were, roses are.

—Lay that out flat, Holger said.

—Ha! said Pascal, coming to join them, to tie his shoelace, inspect his scuffed elbow, and look over his shoulder to see if Franklin was coming, too.

—When, Hugo said, I was a fetching spadger with rabbity teeth and big soulful eyes, out with my scout troop on a lake island, very rocky, cedary place, the air glittering with midges, I remember the heady, summery feel of it all, our scoutmaster undertook to instruct us in the facts of life.

—Facts of life, Pascal said.

—Twentyish, well built, he was a decent chap we all liked.

—By facts of life you mean sex, Pascal said.

—The very same, Hugo said, as set forth in a pamphlet. Which our competent scoutmaster consulted and followed. We sat in a half circle before him. Slapping mosquitoes and waving midges away.

—Here I am, said Franklin, trotting up and leapfrogging Pascal's shoulders, a chaff of grass and leaves stuck to his short blue pants.

—We're hearing about long ago, Pascal said, Hugo's scoutmaster giving the facts of life to his troop.

—What for? Franklin asked.

—So, Pascal grinned, they'd know.

—*Voir est une science*, Hugo said. That's Jules Verne.

Pascal translated for Franklin, cupping hands over his ear and whispering.

—But, as I remember, it wasn't facts we were hungry for, but a sweeter knowledge. Not long before this I had been initiated by one Gretta into the mysteries of kissing, in rather a crowd of us who flocked to one house or another that was free of grown-ups for an afternoon or morning. Some of us were spies who reported the techniques of older brothers and sisters. Gretta knew about kissing in the manner of the French.

—Which is what? Franklin asked.

—Kissing open-mouthed and wiggling tongues together.

—Like you and Mariana. Icky, if you ask me.

—Yes, Hugo said, but what Holger and I were discussing at a philosophical level before we were joined by chirping mice in blue pants and yellow kerchiefs, is that knowledge is furtive and experimental, in the idiom of nature rather than that of diagram and axiom. A verb before it is a noun. In any case, the facts of life were Gretta's kittenish tongue and hugs and caresses, which grew less tentative in the course of things. And there was the electrifying afternoon when, as we nudged each other to take a look, a look that made my mouth dry, Hjalmar Olsen, who was on hour-long French-kissing terms with three girls, all of whom were friends and compared notes and kept score, sneaked his hand into Charlotte Heggland's knickers, with her warm approval.

—Whee! Franklin said.

—So our lecture in a mist of midges lacked that grip on reality the young mind prefers to science from a pamphlet.

21

At afternoon, the weight of molten metal risen in the belly of the volcano hill (which is vulcanic powder wall and old lava veins, and like the plasterer's puddle in his pan of sand) had eaten away, and leaking at mid-height through the corroded hillsides, there gushed out a cataract of lava. Upon some unhappy persons who approached there fell a spattered fiery shower of vulcanic powder, which in that fearful moment burned through their clothing and, scorched to death, they lived hardly an hour after. A young man was circumvented and swallowed up in torments by the pursuing foot of lava, whose current was very soon as large as Thames at London Bridge. The lower lavas rising after from the deep belly of the volcano, and in which is locked a greater expansive violence, way is now blasted to the head of the mountain, and vast outrageous destruction upward is begun.

LOCKER ROOM

—You have so many more resources, Holger said, as if nothing ever bothered you, a stranger to doubt.
—Doubt myself, you mean? Hugo asked, sifting talcum across his toes. Insofar as doubt's skepticism, I live from moment to moment doubting everything. You mean depression, which is the same as despair, a sin, you know. Despair is the enemy's most effective weapon. But despair is itself an enemy: the weapon makes the warrior. Except that depression, despair, the feeling that everything's helpless, is not a warrior but a sneak behind the lines. His great lie is that things are necessarily so. All power stands on the necessary despair of the ruled.

23

Before the morrow the tunnel and cup of the mountain had become a cauldron of lavas, great as a city, whose simmering (a fearful earth-shuddering hubbub) troubles the soil for half a day's journey all around. The upper liquid mineral matter, blasted into the air, and dispersed minutely with the shooting steam, had suddenly cooled to falling powder; the sky of rainy vapor and smoke which hung so wide over, and enfolded the hideous vulcanic tempest, was overcharged with electricity; the thunders that broke forth could not be heard in that most tremendous dinning. The air was filled for many days, for miles around, with heavy rumor, and this fearful bellowing of the mountain. The meteoric powder rained with the wind over a great breadth of country; small cinders fell down about the circuit of the mountain, the glowing upcast of great slags fell after their weight higher upon the flanks and nearer the mouth of the eruption; and among them were some quarters of strange rocks, which were rent from the underlying frame of the earth (5000 feet lower) upon Vesuvius, they were limestone. The eruption seen in the night, from the saddle of the mountain, was a mile-great, sheaflike blast of purple-glowing and red flames belching fearfully and uprolling black smoke from the vulcanic gulf, now half a mile wide. The terrible light of the planetary conflagration was dimmed by the thin veil of vulcanic powder falling; the darkness, from time to time tossed aloft, and slung into the air, a swarm of half-molten wreathing missiles. I approached the dreadful ferment, and watched that fiery pool heaving in the sides and welling over, and swimming in the midst as a fount of metal, and marked how there was cooled at the air a film, like that floating web upon hot milk, a soft drossy scum, which endured but for a moment, in the next, with terrific blast as of a steam-gun, by the furious breaking in wind of the pent vapors rising from the infernal *magma* beneath, this pan was shot up sheetwise in the air, where, whirling as it rose with rushing sound, the slaggy sheet parted diversely, and I saw it slung out into many great and lesser shreds. The pumy writhen slags fell whistling again in the air, yet soft, from their often half-mile-high parabolas, the most were great as bricks, a few were huge crusts as flagstones. The pool-side spewed down a reeking gutter of lavas.

GYM

Folding in, Holger said to Hugo, folding out. What one learns from the American geographers Ullman and Sauer is that if you really know anything, everything else comes into your subject. This is because, I think, you're on speaking terms with lots of other minds and consequently able to converse with yourself. I've often felt, you know, that I have not met parts of myself. I don't mean to be mystical. Scientific, rather, as the self in modern psychology seems to be a kind of averaging of several personalities.

25

Two raps on the door, Pascal with his complete turn on his axis, closing the door by backing against it. A bright look, as always, by way of hello. Holger, reading, gave his happy grin of welcome. Pascal took a deep breath, as of resolution, marched over with exaggerated steps, halted, heaved another resolute breath, and, leaning, kissed Holger on the cheek.
—Because, he said quickly, Franklin gives Hugo and Mariana a kiss when he comes in. Christians, way back, kissed when they met. Besides, Franklin said I should.

LAURELDARK TRAILWAYS

—Eglund, Hugo said to Holger, is all for drawing classes, and I threw in photography and printmaking as well while I had him in a good mood, and academic listings will soon sport an ad for a Grundtvig art teacher. Meanwhile, Jos jumped at the chance to sit for studies and an oil. And is right on time.

In floppy long sweatpants that rode low on his hips, so shallow in the seat that when he sat, as now, affable and open, the fact was shaped in compliant cotton soft from many launderings that he was the happy owner of two large testicles and a stout penis wide of rondure at the glans, Jos looked from Holger to Hugo to Holger, clowning pouts, smiles, and solemn faces.

—Off everything, Hugo said.

Jos peeled the tight tank top from the mounds of his pectorals, forced off his heavy gym shoes and thick socks, untied the drawstring of his pants, which he pushed to his ankles, and stood brown and naked, as unselfconscious as a dog. There was, near him, a spicily acrid musk, causing Holger to discover that Hugo always smelled of some expensive and far-fetched soap or gentlemanly lotion, lilac and cucumber, and that Pascal gave off whiffs of mown hay and peppermint toothpaste.

—You could take photographs of me, Jos said, and sell them in Copenhagen for God knows what.

With a merry smile for Holger, he asked if he were the chaperon.

—For me, not you, Hugo said.

—I'm here, Holger said, to see Hugo draw. I stand in awe of his talents. I was so wrongheadedly mistaken about him when he first joined the faculty, charming as he obviously was.

—Theology and classics mark a man, Hugo said. Here, Jos, put your weight on both feet, that's right, and cross your wrists on top of your head. I'll draw as fast as I can. As well as I can.

27

—I've been thinking about your question, which I answered so peremptorily, Hugo said, and thought you might have felt I was dismissing rather than answering it.

—Question? Holger asked.

—About Pascal and whether you might take him with you on one of your weekend camping jaunts.

—Oh, that, Holger said. I'm certain I shouldn't.

—I'm certain you should. You asked Franklin and me to take him camping with us, back in August. He enjoyed that immensely.

—And made friends with Franklin, who has caught his imagination.

—In a lovely way, Hugo said. As improbable a friendship as one can be, but decidedly one dropped down from heaven. I watch it with a measure of disbelief, learning more from it than any course in education I've yawned and daydreamed through. Franklin, you understand, likes Pascal for himself, as I think you do. What popularity Pascal has had has always been for his brains, and maybe some for his sweet shyness, but I don't think he's ever had a real friend. And Pascal adores Franklin for his knuckly toughness. Genius and guttersnipe.

—I like your saying this, Holger said, because you understand my wanting Pascal to be happy, to have as many good things as he can. I'm as protective of him as I can be without drawing attention, which would make him vulnerable in another way.

—But for yourself, Hugo said, you must take him on one of your weekends, lots of your weekends.

—Just the two of us?

—Just the two of you.

28

—I did it! Mariana said. And I'm alive to tell it, and maybe even a bit proud of myself. What's worse, I liked it!

—I who believe you can do anything, Hugo said comfortably from his chair, am not surprised.

Holger, sitting with his arms on his knees, books and magazines around his feet, scrambled up gentlemanly, startling himself in calling her Mariana.

—I may, mayn't I? he asked.

—Lord, yes, she said, especially as I think I've called you Holger from the start. What Hugo calls people, I do too. Fru Eglund, you remember, introduced herself from her garden, and said I must come to tea. Well, I've been to tea with fru Eglund, telling myself that I've done braver things. She's a sweet woman, you know? We talked flowers and curtains and rugs, and then she got me talking about the daycare center, and children, and then there was tea, which I didn't spill, or rattle my cup in the saucer, and I really do believe, if I haven't dreamed it, that we pecked each other affectionately on the cheek when I left.

—Wondrous and mysterious are the ways of God, Hugo said.

—And I didn't pee my knickers when Eglund himself came in and shook my hand. *Stabilizing* he said you are, big Hugo. I swallowed my tongue and smiled like an idiot. He said you're a stabilizing force at the school. And then he said a lot about your being a Christian in a bold and advanced way, and a solid classicist. Let's see what else he said. I was fogging over as he went on. Athlete, scoutmaster. Sensitive, responsible. Handsome young chap. And fru Eglund, she says I'm to call her Clarissa, said in a wonderfully motherly voice, Edward dear, I really don't think you need to commend doktor Tvemunding, *doktor!* to frøken Landarbejder. And *he* said, puffing on his pipe, my dear, everybody likes to hear good words about people they love, and I like to give people their just due. Clarissa said outside that I turned a sweet and becoming shade of pink. That's when I gave her a peck on the cheek.

—To understand all this, Holger, Hugo said, you have to know that Mariana hates all women.

—I do, Mariana said, they're cats. They have their heads up their behinds. I don't *believe* my mother. I've never had any girl friends. I prefer men, all of them.

She made Holger flinch by kissing him on the forehead. She kissed Hugo on the forehead, for symmetry's sake.

—Are Franklin and Pascal here? she asked. I need to hug them.

SICKLE SHEEN FLINTS

—Wolfgang Taute, Pascal said, says the Gravettian leaf points of eastern Europe, upper Paleolithic, got their tangs as they moved west, and became the willowleaf Swidry point. And probably were in touch with the Ahrensburgians.

—Tanged point technocomplex, Holger said. Reindeer people. The air blue with snow and ice splinters on long whistling winds that hit you like a plank. And in the summer, long marshes of yellow sedge.

AXIOM

All problems, if ignored, solve themselves.

31

—Having talked more openly with you than with anybody in my whole life, Holger said, I'm willing to go along with you in this baring of bosoms. I think you're trying to show me that I need to be liberated from something in myself.

—While keeping your privacy inviolable, Hugo said. I'm not prying. We've talked in abstractions. You were interested in Freud's enigmatic statement that *where it was, there must I begin to be.* The oyster makes a pearl around an irritant grain of sand. Nature compensates. A tree blown over will put out a bracing root to draw itself upright again. Deaf Beethoven composed music more glorious than when he could hear. Stutterers write beautifully. That is, one source of strength seems to be weakness.

—Surely not, Holger said. That sounds like the suspect theory that genius is disease: Mann's paradox. It's romantic science, if science at all.

—No, no, Hugo said. Freud meant that a wound, healing, can command the organism's whole attention, and thus becomes the beginning of a larger health.

—Wounds in the mind Freud would have meant.

—Yes.

—I think, then that I know what he means.

WILLIAM MORRIS IN THE FAROES

These wild strange hills and narrow sounds were his first sight of a really northern land. The islands' central firth was like nothing he had ever seen. It was a place he had known in his imagination, mournfully empty and barren, remote and melancholy. In a terrible wall of rent and furrowed rocks, its height lost in a restless mist, he saw that the sublime can be hard and alien. There was no beach below the wall, no foam breaking at its feet. This gray land, without color or shadows, so fiercely defined as to mass of stone and harshness of detail, knew nothing of doubt, of the tentative, the gradual. Its geological decisions had been resolute. As his ship pitched and rolled toward the Icelandic coast, an eagle began to circle above them with plunges and rises of noble composure, wheeling wildly only when it was joined by a raven teasing and reproving. But both were free in the steep cold of a sky without barrier or restraint.

33

Outside his door, when Holger opened it, were Jos in a minim of sparely adequate briefs and Pascal gleefully piggyback.

—I'm delivering, Jos said, one gray-eyed toothy spadger, who has something to show you, and is about to explode.

—Holger! Pascal said, handing an envelope over Jos's shoulder, read it!

The long envelope bore the return address of the Royal Danish Geological Society and was to Professor Pascal Raskvinge. Inside was a letter accepting for publication Professor Raskvinge's paper comparing the geology of the Galapagos and Iceland.

—They don't know! Jos said, swinging Pascal around in a leggy swirl. Isn't it the damnedest, sweetest thing anybody's ever heard of?

—Do we, Pascal asked, have to tell them? That I'm thirteen, I mean?

—You're twelve, twerp, Jos said.

Holger signaled them in and sank into a chair to study the letter.

—I didn't say I was a professor, Pascal said, honest I didn't. I just sent the article, to see what they would say.

Holger leaned back in a robust fit of laughter.

—Rich, isn't it? Jos said, closing the door with a long push of his leg. Hug the scamp.

He lifted Pascal onto Holger's lap.

—Let's not tell anybody, Pascal said, until it's actually published, and even then I'll be revoltingly cool about it.

—Style, Jos said. Pascal and I are the only ones around this dump with real style.

—Franklin I'll tell, Pascal said, and that means Hugo and Mariana, too. Will you ask them not to tell, Holger?

—May I call you Holger, too? Jos asked. I'm not a prude and I don't blab. Professor Raskvinge!

34

Skipping and bouncing sideways, hands deep in his jeans pockets, Jos was saying to Meg and Rutger striding along with arms around each other's hips that he wished them a juicy tumble in the bracken. As for him, he had an hour's workout in the gym, a look at Anders's film now that some of it was spliced and edited, a half hour's posing for Tvemunding, and that if Meg would give him a kiss, friendly like, he would have the rest of the day by the balls. Meg without breaking stride hugged him in for a supple-tongued kiss which Jos secured for three long steps.

—Golly, she said, dancing her eyes.

—Slut, Rutger said.

—One more, Jos pleaded, trashing Rutger's hair. To give me a better excuse for the doltishly prolonged jacking off I've just added to my agenda.

Meg pushed her hands under his sweatshirt, playing a caress up his wide back and down to his lean hips.

—That's gross, Rutger said. Never mind that you're being studied by two nippers with big green eyes and their ears on backward. Hi, Franklin. Hi, Pascal. The embrace you're gawking at is purest theater. Or was. Quit that!

Meg, all innocence, dived at Rutger, tickled him in the ribs without mercy, and marched him off, blowing a kiss to Jos over her shoulder.

—Give yourself a fit, she said.

Jos spun on his heel, stomping.

—She ran her hand down inside your pants, Franklin said.

—With a raunchy squeeze, Jos sighed. His eyes closed. Wiggled her fingers on it, and then squeezed.

PASCAL'S GRUNDTVIG CAP

Holger, climbing out of the gym pool, knocked water from first one ear and then the other, breathing through his mouth.

—What interested Montaigne, Hugo said, shaking water from his hair, was precision of emotion. The alert eye and attentive ear are cooperating with God and with the logic of creation.

—Precision of emotion, Holger said.

FIGURE AND GROUND

Franklin exchanged caps with Pascal, and Holger had better sense than to ask why.

—You know, Pascal said, you have an island, and in the island a lake, and in the lake an island.

—And, Franklin said, taking off his jacket, folding it, and laying it at his feet, in that island a pond, and in the pond an island.

Pascal took off his jacket, folded it, and laid it beside Franklin's.

—On the island in the pond is a spring making a pool, with a big rock in the pool, a frog sitting on it.

—A frog named McTaggart.

—What you're about to ask, Holger said, sitting, as their ramble around the park seemed to have become a milling about in one spot, with Franklin kneeling to untie a sneaker, is whether the earth is all an ocean with island continents, or is it all rock with ocean lakes?

—Yes, Franklin said, untying and prying off the other sneaker, but there are big lakes inside continents and big islands, like Greenland and England, in the oceans.

—The zebra problem, Holger said. And why are you unbuttoning your shirts?

—Who knows? Franklin said, I'm unbuttoning mine because Pascal's unbuttoning his.

—Correct distance, Pascal said. Talk about neat. Hugo says that the primitive mind is fussy about anything's being too far or too near, and that all our sense of distance is very old and basic. But what's neat is that primitive people and kids have the same sense of distance, correct distance I mean, and Mariana says it figures, as they're both cannibals. And then Hugo said correct distance is what civilization is all about, and that not having a sense of distance is feminine.

—There are two ways of doing this, Franklin said. Right now we can swap socks and shoes, and then shirts, until piece by piece we're in each other's clothes.

—While Hugo was talking, Mariana quietly tiptoed behind him and poured a glass of water over his head.

—Or we can skin ourselves to the knackers.

—Hugo didn't even flinch, water dripping from his chin and ears.

—That's from Lacan, Holger said, as well as from Lévi-Strauss. Women, as far as I know, have a more sensitive response to correct distance than men, in general, I would say.

Pascal, handing his shirt to Franklin, said that Hugo explained it wasn't a matter of gender but of male and female patterns amongst a bunch of people, like savages and kids.

—Oh well, Franklin said, oh. Hugo can explain everything except Hugo. It takes Mariana for that, but only when she's in her right mind.

PASCAL'S BLUE PINSTRIPE SHIRT
With white collar and glass buttons.

—Freedom from kinship, Hugo said, figures in all primitive ideas of paradise. A free choice of kinship, as in love or friendship, is a longing in us all. And this reshuffling of loyalties and attractions must be a finding, an invention. It's one of Yeshua's *logia*, also. Fate is, after all, a strategy.

WOLF LIGHT

—Griddle the Witch was making a stew. Into it, for stock, she had put some kelp, some hoptoads, some cockroaches, several birdsnests, some green scum from a pond, and bethought herself that a nasty juicy boy might be just the ingredient to round everything out.

—Me, probably, Franklin said, fluffing out his hair with his fingers.

—So, Mariana continued, she jumped onto her besom, taxied down the footlogs across the swamp, gave a neck-tickling cackle, and shot up into the middle air.

Pascal, Franklin knuckling his ribs, rolled backward and kicked over upright.

—What I want, Griddle said to herself, is a boy who has just stuffed himself with buttery hot cinnamon toast and drunk a mug of thick frothy hot chocolate, given him by his pretty big sister, who's fool enough to love him, and it would be even better if this nasty boy full of toast and chocolate had a friend just as nasty and just as full of toast and chocolate. They will stew up nice, those two.

—Door! Pascal said.

—Hugo, Franklin said, waffling the flat of his hand.

—Hugo and Holger, Mariana said.

—Britches, Pascal said. Where are my britches?

—Why? Franklin said. Holger'll blush anyway. Hugo won't notice.

—What a day, Hugo said, swiveling rain from the east, sleet from the west, wind straight down, with wild snow to make the mixture thoroughly idiotic. Spring, it calls itself. Here's Holger with me. What's going on here?

—Mud, Mariana said. Soccer practice got as far as mud from thatch to toes, and rats rolled up who turned out to be Pascal and Franklin under the muck once I'd peeled them and stuck them in the shower. No dry clothes for Pascal, so they snuggled in the bedroll and had what they call a nap.

—Nap, Hugo said, giving Mariana a kiss. When Franklin looks that radiantly innocent, he has been diddling the system one way or another. Hello, Pascal.

—Hello, Hugo, Hello, Holger, Pascal said. Mariana made us stand side by side on a newspaper while she undressed us. Franklin said Jos would like it, so I liked it. Everything's different over here. Then she put us in the shower together.

—Here Pascal, Franklin said, one of Hugo's T-shirts. Says Boy Scouts on it, and will come down to your knees. Fun. Me, I like

—Showing off, Mariana finished his sentence. And your dick and ballocks.

Hugo gave Franklin a kiss, and, to be fair, Pascal too.

—No favorites, he said.

—Thank you, Pascal said.

TABLETALK

There are no greater and lesser works of God. Creation is all one work, in a single style, from electron to star, we think, as a dog might suppose that the world extends from the orchard to the river.

PASCAL'S UNDERSHIRT

Narrow shoulder straps piped with a hairline of blue cunningly stitched.

Holger, his blue tent trig, its neat spare interior warm with congenial afternoon light under brailed flaps, pondered the moment, light as a function of time, the vibrant clarity of his pleasure in being alone in an expanse of wood and lake and sky, at peace with himself. The stillness was resonant and alive. Barefoot, he kept to his habitual decorum, however wildly unlikely it was that any other might intrude. By parachute? Pascal would ask.

No, that was Franklin.

Wildly unlikely, his own phrasing, was what Pascal would say. With an edged smile, he took off his jeans and the rakish briefs he'd bought because Hugo wore a pair like them, and Pascal had said with approval that everybody admired Hugo's racy underpants, and savored the freedom of his comfortably frayed and creased soft cotton shirt as his only garment. He felt both ascetic and immodest.

Sweet and crazy, Franklin would say.

Comfortable, Pascal.

But, my dear Icelandic Lutheran Reformed Evangelical Holger, he could hear Hugo saying with breezy candor, have the lucidity to see that you're emulating handsome Jos, who roves about the dorm in a ratty pullover, his Eagle Scout dick wigwagging as he treads.

A precise memory charged with redundant imagination:

Jos in Rutger and Anders's room arguing an assignment in trigonometry, his briefs rolled down in a ropy twist across his thighs, trifling fingers tugging his thickening penis as complacently as if petting a dog. Holger never entered a room, door open or closed, without knocking. Rutger's door was open.

—Don't mind Jos, Rutger said, our resident savage, probably noble.

—Whichwhat and since when? Jos said. Mind what?

And when Holger was back in his rooms, a smart rap on the door announced Jos, decent but with the bunt of his briefs strained forward.

—Honest, he said, I wasn't being cheeky just now. Awful to have to admit it, but I really wasn't aware I was monkeying with my dick. Anders says you'll think I was being impudent.

—Apology unnecessary, Jos. I should apologize to you for thinking it charming.

Jos, mouth opening little by little, gawked.

—You did? I know Tvemunding would, but he's crazy. You don't love me or anything like that, do you, hr. Sigurjonsson?

—Nope, Holger had said with grinning confidence, astonished that Jos's question had not upset him. What I find charming is my subjective prerogative, isn't it, and I thought you asked to call me Holger when you brought Pascal in to tell me his article was accepted?

—The secret article, Jos said. Oh yes, well, Holger then.

—I like that.

—We're talking crisscross, I think, Sir. I mean, Holger. It wouldn't bother me in the least if you loved me. I'm broad-minded that way.

—You're a good boy, Jos.

—And charming. By subjective prerogative. I've got to know what that means.

—Subjective, in the privacy of my mind. Prerogative, that what I think is my own business. Our apologies are symmetrical: both for a disrespect.

—Where's the disrespect in my subjective prerogative charm? Love those words!

—You're supposed to resent it, I think.

—Not me! Who says?

—Something called the world.

—The world can stuff it.

A double rap on the door: Pascal spinning in on his heel.

—Oh wow! he said. Big Jos, and in his nappies.

—Hi, squirt, Jos said.

PASCAL'S BRITCHES

—Iceland, Pascal said, is a nest of volcanoes, like the Galapagos Islands. The bases of the volcanoes flowed together, like chocolate sauce in a banana split, to make a plateau. In Iceland the plateau is above, the Galapagos, below sea level. Where you have meadows and sheep and Lutherans in Iceland, you have the ocean between hilltops in the Galapagos, that is, between islands.

After a victory celebration of banana splits with Holger and Jos, Pascal chose as more reward to spend the night with Franklin, at Hugo's. But, Pascal insisted, not to tell about the article's acceptance, for which he would choose his own good time. Jos agreed.

—A good secret is something sweet up the sleeve.

Franklin met them at the door wearing a gray sweatshirt and white gym socks, otherwise naked, his lizardy stripe of a penis poking straight out over a roundly solid scrotum.

—Hi, Holger, he said. Hi, Pascal.

—The ingenuous state of nature in which Franklin greets you, Hugo said, was devised by its exemplar soon after you called.

While Holger made his devoirs to Mariana, who was sewing buttons on shirts, and to Hugo, who was writing in a bound notebook with gridded pages, Pascal with studied unconcern doffed first his short pants and briefs, which he folded pedantically as he talked about the subglacial and undersea lavas of Iceland, and placed with Franklin's clothes in an oblong wicker basket, and then sat to untie his shoes. Franklin helped.

Above the basket, on a shelf, was a triangular Cub Scout neckerchief, its blue border punctuated with chevrons, wolf face, and *fleur de lys* in a square, a blue beanie, the German magazine *Philius*, an aluminum canteen in a canvas jacket, with strap. Above the shelf, Hugo's painting of Tom Agernkop.

—Nested order, Holger said.

—I'll buy the nested part, Mariana remarked, biting thread.

Pascal, pulling on a T-shirt, said:

—I don't go around the dorm like this. Exactly the opposite, interestingly enough. This is my and Franklin's uniform over here.

—Who's your roommate at the dorm? Mariana asked.

—I'm the only Grundtvigger, Pascal said, with a room to myself.

—Because, Holger explained, by age he's lower school, but academically upper.

—And if, Hugo said archly, somebody who's presently inspecting his virile member as if he'd never seen if before and is wondering what it's for, gets his grade average up, not your v.m. but your grades, he can move in with Pascal, and Mariana and I won't hear mouse squeaks, squishy slurps, and puppy yelps half the night.

—You've scandalized Holger, Mariana said, and he's leaving.

—Can't be away any longer from the dorm, Holger said. Jos is in charge, but his authority runs thin.

—Wait! Pascal said, turning Holger around to hug him.

A whisper from Mariana, and Franklin scrambled up from the floor and added his hug.

Hugo walked Holger back to the dorm, talking about Aramaic phrasing discernible in New Testament Greek.

PASCAL'S UNDERPANTS

Delay of iodine in kelp, rondure of acorn, fit of cup, flex of mouse, nod of helve, tilted pileus mushroom warp, tangle of floss, musk of straw, dent of cowrie, attar of olives, nubby scammony nuchal pink warm under spun cotton knit fine.

43

Jos in a dingy workout shirt foxy with sweat and parting at the shoulders, slim jeans, and scruffy sneakers, asked Holger in the hallway, between classes, if he could have a quick word with him, please.

—I need, he said, to cut German and English, which I'm up on and fluent in, anyway, and gym, which Hugo will have my butt for, though I work out more than anybody in this dump. I got through chemistry, but I'd like to catch some sleep. Would it be too much to ask if I could sack out on your floor for an hour or two?

—If you need to, Holger said. You aren't into narcotics, are you, Jos?

—Oh Lord, no! Jos said.

—The apartment's been cleaned for the day, Holger said, shutting the door. Nobody will bother you. Insomnia?

—Well, no, Jos said. Night before last, we won't go into that, I skipped lots of sleep, and didn't sleep at all last night, and it has caught up with me. If I could stretch out on the carpet here, with maybe that thingummy across the back of that chair for a pillow?

—You'll be more comfortable in bed, Holger said. Clean sheets, even.

—You're a brick, Jos said, undoing the brass buttons of his jeans. Fact is, he added with a rueful look, I jacked off all fucking night. Decidedly retarded, and not recommended by the Boy Scout handbook, but there we are. Sorry, no underbritches.

—Lend you pyjamas, Holger said.

—Mna. Maybe a top? This sweatshirt smells like the zoo.

MAX BILL

Horizontal blue, diagonal red, vertical green.

45

—In the bedroom, Holger said to Pascal when he twirled in, we have Jos, who said he was dead for sleep, and whom I've let snooze through dinner.

—Crazy, Pascal said. Jos in your sack. So we start bed check here.

—Let's see, Holger said, if he isn't ready to get up. We can make him a snack.

One arm over his head, the other out straight, Jos, smiling awake, peeped at Holger and Pascal from narrow eyelids.

—Where am I? he asked. What time is it, and who am I?

—A long boy name of Jos, Holger said, with a pair of handsome eyes, feathery eyelashes, and wrecked hair. The rest of him is rather operatically twisted into the covers.

—And, Jos said, is this The Buttermilk Elf?

—Hello, Jos, Pascal said. You're wearing Holger's jammies.

—Only the top, Jos said, kicking loose from sheet and eiderdown, swiveling out of bed to stand on his toes, stretch, and yawn.

—Like a lion, Pascal said.

—Be nice to me, friend Pascal, as nice as Holger's been. I'm feeling sort of unreal and discontinuous.

—Scramble you some eggs? Holger asked. Toast, marmalade, a sausage or two? You've dreamed right through dinner, where your absence was commented on, imaginatively.

—I'll have some of the marmalade and toast, too, Pascal said. I know where everything is, and can do the eggs. You run them around in the pan with a fork, right? Lots of butter. It there a spring in your dick, Jos, that makes it bounce like that when you walk?

—Somebody, Jos said, is not as undescended of balls as he used to be, and probably has high-octane hormones squishing around inside him, wouldn't you say, hr. Sigurjonsson? Holger, I mean. Feels good, doesn't it, Grasshopper? Was it getting taken for a senior academician with beard and dandruff, one soon to be published in a magazine big as a phonebook, that made the sap rise from your pink toes, upward, and upward?

Pascal danced a tricky step, grinning and snapping his fingers.

—I like you to kid me, Jos. It gives you such pleasure.

—Easy on the salt, Pascal, Holger said.

—Why, Pascal asked, did you sack out here all afternoon, as long as we're being personal?

—Because, Mushrump, I didn't sleep for two nights in a row, one given generously to guarding Rutger and Meg while they did it more or less all night, whimpering and sighing with approval of each other's anatomy, that's quite a story, and then last night I practiced self-abuse, as they say, from beddy-bye until I heard birds twittering. Thought my mind had gone, but they were real birds, and it was daylight, and my bold fellow here, who, yes, does have a spring inside to make him waggle like this, was still ranting to make a baby. Nature's awful, you know. No regard for decency or model behavior.

—Whether we're to believe this, Holger said, is up to us, isn't it, Pascal?

—I'm jealous, Pascal said. I can say that, can't I, Holger?

—Ha, Jos said, you have a room all to yourself. Asgar slept through it all, but woke up, all eyes, for the last gusher, which was as sweet as deep up a girl, and called me a pervert and a maniac. Not, you understand, for jacking off, as he was careful to explain, but for when I was jacking off, before breakfast. You did good with those scrumpled eggs, Professor Raskvinge, and is there more milk?

STUDIO

Jos's eyes, lakeblue discs in eyelashes like the outline of an elmleaf drawn with a drenched Chinese brush, stared in so short a focus at Holger's they seemed slightly crossed.

—Do I really look like that?

—It's a splendid likeness, Holger said. Yes, you look like that.

—It's still only a study, Hugo said. Can't call it a painting when it's just Jos with his wrists crossed on top of his head, weight on both feet.

—And my eyes look like that?

—Yes, Hugo said.

47

—What Iceland has that's really wild, Pascal said, is volcanoes erupting under glaciers.

—Crazy, Franklin said.

—Blows hunks of glacier into the air, melts the glacier, boils the glacier into steam. Drowns Lutherans for kilometers around.

THE PRESENT IS ANOTHER COUNTRY

—Well, Jos said, so he does have bits of eggshell still sticking to his curls. That's all the niftier.

Holger had walked Pascal to Hugo and Mariana's after bed check, had visited awhile, and on his return to his rooms found Jos sitting against the door, knees up, cricket cap on backward, in his low-waisted sweatpants, lumpy white socks, and gymnast's tank top.

—Can I come in? he said, sliding his hand from inside his pants, tying the drawstring, and getting up with a nimble bounce.

—Absolutely, Holger said. I was just seeing Pascal over to spend the night with Franklin Landarbejder. One of our modern improvements on the past. They snuggle, I suppose, in a sleeping bag.

—Over where Franklin's clothes are, in the wicker basket, Jos said, and his scouting gear, next to me in paint on Hugo's easel, and with Hugo and Mariana making the bed creak and jiggle.

Holger shrugged.

—Cocoa, milk? Even beer, which I'm not supposed to offer you.

—I won't snitch, Jos said. I need to talk a bit. Pascal would want me to have a beer, the sweet little nipper.

—In which case, Holger said, we'll follow Pascal's wishes.

—What I want to talk about is sort of raunchy, so I might as well throw in, to see how you're going to take this, that I think you and Pascal being pals is a good thing.

—Am I supposed to know, Holger asked, what you're talking about, Jos?

—Well, Jos said, so he does have bits of eggshell still sticking to his curls. That's all the niftier.

—My question remains the same.

—OK, Jos said, smiling amiably and sitting on the floor, knees up, his back against a chair occupied by books, new botanical and geographical journals, a rolled map, a soccer jersey, and a musette bag.

—Let me clear the chair for you, Holger said. You don't have to sit on the floor.

—Prefer it, Jos said. Good beer. And you're a good man.

Holger sat in his leather reading chair across from him, having shuttered the venetian blinds, replacing his shoes with bedroom slippers.

—I'll blurt it all out, Jos said. I don't know, maybe you can tell me why I want you to know all this, but I do. A kind of sharing, as you'll see. It's nothing scary, and not a problem. About two weeks back I fucked Meg. Not *made love to* or *slept with*, those stupid words, but fucked. That is, Rutger and I fucked Meg. He's fucked her just about every day since he's been here, and they'd been doing it well before, wholly into each other.

—As the whole school knows, Holger said, with the possible exception of the Master and fru Eglund, McTaggart, and the kitchen cat.

—Well, Jos said, I've never been what you would call buddies with Rutger, as friendships go, though we've gotten lots closer this term, and I've sort of fallen in with him and Meg together. Three friends are different from two friends, you know? Why the smile?

—Thinking of something else, Holger said. Go on.

—Got to piss. Your bathroom's down the hall, isn't it?

—On the left.

—Your rooms are like a comfortable house, Jos said over his loud midbowl stream. It's good to get away from my Spartan jail cell. I'll leave in a bit, huh?

—It's early, Holger said. I've nothing I have to do before bedtime. Your beer's where you were sitting.

When Jos came back to the sitting room his sweatpants were rolled into a wad which he tossed onto the chair.

—Very becoming, Holger said, undershirt and socks.

—Wasn't wearing briefs. You don't mind? You come and watch Hugo paint me in Fanny fuck all, though my weewee is in its hang position there. It has, however, come within a hair of standing straight up. There was the afternoon Mariana came in with groceries, and kept saying how handsome I am. It gave a jump, and nodded, which she saw, and let me know with a sweet wink. Which made him jump again. And I keep having the feeling that Hugo, if I gave him a little encouragement, would haul me on his shoulder over the bed and love me until we both passed out. Holger, what are those two books over there, *Growth and Form*?

—D'Arcy Thompson, a British scholar, on the laws governing natural structures. It's a book to know. Pascal has read it twice, I believe, and it's one of our favorite books to talk about.

Jos took the books down and opened them in the pool of lamplight on the carpet by Holger's chair.

—Do you know R. Buckminster Fuller's work? Holger asked.

—Geodesic buildings, Jos said. Sticks held in suspension by wires. A new kind of solid geometry. And a world map in triangles. Pascal has one on his wall.

—And Klee's notebooks? Holger asked.

—No. You have them here?

Holger fetched them, and sat with Jos on the floor.

—The Botany Club, he said, is going to start a project in which I take them through Leonardo, Fibonacci, and Klee.

Jos pointed to the framed Klee on the wall.

—Hugo and Mariana admired that the evening of the battle Adam and Franklin had down the corridor. They took it, I'm afraid, as evidence of my appreciation of the fine arts, but it's there for its accuracy of botanical forms.

—Show me, Jos said.

THE BLIND FOLKSINGER

A steady clatter of rain on the skylight accompanied a Bach partita on Hugo's phonograph.

—Earliest memories, Hugo said, are problematic. They can be constructed from later information, from family folklore.

—Not this, Holger said. What I remember is a sunny room, vivid colors as of cloth, greens and blues, and a window brilliant with the light of an Icelandic spring. In this scene I am in a woman's lap, perhaps my nurse, perhaps my mother. I had just been bathed. The oval porcelain tub is nearby. A clean fluffy towel and the odor of talcum are part of the memory. And this woman played with my penis, bouncing it with the flat of her hand. It is a very happy memory, you understand.

—Was she, Hugo asked, perhaps only drying under the foreskin, which can be a tight fit in a baby, and you were enjoying it?

—The odd thing is that I see this memory as if I were a third person, looking on, yet enjoying the pleasure of having my penis fondled.

—You're remembering a mirror, Hugo said. A woman would sit with a charming baby so that she could see herself in a bedroom mirror. Our culture has conditioned us to dwell on the image of a happy mother and winsome infant. How old were you?

—Not more than two, as I figure.

—Does this come in a dream?

—No. It's a waking memory, but it visits regularly, as in Proust. Shaving, bathing, or in a sunny room.

—The psychological weather.

—Yes. But what I've got up the courage to narrate is not this, but an event much later, when I was ten or eleven. Saturday is always a fateful day, and this was a Saturday. I remember the clothes I was wearing, because they were new, bought for the beginning of the school term: a blue wool sweater. I was vain of the fit, and of its quality. It was of heavy wool, with flecks of red and gray in its strong Icelandic blue. And I had new long corduroy trousers, which swished. And all of this finery fitted in with an outing my favorite uncle had arranged. We drove into the country, to see a man my uncle had met years before, and wanted to see again. My uncle was a schoolteacher and keen on Icelandic folkways, legends and ballads, that sort of thing. A ride in an automobile was exciting enough, over country roads, but to be going to a farm was even more exciting. But I mustn't draw this out.

—As you will, Holger. But I gather this is for my ears only, and Mariana will be along, and Franklin with his double.

—The essentials, then, and we can deal with the implications in good time. The blind folksinger my uncle wanted me to meet, and hear, lived with his sister and her husband on a farm about as remote as you can get. Dingy sheep with black legs, ponies, green hills all around. A very old white stone house, with barns and pens and sties also of stone. Dogs barked us in for half a kilometer, and I remember rings of hawks in a cloudy sky. The people were simple country folk but with those deep traditions which contain respect for scholarship and a familiarity with the Bible. There was a radio, I remember, which picked up Reykjavik. The interior was purest Ibsen, reeking of the past. Why are you smiling?

—Because I'm enjoying the tale.

—I don't see how you could be. The Bach partita helps. Well, country people, a blind folksinger. I'd never met a blind person, but I understood, before we left, how he lived in a world of familiar surfaces and spaces, and how his ears served as his eyes. He sang, accompanying himself on just such a harmonium as you and Mariana have, which you've taught Franklin and Pascal to sing so prettily to. I remember some lines of a spooky ballad, sung in a high, keen, perhaps falsetto voice.

—Countertenor, Hugo said.

—Yes, countertenor. The lines were:

Long is one night,
But longer are two,
O how can I wait for three?

When, later in life, I saw a photograph of Walt Whitman, I realized that they could have been taken for twins, right down to the shape of beard and hair. The faces, especially the eyes, were the same, strange as it is that blind and seeing eyes should resemble each other. He made his sister describe me to him, and I must have blushed wildly to hear myself itemized and assessed. Red-brown hair, sweet eyes, freckles, the handsome blue sweater, which the folksinger asked to feel, the new corduroy trousers, whose sound he'd wondered about. He ran his fingers over my face, and held my hands in his for an uncomfortably long time.

The phone rang. Hugo said into it:

—Lovely. Holger's here. He's telling me about his childhood. Oh yes. We'll have a fire, against the damp.

And to Holger:

—Mariana. She'll be along in a bit. Says hello.

—Well, then, to get to the substance of all this. There came a moment when Uncle and the sister were searching out old hymnals and some kind of folklore journal, these being in long chests painted over with trolls and floral swirls, and the folksinger enticed me over and whispered that he would like me to walk him to the outhouse. It didn't occur to me until later that he would have known the way perfectly, but I felt a measure of virtue in leading the blind to a call of nature. He kept his hand on my shoulder all the way. I won't try to describe the outhouse, a new experience for me. Once inside, he asked if anybody were near, and when I said no, he said that I should make water first, his words, make water. I did, feeling very sure of myself as a child of the city among such countrified and primitive people. My new togs enforced my sense of superiority, as the speech of these farm people was as antique as their strange clothes from the century before. The blind folksinger's trousers came up to his chest, and his shirt had pleats and a frill of lace at the collar, and his coat had the biggest buttons I'd ever seen. And then, when I was about to tuck in and zip up, the old codger fumbled for my penis, and got it. I'd never felt a hand other than my own on that tender organ, and I was mystified, scared, and obliging all at once. I won't try to analyze my emotions, except to say that my fear gave way to pleasure, and to the sweetness of stolen pleasure, at that. I want to be very truthful, Hugo, because I think this is a key to something that will probably be obvious to you, but which as yet isn't to me.

—We'll see, Hugo said. This gets better and better.

—He was an astute old cooter, and said we mustn't dally in the outhouse, even though my little man, as he called it, was springy stiff and feeling wonderfully sexy. His age, by the way, was probably late thirties or early forties, that is, an old man to my few years. So I zipped up, with my erection making a bump in my new corduroys, and as we walked back he sang some lilting ballad with a jolly refrain. He held me hard by the shoulder. When we got back to the house, he went no farther than the door, through which he said in a loud voice that the young gentleman wanted to see the black-faced sheep in the upper pasture. Where we walked, and when he asked if we were out of sight of the house, or of anybody, he mastered, by touch, the working of my zipper, while I stood in a kind of trance. He kept asking, in the kindest of voices, if I liked what he was doing, and I answered, quite truthfully, *yes*. He wanted to know if I did what he was doing by myself, and I remember how wonderfully wicked I felt when I replied that I did. But when he wanted to know if I had friends who did what he was doing, I said no, and he said that I must get new friends who would. He made me promise that, that very night, when I was home, I would play with myself, as he called it. We walked farther into the pastures, with sheep and cows staring at us. On top of a knoll I realized that we were walking in a great circle around the farm. And I must tell that not long after he'd jacked me off, he asked if I would like it again, and I eagerly unzipped for a replay. This time we did it together, his hand over mine, and he kissed me on my head as I reported on my rising pleasure.

—Good God, Holger! Hugo said. You were initiated into the boyish mysteries by a wizard of the *huldufolk*. Your cock's probably magic. I don't dare tell Mariana.

—You're the only person I've ever told this, you understand. At the time, it was not something I could tell anybody. It was, indeed, a rite of passage. That afternoon ended with the folksinger saying that I was not a boy but an angel, with everyone pleased that I had brought joy to the house for a few hours, and there was a long ballad before we left, which interested my uncle, as he'd never heard it, and asked to return to take it, and others, down. So there you have it, friend Hugo: a kind of primal event, as clear as I can tell it.

—Did you return?

—Yes, several times, and with similar ruses for being out of sight long enough for our stolen pleasure. And I was faithful to his injunction. That was a lovely secret that I hoarded: an adult who wanted me to feel sexual pleasure.

—He didn't take you in his mouth?

—Well, yes, he did. I was trying to spare you that.

—I can't think why. And the real question is why you wanted me to know this rustic tale from wildest Iceland.

—Isn't it the Freudian *es* of the formula? Where it was, there must I come to be.

313

—I couldn't possibly say. Holger, old boy, I know exactly nothing of your emotional life.

—There isn't any. I was engaged for a while when I was at the university, but broke it off when in a dismal revelation all I could see was a prospect of gin, bridge, and television. Moreover, she was Catholic, with transparent designs for my conversion. And smoked.

—You should be cheerful the rest of your life for so narrow an escape. No wonder you love to hie off on weekends to the darkest forests. As for your psychological backtracking, I see more in the earlier memory. It's a painting by Mary Cassatt. Only thing in my past I can put beside it is the day I showed the postman my dick. Everybody in Kindergarten had liked seeing it, and I was sure he would, too.

BYGGVIR THE BARLEY

The light that had been so radiantly pellucid all afternoon took on bronze tones in the pinewood. On the slow rise of a slope soft with a flooring of pine needles Holger, Pascal, and Jos laid out provender.

—A good ten kilometers, Jos said.

—I've never walked so far, Pascal said. Not all at a go, anyway.

A long walk is one of my ways of keeping body and soul on speaking terms, Holger said.

—Neatest of ideas, Jos said, to take the bus to Tidselby and walk back to Grundtvig. You didn't think I'd come along, did you, Holger? Couldn't say no to Pascal, though I did come and ask if you really wanted me. I mean, it's your walk, with Pascal. Deviled eggs! Chocolate squares!

—Catered, Holger said. Fru Vinterberg, for a modest fee, composed this feed: sandwiches, buttermilk, coffee, deviled eggs, cheese, no end to it. Paper napkins, even. And gave her motherly blessing to a picnic in the country.

—Didn't comment, did she, Jos asked with his mouth full of sandwich, on how you spoil Pascal rotten?

—Jos, Holger said to Pascal, pointedly, is a horrible example of the kind of person who knows no ground between a very correct formal politeness and unbuttoned familiarity. The old Jos used to be a model Danish schoolboy to his housemaster, and the new Jos treats him as the sailor next bunk over in the forecastle of a herring trawler.

—So? Jos asked. We've sat up all night talking about a hundred things, and I've slept off a carnal binge in your bed, and you like to see me being drawn and painted by crazy Hugo.

—It's a good picture, Pascal said. Are those pickles in that paper boat? He's going to paint me, too, skinny as I am, and Franklin, but maybe with clothes, or some clothes on. He's done Franklin nude several times.

—Is he a good painter, Holger? Jos asked. I think he is.

—He says, Pascal answered, that painting is his way of showing others what he sees. If he were a poet or a writer, he could say what he sees. Franklin and I asked why he didn't just photograph things, and he said he might, at that. But wouldn't quit painting. There are lots of sketchbooks all of Mariana.

—It is my opinion, probably worthless, Jos said, that everything Hugo does is sex, one way or another.

—Talk about seeing yourself in others, Holger said.

Pascal grinned around a deviled egg.

—If I weren't me, I'd like to be Hugo, Jos said. I don't know about looking after all those scouts, or teaching Sunday School, but I'd like to do the brainy things he does with the big dictionaries and books, and paint, and bounce Mariana four or five times a day, and maybe even love on Franklin. Does he do that, Pascal, love on Franklin?

—Do you think I know, Jos? Pascal asked, putting a foot against his knee and pushing.

—Boys, Holger said.

—Probably does, Jos said. Is there any more buttermilk?

—Finish mine, I think these soft pine needles, so lovely warm and crunchy, want me to stretch out on them and have a lazy rest, good for the digestion.

—Holger's ideas are unfailingly top-notch, Jos said. First, a wild bus to Tidselby, with its sights, cabbage patches on the high street, and a row of piglets having lunch on fru Pig. Secondly, a nifty hike, very comradely, and with news of the flora and fauna along the way. If Pascal is as educated at twelve as Holger is at twenty-whatever, what in the name of sweet Jesus will Pascal sound like when he's Holger's decrepit age? Thirdly, a picnic in the woods. And now pallet drill on sunny pine needles. May I be totally comfortable, Holger?

—What now, scamp?

—Discard my pants? Which are Asgar's anyway, and are biting my hipbones. Mine, with the slit pockets, were too nasty for an outing among moral Danes. Shirt off will feel good, too.

—Dapper undergear, Holger said.

Jos, brown and smiling in a jockstrap with a finely meshed net pouch, tapped his broad and thick pectorals with admiring fingers, the knobby furrows of his ribs, the grooved plane of his long abdomen.

—You're beautiful, Jos, Pascal said. An ancient Greek.

—Work hard enough at it, Jos said. High-tech tough, the supporter. The fit is perfect, as the waist and cinches latch together with Velcro facings, the cup too. See?

—So you assemble it on your person?

—And rip it off, Jos said. Infant friend Pascal, if you'll lie on that side of sleepy Holger, at right angles, like, I'll lie on this side, using him for a companionable pillow, all of us wickedly close.

—Feels naughty, Pascal said.

—Friendly, Jos said.

—Slit pockets, Pascal said.

—I knew that hadn't slipped past Pascal, Holger said.

—For making my dick happy in class. Ankle on knee, book propped just so, and one can frig away fifty minutes which otherwise would be the dullest in northwest Europe. Tom and I sit beside each other in five classes, and inspire and encourage each other. Should Pascal hear this, Holger?

—Nerd! Pascal said.

—Should *I* hear it? Holger asked, running fingers into Jos's hair, and into Pascal's.

—Holger can hear it, Jos said, if he won't snitch to housemaster Sigurjonsson.

—Which of those two is being lain on by two Grundtviggers in the sun, deliciously warm?

—Holger, Pascal said. Housemaster Sigurjonsson won't exist again until we're back. Masturbation was invented by the god Hermes.

—Jesus, Jos said.

—Hugo told me that, Pascal said. Me and Franklin.

—He's the one who delivers telegrams from Olympus, isn't he? Jos asked. Wears a derby with wings, and has cute little wings on his ankles, and clears his way with two snakes fucking on a stick? Otherwise dressed for a bath?

—That's him, Pascal said.

—Is it still Holger, Jos asked, who's messing with my hair?

—Still Holger, Holger said.

—Thing is, Jos went on, is not to mind if you come, and to brazen out looking as if you've broken an egg in your pants. Tom, the god Hermes of NFS Grundtvig, worked out the technique. No underwear, old pants with the pockets scissored out, and the degree of covert operation required. In McTaggart's world's dullest class, you can unzip and jack away in the open, behind the big English anthology. Latin and Ethics, inside, and stay on one's guard. Geometry's a ticklish business also, with caution and vigilance repaid, especially as Walliser is some species of religious fanatic. But Art Appreciation is a snap, what with the room darkened for slides.

—How, Pascal asked, can you pay attention?

—What, Cricket, do you think about when you whack off?

—Nothing, Pascal said.

—Holger still with us? Jos asked, rolling his head under Holger's fingers.

—Still here, but barely.

—Sigurjonsson not likely to come back suddenly? Paying attention's no problem. I pay better attention in Art Appreciation and Geometry for having my dick feel like the last movement of Beethoven's Ninth. In Ethics and English

I'm making up for the scarcity of spirit in Bakke and McTaggart. Tom, what a champion, can come while sight-reading Latin.

—The tenacious diligence of it all is what gets through to me, Holger said. The biology is plain enough.

Pascal reached back and laced fingers with Holger.

—For all our whiffling our peters as a pair, Jos said, like before Latin when we're good at happening on each other in my room or his, to work tone into our members, you know, and breeze, he's never made a pass at me, loyal to gawky Lemuel all the way. Who, Lemuel I mean, is of a reticence, circumspect, except, natch, with Tom. Lacks imagination, Lemuel.

—Are you being depraved by all this, Pascal? Holger said. I am.

—If I am, is it OK?

—Why not? Jos said, rolling over and propping his chin in Pascal's forehead. Pascal has lots of rascal in him.

—Franklin, my buddy, Pascal said, found the rascal, and likes him. He's a nice rascal. I can talk Jos Sommerfeld, too.

—And, Holger said, Pascal's finding the brainy boy in Franklin.

Jos rolled back over, resting his head on Holger's abdomen.

—Not being too familiar, am I? he asked with an indicative bobble.

—You're an affectionate person, Jos, Holger said.

—Shameless, Jos said.

—But with style, Holger said. Much would have to be forgiven you, except for style, shouldn't we say in all candor?

—Housemaster Sigurjonsson has returned, Pascal said.

—Mna, Jos said, rising to hands and knees, he's taking the afternoon off.

He crossed Holger on all fours, stood and rolled his shoulders, cupped a hand over the pouch of his jockstrap, appraising its swell, clucked through puckered lips, prodded Pascal's shoulder lightly with his toe, and sat beside him, shoving a hand with walking fingers under his shirt.

—Talk about being familiar, Pascal said.

—Nobody's looking, Jos said.

—Somebody's untying my shoes, Pascal said. And winkling off my socks.

—Holger's still here, Holger said, but how much longer I can't promise.

—That's my zipper!

—Squeaky clean didies, Jos said, extra small. Shake him out of his shirt, Holger, while I deprive you of your shoes. We're all, before hr. Sigurjonsson comes home, going to have a big rough threeway hug, just as God made us, because the world is full of hopeless nerds afraid of being touched and too fucking mean to cuddle a puppy, and we're sweet daffy friends, yes? Oh yes!

—Oh wow! Pascal said.

—Undo Holger in various places, Jos said, and skin him to the balls. He's more or less covered with red hair all over, which will tickle.

Holger, crimson, nevertheless stood for Pascal to unbutton his shirt with awkward fingers. He unbuckled his belt himself, and had begun on the brass buttons of his hiking shorts when Jos took over, deftly, and hauled down shorts and briefs together.

—Jim bang goofy! Pascal said, Jos lifting him into Holger's arms.

—That's the spirit, Jos said, collapsing them onto the pine needles with a robust, pulling hug. Pascal between them, Holger and Jos, hands locked in the small of each other's backs, rocked into momentum enough to roll over twice.

They lay still. Jos, caressing Holger's back, nuzzled his face in Pascal's hair. He kissed the back of Pascal's neck, relinquishing the doubleness of his embrace to hug Pascal alone.

—Your turn, he said, rolling away.

Pascal wrapped arms and legs around Holger.

—That's the style, Cricket, Jos said. Nothing shy. I'm right here, greedy, when you've squeezed Holger breathless.

—OK, Pascal said, tousled of hair, dazed and vague of eye, but you and Holger have to hug, too, next.

They complied, laughing happily, Jos drumming his heels on the ground.

—We're stuck all over with pine needles, Jos said, sitting up and gasping. One on my dick. Tell you what: I started this, and I see how to wrap it up before hr. Sigurjonsson puts a stop to it. I get one more warm and wild hug from Pascal, and Holger gets one, exactly as warm and wild, and then we turn back into stodgy Danes out hiking, huh?

Warm and wild hugs hugged, Holger brushed and picked pine needles off Pascal with a dreamy gentleness, and held his underpants for him to step into, and settled their fit.

—You're going to dress me?

His question was quiet, matter of fact.

—Mind?

—What is there to mind?

Pascal ran his arms into the sleeves of his shirt, and looked pleased and proud as Holger buttoned it on. Hiking pants, socks, shoes, followed.

—I can tie my shoes, at least.

—No, Holger said, I tie them.

—Friendly, Jos said. I'm loving this. My Christian feast of neighborliness worked, you see.

51

The next Ice Age began in the fourteenth century. Cold wet winters advanced the prows of the glaciers. Harvests in the north of Europe failed year after year, until the vineyards of England were abandoned. In Scandinavia and

Iceland wheat and barley farmers became fishermen. Art became speculative and ironic.

LIONS HAVE NO HISTORIANS

He drank only well water, the blind folksinger, never spirits. Is your hair coppery gold, he had asked, or is it the white of meal, as with the old stock? He believed in the hidden folk. I know too much about them to doubt that they are. They are, you know, he had said, with a squeeze for Holger's shoulder. They are wise. Your smallclothes are cunningly sewn, he had said, and your hands are as soft as a girl's. The hidden folk sent you to me, and the debt I owe them is large.

53

—Holger! Jos said, coming in without knocking, what the fuck happened?

—Sprained my ankle, Holger said. In the gym.

—Lemuel said you'd met Biology on crutches. Here I am. What can I do? Where's Pascal?

Holger was in his easy chair, his bandaged foot on a stool.

—The horse, Holger said. I was getting good at it, and next thing I knew I'd come a cropper, with a shooting pain in the ankle. Hobbled over to the infirmary, where Matron tied on twenty or so meters of gauze, as you see, issued me crutches, and commanded me to stay off my foot for three or four days.

—Awesome, Jos said. And not like you. You're as unbreakable and permanently healthy as crazy Hugo.

—Jos, Holger said, the front of your pants, which look as if they have been worn in a ship's galley by six generations of teenaged apprentice cooks, is sopping wet.

—Don't change the subject. I want to know what I can do to help. I'll move in, bring you things, pour and stir your medicine. Didn't you get any medicine?

—Aspirin.

—Two loads, Jos said of his pants. Came in English and in Ethics. I didn't take time to change. Apologies, if needed.

—Of course not. See who's at the door.

It was Mariana.

—Holger, poor baby! she said. Hi, Jos. Holger, Hugo called and said you'd fallen ass over heels doing gymnastics but that you hadn't broken anything, only wrenched a tendon in your ankle. What did Matron, the bitch, do for you?

—Bound it up. Says to stay off it.

—Didn't put anything on it?

—Nope.

—Not even Baume Bengué? I suspected as much, which is why I'm here, on my lunch hour, with the goods.

She took from her purse a large bottle.

—The liniment of Sloan. It's really just turpentine and red peppers. Comes from Pastor Tvemunding, who swears by it. What's more, it works. I daub it on Hugo all the time. It did wonders for an ankle I sprained last year. Got any cotton swabs?

—In the bathroom cabinet, Jos.

—Also, Jos, put on a kettle, Mariana said. Have you peed your pants? Bring a washcloth, a basin for the hot water, and I'll unwind this silly bandage.

—I'm not used to all this attention, Holger said. Florence Nightingale and Jos. I wouldn't ask about his pants again, if I were you.

—Oh come on, Holger, she said, busily unwrapping gauze from his foot, I wasn't born yesterday. Does it hurt?

—Throbs.

—Kettle's on, Jos said. Basin and washcloth here, plus a sack of cotton balls. In which drawer are your briefs, Holger?

—Top left.

—I see your gym shorts on the bed, if I may borrow them, and a pair of underbritches, and then frøken Landarbejder will be spared my depraved pants.

—With bottomless pockets, Mariana said sweetly. I do happen to be Franklin's big sister.

ONE HUNDRED STARING SHEEP

Long slopes of bluebells and buttercups under windy running clouds. The ranny mouse, the blind folksinger said, let us free the ranny mouse from his sweet nest in the bag of your smallclothes, that smell so clean and are of such soft fabric, so neatly sewn. What a nice sleeping mouse he is, and grows so fast when he wakes.

55

—Couldn't get here before now, Pascal said, and have rather disgraced myself, at that. I heard you'd been to class on crutches, and then that Hugo was taking your geography class, and I asked McTaggart to be excused from English, as I'd heard you'd had an accident, and McTaggart asked what that had to do with anything, least of all cutting his class. And when I said you might need me, he laughed, and I already had my foot back to kick him when I was smart enough to see that kicking the English master, as he deserved, wasn't a bright idea, so I had to stay, but Hugo, of course, excused me from gym without my even asking. Go look after Holger, he said.

—He sent Mariana at noon, Holger said. The odor of turps pervading the room is Sloan's Liniment, as per the bottle of it there, which Mariana and Jos dabbed on my foot, which is only sprained, after soaking it in boiling water. Cooked it, I think.

—Jos?

—He was here first, after I hobbled from the infirmary. Mariana, who has a degree in nursing children, you know, was incensed at Matron's treatment, and did it all over, her way, or, rather, Pastor Tvemunding's way. Sloan's Liniment is Capsicum oleoresin, methyl salicylate, oil of camphor, pine oil, and turpentine.

—Mexican red peppers in urinal cleaner, Pascal said. Oh wow.

—What about some tea and toast with marmalade, friend Pascal? I'm to stay off my foot. I've been hoping you'd turn up.

—Don't dare get up. I know where everything is.

Halfway down the hall, he turned and ran back to give Holger a hug and nuzzled kiss, getting hugged in return.

—Cups, saucers, plates, Pascal said after an interval of putting the kettle on and buttering bread for the oven, cream and sugar, spoons and knives. Let's move the coffee table here. I can sit on the floor. Holger, are those Jos's pants over the foot of your bed?

—Sodden with sperm? Pocketless? Those are indeed Jos's pants. He came directly here from class, when news of my crash spread through the school like wildfire, without changing into decent attire. When Mariana turned up, Jos borrowed a pair of my gym shorts, as well as briefs, but not before Mariana got an eyeful of handsome Jos in the article of clothing under discussion, which in the first instance define how generously he's hung, and in the second, that over two classes this morning he drenched them twice, liberally.

—Jos, Pascal said, Jos. I like Jos.

—Jos likes you. He would have gone ahead and kicked McTaggart, I fear. And McTaggart kicked by Jos would be in the hospital rather than in his rooms waited on hand and foot by the eminent geologist Pascal Raskvinge.

—Nobody would give a hoot if McTaggart sprained both his ankles. Kettle's boiling! Somebody's at the door! Toast is probably burning.

EN TO TRE

Firstness is such as it is, a mode of being positively and without reference to anything else. Secondness is such as it is, a mode of being with respect to a second but regardless of any third. Thirdness is such as it is, a mode of being bringing a second and a third in relation to each other. I call these three ideas the cenopythagorean categories.

57

—Holger's having a nap, Pascal said. Be quiet.

Jos slipped through the door and closed it softly.

—Hello, Jos, Holger said. I wasn't asleep. Pascal glutted me with marmalade and toast, and I sort of snoozed off.

—I'm back. I went first, as I thought I might be needed here.

—First what? Pascal asked. Help me wash up.

—Never mind what first, Jos said, putting his hand on Holger's forehead. No fever. I could carry you to your bed.

—I'm fine, Jos, Holger said. My only problem is that to walk I have to hop on crutches for a few days.

—I can sleep here, on the floor by your bed, in case you need something in the night.

—Pascal! Holger called. Come and throw Jos out of here.

—Whichwhat? Pascal said, a dishtowel around his neck.

—Explain to Jos that I am not helpless, or senile, or weak as a kitten, and that I intend to live to a ripe old age, please.

—Did I leave my sticky pants here at noon? I'll change back, and return your gym shorts, for the loan of which, thanks, and your briefs, which now smell of inside a girl, and of me.

—Let me see, Pascal said. And come wash cups and saucers.

SYNERGETICS 529.10

It is one of the strange facts of experience that when we try to think about the future, our thoughts jump backward. It may well be that nature has some fundamental metaphysical law by which opening up what we call the future also opens up the past in equal degree.

59

—It's time for another soaking of my wrenched pedal extremity, Holger said. So back to the kettle.

—I'll do it, Pascal said.

—I'll pat on the Liniment of Sloan, Jos said. Official paramedic on the staff of frøken Landarbejder is what I am. She cures by just being here. I could see Holger get better as soon as she rolled up.

—Jos, Holger said, do your pants stay up by faith alone?

—They're stuck on, Pascal said from the kitchen.

—Forgot to zip up. Dick acts as a wedge. Did I forget to say that they're coming to see you, Hugo, Mariana, and Franklin?

—Basin of scalding water! Pascal said. *En garde!*

—I can undo the bandage, Jos. I'm not helpless, if I can ever get you to believe it.

—We like waiting on you, Pascal and I. Put your foot in the water. Cricket, where are the rabbit scuts?

Pascal jogged down the hall, humming the grand theme from *The Reformation Symphony*, and came back with Holger's pyjamas, plaid dressing gown, and one bedroom slipper.

—But, Holger said, there's dinner to hobble to in an hour.

—We're going to bring it to you, Pascal said. Fru Vinterberg will make you a tray, make us all trays, as I told her we had to eat here with you.

—God in heaven, Holger said.

—Off your shirt, Pascal said, and britches and undies. I found the jammies under your pillow.

—What you're doing, Holger said, is playing hospital. Pascal suffocating me with a pyjama shirt while Jos slathers liquid fire on my foot.

—Wrapping the bandage back on is the big thrill, Jos said. Let's get you into the bottoms before I do that. Wonderful aroma, the Liniment of Sloan.

RUE DE FLEURUS

Human nature is not interesting. The human mind is interesting and the universe.

PAPYRUS

Yeshua was the shepherd who abandoned the nine and ninety sheep to find the one sheep which was lost. There was delight in his heart when he found it, for nine and ninety is a number of the left hand, and if one is added to it, it passes to the right.

62

—Question 1, Comrade Jos, Pascal said, is are you going with me to get our dinner trays in those gummy pants with the snail tracks all over the front, and question 2, is, if you are, how are you going to carry a tray with both hands in your pockets?

—Quite right, O demiliter moral guide. Have to reborrow Holger's briefs and gym shorts. Must look clean-cut and handsome for fru Vinterberg.

—What I fear, Holger said, is that Jos is going to feed me like a baby bird, and put me in the shower afterward, and wash me, and put me to bed with a hot-water bottle.

A STARFISH IN STRING

Greek exercises on Hugo's worktable Holger on crutches saw, corrected in Latin, skylight muntins and stiles grid of shadow and square panes, bright, on them, yellow and blue pencils in a James Keiller & Son Ltd Dundee Orange Marmalade jar. Clothbound notebook, Hugo's skilled calligraphic hand. A magazine *Le Petit Gredin*, its cover a meticulous drawing of a scalawaggish urchin with mussed hair, fleshy penis the swarthier for jutting from the pale trace of small swimming trunks. *Centre pour Recherche*, and a little girl with merry eyes on the cover of *L'Espoir*, naked with butterblond hair, genital mound pudgier and more distinctly cleft than Holger would have imagined, *pour une enfance différente*. Manila envelope with Belgian stamps. Franklin's sneakers, mustard and blue, stuffed with white socks, under the table.

64

—Antinoos and Eros, Hugo said. I think I'll sprain my ankle, too.

—Eglund called just now, Holger said, and I assured him that I can stump to all my classes on crutches, and that I'm not in the least out of commission. What we're to make of last night I'm not certain.

—I'm proud of Franklin for insisting that Pascal stay here.

—Well, it went this way after you, Mariana, and Franklin left. Jos absolutely insisted on seeing me safely to bed, tucking me in, putting the crutches against a chair, setting a lamp with tilted shade on the floor for a night light. Then I shooed both rascals out, commanding them to go to bed. I was reading myself to sleep when here came Jos with blankets and pillow, saying that he was going to sleep on the floor by my bed, wearing only one of those sweatshirts of his that seem to have survived unlaundered and unmended as hand-me-downs from his brothers and to have been worn by several strenuous contenders over the last two or three Olympic tryouts.

—Lovely, Hugo said.

—These kippers were cooked by Pascal, who has just left, towed away by Jos. Once Jos, you see, had made his pallet, wrapped in blankets like a red Indian, he remarked casually that Pascal was brokenhearted because Jos had convinced him that the two of them playing field hospital here would be a nuisance rather than a help. So, idiot that I am, I gave him the choice of going back to his room or of fetching Pascal.

—But absolutely, Hugo said. I can't think that Jos was being mean. He just wasn't thinking.

—May I report, for your ears only, that Pascal had been crying when Jos went and brought him in, more or less across his shoulders?

—Pascal, Hugo said, pouring himself a cup of coffee, has obviously existed forever, to look at him, a tall twelve-year-old with the singular, intelligent beauty you see in northern Italians, and is just as obviously growing in front of one's gaze from an awkward, dreamy little boy into a graceful adolescent. Nothing of the ox in him. Father's a diplomat, living apart from his mother, who's some species of psychiatrist. He has depended on his acquisitive mind to stock his heart, and would, I think, be terribly lonely without you and Franklin. He's latched onto you, Holger, because you're all brain, too, and have kept the passion for learning and knowing which is burning so brightly in him.

—Italian? Holger asked.

—Pascal's mother is Genovese. His father's as Danish as a Holstein.

—Pascal was radiant when I woke them this morning, wrapped in the same blanket and with their heads on the same pillow. Foot's much better, I think, by the way.

—Even so, Mariana says you're to stay off it for another two days. The efficacy of Sloan's Liniment is largely imaginary, but Papa believes in it, and Mariana. So it works, like everything else they believe in.

SOCIETAS AULUS GELLIUS

If Anders, then Kim. The Alumni Room, regular meeting place of the Latin sight-reading club, was preempted by old boys and directors, and Hugo had commandeered the boathouse loft, which the Ungdomsfrihed Band had made their clubhouse, an oblong white room with red and blue rafters, square barn windows, bare floor as scrubbed and uncluttered as a deck. German and Dutch posters for the Cause on the walls, and photographs by Hajo Ortil and Jos Meyer. A red bookcase made by Anders contained in neat stacks copies of *Signe de Piste, Pan, Libido, Le Petit Gredin, Juvenart, Blue Jeans*, and *Pojkart*.

—We sit on pallets, the ones stacked over there, Hugo said. About half of us belong to both clubs, so it seemed logical to ask to meet here, and everybody agreed.

—Quit looking as if you'll catch something, Harald, Anders said. Nobody's going to put his hand on your knee.

—Why not? Tom said. Harald's knees are nice and boxy.

—Watch it, Harald said.

—So, Hugo said, if we're all comfortable, let's go with line 189 of the Ausonius, where the poem becomes Monet, as I was talking about last time, and Hjalmar has brought two books with Monets that have reflections in rivers.

—*Glaucus*, Marcus said, is a color adjective, for sure, but what color?

—The color of a river in summer, Harald said, under a clear sky. Green, blue green, silvery green.

66

—You'd think, you know, Pascal said, that Jos and me in a blanket by your bed adds up to two, huh? Not a bit of it. Three. Jos, me, and Jos's hangdown, which didn't.

—Is it having the highest IQ at NFS Grundtvig, Tiger, Jos said, that makes you warm as a stove?

—I'm not listening to you two, you understand, Holger said, but if I were, I wouldn't know whether I was hearing grousing or bragging. A little of good

Pastor Tvemunding's snake oil goes a long way, Jos. So, easy.

—Got to get you well. It makes Pascal low in his mind for you to be a cripple.

—Does not, Pascal said. Makes me happy I can help. That's Franklin at the door.

—Hello, Jos Holger Pascal, Franklin said, darting in to shake Holger's hand, touch foreheads with Pascal, and be grabbed, hoisted, and kissed on the tummy by Jos.

—What was that all about? he asked.

—Just feeling friendly, Jos said. Holger and Pascal are shy, being respectively a dignified housemaster and an infant genius, whereas you and I, Citizen Franklin, are rogues, *jo?*

—I shook Holger's hand, Franklin said. And how's your foot? I was forgetting that part of it. Practiced on Mariana. And then Jos, you're to pose at four, Jos, Hugo said to tell you, Jos fucked up my hair, combed it twice. And Pascal and me and Holger are to come to supper at six. I'm to be here with Pascal until then, unless Holger doesn't want us. Then we could go swimming or something, or something, you know.

—Swimming it is, or the various somethings, Holger said. Off with the two of two.

—Will you be all right? Pascal said.

—No, never. I'll fall out of my chair and get gangrene and die of thirst and loneliness. And take Jos with you.

—I'd thought, Jos said, I'd have a little nap here beside your chair, in case you need something, until four.

67

I crossed the Neva, muddy and in spate, at Vincum, an old town with fine new Roman walls. It was here that the legions trounced a revolt of the Gauls as thoroughly as Hannibal crushed the legions at Cannae years before. The peaceful fields I walked across, sweet with hay and with nothing more than the lowing of cattle and the whistling of larks to ruffle the quiet, were once strewn with black corpses of the Treveri, flocks of carrion birds cawing and pecking.

A deep forest to get through beyond the fields, pathless, dark and thick. Here in the northern reaches of the empire these wildernesses maintain, forests without roads, unmapped marshes, wooded valleys with no human beings for miles and miles. The town of Dumnissus, I knew, lay over to my left, and the springs at Tabernae: lands recently settled by Sarmatians, barbarians brought into the empire to learn farming and to pay taxes.

On the other side of the forest I could see the Belgian town Noviomagus, Constantine's headquarters when he brought the Franks and Alamanni into the peace of Rome. The sunlight after the dark of the forest was wonderful under a blue and open sky, making me for a moment feel that I was in my own country, and half expected to find the vineyards of Bordeaux, steep radiant skies, broad blue rivers, the red roofs of country villas. For the Moselle of the Belgii is the Garonne here in the north, and Roman civilization has made it even more like. Here are Roman vineyards on slopes, green pastures cleared along the river, which is deep enough for ocean vessels, and the tide comes far upstream. This is a watery part of the world, rich in creeks, lakes, springs. No cliffs, no river islands, no shoals. Boats can move freely by current, by oars, by rope and towpath, and the river is fast, unlike the unhurrying, the majestic Garonne with its slow bends and long promontories that impede its progress to the sea. Nor does the Moselle silt up its banks or have swamps of reeds along it. Here you can walk on dry ground to the river's edge. There are even beaches of hard sand, like marble floors, taking no footprint.

A DIAL HAND, NO PACE PERCEIVED

The tent by lantern light, side flaps down and secure, had the temporized homeliness of nomadic space. The silence of deep dark for Bach, Spartan disregard of the ground's hardness for comfort, accuracy of memory. No depths, Hugo had said, there are only distances. Jos's clinically white jockstrap, that bulked his genitals into a double fist, thumbs out, was the more erotic for being without any decorative line. It remembered archaic basketry, the harmony of its coarse meshwork finely woven, form without style. A little other.

Holger listened to the night, hearing a badger, perhaps, perhaps a stoat. The lake lay as still as mercury.

69

And the river is transparent right to the bottom, where one can see with perfect clarity ribbed and furrowed sand, blue-green watergrasses combed flat by the current but undulant, stitched by zigzagging fish, or clean stretches of pebbles, or whitest gravel with patches of moss. And toward the estuary, seaweed and pink coral, and mussels with pearls, as if nature, which wastes with a prodigal hand, and which owns with indifference all that mankind lusts for, had strewn jewels and the baubles of the rich along the river bottom.

Chub swarm here, a toothsome bony fish, best when cooked within six hours of catching; trout speckled purple and silver; roach, whose bones are not the needles of most fish; grayling, shy and hard to catch. And barbel, who comes down the Saar, a river that rushes through gorges, and is happy, once it has swum past the three-arched Consular Bridge, to be in the calm Moselle. The barbel alone of living things improves in taste with age.

And salmon, with its rose flesh, whose robust tail even at middepth ripples the surface. Who, at a meal of many dishes, has not asked to have the salmon first? Fat, savory, silver-scaled salmon!

And the eel pout is here, too, brought from the Danube to stock another noble river, a welcome immigrant, and one that has thrived. Nature, the master designer, has speckled its back with spots, like the first raindrops of a storm on stone, and each spot she has ringed with a saffron circle. The lower back she has made skyblue. And perch, the only river fish that can vie in taste with those of the sea, delicious as red mullet, and like it filleting easily into halves. And pike, whose local name has given way to the Latin *lucius*, eater of frogs, who keeps to creek mouths and pools, fancier of marshgrass and mud, never seen on the gentry's tables but a frequent fellow in taverns and peasant kitchens, fried golden brown in deep fat. And with him other hardy fish of the people: green tench, and the bleak, favorite of boys at their campfires, and shad, delicacy of the humble hearth, the poor man's salmon or trout. And gudgeon.

And catfish, that genial monster, defying classification. Is it the smallest of the whales and dolphins? Is it the last of a primeval order of nature, living on beyond its epoch?

FRIEDRICHSTRASSE 1927
Gunther in a secondhand belted jacket the color of oatmeal, a blue pinstriped blouse a size too large, scruffy shoes, wide-brimmed straw hat, short pants. Hair feathery and full at his nape. All of an afternoon Holger had read *Der Puppenjunge*. Hugo had brought it to him, saying that it was a book he ought to know. Narrative is the music of prose, and prose the mute inner thought of poetry. Holger found such statements annoying, neither fact nor theory. They were valuable, however, because Hugo said them. The meaning, Hugo had said, is in the narrative.

71
Look up. Every slope is a vineyard, as if we were in the Campania, Rhodope, or Bordeaux, where our vines are mirrored green in the yellow and silver Garonne.

From the highest ridge down to the Moselle, grapes. The tenders of them shout jovial obscenities to the barges and travelers on the river road. Voices carry over water, and the hills make a natural theater for coarse laughter and rival wit. This *scaena*, a poet might say, includes men half goat and blue-eyed watergirls locking eyes in brambles on the bank, swimming saucily away. Panope, the lady of the river, steals with her daughters, as stealthily as mist at dawn, to nibble grapes, and rude fauns with the gourdish testicles of rams and a bullwhorl of hair between their nubby horns, chase them back into the river. Peasants have seen them dancing all of a summer night, and more, which I will not repeat. *Secreta tegatur et commissa suis lateat reverentia rivis.*

More fit for human gaze is the grove on the hill reflected upside-down in the blue river. The illusion is of trees and vines flourishing deep in the water, swaying with a liquid motion. Barges floating through treetops!

Oars dipping into grapevines!

Sinuous silver slices limb from limb, instantly rejoining them in a rippling dance.

—We should be reading this down at the river, Asgar said.

—Naked, Halfdan added.

And across this inverted landscape comes a battle of boys in skiffs, oars dipping deep, their boats circling each other, the one driving the other into the bank. Workers in the vineyards stop to watch, and cheer their naked sons and brothers on, boys browned by the summer sun, with copperbright hair. When the ships of Caesar Augustus defeated those of Antonius and Cleopatra at Actium, Aphrodite declared games to celebrate the victory at Apollo's temple. She commanded Eros and his stripling friends to re-enact the battle in toy triremes, with tenor shouts mimicking the cries of marines and sailors, and all against a background of the vineyards that slope down Vesuvius, the hanging black cloud of which represented the smoke from burning ships. So the Euboians replay Mylae with charming adolescents in boats. Here on the Mosella, if we look at the inverted reflections of country boys shoving each other's boats with oars, shouting battle cries, we can imagine we are seeing naked Eros playing Roman sailor for Aphrodite's delight, Hyperion embracing them.

And their sisters, watching from the bank, use the river as a mirror to reset the combs in their hair, and to blow kisses to their warping reflections, and wind a curl onto a finger, and study the effect, and complain that their brothers are shaking the river so.

A fishing boat with nets comes along, and boats with men fishing with pole and hook. The boys leave their play to help with the cork-buoyed seines. The catches are laid out, panting and gasping, on the rocks, to drown in air.

72

Whisking rain on the window, weak daylight ruling a stack of thin slits in the blind, the room chill, Jos, rolled in blankets with Pascal on the floor beside Holger's bed, propped himself on his elbows, and craned his neck to see if Holger was, by luck, awake.

—Holger! he said softly.

Pascal ruckled in his sleep.

—Jos? Holger said.

—Half an hour before reveille. The floor has gotten much harder than it was night before last, and twice as flat, and it's cold down here. What about I stick a whippet of a boy in bed with you, followed by myself? Nobody's looking.

—Sure, Holger said.

—I'll take off my doggy sweatshirt, and add our blankets to yours. Pascal smells as sweet as a shampooed and talcumed baby, and has been cooing like one. Is there room on this side? He's sound asleep. I'll huddle in on the other.

—Charming, Holger said.

—Apply an arm around our sleeping friend, or he'll miss me.

—You can keep your sweatshirt on, Jos. I'm not finicky.

—Oo! Jos sighed. It's warm under here, and most of all it's not the hard-hearted floor. Listen to the rain.

—Go back to sleep, Holger whispered.

A surge of weightlessness had tossed through his genitals as he slid his arm over Pascal's shoulders. Pascal snuggled his hair against Holger's cheek, and stretched a leg across his thighs.

—It's too nice to go back to sleep, Jos said. Just need to lie here and soak the ungiving floor out of my back and butt, and feel warm and affectionate, and think about people already up and out in the rain. Hugo, about now, is lugging his overworked cock out of a sore and overfucked Mariana, saying his prayers in Greek, to run six kilometers through the wet, singing Lutheran hymns. Franklin's probably with him, hair stuck flat to his head, happy as a piglet at the teat. There are fat and farting politicians out there, dreaming of money. First thing they'll think about when they get up is new ways to steal, start wars, starve the people.

—Starve the people, Pascal said, wrapping both arms around Holger.

—Thinks you're me, Jos said. He gropes, I might warn you. Nothing personal. Dreaming of Franklin.

—Who's dreaming of Franklin? Pascal asked, awake. Hey! Where am I? What is this?

—Good morning, Holger said.

—Holger, Jos said, took pity on us on the hard floor, and has put us in his soft bed, picking us both up at once, you under one arm, me under the other, despite having to hop with us on one foot, and has distributed us around on this supercomfortable mattress, with him in the middle, to keep you from throttling my dick and depraving me.

—How long have we been here? Pascal asked in a small voice.

—All night, Jos said. You had wet dreams the whole time. Couldn't tell which was the rain outside and which the pitterpatter of Pascal sperm under the covers, splashing all over us.

—Good old Jos, Pascal said. Is this all right, Holger? Us in the bed with you?

—Of course not, Holger said. The headmaster would go weak in the knees and have several heart attacks. One boy in my bed would have the same effect on him. And I have, by last count, two.

—Went to sleep on the floor, Pascal said, Jos and me, and I wake up in a bed. Did Jos wake up when you put him in?

—Jos put you in, Holger said. And put himself in. Me, I'm an innocent Icelandic Reformed Evangelical Lutheran, bachelor and hermit, with a tender foot in a bandage, piled all over with naked boys.

—Let's see it with kippers and marmalade, Pascal, Jos said. Eh? Toast and coffee.

He rolled out of bed onto all fours, prowling over to fetch Holger's crutches, which he brought to him ceremoniously. Of his erection he said that it was like his heart.

—Upright and loving God.

73

And along the winding course of the beautiful river country houses sit in orchards.

Once the admiration of mankind was for turbulent and wild waters, such as the strait Sestos faces, the Hellespont, or the treacherous channel between Euboia and Boiotia, where Xerxes crossed into Greece. Now we admire rivers such as this lovely Mosella, where one language flows into another, where merchants, not soldiers, meet, a river narrow enough to talk across.

With what eloquence can I describe the architecture of places? Here are palaces worthy of Daedalos, that man of Gortyna who flew; and temples worthy of Philo who designed the portico at Eleusis; fortresses worthy of Archimedes; and worthy too of the architects in Marcus Terentius Varro's tenth book. Did Metagenes and Ktesiphon of Ephesus inspire the Roman work hereabout, or Iktinus, architect of the Parthenon, who painted an owl of such magical realism that its stare could drive living owls away? Or Dinokhares, who built the Egyptian pyramids which swallow their own shadows and made an image of Arsinoe, the sister and wife of Ptolomaeus Philadelphus to stand in the middle of the empty air under the roof of her temple at Pharos?

All of these might well have built the marvelous structures here in the land of the Belgii, to be ornaments along the Mosella. Here is one high on a cliff, another built out over a bay, another sits on a hill overlooking its vast estate. And here is one flat in a meadow, but with a tall tower. Another has fenced in a portion of the river, for private fishing. What can we say of the many villas with their lawns flowing down to river landings? The marble bathhouses, with steam rooms and swimming pools, where one can see happy and athletic swimmers, some preferring the river itself. A chaster, healthier Naples.

I feel at home among these people, and wonder if the old poetry can picture them, their neat gray villages and winding green rivers, with a proper tone. I have confided in my friend Paulus my misgivings in this matter.

Vergil, yes, and Flaccus, their art will serve me, as it has, in making poems of these northern woods. But their center of gravity, to be Archimedean, is in Greece, halfway around the world, and that center is shifting. The young Gratianus, my pupil, and his little brother, know Greece by rumor. It is a fading rumor, and we are moving away from it. This new religion of the imperial family, with its Zeus who was born as a human infant and taught phil- osophy in a tropical and zymotic province until he was crucified as a common criminal, fits strangely into the order of things. In utmost privacy I have hinted that it is making a prig of Gratianus.

I am myself part Celt, part Roman. The culture of Bordeaux, of which I like to think I am as good an exemplar as one can point to, is a fusion, beau- tifully proportioned. Of Rome and Gaul. Perhaps, as Aristotle says, any two things generate a third, and it is that nameless third quiddity I think I feel in these northern and western reaches of the empire. It is something I see in my Bissula, her braided yellow hair and frank blue eyes. She was a charming slip of a girl when I bought her. Her language was that of the Swabii, and her first lispings of Latin gave me more pleasure than hearing the royal princelings mouthing Greek, their suspicious priest with us in the nursery, cutting his eyes at me if one of our texts alluded to the firm breasts of an Arcadian girl or the hyacinthine hair of a Sicilian shepherd.

Bissula, Bissula, child of the cold and turbulent Rhine. Eyebrows were raised when I freed her. I could not abide the slave's collar around her tender neck. From the slaughterhouse of war, pain, and desolation beyond all pow- ers of a poet to describe, they brought her to me, a promising little scullery maid of a slave, who might also be warm in bed. I freed her before she could know what it feels like to be a slave, and put her in charge of my quarters, diminutive housekeeper that she is, spoiled as she is. The emperor's officious staff can have no notion that she gives me more pleasure to talk to, to watch, to admire for her beauty, than all the princes and fellow grammarians, and these Christiani with their fasts and mystical feasts of magic loaves and wine, among whom I have to move.

The Greek and Roman poets talk about the color of faces, reciting one another's formulae about roses and lilies. By Jupiter! they could do nothing just for Bissula. She has freckles across her nose, like a trout's flanks, and her skin is now clear, like the air itself in the lower sky, now pink, now the brown of breadcrust, when she has been in the summer sun. Her smile is of the north. She is not a miniature woman already skilled in the politics of a family, as in Rome, nor yet a little vixen babbling of fashions in hairdos and roman- tic alliances, as in Bordeaux and Arles. She is a child.

She has a puppy, name of Spot, and a cat named Grace, and a pet chicken wittily named Imperatrix. She reminds me of my grandson Pastor with his honest eyes and frisky ways. I care nothing for the looks askance and the gossip. She is firmly the mistress of my household. If you want a bottle of Bordeaux, she has the keys to the winecellar on the belt around her trim waist. If you want to be paid for vegetables or a hare, for grooming the horses, my purse is on her hip.

She is, in some sense poets and peasants can understand, but not the corps of diplomats and soldiers with whom I dine and whose rank I share, she is the Mosella. She is the spirit of this land.

At table we talk law and economics, engineering and taxes, politics and Rome. Everything always comes back to Rome, to the Senate and Caesar. It does not exist, this Rome. It must be made up, hour by hour. Two legions of barbarians who have learned to march and attack in our way: Rome. Paved highways with couriers and goods trains: Rome. And now priests and bishops with their Hades of eternal damnation and their Elysian Fields with golden streets and a gate of pearls: Rome. A bronze eagle on a standard: Rome.

This Rome will melt, as all the others have. The most ancient Rome, the one of red terra-cotta, born of a she-wolf, melted in the pulse of time to become the seven hills ruled by lightning and the entrails of cows, by philosopher kings conversant with gods who lived in the forests and marshes. But this Rome is that of the hobnailed boot, the tax collector, and the new religion from the east, always from the east, one religion after another, Cybele and Attis and the Magna Mater and Mithras, with stranger and stranger rites.

But my Bissula is the world itself, for the world has a soul. It has no tongue, no language, this soul of the world. We live with it in us all our lives, no matter how we try to translate it into laws, violence, arrogance, power over each other, preposterous fables, and ridiculous observances. The political world lurches from slaughter to slaughter. Mankind has become a roost of vultures.

Bissula hates water, and says she should be smeared with tallow under her wool dress. But she is tractable, and I explain in words she listens to gravely, understanding nothing except the music of my voice, that she must be of the new world. Her northern vigor will not be diminished by a Roman bath, nor her desirable toes by sandals. I tell her about the forests of masts in the harbor at Bordeaux, the parks with flowers, the dogs, the streets shaded by trees against the sun, and all of this makes her laugh. *Effulgens.*

74

At Oporto, out in front of the colors, with the fife and the Serjeant Major, he had brought the Eleventh, the bloody Eleventh, down the gangway to *Lilliburlero,* with the sweet fuckers whistling along, for no regiment of foot has ever been formed on God's earth handsomer than a Devonshire regiment.

He had almost got to Salamanca, and had seen sights Hell itself knows nothing of.

And now a roll of drums, and he in his good shirt already drenched and cold with sweat, and the minister with him, and a churchbell ringing the quarter hour. He saw the gallows at which he had not meant to look, with two nooses. He had meant to look only at Ensign Hepburn, who was to die beside him. Why had so many people come to see him die?

He had not slept, had shivered all night, and had puked up the rum the jailer gave him.

The scaffold was in the street, in front of the Debtor's Door, Newgate Prison. In the crowd on both sides of the gallows were Lord Yarmouth, Lord Sefton, and the Duke of Cumberland, the Regent's brother, and Byron's friend Scrope Davies.

The crime for which Ensign James Hepburn, 25, and Thomas White, 16, were hanged on 7 March 1811 had been committed in a room above a public house on Vere Street two months before.

Ensign Hepburn had seen Tom White in St. James Park, and liked the beauty of his sixteen-year-old body enough to send a young friend over to him to sound him as to his willingness to be fondled. Tom White, sizing up Ensign Hepburn, replied that there was a room in Vere Street to which he might be followed. He was fair and well-knit, with a straight back and long stride that had got him chosen as a drummer boy in the Eleventh North Devonshire Fusiliers.

Ensign Hepburn had bought him a pint of bitter and a cold breast of hen between two slices of bread, and these he drank and chewed as his breeches and stockings were removed, with fine compliments for his manly equipment and the firm make of his backside and legs.

And now his eyes were blind and burning, so that he stumbled on the steps. He pulled his sleeves over his wrists.

—Goodbye, Tom, he heard Hepburn say, and he tried to say *Goodbye Jim* but was not certain that the words came out, as in a dream.

While his hands and ankles were being fastened, and the noose fitted over his head, he hoped he was repeating after the minister *For I am the resurrection and the life: he that believeth in me, though he were dead, yet shall he live.*

III

Pascal was still asleep, a bubble between his parted lips, his hair as graceful tangled and matted as when it was combed. Dawn, chill, would give way to summer warmth, a blue sky. Holger, who had expected to sleep tense and anxious, was surprised that he had slept in an easy happiness. Pascal had jabbered, excited and vivacious, in the car all the way to the campsite, as if he had left his solemn composure behind. They had put the tent up well before dark, giving them time to explore and to feel that they were in full possession of their territory.

—We establish a residence, Holger had said, so that this becomes our home, for however short a while.

—Today and tomorrow and the day after, Pascal had said. When I was out with Franklin and Hugo it was like we'd lived there in our camp all our lives, you know, and it was ours. And this is our place. The car, the tent, the lake, the woods. All ours.

—Every bit of it.

—Mama said, How wonderful! And that I didn't need to call Papa.

Holger eased out of his sleeping bag and the tent, stealthily, on all fours. Outside, he dressed in jeans and a sweater. He laid a fire and filled a kettle with water they'd brought.

—Pascal! he called.

—Yo! You're up.

And there he was, knuckling an eye and yawning, in the thin-blue-striped T-shirt and slight briefs he'd slept in.

—Hello hello, he said. Got to pee.

—Anywhere, Holger said. We have the world to ourselves.

—I peed in the ferns last night. Pine needles today. Hugo and Franklin peed together on our outing. They're like that.

—Cinnamon and raisin buns, with butter, with tea, with gnats, for breakfast.

—Being shy is actually pride, Pascal said, facing Holger and making a crystal arc to which he gave a whipped wiggle, gnats on cinnamon, yum. Lots of milk in my tea.

—We'll go over to that island, shall we, in the boat, once we've squared away?

—The one all blue in the mist?

—That one.

—What's on it?

—Don't know. I've never been over. When I come out by myself I'm content to stay here, wallowing in the quiet and the peace, reading, making notes, with a walk and a swim when I want to. I hope you're not going to find it duller than dull.

Pascal looked out of the sides of his eyes.

—Dull? I'm happy.

Holger chewed awhile and drank a long swallow of tea.

—So am I.

—Is there anybody on the island?

—I shouldn't think so. I'm pretty certain not.

—Then can I go bare-bottom?

—Absolutely.

—Franklin would. And Hugo, to swim. Franklin does it for the fun of it.

—You're wearing a life preserver till we get there. They're in the back seat.

335

I'll get the boat down. We want a jug of water as there's probably no spring on the island, and the net bag, also in the back, for, let's see, bread and cheese and a thermos of tea, the first-aid kit, the binoculars, my notebook.

—I'll put my T-shirt and underpants in too, Pascal said, taking them off, should we meet anybody, I guess.

—And your short pants, friend. And caps for us both.

—You don't mind I'm britchesless, do you, Holger?

—Of course not.

—You're blushing, you know, real strawberry.

—I'll only blush worse if you keep mentioning it, Holger said. Here, let me get you into the preserver neat and trim. Woof! What's the hug for?

—For bringing me camping.

—Consider yourself hugged back, for coming along, but right now I want you in this cork jacket so securely not even Hugo could rig you better.

—Doesn't matter that I can't breathe?

Holger at the stern, Pascal in the bow, they paddled over to the island, singing *The Owl and the Pussycat*, Pascal looking over his shoulder from time to time to grin.

—In between those two big rocks, Holger said.

Pascal jumped neatly into clear pebble-floored water and pulled the prow onto the shale shingle beach. Holger helped him draw the canoe ashore.

—Rift rocks, very old pines, meadow grass and flora. Wonderfully lonesome, isn't it?

—I like it, Pascal said. Butterflies. How do I get out of this DayGlo-orange straitjacket? Stash the paddles here? If we climb the big rock at the other end we can see the whole island at once, wouldn't you say?

They walked through cool and dark pines in the saddle of the island, coming out on the other side onto a sloped bright meadow that slanted up a sunny shaft of gray rocks where they could see across to the tent and Volkswagen, which looked strangely unfamiliar from this wild vantage.

—A feeling of being very far away is what I have, Pascal said.

—Yes, Holger said. That's why I like getting away. There is decidedly no such place as NFS Grundtvig. Never was.

Pascal laughed.

—Our voices sound different.

—I think we are different.

—Over the edge, said Pascal looking, is steep straight down to the lake. Some enterprising bushes growing right out of the side of the rock. It's nice and hot up here.

Holger sat, unlacing his sneakers.

—The binoculars, Pascal said. Hey, you brought your camera.

He surveyed the full horizon.

—People on the far side. Scouts, I think. Blue and khaki. Tents. They couldn't have come up the road we did.

—You have to know, Holger said, about the gate in the fence, and the cow-path we drove along the last three kilometers, to get to where we are.

Holger pulled his sweater over his head, bare torso beneath, chest hair thick, a gold chain with pendant coin around his neck.

—Why the wicked smile? he asked.

—Not me, Pascal said. What's the medal?

—A tetradrachma, museum reproduction, Artemis and four dolphins, chariot with four leggy horses on the obverse.

Pascal leaned to study it.

—It's beautiful.

—A friend gave it to me. I've worn it for years. You're beginning to turn pink from the sun already.

—You blush, I tan, same shade. We could both tan.

—*You* won't blush, friend? These jeans are all I'm wearing.

—Pride, as I said, is what shy is. Actually, what Hugo said.

Holger stood, nimbly, unzipped his jeans, stepped backward out of them, folded them into a square for a pillow, and lay on the slant of the rock, his fingers knit behind his head.

—Hugo is your real teacher, isn't he? Did we get here with sunglasses? He has caught your imagination.

—Sunglasses, sunglasses, Pascal said, scrounging in the net bag. Thermos, comb, whyever a comb, film, is there film in the camera? Bathing suit, my underpants and britches, sunglasses. Here. Can I have your sweater for a pillow? Except that I get the fidgets lying still.

—So don't lie still. Walk on your hands, do jumping jacks.

—Jump you flatfooted, across your chest. One and two and three!

—Good sense of space. I'm not stomped to death and your heels are touching.

—Next, over your belly button. One's all, two's all, zicker-zoll zan! Neat. This is something Franklin would do, you know?

—I've noticed you turning into Franklin.

—Franklin's trying his best to turn into Hugo. I like Franklin. And he's really the only person who's liked me. At Grundtvig, I mean.

—I like you.

—I know that, Holger. Now over your middle. Humpty Dumpty is ninety-nine, and one's a hundred, plop. Over your knees, next, sinctum sanctum buck. Hairy feet. Whoof! Now I can lie down and be civilized. I'm shy.

Holger looked at his watch.

—Another five minutes, and we do our backs.

—Methodical. I like going without clothes. I didn't think I was this kind of person.

337

—What kind of person would that be?

—I don't know. I really didn't know I had a body until Franklin showed me. It was something my folks owned and operated, not me, something with ear-aches, constipation, runny nose, clean fingernails, eat your vegetables and drink your orange juice. There's Jos with his muscles and weights and big shoulders, and Rutger and Meg, and Kim and Anders, and Hugo and Mariana.

Pascal sat cross-legged beside Holger, one knee pressing on his thigh.

—Sun and breeze together, Holger said, and such incredible quiet.

—I get kidded a lot because you like me. But it's only kidding, though Franklin had that fight with Adam because of it.

Holger lifted his sunglasses and looked hard at Pascal.

—Jos got Adam the next day and scared the living lights out of him.

—The things I don't know, Holger said.

—But Jos jollied Adam around again. He doesn't like hard feelings.

—I'm not certain I understand any of this.

—What's to understand? Franklin came over, from Hugo's to see me. Adam, who's a prig, which is what Jos called him, and thinks Franklin is not one of us, and is jealous if you ask me, said something nasty, Franklin won't tell me what, that made Franklin so mad he hit him.

—We should have brought Franklin along.

—Oh, no. If Franklin were here, I'd be with him, not with you. that sounds awful.

—Now you're blushing.

—I hear a boat, Pascal said, reaching for the binoculars. It's the scouts, and they're rowing this way, three boats. Come look.

—Our island, Holger said. What wars are all about. Our place that we thought we had to ourselves is about to be invaded. Perhaps if we show them we're here, they'll have the good manners to give us a miss.

—They can see me, Pascal said, nipping over to the net bag for his briefs and Holger's bathing slip. Semaphore flags, he said, for a signal from one naked skinny boy perfectly visible against the sky.

Right arm straight out, flapping briefs, left hand with slip over genitalia: *B*. both arms up, the body a *Y*: *U*. both hands at genital level, a shift to the left: *G*, twice. Left hand up, right over genitalia: *E*. arms straight out: *R*. left hand, across chest, arm right up: *O*. right over genitals, left straight out, twice: *double F*.

—They're answering, acknowledge and repeat. Wait a sec. That's a *hello*. They're landing, anyway. Ten, I count. Nine scouts and their keeper.

Holger came to the ledge, hands on Pascal's shoulders to peer down at the boats. Pascal placed his hands over Holger's. Solidarity.

—I suppose we should be grateful that the intrusion is as benign as scouts. Even so.

—Pests, Pascal said.

—Heigh ho! came a jovial voice from the foot of the slope.

—Hello! Holger called down.

The first of the landing party to appear was a freckly ten-year-old in gold-rimmed specs, red bandana around his head, piratically knotted, in short blue pants and webbing belt hung with a canteen and a hatchet. He stopped short, silver braces gleaming in his open mouth.

Behind him arrived an older boy in a beret and red briefs, a mop-haired spadger in sneakers and shorts, carrying a butterfly net, and their scoutmaster, who seemed nineteenish, sturdily athletic, with cropped blond hair and smiling green eyes.

—Thought I ought to apologize, he said, before obeying your semaphone. Also to introduce myself, Sven Berkholst, with my troop. We'll keep to the other end of the island, unless you're camping there.

Nine scouts with fox eyes stood in a line behind him, staring.

—Holger Sigurjonsson. And this is Pascal. We're camped over there on the other side of the lake. We rowed out to see the island, and to have our lunch in a bit.

—Your son?

—Friend. We're both from NFS Grundtvitg.

Pascal slipped his arm around Holger's waist, causing elbows to nudge among the scouts. Holger placed both hands on Pascal's shoulders.

—We're from Tarm, Sven Berkholst said. We're out for butterflies, and some elementary marine biology around the shore. Nice meeting you, and we'll push off. Troop, about-face. I'll keep the boys away from up here.

—No need to, Holger said.

Pascal tightened the squeeze of his hug as the scouts left, some looking back furtively. Watching their heads bob among bushes and be lost to sight among the pines, Holger, surrendering to an impulse, hoisted Pascal with a clean swift heave, turned him around in the air, and, clasping him tight shoulder and butt, held him bravely, nuzzling his midriff before easing him down.

—Let's have lunch, Holger said, or whatever midmorning meals are called. Did I do that, hug you, I mean?

—Somebody did. Kissed me on the tummy, too. Why are you putting on your jeans?

—Dressing for dinner, Holger said. It seems sublimely silly to eat in the altogether. Not you, me. Stay in your Adam suit. Bread we have, cheese we have, hot tea with milk we have.

—I'm staying naked all day, Pascal said, especially if I'm going to get hugged. Two plastic cups, cheese in foil, good chewy bread. I thought it was exciting enough getting here yesterday, and putting the tent up, and having our supper, and talking by the fire, and sleeping in a tent, but today, so far, runs rings around all that.

—Oh, I agree, Holger said. This meal, on Hugo's authority, is Epicurean. Epicurus has a bad reputation for high living and outrageous gourmandise. Hugo says, however, that he ate as simply as possible: goat cheese, bread, cold spring water.

—It's good, Pascal said with his mouth full. Hugo hugs Franklin all the time. Mariana makes a joke of being jealous, but of course she isn't, really. Other things, too.

—What other things?

—Just things.

—Clouding over, would you look?

—Good old Danish weather. Drown the scouts, maybe.

—Well, I don't think we'd be that lucky, but I do think we'd be wise to row back to the tent before it rains. Police the area, scamp, and I'll pack.

—Wasn't there, Pascal asked, some chocolate?

—Dessert in the tent. You don't have dessert with a snack, anyway. Thermos, your clothes, such as they are, camera. Wait. Let's photograph you here on the rock. Stand over there. Smile. got it.

—Can I show the picture to Franklin?

—Why not? Oh boy, is it ever going to rain.

As they crossed the wood they began to hear scouts' voices near the cove where they left their canoe. Smells of turpentine, deep humus, the straw odor of pine needles. The wood was cool and dim, with laurel undergrowth toward the edges, so that one did not suspect the closeness of the lake. Pascal walked in front, the net bag slung over his shoulder. It was the merest chance, as his eyes were happy to keep to Pascal, that Holger took in at a glance, and that peripherally, two scouts in the laurels over to the left. One, with a bear-brown richness of hair raked forward, recurving into a snub-nosed open-lipped profile, had shoved down his shorts and briefs. His penis was rigid, scrotum bunched tight. His head was close to that of another scout, whose hands were busy. Holger kept silent, and for a few steps doubted what he had seen, though the boyish profile and prosperous erection remained as a clear afterimage.

They saw the scoutmaster on the far slope, and waved to him. Two scouts were bottling something, knee-deep in the lake. They secured themselves in their lifejackets, shoved the canoe into the water, and made off. Halfway across, the rain began, soft and swiveling.

—Rain on my peter, Pascal said. That's a new experience.

—And that's something Franklin would say.

—What if I turn into Franklin all the way? Like in science fiction, huh? He's very smart, but hasn't read a great deal, not yet.

—Has it occurred to you, small friend, that Franklin can just as well turn into

Pascal, with the highest IQ at NFS Grundtvig, and be voraciously interested in the whole curriculum? I've heard Master Olsen say that he thinks you're doing Jos's algebra for him.

—A swap, Pascal said over his shoulder, looking around with flat wet hair. I do his algebra and he lets me see his magazines.

—I'm not asking what kind of magazines, not out in the middle of a lake, wet to the skin, with waves beginning to chop.

—You don't want to know, friend Holger. Boys are nasty.

—That's why I have to get away to the woods for a few days every month.

—And bring one boy with you. I hope it's dry in the tent.

—There's nothing cozier than a tent when it's raining, as you'll see in two shakes of a lamb's tail. Hop ashore and steady the prow.

They unrolled the sleeping bags to sit on, and Holger wrapped Pascal in a blanket from the car before he stripped and dried, put on an outing shirt and pyjama trousers.

—The scouts should be thoroughly soaked by this time, Pascal said.

—No wetter than us. Is your hair drying? You look like a baby bird in its nest, with only your face and frizzled hair outside the blanket. So much for going bare-assed all day.

—I'm naked in the blanket, if that makes any sense. Feels good, a rough blanket. I feel good, anyway. I'll bet you didn't see two scouts over to our left when we were crossing the pinewood, taking off each other's pants.

—I did, as a matter of face. Mostly out of the corner of my eye, but an eyeful nevertheless.

—They had stiff peters, you mean.

Holger answered with a forgiving shrug.

—Our place, Pascal said. Our tent. We're dry after being wet, warm after being cold, and we're all by ourselves after uninvited pests.

The rain quit midafternoon. They explored the deep wood on their promontory, Pascal wearing a sweater and sneakers only. They found a wildflower Holger could not identify, and a moss and fern of uncertain name. Pascal gathered leaves to press and learn. They peed together, mingling and crisscrossing streams. When Holger was laying the fire for supper, Pascal gave him a generous hug from behind.

—I'm being silly.

—I don't think so, friend Pascal.

—I don't even hug Franklin. We josh and grab each other.

—You're lovely, you two.

Pascal puffed out his cheeks in bemused puzzlement.

—Hugo says we're pukey, and Mariana, depraved.

—That's affectionate teasing.

—I know that. But Pastor Tvemunding, Hugo's papa, said like you that we're lovely. Jonathan and David, he said we were. That set Hugo off. He and his papa talk about everything: it's wonderful. They know the Bible off by heart, in Hebrew and Greek, and history and science. They make everything seem different. And they're very funny. They can sit and read each other things out of the newspaper and books, and set each other laughing. Franklin says it's some kind of code, and we've never figured out what they laugh about. Pastor Tvemunding says the Devil has no sense of humor whatsoever, and that you can always get his goat by laughing. Me, I asked him if he really believes there's a Devil, and he cocked his head, cute old man that he is, and said that the Devil's only claim to existence is our belief in him.

—What do you suppose he means by that?

—Hugo took over, and said that the Devil is precisely nothing.

—Soup in a cup, Holger said. And sandwiches of any of these, in any or all combinations.

—Sardines and cheese. Hard-boiled eggs. Franklin would love a sandwich of a chocolate bar and sardines. Soup's good.

—I'll light the lantern in a bit, and we can move into the homey tent, out of this damp. And snap the flaps closed, as I'd say it's going to rain again.

—Terriff, Pascal said, his mouth full, and super. You got some sun, you know.

—I also know that neither of us has had a bath today.

—Do we have to?

—This is our weekend for doing what we want to. But we'll wash up these supper things in the lake, and pick off some of the pine needles stuck to your behind and brush our teeth.

The tent by lantern light was snug. Fog had risen on the lake and a soft, meditative rain made a whispery rustle against the tent.

—In the buff all day, Pascal laughed, here I am putting on pyjamas to go to bed.

—Life's like that.

—Wildly illogical.

—What a fine sound, the rain.

Holger with his jeans and sweater for a pillow, Pascal sitting cross-legged, they talked about the island, its geology and vegetation, the scouts across the lake, the freckles on Franklin's nose, Paul Klee, Icelandic ponies and meadows, Holger's briefs, the label of which Pascal held to the lantern to read, double stars, Kafka, toenails, zebras. Jos Sommerfeld's symmetrical physique and asymmetrical mind, butterflies, the depth of the lake, Pascal's mother, Hugo and Mariana, masturbation, causing Pascal to slide his hand into his pyjama pants with an impish look of greenest innocence, the fight between Adam and Franklin, irrational numbers, petals and sepals in crocuses, whether Iceland is the first part of the New World to be settled by Europeans or the westernmost country of Europe, what it means that friends are another self, as Pastor Tvemunding says, Hugo's room over the old stables, its photographs and paintings and the organization of its space, and what make of microscope Pascal should inform his father to buy for him, as promised.

—And if we're going to be up early tomorrow and explore the other side of the wood, or maybe go back to the island, we should douse the lantern and listen to the rain and get some sleep, wouldn't you say? What are you doing, mite?

—Taking off my pyjama bottoms.

Holger, on his knees, extinguished the lantern.

—Now what are you doing?

—Getting into your sleeping bag with you.

IV

PAULUS' BREV TIL EFESERNE VI.12

Thi den kamp, vi skal kæmpe, er ikke mod kød og blod, men mod magterne og myndighederne, mod verdensherskerne i dette mørke, mod ondskabens åndemagter i himmelrummet.

77

—Liked having breakfast with you this morning, Jos said. All that neatness. You could run a hospital or a submarine. And Pascal neater than you. And the good talk. Is it awful I'm jealous, or envious do I mean? Napkins, real cloth napkins.

—Everybody's to get a breakfast, Holger said. The vulnerable meal, but with built-in leaving time.

—With Pascal at all of them? You're becoming Hugo for dash and facing down Eglund.

—I run before breakfast, Pascal, Hugo, Franklin and I. I write before breakfast. Plan classes. The things one learns on a morning run.

—You're becoming me.

—Like now, lifting weights.

—You're really going to the boathouse to lay a talk on the revolutionaries?

—Sexiest part of you, Jos, is the way your top lip makes a beveled wedge in the middle. And your back. Like your back.

—Conversation stopper if ever I heard one. No, I can return the serve. It never gets me anywhere to say something like that to you.

—Count.

—Sixteen more. Looking good. I'm making you and Pascal do the same routines, you with more iron.

—Turning into Pascal, too. An article on Carl Sauer accepted, American geographer.

—Good hollow scoops on the outsides of your butt; leg lifts and running to keep them that way. Wicker chairs, Cretan shawl, flowers in a vase, bowl of roses. Nicest room in all Grundtvig, you know. Thorvaldsen and Kierkegaard on the wall.

—They make a chord. Hugo opted for Georg Brandes and Kierkegaard. He says they solved for Denmark the social and psychological problem of inside and outside.

—There, sixteen. What the fuck is inside and outside?

—Inside is the privacy of the imagination, which the Bible calls the heart, where the fool has said there is no God and where one can be angry with one's brother, secretly, and be a murderer, and lust after a deer-eyed woman and be an adulterer.

—Bullshit, Jos said. Hook your feet under the strap and do fifty sit-ups with your hands behind your head, knees well bent.

—The invisible heart has always been a hard place for moralists. The church has always tried to monitor and censor it. So has psychiatry, and fru Grundy, parents, and other busybodies. Hence our search for new kinfolks. We find them most of all, Hugo says, in people who can make their inside outside, that is, artists and poets, sculptors and composers, who moreover have the ability to show us our own insides, our imagination.

—Don't jerk when you lift. Make one clean deliberate movement. If you made a movie of my imagination, you couldn't show it even in Denmark. Germany, maybe, but they wouldn't appreciate it, being nerds.

—All meaning is narrative. Hugo, again. So we Danes decided, following Kierkegaard and Brandes and others, that we could tolerate everybody's inside difference provided we all respected that difference, and made the respect an outside sameness. That's why you can roller-skate around the parkering and the peripheral road with your dick out through the fly of your jeans.

—Heard about that, have you? Have to keep them on their toes, you know.

—Franklin told it at supper, admiringly.

ENTEN ELLER

—All systems, like Kierkegaard's thought that anhelates toward the paradox of the unthinkable, Jos said, have hiccups of chaos in them, as turbulence is new information and a specific against entropy. Do I, or don't I, sound like Pascal?

—Very Pascal, Pascal said.

—More like Pascal, Holger said, than Pascal.

—So these wide-eyed revolutionaries with their den over the boathouse who treat Sebastian as an ichneumon.

—Catechumen, Pascal said.

—Whatever. I took him, high-handedly, as you can't go without a comrade. High-handedly, as I'm not a member myself.

—With your and Sebastian's jeans and underpants rolled under your arm.

—Very Gray Brothers. Kim was in stitches.

—Franklin is right, Holger said. Sebastian would find Hugo's wolfcubs more exciting.

—It's the principle of the thing, Jos said. How was I to know that Anders was going to read a paper on the architecture of grebes' nests? Made of sticks on the water. At least Sebastian thought that was neat, and has been talking grebes ever since. They run on the water, grebes, like Jesus in a hurry.

—Go back to your being pantsless.

—Grand success. Everybody followed suit, once we'd heard about grebe sticks. Tom then gave the news from around the world on what Fascist government has passed what laws against who can hug and kiss whom, and where. Lard butts with terminal halitosis in Washington who are willing to kill every man, woman, and child on the planet with napalm, poison gas, and hydrogen bombs, write laws against taking your dick out even to piss. So I joined them then and there, Sebastian too, contraband as he is. I don't even like Sebastian, much less love him. That's when Tom had a laughing fit, as it turns out that Sebastian had already joined, twice before, in fact, once with Franklin as his bonded mate, and once with Pascal, ditto.

79

The wooded knoll above the bend in the river, a Chekhovian place, wicker beehives just beyond the hawthorns, a tinge of honey in the light. Franklin, nothing shy, at least offered authority for his presumption.

—Pascal said.

He had grabbed and fought his arms into the sleeves of a hooded jacket as soon as Holger had said he needed a ramble.

—Me too, Franklin had said, causing Hugo to look at the ceiling.

—New style, holding hands. Jos said it's sissy, and then he held hands with me across the quad. He'd also just put down kissing as perverted, and then smooched Sebastian on the mouth. Butterscotch and foreskin he said it tasted like.

—What happened to Sebastian's hair? Holger asked.

—Well, Franklin said, I cut it. Looks good, wouldn't you say?

—Franklin, it looks awful.

—Never cut anybody's hair before. There was general opinion at the club-house that he had too much of it, and that he would look less like a girl with about half of it scissored off. Guess I got more than half, didn't I? Pascal cut a pair of his jeans off good and short for him. Now the pockets show.

—Could you find Sebastian, do you think, when we get back?

—Sure. What for?

—To take him to the barber. And, friend Franklin, if I sent you and Pascal to Jorgensen's on the bus, would you get Sebastian a pair, two pairs, of niggling britches with a snide fit, like yours?

Franklin made his face a rabbit's by rucking his upper lip, catching the nether under his wedgy teeth, rounding his eyes, and wrinkling his nose.

—We could, you know, get him some tough sneakers, too, and ballsy socks.

—Better and better.

—And some underpants that don't sag or come up over his belly button.

—You're being brilliant, friend Franklin. And how will he take all this? Will it hurt his feelings?

—Might, at that, come to mention it. Pascal can say he's sorry he ruined his jeans. He'll think of something, too, for the sneakers and socks and nappies.

—Just what is going on with Sebastian?

—Like at the clubhouse? He hasn't a clue what the meetings are about, making two of us, as I don't either, when it's my turn to go with him. I mean, book reports! An old fart from England bleating about what's against the law in Germany or Belgium. In *engelsk*, to boot. He wanted to interview, he called it, Sebastian, who he'd been staring at all along, maybe because of his haircut but probably, wouldn't you say, because he looks as if he's escaped from his babysitter. Didn't Pascal say you were coming some Wednesday soon?

—How does anybody get around Pascal?

—You don't.

—You'll be fun, like the loony Dutchman we all peeled to the knackers for, and who kissed us, hilarious, and grew a bone. I'll find out what they did after they threw me and Sebastian out. Tom and Kim, the two I've asked, answered with a shitty smile.

—Pascal wants me to talk about time and territory.

—Sounds as sexy as matron in hair curlers.

—The body as a territory and as an organism in time. The body as narrative and event. As figure against a ground, against history. Wittgenstein in an intriguing *Zettel* comments on the surface temperatures of the body, without particulars. Cold elbows, warm armpits.

—Hugo hollers about Mariana's cold feet.

80

—Really should have brought Barnabas, Franklin said. But Mariana would have had to come along too, for him to drink from. And if Mariana, Hugo, to fuck Barnabas a little sister. Find one thing wrong with this tent, Sperm Breath, and we'll see my footprint on your butt for the next two days.

—Right back peg's not in line, Pascal said. I'll mention it before Holger does. Oof!

—Warned you.

—Boys, Holger said.

—The last weekend that can be called summer, Pascal said, by any stretch of the imagination. You'll like the foul-weather times, friend Franklin. We've even been crazy enough to go over to the island with rain coming at us sideways by the bucketload, and inside the tent is wonderful when there's a nasty drizzle.

—Which is what we'll get when and if we talk Holger into bringing us out with Alexandra, some Friday, returning on Sunday afternoon to collect the limp bodies, eyes rolled back in our heads, sweet idiots.

—There's got to be a weekend, Holger, when you've had it with Pascal, can't stand the sight of him, and will be all for hauling us out here. Won't need to provide anything but transportation and tent. We won't eat.

—The contingency, Holger said, will have to be something else, such as my generosity, or simply because I can't say no to Pascal.

—Hugo and Mariana are always saying they'll sell me to the Gypsies, first offer. Sometimes it's give me to the Gypsies. But it would take Israeli Commandos to pry Holger loose from Pascal.

—Aren't you sort of forgetting, Holger said, that you and Pascal can, without a word or sign, get each other's britches off? When was it, last Tuesday, I was grading papers, Pascal was typing at the desk, his back to Franklin, who was lettering in his map assignment on the floor.

—Good afternoon, Pascal said. Grace abounding.

—Agreed, but Franklin sat up, watercolor brush in teeth, unbuttoned his jeans, and went back to making the Balkans green and yellow. Then Pascal, between shifts of the carriage, undid his belt and when he could spare a hand, kept edging his zipper down. The *a* of Bulgaria finished to his satisfaction, Franklin stretched prettily in the afternoon sun, with a sunny smile for me, serious thoughts in his eyes, which I took to be about the geography of the Balkans.

—Holger, Pascal said. You were supposed to crook your finger, and get climbed all over.

—Well I, at least, was thinking geography. So Pascal quit typing, slid out of his chair as casually as you please, and without so much as a half glance over his shoulder, walked backward until his butt was against the back of Franklin's head. I saw all this with my own eyes. Then the two of you had your jeans and underpants off in something under three milliseconds, and in three more were wrapped around each other on the floor.

—Could be, Franklin said, we're horny all the time. Fact is, though, I mean aside from being horny all the time, we know what the other's thinking. Like what flavor of ice cream. It's not done to have to ask. We never miss.

—Holger's only pretending he can't read our minds. Mariana can.

—I can't, though, Holger said.

—We can teach you, Franklin said. Look. I'm closing my eyes. Better, Holger's going to blindfold me with a handkerchief or something. And bang two pans together so I can't hear footsteps. Pascal's going into the woods, out of sight, so Holger, even, won't know where. Then I'll walk right to him, OK?

—Challenge taken, Holger said. This is going to be good.

—I warn you, Holger, Pascal said. He can do it.

—Of course he can't do it, Holger said. I'm tired of these irrationalities in students I'm trying to teach science.

Pascal shrugged and trotted off as Holger was tying his handkerchief across Franklin's face. He tiptoed for a while, doubling back from entering the undergrowth to sneak along the edge of the lake. Here, he took off his shoes and socks and waded some meters out, thigh-deep. Holger the meanwhile clashed two frying pans close to Franklin's head. At a signal from Pascal, he said:

—Ready. Go find him.

Franklin stood still for a full two minutes.

—Untie my sneakers, he said. You'll think I'm peeping if I bend over.

Barefoot, he did an about-face and walked toward the lake, off course by ten degrees at first, correcting with confidence as he walked. At the water's edge he felt around with his foot before striding in.

—Fuck, he said cheerfully.

Approaching at a different angle than Pascal's, he waded through deeper water, up to his belt.

—Really shitty of you, you know, he said, hugging Pascal.

—OK, Holger called. I'm sending back my diploma to the university. Hey! Watch it!

Franklin with a sturdy shove pushed Pascal under the water, to be himself pulled under by a thrashing Pascal. Muddy and sodden, they walked hands over shoulders to shore, spitting lake water.

—Wring everything out, Holger said. I'll put up a clothesline while Franklin tells me how he did it.

—I knew where he was, Franklin said.

—But how?

—Knowing is knowing. We've got goose bumps.

—Towel, Pascal said, tossing one.

Holger caught the towel in the air, and began drying Franklin with a rough swiftness, the quicker to get to Pascal.

—Work on your hair some more with the other towel, Holger said, and wrap the blanket around you.

—Save room for me, Pascal said.

Holger, having run a spare tent rope through the belt loops of their wet hiking shorts, the arms of their jerseys, and the leg scyes of their briefs, tying the rope between two birch saplings, discussing Franklin's prescience with, as he said when he looked over his shoulder, the woods, lake, and sky, finished to find Pascal and Franklin rolled tight in their blanket, all but the tops of their blond heads.

—Kissing, Franklin said, except that I can't see that it gets you anywhere. Crawl in with us, Holger.

81

Over the summer the hallway between Holger's living room and bedroom had been restructured into a large, square study with two glass walls. This elegantly modern extension was into a small garden surrounded by a brick wall high enough to make the study a private and sunny room. Bookshelves had been built from floor to ceiling on one of the walls that was not all window, and a Rietveld worktable, three by two and a half meters, stood along the other. A glass door opened onto the flagstone terrace. This renovation was Hugo's idea, and design, agreed to by Eglund, paid for by the Alumni Fund.

—The corridor, Hugo had said, will grow sideways and be a third large room, its darkness becoming a splendid cube of sunshine and airiness, with an inside-outside feel.

—And, Holger said, it is ten times lovelier and sweeter than I could picture it. It is, quite simply, wonderful.

—Well, Hugo said all I had to do was remind Eglund, who's nobody's idiot, that your geography book, and the edition of Horrebow, would precipitate offers from universities and other schools. I kept silent about your decision to lead a scholarly and circumspect life at Grundtvig.

—But, Hugo, dear soul, what with your being chosen to be headmaster once Eglund retires, all the money in the world, nor all the prestige, could entice me away.

—*Lovelier, sweeter, wonderful,* Hugo said. Three non-Icelandic words uncharacteristic of your diction, as was.

—Have I changed so much?

—Yesterday, when you were watching, and helping, Franklin and Pascal change Barnabas, you were as different, advanced is what I mean, from the Holger I first knew, as a tree laden with apples from its sapling. The four of you were of an average age, which would be what, thirteen, Barnabas's one rather bringing it down. And after all the promiscuous kissing of Barnabas, spout and all, you pleased Mariana tremendously by sitting with your chin on her knee to gaze at Barnabas at the teat.

—Beautiful breasts Mariana has. Barnabas is Eros himself. Those eyes!

—Barnabas thanks you for the compliment, but begs to second his father in noting that if there's a clone of Eros about, it's Pascal. Does he glow in the dark? I overheard one of the new kids pointing him out to another. The argot in which they parsed his beauty I'll spare you, but the rest was that he publishes articles in journals his teachers can't get published in and gets taken on long trips by the biology and geography master.

82

Cornflowers and red valerian in a marmalade jar. Rye biscuits, cheese, red Dubonnet. Wet autumn leaves stuck to the glass walls of Holger's studio.

—Pascal's making a happy idiot of me released all kinds of energies, Holger said. I began a notebook at the beginning of the summer, after discovering Auden's *Letters from Iceland*, seeing that there's a species of writing where any and everything fits in. So that's what I've done, as you've seen. I've tried, Hugo, to follow your injunction to write exactly what I wanted to. So my work on arctic mosses, the essays on Sereno Watson and Sauer, fossil flowers and insects, are in with Pascal's toes.

—Nice toes, Mariana said, but not as sexy as Franklin's.

—Please don't get us tossed out on such a cozy afternoon, Mariana sweet, Hugo said.

—You can stay, Holger said, as long as Barnabas is so blissfully asleep.

—You hold him better than Hugo, Mariana said. Hugo is likely to look up something in the dictionary, with Barnabas upside-down under one arm. He's not wet, is he?

—Have we pissed ourselves, Tiger? Not us. We're dry and aromatic: talcum and hyacinths.

Hugo leafed back and forth through Holger's manuscript.

—Samuel Johnson in the Hebrides. Lavas, gannets, mosses. Pascal's knees. Doughty in the Finnmark. *If we look to nature, we see nothing human, and if to the human, nothing natural.* Baltic islands, their wildflowers and butterflies. Pascal's eyes. Iberomaurusian harpoons. Jeremy Bentham. Icelandic trolls.

—Trolls in a bramble I had to pass on the way to school, Holger said. I became convinced that there were elves in it who would do me a mischief if I didn't think kindly of them as I drew near. They are the opposite of Pascal. Over the summer something changed in me that's so peculiar I don't know what it is. I was taken apart and reassembled in a new geometry. Suddenly I could talk and write in a new way. I have stopped the car to make notes of ideas, have dictated to Pascal while driving. Better still, I've allowed Pascal to do some of the writing. He says he can read my mind, and that there are things which he says I know the trolls in the bramble will get me for writing, which he has written for me, like the paragraph about tongues under fore-skins, just after John Burroughs on winter sunshine and squirrels. And before Goya and the humanity of children.

—That's Franklin with the freckles, Mariana said, and warty knuckles and round-eyed gaze at his dink when he's galloping it, and who believes that if he doesn't jack off at least thrice a day he'll go into a decline and waste away, and that six times a day keeps him sound and happy.

—Pascal is my daimon. Franklin, Pascal's.

—Who's Franklin's? Hugo asked.

—You, Mariana said. And you have more daimons than can be counted. Your father, handsome Jos, your scouts.

—No, sweetheart, Hugo said. You. You and Barnabas, now that he's here.

—Hello, Barnabas, Holger said. Decided to open your big blue eyes, did you?

—In which that wondering look, Mariana said, means that he's having a serious pee. Aren't you, Lamb?

—I'll change him, Holger said. I'm not as good at it, yet, as Franklin and Pascal, but Barnabas doesn't seem to mind.

—He likes Bedstefader Augustus most of his admirers. He has a Faroese magic charm he chants to mesmerize Barnabas into cooperation. Misses having his dink kissed and trifled with by Pascal and Franklin, though.

—Do I change in the manner of Pastor Tvemunding or of F. and P.?

—Go for Pascal's style, Mariana said. It's our big afternoon out with Holger and cheese and crackers and potent Dubonnet. And if I read Hugo's mind accurately, he's planning to leave Barnabas here for the next hour or so, to provide him with a little sister, or brother, or both.

—Besides, Hugo said, I see a long brown leg coming over the wall, and a blond head and able arm, Pascal as ever was.

—They do that, Holger said. Means there's another. Handsome leg over first is achieved by Jos's or Franklin's back. Otherwise you see hands first, then head, a knee, and you have a boy in your garden.

—It's Jos, Mariana said, wearing Pascal's cap. What a leap!

—Thus the use of gymnastics, Hugo said, to fly gracefully over a wall into your housemaster's garden.

They mimed idiotic delight, peering in through the glass wall, wiggling fingers at their ears, cross-eyed, tongues stuck out.

—Hruff! Pascal said, rotating through the door, we've lucked onto Mariana with the giggles in her eyes, lucked onto Hugo full of cheese, crackers, and Dubonnet *rouge*, lucked onto Barnabas with his dick on the snoot. Are all babies' balls so fat?

—Come on, Hugo, Mariana said. Barnabas can tell us the rest of this when he learns to talk.

—Gym, Jos said. Pascal did a triple set of fifty presses without a gasp. Whack his tummy and break your hand. Feel the definition of his pectorals.

—Me, too, Mariana said. Why, Pascal, are you in Jos's hopeless sweatshirt that's parting at the seams on the shoulders and that a billy goat would think was his father?

—Because he let me. Also his jockstrap with the mesh pouch, see, and his ratty socks. Not for the finicky.

—Holger, Mariana said, darting a teasing glance at Pascal's happiest of grins, if Barnabas stages a tearing snit, send him over by whoever's coming our way. Quick, Hugo, before Pascal takes everything off.

—I see what you mean, Hugo said.

—Barnabas couldn't care less. He thinks he's joined the navy.

—I'll walk you over, Holger said.

—We're not walking, Hugo said. We're running.

—Fine and dandy, Jos said. Off to place an order with the stork. Would you look, friend Barnabas: as soon as your mummy and daddy are out the door, here's Pascal, bosom friend of Uncle Franklin and all of whose clothes seem to have fallen off, butting the crotch of Holger's jeans, and getting a subarctic glare for it.

—The *huldufolk*, Pascal said, are in the bramble, looking out with elvish eyes.

—And, Holger said, gathering Pascal into a comprehensive hug, the owl is in her olive.

—Holger, Jos said to Barnabas, was born and raised in Iceland, where neither the sheep nor the Lutherans approve of sex, and make rather a long face when it intrudes into their decent daily round.

—Crazy horny, Pascal said. Jos's sweatshirt is magic. It belonged to his brothers before he got it. Smells of all three of them. Has Jos sperm all over it.

—How do you put a baby to sleep? Jos asked. Don't you bounce it on your shoulder, or something, while humming Brahms?

—Let me show you, Pascal said. You put his head like this and jiggle him gently, gently, and recite Vergil or the yellow pages, he doesn't care which. He'll either drift off to sleep or stick his fingers in your eyes. Sometimes he pukes into your collar.

—Sweet little buggers, babies. It looked for a while this summer that I'd made one on Suzanne, and one on Fresca. If Rutger could get pregnant, I'd have had to sweat him out, too. False alarms. God is kind to idiots.

—Rutger, Pascal said.

—We did two weeks of backpacking in Germany, Black Forest and around. Youth hostels. Wildflowers. Swedes with big blue innocent eyes fucking all night, squish squish. Awesome silences at noon. There was this girl who—

—I've heard all that, Pascal said, and I believe some of it. Tell about Rutger.

—Not with Barnabas listening. Look, if you two want to fall on each other, ease Barnabas into my arms and we'll have a nap here in the sun on the floor, or take him down to my room. Rutger has probably never seen a baby. Sebastian will like him. Would Barnabas enjoy being jacked off?

—Are you certain, Jos, Holger asked, that you know how to hold a baby?

—No, but I can learn real fast.

—Your shoulder's his pillow, Pascal said, and your arms and chest his cradle. Cradles rock. So rock him sweetly, like this. Hum *A Mighty Fortress Is Our God*, and he'll think you're Pastor Tvemunding.

—Crazy. Will he piss me?

—That'll mean he loves you. I hear Holger turning down the bed and zipping down his jeans. Jos?

—Hello, Barnabas. Like me, huh? Yes, Tiger?

—Shall I?

—I'll hold my breath.

Pascal, padding down the hall, stopped, spun on his heel, returned to kiss Barnabas on the cheek and Jos on the mouth.

—Local custom, he said, trotting off.

—Lucky bastard, Jos said to Barnabas, having Mariana for your mummy. And handsome me for your babysitter. And Holger the Icelandic Lutheran and the wizard Pascal, though those two are this very minute licking each other in susceptible places, and being wonderfully friendly and tender. And now the rousing stanzas of *A Mighty Fortress Is Out God*, as sung by Jos Sommerfeld, Eagle Scout.

Arise O captives of starvation!
Arise O wretches of the earth!
For justice thunders condemnation.
A better world's in birth.

It is the final conflict,
Let each stand in his place,.
The International Party
Shall be the human race!

—Jos! Holger said, looking around the door, with Pascal behind him.

Arise O workers of the world!
Throw off the foul disgrace!
And the International Party
Shall be the human race!

—Isn't it a grand tune! Comrade Barnabas says I'm the only babysitter he'll be a good boy for, here on out.

—Jos.

—Huh!

—Jos, Holger said, come on back, with us. Give me Barnabas.

Pascal, fiddling with the drawstring knot of Jos's sweatpants, said:

353

—Where do you learn such knots? From sailors?

—Knackers never been tighter, Jos said. Pat Pascal on the rump after gym, get butted in the tummy by his sweet lovely head, grope him and get groped before climbing the garden wall, and you find yourself in Holger's bedroom, and bed, I hope.

—Tilt the lampshade, Holger said, so the light's not in Barnabas's eyes.

83

Holger, spent, recited genera and species of Norwegian forests, asking between *Betula pendula* and *Fraxinus excelsa* if there were any cold bubble water a handsome boy might bring him.

—In a sec.

—I'll get it. You're busy.

—Hooked. That Italian town that was so green and open in its piazza, buildings so mellow and sunny, where we arrived one noon. If you're finding bubble water, I need a sip. You went to find us a room with matrimonial bed, as they say, the Italians, and I checked out the magazine kiosk and had a pee in the shady corner of a wall, observed by an appreciative old gentleman around the side of his newspaper. Well, there you were across the square, and it hit me, one of those sudden flip-flops of the mind, that this was the longest distance we'd been from each other in maybe a month, you know, and that you were Holger Sigurjonsson, from Iceland, geography and botany master at NFS Grundtvig, needing a haircut, wearing khaki shorts and sneakers without socks, and a tank top with the Dansk Ungdoms Fællesråd insignia on it, and you were smiling, blissfully happy. And, this is the spooky part, you were a bit unfamiliar, a stranger for a second or so, someone I couldn't place right off, and so was I, seeing my reflection in a shop window, a sprout of a boy whose feet seemed too big, legs too long, also needing a haircut, probably going crazy from hyperejection of sperm, blue smudges under my eyes, but more likely becoming a moron from being too happy. And there you were, walking across the square, drenched in Italian sunlight, somebody I knew but couldn't quite place. You ever have such moments?

—All the time. Heart skips a beat every time I see you. I'll do odd things on the tennis court, and Hugo sighs and smiles. Shall we resume our game, he doesn't need to say, when Pascal is out of sight?

—Awful.

—There was a blind folksinger in Iceland when I was your age. He lived on a farm with his sister and brother-in-law. An uncle who knew him used to take me out for a day in the country from time to time. He would ask me to describe meadow flowers, colors and shapes and distribution over the pastures. He could remember them from before losing his sight. I would pick them for him to feel and smell.

—So you're a botanist. Poor fellow, the blind man.

—A sweet, gentle man. With a fine voice and a great repertory of songs, probably medieval, some of them.

—A good photograph that would make, Pascal said, the slats of late afternoon light across the bedtable. Underpants, the book of Isak Dinesen's flowers, one sock. Russian Constructivist, all the diagonal lines. Tell me more about the blind folksinger.

YELLOW MAPLE, AUTUMN MIST

Alexandra, blue silk scarf fluttering at her throat, was on the far side of the soccer field, white jeans, red sweater, in dialogue with Franklin by arm semaphore. Pascal, coming from the gym, hair wet, sneakers fashionably untied, joined in. Franklin to Pascal. Pascal to Alexandra. Alexandra to both.

—*Kære gud!* Joe said to Holger. Did you read that?

—Afraid so.

85

Across a slant and mellow radiance a spider had knit her web in the barley. Further along, grebes foraging. Holger thought of the mosses and gannets of Iceland, of *huldufolk* in a bramble, of Pascal at sixteen, at twenty, how handsome he would be. Shared time doubles.

CHARLES IVES: STRYGEKVARTET NUMMER 2 1907-1913)

A smiling Jos said after the concert by the Copenhagen String Quartet in the auditorium that however the music went down with the Grundtvig smart set and all the townies they at least got to see him in a jacket, shirt and tie, Sunday trousers, and shoes. Hair combed, too. Shirt and tie were Rutger's, but the rest was his own togs.

—Not only me in my finery, but in Holger's company. Didn't believe it when you asked me. Underwear and socks, Rutger's, too. Tie clasp. Did I behave?

—Exemplary, Holger said. And seemed to like it, even.

—O ja! Love fiddle music. Got to pee.

—Here?

—Not to play the game. Modesty's pride. Pride's class hegemony. Very bad, according to Nils.

—*Kære gud!* Hugo said, coming over from the dispersing crowd, the Ives, the Ives! Every so often something other than Whitman, cornflakes, and blue jeans comes out of the USA. I'm not saying a word, you'll notice, about Jos watering the oleanders, though he is facing away from the Eglunds and Pastor Bruun.

—Being Danes, we had to have the Nielsen, and being lucky, we got to hear the Ives, but what sin were we being punished for with the Stravinsky? Ho,

Mariana!

—It's sexist to piddle in public, she said, as you know I can't.

—Why not? Jos asked. Meg would, and has, if you count the woods and ferns. The showers. Scandalized Asgar.

—I'd ask you over, Holger said, except that Pascal and Alexandra are there.

—Horrifying, Jos said, zipping up. Isn't Pascal going to have to go to a rest home with an ice pack on his balls? Diet of thin gruel and wheatmeal biscuits? Babbling.

—Can't, anyway, Hugo said. We promised Franklin, who's sitting Barnabas, we'd be straight back. I gathered from some concupiscent observations he was making to Barnabas, who gurgled his approval, we can only suppose, that Alexandra had planned to be ravished by him this evening. But you say she's with Pascal.

—Worse and worse, Jos said, Hugo pretending to have forgotten the facts of life. I'm going to Holger's, infants fuckering in the middle of the floor or not. Mariana is going to kiss me goodnight.

—So's Hugo, said Hugo.

—*Ork jo*, Jos said. Style's all. When I have more style than anybody else in Denmark, the papers will ask me how I did it, and I'll say some from Mariana, some from Hugo, some from Holger, and NFS Grundtvig will be famous for something other than scouts who hold hands and thirteen-year-olds who are mistaken by the Geological Society for professors with beards down to here. Do we barge in, or is there a signal? We could go over the wall and give them a rude shock just as they're squishing in bliss. Barnabas has an orgasm from the top of his head to his pink toes when he's feeding at Mariana's teat, and so would I.

—Door's unlocked, Holger said.

—Ho! Jos called. Cultivated intellectuals back from the concert! Decent Lutherans wearing neckties!

—Alexandra's in the bathroom, Pascal said, getting dressed. Jos looks like the Stock Exchange.

—Why is Alexandra getting dressed? Jos asked. Why do I look like the Stock Exchange? Why are you kissing Holger and not me, too? Why don't you have on any clothes?

—Holger, hi, Alexandra said, tidying the sleeves of her sweatshirt. Hello, Jos.

—Hi, sprat. We, Holger and I, have been to hear the København Strygekvartet.

—They're lovely, Alexandra said.

—Hence these togs. At least one person, McTaggart the goofy English master, didn't recognize me. So what have you two been doing?

—Mind your manners, Jos, Holger said. I didn't recognize you when I first saw you this evening. Your eyes are shining, Pascal.

—Jos has manners, Alexandra said. I couldn't be the only person to see through Jos. He does everything a nice person can think of to be thought a big happy lout, whereas he's as gentle and well-bred a Grundtvigger as there is.
—And handsome, Jos said. Don't leave out handsome. So what were you doing?
—Well, Alexandra said, sitting and curling her naked toes, Pascal read me some of Holger's book, about fossil flowers and leaves, and some of an article of his about *une enfance différente, un peu effrayant mais pour la plupart sensible et bien pensé.*
—Style, Jos said. That's what I must work on. Style. Even Rutger has style. Nature's busy imperative stiffens his member when he sees Meg, but he talks a little politics and what's new in shirt collars before he shoves it in. Pascal and Holger snuggle in a sleeping sack in the wilds and talk about Finnish mosses and the poultry of Armenia.
—*Welwitschia mirabilis*, Pascal said, cogging his fingers among Alexandra's toes. Gnetophyta, country cousin with buck teeth of the conifers three hundred million years back. Genus with one species, as with angels.
—As with human beings, Holger said.
—They talk like this all the time, Alexandra sprite, and I'm going to talk like this, too, when I get the style down. As Pascal, who grew up with his nose in a book, turns into me, I need to turn into Pascal. I've worn the paper cutout wolfcub mask, crepitating on all fours, in red sneakers and whiffety blue pants, whining like a puppy, yapping silver yelps, and wagging my behind, sexy little tyke, and people were always taking my whiffety blue pants off, for one reason or another. This summer I sailed kites over at Malmö, in a park. All you wear's a pod of gauze strapped around the hips and up the crack of your butt. And bounced over the bay on a sailboard naked as I was born, curveting and skimming, hugging and tacking. And here I am, wanting to be Pascal, so's I can be an anthropologist and know all about people.
—I can't decide, Alexandra said, between anthropology and archaeology. I imagine I have a romantic view of both. I do, I'm afraid, of most things.
—Some more than others, Pascal said.
—What I want, Alexandra said, is a world where difference is not a way of being the same.
—Wait, Jos said, till I figure that out. I'm different, and stick out in the Grundtvig sameness. Why is Holger smiling?
—The really different person an outsider sees at Grundtvig is Mariana.
—*O ja*, Jos said. We all pant for Mariana, and slobber.
—Don't play the lout, Jos. Over at ES Brugge we're all being groomed for men like Hugo, even if they're too feminist to admit it, and Hugo goes for a woman who.

—Girl, Pascal said. Mariana's a girl.

—A woman who's decidedly lower class and of no family, as unsophisticated as she is ungrammatical.

—I hadn't noticed, Holger said. I mean, Mariana is Mariana. Hugo loves her. Clarissa Eglund consults her about hats, flowers, and sauces.

—Owl call, Jos said. Owl name of Franklin.

—Lend a back, Jos, Pascal said, to heave Alexandra over the wall.

87

Walt Whitman, sending some doughnuts to Horace Traubel's mother, wrote on the bag *not doughnuts but love*. It is, Holger said to Hugo, a useful formula. Of the yellow maple there in this autumn mist we might say *non acer est sed angelus*.

—It is, indeed, Hugo said. The opposite of a troll, wouldn't you say?

88

To *The British Grenadiers* on Pascal's fife and Sebastian's drum, followed by Kim with the guidon and Hugo with Barnabas on his back, the NFS Grundtvig Frispejderne, Tom White Gruppe, in two files of pairs holding hands, marched by Headmaster Eglund's house, out across the soccer field, and onto the country road.

—Aren't they, the headmaster asked Mariana, who was gathering roses with Clarissa Eglund, in different uniforms? I thought scouts were green and brown, not yellow and blue?

—And, Clarissa said, unless my eyes are deceiving me, little Barnabas has a uniform like the others. Did you see, Edward dear?

—I made it, Mariana said, exactly like the others, but with buttons on the blouse to anchor it to the pants. The pockets, of which there are six, gave me fits. Also made the flag. They're only going down the road a bit, for a practice patrol, and will be back in an hour or so, or Barnabas, who's the mascot, wouldn't be along.

—Sebastian, I believe, used to be a Tivoli drummer? What spirit to a drum and fife!

—Barnabas agrees, Mariana said. He does a kind of devil dance when Sebastian and Pascal practice. Hugo worked it out over the summer, I thought you knew. He made a scout troop of the revolutionaries. Denmark has about forty different kinds of scouts, Baptister Spejderkorps, Frivilligs, Communists, the Socialdemokratiske Ungdom, the fellowship this and the fellowship that, Greenland Pioneers, and whichwhat, so here's another. His own troop remains, the green and browns, with blue for the cubs, hr. Eglund was speaking of.

—Edward, please. So what are the mustards and slate blues?

—The Tom White group. They're like the Theban Band, it's called, in ancient Greece, pairs of friends. That's why they march holding hands, two by two. Jos keeps an eye on them, as an anthropologist he says, and Hugo has them all wanting to learn Greek and history, and Holger gave a wonderful talk to them on sharing time and space. A friend is another self, he said. Used words like respect and adoration and loyalty. Hugo said it was a sermon his father might have given. Barnabas, who was there with me, slept through lots of it.

—It's all well over my head, hr. Eglund said. Shall I do a bowl of roses, Clarissa dear? Anything to keep them out of mischief.

—Why, Clarissa asked, are they named for Tom White, and who was he?

—Somebody in the English army, I believe, Mariana said. Back when they wore red coats. Died terribly young. Hugo can tell you more about him.

—Yes, Edward, a bowl of roses for the table would be splendid.

89

—See? Pascal said, handing Holger a bunch of chicory and red valerian, they're flowers, for you, because Franklin brings them to Hugo, who puts them in a jar of water and says he likes them. They're sort of from the edge of fru Eglund's garden.

Holger laid a postcard in Kierkegaard's *Philosophiske Piecer*, to keep his place, and stared at the disarray of Pascal's hair, the livid welt on his cheek, his swollen lip that he played his tongue over.

—So will I put them in a vase, Holger said, if I have such an article. Which I absolutely don't.

—The marmalade, Pascal said, is down to just about enough to go on a slice of bread, with some butter, and then you'd have that to put the flowers in. Hugo keeps pencils in a marmalade jar.

A tear fattened in the corner of an eye and slid down his cheek, over the reddening welt.

—Ingenious solution, Holger said. And who do we know fossicking for tucker to finish off the marmalade with a cup of tea, perhaps?

—Milk, a big glass of cold milk. There's half a bottle and one not opened yet. You've been grading papers, all done, with the rollbook on top and a rubber band around the lot. And reading.

—Kierkegaard. Danish grasses and wildflowers, the papers. Now tell me what in the name of God has happened to you?

Pascal, eyes as round as kroner, was wiping marmalade out of the jar with his fingers.

—Franklin and I have had a fight. Alexandra's his girl only, now. I had it coming to me. Everything's OK, sort of. That is, we hit each other pretty hard. But he caught up with me afterward, when he cooled down a bit, to see if he'd hurt me. So we kissed and hugged, sort of.

His sandwich built of wedges of butter and runnels of marmalade, Pascal took as large a bite as he could, for the comedy of it, accepting a tumbler of milk from Holger.

—Pascal?

—All yours. Forever.

THE RINGDOVE SIGN

I

The Arctic Circle, Mariana said, and here's that light again. It's like nothing I've ever seen before. We're deep in conifers and aspen, and when their shadows begin to stretch out long, as now, all the hard accurateness of the light out here in the woods becomes this brilliant softness that lasts for hours, greens going blue, the sky violet, with neat lines of gold on the edges of things. Splendid is the word, Hugo said. And the midges dance out in hordes. Their jigs in spirals, their jigs in rounds. The gnats and leafhoppers here, Hugo said, are so many silly innocents compared to the ferocious samurai mosquitoes up north. On the Arctic Circle. You'd think the silence at the top of Sweden would be absolute. Not a bit of it. For one thing, the silence itself is an oppression, a density in the ear, so that the whine of mosquitoes and the hum of big black flies make a drone you wouldn't otherwise hear. We'd got to Boden by train, and marched out to the Circle in stages, great fun at that age. A devil, Mariana said. No I wasn't, I was sweet and shy. Ask Papa. We were joining a troop of Swedish Scouts, boys and girls together. A fine August day. For the North Pole. Which is considerably beyond, Smarty. On the Circle all the trees are dwarfs, as they grow so slow in that climate, getting root water only a few months of the year. Swamps of peat, fields of moss all warped and wavy. The evergreens are giving way to birches. When the Swedes saw our guidon down the path, the loneliest scraggiest worn path in the world, they turned out their brass band, and chose to greet us with *I Fratelli d'Italia*, Garibaldi's battle hymn, as handsome a piece as there is, always excepting *Wilhelm of Nassau*. I remember that the band all looked alike, peas in a pod, longish blond hair and cornflower-blue eyes, and almost uniform. The cornet was barefoot, and here and there one saw a shirttail out and an unbuttoned button, an unzipped fly, a haywire shoelace. But they played with spirit and dash, and to be met in that

361

northern emptiness, that world of scrub and wild desolation, made us feel wonderful. We formed into a double file, and marched in to the music, left foot in time to the drum. Our scoutmaster, a freckly math teacher in steel-rimmed specs and a race of coppery hair across his forehead, to be in style with his charges, saluted the Swedish master, or mistress, for she was a woman, and shook hands. The Swedes have the damnedest sense of humor. They told, over and over, with richer merriment every repeat, how the band got into its uniforms faster than it had ever before dressed, and how the trombone could not for the longest be found, and how they had a squabble as to whether they should play *King Kristian* or *Du Gamla, du Fria*, and compromised with Goffredo Mameli, as symbolic of idealism, youth, and liveliness. Mariana said, I've seen Franklin laugh at the bubbles in Perrier water.

2

When a mouse looks at the world, Einstein said, the world does not change. Yes it does, Niels Bohr replied. A little.

LONG SHADOWS BEFORE THE FIRST STAR

The Summer Box, Papa calls it, Hugo said. I can remember talk as to whether it's a cabin or a hut. We came here for a month at least every summer, Papa and Mama (you would have liked her, and she would have liked you) and I, and on the odd weekend, when I could bring along a friend. The inconvenience of it is its charm for Papa, having to survive on what you bring. He divides people into those who like coming here and those who don't. Put me in the first lot, Mariana said. And Franklin and Pascal when they get here, day after tomorrow, isn't it? If they get on the right train, if they get on the right bus, if Pascal's folks delivered him at Papa's. Those two, Mariana said.

BLUE RIVER WITH WILLOWS

My buddy Asgar and I were certain our scoutmaster was largely unacquainted with the female of the species other than his mother and aunts. He'd certainly never before seen a woman scoutmaster, especially one who laughed at the bubbles in Perrier water. it took a while to sort out the sex of the Swedish Scouts. They were all dressed exactly alike, had the same length of hair, and names weren't all that much help. A girl I thought for sure was a boy turned out not to be. We were supposed to communicate in Esperanto. We fell back on English. We pitched our tents in a line facing theirs and went off to a blue river lined by willows. There's no underbrush up there, no ferns like here, or berry bushes. Only moss, rock, stunted grass. The Swedish mistress said we must undress quickly, and get into the water, or the mosquitoes would quite literally eat us alive. Was she ever right.

TRACTATUS I.21

Any one fact can be the case, or not the case, and everything else remains the same.

AUGUST

Hayfoot strawfoot, Hugo said, crunching larch cones, Pascal copying Franklin, off the forest trail to our campsite on the river. That's lovely, Mariana said, Pascal copying Franklin. I wouldn't have guessed that anybody would copy Franklin in anything. It's Franklin who's the champion copycat. After you appropriated me, which has, willy-nilly, involved appropriating Franklin too, he has taken you as the authority for all of life's surfaces and corners. He brushes his teeth, bathes, combs his hair. And now here's a well-off tyke at Grundtvig who seems to be the apple of his housemaster's eye and who talks like a book and as you've told me has the highest IQ in the school looking up to Franklin. Oh it's more than lovely, Hugo said. It began, you know, with that fight when Franklin took Pascal's side, wholly inexplicably, and then Holger asked me if I would take Pascal on an outing, to give him some sense of the practical and some measure of self-confidence. So when we had our tent pitched, the flaps reefed, and ringed rocks and set up a spit, we were in thick summer pastoral peace: frogs talking to each other across the river, a raven cawing, dragonflies glinting green. Pascal was whistling Mozart as we made camp, and so was Franklin, a musical ear I hadn't suspected. So the copycatting goes both ways. We'd crossed paths earlier on in the afternoon with some *Wandervögel* from Stuttgart, rather raunchily ahead of the times. One of them, sienna brown and as towheaded as an English sheepdog, eyes china blue, was wearing jeans shorts that would have fitted Franklin better, and their zipper was on the fritz so that the pod of his briefs, rusty yellow, stuck out through his fly. His girl, freckled pink and gold her whole face over, seemed to be wearing his shirt and nothing else. There were two boys in scarcely anything except packs and red caps who were holding hands. Another girl was sweetly barebreasted. They hailed us jovially. Pascal had questions, to which Franklin made up answers of an outrageous sort.

7

Tuesday, Mariana said, and whistled two long notes. I suppose the angels recorded it, they'd have to, blushing. If we came out here to love each other into fits and for you to pull together your crazy thesis, I hope the crazy thesis gets pulled together as well as the loving each other into fits. The angels won't blush, Hugo said. They probably wrote it out as music, or in annotations of which we know nothing. Or maybe as bald facts. Only hours after making love deep into a summer night, Hugo woke Mariana with his finger, causing her to talk salaciously in her sleep. Birdsong. A skimpy breakfast, after making love, scarcely interrupting renewed affections. Made love all morning. Lunch forgotten. Made love all afternoon. A walk in the meadow, naked as Adam and Eve.

8

Well, Pascal said once we were all shipshape with site and tent, as a matter of fact I call Housemaster Sigurjonsson Holger when we're by ourselves, never any other time. Hugo, Franklin said, is always Hugo. So, hr. Tvemunding, Pascal said, I'll call you Hugo. Very spadger, his ribs, with something baby bird in the shoulders, something goblinish about the back of the head. There was a tadpole flexibility before this gawkiness. A sturdy symmetry to follow. From Maillol to Soutine to Kisling. Franklin's stage ahead with his prat pout and flat tummy, foxy eyes with the contour of an almond. Maillol, Hugo answered Mariana's question. Chloe. You are my goat, Mariana said.

HYACINTHUS INDICUS MINOR

The root of this Iacinth is knobbed, like the root of arum or wakerobin, from whence spring many leaves, lying upon the ground and compassing one another at the bottom, being long and narrow and hollow-guttered at the end, which is small and pointed, no less woolly or full of threads than Hyacinthus Indicus Major. From the middle of these leaves the stalk rises long and slender, three or four foot long, so that without it be propped up, it will bend down and lie upon the ground.

10

Their two voices, Pascal's burgher correctness and school slang, Franklin's proletarian grittiness and complex grammar, began to swap locations and tones. I adjudicated. I'll bet you did, Mariana said. Franklin said that I talk all sorts of ways, and that Pascal should hear me talking with my father, whom Franklin identified as a pastor and his personal friend. And that he should hear me talking with you. To barf, he added, immediately bragging about my teaching you English. I'm much more interested, Mariana said, in the Swedish Scouts at the North Pole, as I have a feeling that there was mousing from tent to tent in the night. There was no night, Hugo said. The sun stays up all day, sinking to the horizon and rising up again. The mosquitoes had attacked in rolling singing hungry swarms despite our nimble scramble into the blue river with willows, and we all smelled of witch hazel and iodine. Of course we had to sing folk songs around the campfire, eating ashy sausages. So, Mariana said, you began a life of tents and campfires. Did I? Hugo asked. Does that mean something? Deep in a forest makes for good talk and good fellowship. Objecting I wasn't, Mariana said.

SILVER DRAGONFLIES

Holger says, Pascal said, we're all defeated by the inert violence of custom. This with a siffling sigh while Franklin was shedding every stitch. Shirt off, thrown down. A stare from me, a *sorry* from Franklin, and the shirt got hitched by its collar on the ridge pole. Pascal, imitating Franklin jot and tittle, doffed his togs. Blue Cub Scout short pants, identical as to red Swiss Army pocket knives pendant from belt loops, sheathed camping knives on left hip, canteen right hip, scut packs with nylon impermeables, compasses. Holger had seen to it that Pascal was to have precisely what Franklin was to wear right down to underpants (blushing), off, folded on mesial axis, and stashed in tent corner. It pleased Franklin to stomp around in shoes and socks only. This was when Pascal quoted Sigurjonsson quoting Sartre.

12

Perhaps what cannot be said is the ground on which what can be said comes by its meaning.

BOEHME THE COBBLER

In some sense, love is greater than God.

14

Me, I'm simply lucky, Franklin said. Pascal munching a cinnamon bun at breakfast, up to his neck in my nylon parka, Franklin similarly engulfed in my khaki shirt but with his dinky maleness honestly bare, had said how keen it was to sleep in a tent and run naked and eat on a riverbank. Their wearing my parka and shirt referred to Franklin's saying that when he stayed overnight with us at NFS Grundtvig he wore my undershirt for a gown. Though it is always more probable that the reporter of a miracle has been deceived than that the miracle occurred, this does not obviate the miraculous, and there remains the space where the misunderstood has the force of miracle. There you go, Pascal said, using that word. What's wrong with it? Franklin asked. It's vulgar, is what, isn't it, hr. Tvemunding? Hugo, I mean. It's vulgar all right, I said, but it's Franklin's word. We are our words. We can, however, make the words we use, like poets and philosophers, and people who want to be understood. Most people are parrots, hoping to please by imitation. Squawk! said Franklin, and fell over backwards laughing at his own wit. Pascal waited two seconds before joining the laugh. Language, I persisted, always the explainer, is mostly a matter between friends, and friends can use words they wouldn't before some people, like parents and in public, on a bus, say. My language in class is impeccable, but gets saltier in the gym, looser at home. Holger, Pascal said, always talks the same. We're friends. Franklin gave one of his looks. Satiric doubt.

THE MORE ANGELS, THE MORE ROOM

The second afternoon of an outing is when the roundness of it asserts itself. No need to tell me, Mariana said, shuffling into a dance and snapping her fingers. There's community, rhythm. The outside world has receded out of sight. Out of mind, Mariana said. There are no Kindergartens, no crayons stuck up noses, no peed knickers, no flash cards with Mina Jenssen croodling *dog* when I show the porcupine and *hat* for the letter A. The outside world has been replaced by an alternate one of exploring, swimming, botanizing, telling jokes, remembering analogues of each other's tales. I didn't think I'd like you at first, Franklin said to Pascal, but now I like you. Pascal thought of no reply, poor fellow. Well, Mariana said, a declaration of love from Franklin is not to be taken lightly. He didn't like you at first, was jealous, resentful. When the angels were manufacturing Franklin they broke off big blue pieces of heaven and worked them into his soul. Pascal too, Hugo said, but I don't think heaven has a great interest in mind, which is what the angelic craftsmen paid much attention to in Pascal. I asked myself what cautionary advice he'd had from Holger, who couldn't very well disapprove of Franklin. Probably some comprehensive warning against nastiness, certainly supererogatory in a school like NFS Grundtvig, but then Holger would have only a vague idea of townsfolk like you and Franklin. Who pinned Pascal's arms from behind and nuzzled his nape. Pascal froze, wriggled loose, and regarded Franklin with a look that slid to the tail of his eye. Whereupon Franklin, determined to hug somebody, came and hugged me. I was sitting, writing, I hugged back, and got to my knees and rolled him squealing over my head, and grappled him into a rolling hug that toppled us, and we fell knotted together arms and legs, hooting. Pascal, miserable, contracted his shoulders, one foot on top of the other. I swung Franklin loose, carried him by the armpits and stood him nose to nose in front of Pascal. You two, I said, work on your friendship. I've got notes to make, water to fetch, wood to gather, thoughts to think.

SWEET YELLOW MOTH MULLEIN

The yellow moth mullein whose flower is sweet has many hard grayish green leaves lying on the ground, somewhat long and broad and pointed at the end: the stalks are two or three foot high, with some leaves on them, and branching out from the middle upwards into many long branches, stored with many small pale yellow flowers of a pretty, sweet scent, stronger than in other sorts, which seldom give seed but abide in the root, living many years.

17

Sunlight, once, on their tousled heads beyond the rocks downriver, their voices from the larchwood. Franklin kneedeep in sedge and wild carrot by a granite rockface spritted with mica and dappled with lichen was inviting

Pascal to test the rigidity of his penis. O boy, Mariana said, trust my Franklin. I whistled my arrival. Franklin said brightly that they'd seen a badger trot and a grebe. Saw a water rat! Pascal said. The grebe had a golden craw with silver dots. Franklin was full of himself, talking big. I mussed both their heads, remarked that they were in the Serengeti of the saw-toothed chigger, and wanted both of them to soap up at the river, giving particular effort to their legs, and to smear themselves with insect repellent afterwards. Franklin boasted of an infestation of chiggers the summer before. This, he said, is my whatevereth camping trip. He'd been with me and you, and with the Cubs, and once with my troop. I'm the mascot. Sleep in Hugo's tent, march with him at the head of the column. But I like this better, friends only. Hugo studies God, and is the Greek, Latin, and gym teacher. Thanks, said Pascal, I only go to NFS Grundtvig. I forgot, Franklin said. Holger teaches biology and geography. He's been to Sicily and Iceland. Frogs and maps, Franklin said. Mitochondria and tectonic plates, said Pascal. Hugo's twice as old as me plus a year, Franklin said, and has been fucking since fifteen. His dick's 23 cm. He and my sister Mariana do it every day, because they love each other. Hugo's papa, he's a pastor in the Protestant cult, says it's kin to loving God, who wants us all to love each other. And then Franklin gave papa a grand rating as a very bright old gentleman, pink and scrubbed, nattily dressed, who lives in a big old house with a flower garden all around it, and hundreds and hundreds of books inside, all of which he has read. Wise, generous, and liberal, especially in the matter of boys' monkeying with their peters, which is nature, and nature has God for its designer. Franklin omitted the detail of our visit when Franklin came down to breakfast britchesless and upstanding, and got a kind lecture on the way back upstairs, led by the hand, on conventions, decency, and several other matters. Ah yes, Mariana said, and that's when we heard the little twerp saying that you go around your apartment in nothing but an undershirt and me in nothing at all. I loved your father saying, yes but you'll notice they don't do that here, and they do it because they're very much in love with each other. Mercifully we didn't overhear the rest of the discussion.

CLOVER. BUTTERFLIES.

Not so silly fast, one heard Franklin from the far side of the tent. Like this, if you want it to feel good. At supper they sat shoulder to shoulder, shoving from time to time, with silly smirks. Holger, Pascal said, is shy. He starts to say things, and stops, changing the subject. The water rat was just along the river, where he has a trot like the badger's. Did you know that spiders rebuild their web every day? They eat it at night. Crazy, Franklin said. I hope we hear the owl again. Over the frogs. Don't they ever sleep? When Mariana and me are spending the night, Franklin said to me, can Pascal come over? We could make a pallet on the floor. Thing is, he said to Pascal, is not to be in the way, to move with, like a dog, and not against. Then we won't be underfoot. In wintertime we eat around the fire, like we're doing now. Fried bananas with brown sugar Mariana makes sometimes for a snack at bedtime. With milk. Did, I asked, Pascal like the idea? If so, I could square it with Holger. Pascal, shy, said nothing. What if Holger says I can't? he eventually said. But, I said, it was Holger who thought up this outing, after this rascal Franklin batted his eyes at him one day and said God knows what. Did I? Franklin said. Casually, calmly. The kid is on his way to being one of the world's great actors. O yes, that. I'll come, Pascal said, looking up brightly.

19

But why didn't you tell me, Mariana asked, about this light? And the moths and butterflies and the meadow over the hill? Privacy to love ourselves into fits, yes, and roughing it on the provisions we bring in, and water from a spring, and a cryptogonadal eleven-year-old with an IQ bigger than yours, and my idiot little brother, when they find us, and your father, in time, but not the magic soft long goldeny light. Which, Hugo said, will eventually last all night. That is, it will be the night. I'm not leaving it, Mariana said. I want to live with it, on it, in it, the rest of my life. I must, Hugo said, take you to the Arctic Circle, and maybe this time I won't be bitten by mosquitoes all over my virile member. Asgar, too. Which we made worse by whacking off as usual before falling asleep. Though it would have swollen up and turned purple all the same, I suppose. It was brave Asgar who boldly pulled his pants down for the Swedish scoutmistress next morning when she was daubing mosquito bites. Oh dear, she said, oh dear, what a frightfully awkward place to be bitten so cruelly. But she daubed away, with several other wounded, girls too, looking on with curiosity having overcome every scruple.

THE BALLOON

It was over the meadow beyond the birchwood, descending, its gaudy colors, like those of a circus wagon, splendidly strange against the blue haze of the sky and the soft greens stitched with purple and yellow runnels of wildflowers in the meadow. The wooden paddles of the propeller were idling over. The telescope in its sweep flashed a white disc of glare. The *Jules Verne* was back, here.

CLEMENT TO THEODORE

Add to the evangelium of Marcus: They arrived in Bethany where there was a woman whose younger brother had died. She found Yeshua and lying face down before him said *Son of Dawidh take mercy on me.* Those who were with Yeshua, his followers, spoke harshly to her, which angered Yeshua, who went with her to her brother's tomb in her garden. There they heard a loud voice from within the tomb, and Yeshua lifted aside the stone door, and went in, and took the young man in his arms. He sat him on the coffin's edge and took both his hands in his, and the young man looked at Yeshua and loved him, and begged that he might be with him always. They left the tomb and went into the house of the young man, who was rich. Now six days later Yeshua asked the young man to come to him at night, naked except for a linen cloth. And throughout the night Yeshua explained to him how the world had God for its king, and at morning Yeshua left Bethany and walked to the other side of the Jordan.

MARCUS XIV:51
Adulescens autem quidam sequebatur eum amictus sindone super nudo: et tenuerunt eum: at ille reiecta sindone, nudus profugit ab eis.

SANKT HIERONYMUS WITH OPOSSUM
A sequence of twelve photographs by Muybridge: a dappled horse named Smith with rider, nude. A lithograph of 1887, the flat carbon of its blacks and silvery graphite of its half tones having the authority of both science and art. Smith's tail has dashed into an upward spray by the sixth photograph. The sequence records a single four-legged step, or, in horseman's language, stride. Time lapse between exposures: .051 seconds.

24
There was a dialogue conducted by the furniture, as in a De Chirico, where *Stimmung*, or time with the feeling of music, involves one thing with another, Mariana's flowery scarf, its Indian pinks, mustard browns, and Proustian lilacs, with the feral cunning of the large photograph framed in thin aluminum on the wall of Bourdelle's *Herakles Drawing His Bow*, Hugo's running shoes, their incisive blue stripes slanted like the insignia of a rank coparcenary with the god Hermes, coffee mugs in an event with light, a map of the Faeroes on the wall opposite the *Herakles*, a blue javelin standing in the northwest corner, a Cub Scout neckerchief, yellow and black, Franklin the Electrical Beavertooth Rabbit's, a vase of zinnias, a trapezoidal shaft of soft late afternoon from the skylight to the blue rug, the bed made as neatly as one in a barracks.

MARCUS X:46
[They came to Jericho and the sister of the young man whom Yeshua loved and his mother and Salome were there, but Yeshua would not see them.]

26

Linen is the clue, Hugo said. Johannes the Dipper wears animal skins: that seems to be very important, and when Yeshua is mocked and tortured he is made to wear a purple emperor's robe, to satirize what they think are his pretensions to being a ruler. But otherwise he wears linen. *Byssos*, the garb of Pythagoreans and the Essenes. Angels wear white linen: that's standard. A pure garment: animals have not been slaughtered to make it. And as the tomb on Easter morning, linen linen linen, flashing white, pure. A daimon would wear linen when he is apparent to the eyes of the vulgar in this world, though the structural detail is for the daimon to be naked, like the infant Yeshua, signifying sinlessness. And, Mariana said, her chin on her knees, looking out into the beautiful northern twilight, you think that the gospel writers could not wholly detach themselves from the ancient and pervasive Mediterranean belief in daimons as angelic messengers from heaven to an inspired person, a philosopher or a teacher like Yeshua, and gave him one: he's the adolescent naked except for a piece of linen in the scene of the arrest, and he's the younger brother Yeshua revives and talks to all of a night, and he's the angel at the tomb on Easter. He's all over the place, Hugo said. The revival in the garden has come down to us folklorishly askew. The chap's name was El'azar, or Eleazar, or in Latin Lazarus. Check out daimons with names, like angels. The night's conversation ought to be messages from on high for Yeshua, not Yeshua instructing a rich young man whom he has brought back from the dead. He's also probably the same as the rich young man Yeshua said should give all he had to the poor. And, Mariana said, these things got scrambled around in the writing. First in the telling, Hugo said. Each early community would have had its own history, and over a hundred years details transmute. I tell you an interesting story, but you don't quite get the drift of all of it. You then repeat the story, and account for certain details in your own way, or the way you understood them. A hundred years pass. Versions get written down, some of them in languages not one's native tongue. You see? And the daimon had, in one of the longest traditions we can trace in the Mediterranean, a bird form. A dove. More than any other folktale, Yeshua mentions the sign of Jonas. That is, the sign of the dove. Jonas means dove, Mariana said. I do listen. You're better at this than I am, Hugo said.

THE BOW OF HERAKLES

Up these outside steps, Franklin said. Hugo lives here. It was the top floor of the stables, way back, now a garage and place where the grounds people keep their things. Somebody, a teacher here, who left, he taught drawing and building houses and things, made the upstairs one big room, but with a bathroom and kitchen and a skylight. When Hugo came here, all he needed was a bed and a chair and a table to make himself a place to live. Pots and pans and things. Hugo says that what you own should be a pair of jeans, shoes, socks, and shirt. One sweater. But he only talks that way. He has lots of things. This, around my neck on this shoelace, is the key. Mariana has one, too. You first. That big picture, it's a photograph of a statue in Paris Frankrig, where Hugo bought it. He's been all sorts of places. Greek, Pascal said, a hero from the myths. Yes, said Franklin, you see he was good and strong and he shot bad things with his bow, things that hurt people. He's naked because the *Grækere* didn't wear any clothes most of the time, big balls like Hugo's, but this picture here, which Hugo painted, of my sister Mariana, is naked because girls are pretty with no clothes on. Hugo can paint real good. He has drawn me all sorts of ways, with color pencils, my pecker on view, chinning a limb down by the river, asleep in that chair. A Muybridge, Pascal said, looking at the photograph in twelve frames of the horse Smith. Brancusi's *Torso d'un jeune homme*. Hugo says that has purity, whatever the fuck he means by that. Pascal winced. Now I've said something wrong, Franklin said. Let's have a glass of milk. The *Torso* is beautiful, Pascal said. It has elemental simplicity. In the archaic Mediterranean period the body was shaped that way in Cycladic and Maltese sculpture. Cycladic, Franklin said, Cycladic. Here, Pascal said, taking down a book and flipping through the pages. There, he said, that's Cycladic. You knew it was in that book? Franklin asked. No, but by the title there was a good chance. You could have said you knew it was in the book and fooled me. I don't want to fool you, Pascal said. Good milk. Franklin drank his at a go, and licked the inside of the glass held upside down. As he licked, he squeezed the crotch of his short white pants. Pascal sat in Hugo's reading chair, feet and all, ankles crossed, and sipped his milk. What I think, Franklin said, unzipping, is that you're not balls up inside anymore. It didn't look like it when we were camping with Hugo. You get stiff good. And you say it feels neat to play with it. If it feels half as good as mine, you're getting there. Why would your housemaster friend Holger say you can whack off in moderation if he doesn't want you to do it at all, you know? See, one pull back and one pull up, and I'm bonehard and tingling. Pascal spilt a fat dollop of milk on his shirt and pants. Fuck, Franklin said. Don't get it on the rug. Here, over to the sink. Shirt, britches, rinch 'em in cold water, is what Mariana would do. They'll be dry again in no time. Underpants, too. Your dick's half stiff, you know. What, Pascal said, if hr. Tvemunding comes in, or your sister? What nothing, Franklin said. You don't know those two. They don't think about anything else. And they don't snitch. See, pull back, slide up. Everybody at Grundtvig whacks off two or three times a day. I know that, Pascal said. In the showers, in bed, up over the boathouse. Yours has a more mushroomy head than mine. See, I'm getting hair. Hugo's has big veins all over it, and bumpy ridges. Long as my forearm, and the head's as big as my fist. See, he said he got it that big by whacking off when he was a boy.

28

Do you, Pascal said, know about the nest of crystals in a salmon's brain by which it steers in a magnetic field? Like a radio, said Franklin.

29

The peaches, Mariana said, have been in the spring, in their tin, and so's the condensed milk, which is why they are so delicious and Hugo is smiling at me with designs in his eyes. One design. All the writing's to be done by the time papa gets here, so that he can read it through. He's going to like the hobby-horse. And the structuralist analysis of clothes. Wheat and figs will be nothing new to him, or Gnostic static.

THE GREAT APPLE ROSE

The stock is large, covered with a dark grayish bark except for the younger branches, which are reddish, armed here and there with great and sharp thorns, but nothing so great or plentiful as in the Eglantine, although it be a wild kind: the leaves are whitish green, almost like the first White Rose, and five always together, seldom seven: the flowers are small and single, consisting of five leaves, without any scent, or very little, and a little bigger than those of the Eglantine bush, and of the same deep blush color, every one standing upon a prickly button, bearded in the manner of other roses, which, when the flowers have fallen, grow great, long and round, pear-fashion, bearing beards on their tops and are very red when full ripe.

ACORNS

Earliest dawn, mist, the shine of dew, a single star still in the sky. Hugo could make out the basket of the *Jules Verne* in an open place in the pines, its rope ladder down. Quark, he called softly. Quark, again. He heard a voice speaking God knew what language: it was more animal than human, full of chirps and ratchety gutturals. He called again. Ferns parting before him, a boy naked as a newt, wet to the hips, strode out with wide rolling steps, waving his arms in greeting. It's you, he said. Can we talk? Hugo said. Talk? Quark said. You *are* Quark? Hugo asked. There were the three of them, ten or eleven in age, Quark, Buckeye, and Tumble, voyagers in a balloon of the last century. We are washing in the dew, Quark said, and drying in the air. It's wonderfully *so me tumenge 'kana rospxenava ada zhivd'ape varikicy romenge*, Buckeye! you worthless goosebrained chickenhumper, put me back onto Danish. He fiddles with the adaptors on the thread out of absolute gormless idleness. *El ruaus della dumengia damaun fa*, stop it! Buckeye's radiantly grinning handsome face rose over the wicker taffrail of the basket. I was getting us all into *lingua loci*, Crosspatch, while heating the griddle for pancakes, and reading the newspaper we bought in the village. Hi, Hugo, what brings you out to the ship so early of a morning? Tumble is out milking cows. A little from several: so it won't be missed. Pancakes, blackberries, and milk. Who are you? Hugo asked. Not to say, said Quark. What language is your name? Quark looked blank, smiling. Buckeye! he called. Ask Hizqiyya Band yot asterisk scanner to give us a printout in Latin letters quote what language is your name close quote, with *your* referring to Zoon Hex Dyo Hen. Tapped in, Buckeye called down. Green through, red active, here it comes. Here it is.

QUARK ULT QUERCUS LATIN OAK EVANGEL DODONA CROSSREF IRISH THEOLOGER JAMES JOYCE CRY OF GULL ARCHETYPE DOVE SIGNUM JONAS ALSO CROSSREF ELEM PARTICLE SYNERGIA MUNDI CROSSREF HARMONY BROTHER BUCKEYE MT OAK GENUS AESCHYLUS OR BUCKEYE TREE ALSO CROSSREF BROTHER TUMBLE FREQ GALLIC TOMBER ENGL TIMBER CROSSREF TREE SYMBOL CONNEC VAR MYTHOLOG DRYAS DAIMONES REQ ROUTES REMIND YOU RESTRICTED EXCEPT DESIGNATE POETS PS HIZQIYYAH TO PATROL WHO WANTS TO KNOW?

BOULDERS SEAMED WITH GOLDEN SAMPHIRE

Looking out of the top of his eyes, whistling Mozart, Franklin unlatched the buckle of his Wolf Cub webbing belt, fingered the brass button from its eye, and slid his zipper down. Get chiggers on your behind and balls, Hugo said, if you're about to do what I think you're about to do. Which is what? Pascal asked. I can read Franklin's mind, Hugo said. Several meters back, on the flint path, the Electric Rabbit's paw was squeezing its crotch, and now its unwrinkled brain slips along an obvious and wholly natural line. That's not my mind you're reading, Franklin said. A joke, Pascal said. I'm learning.

A GARDEN IN POMPEII

With a stone Hercules in it, Buckeye said. At one end, where the olive a hundred years old was. And at the other, with the seedlings in perforated jars, the bee balm, polpody fern, amaranth and bachelor buttons, was a stone Priapos. Rose, white violet, dogtooth, wallflower, Tumble said, bergamot, thyme, saffron crocus. The Perfumery of Herakles was the sign above the door, across from the shop whose sign was Cash Today Credit Tomorrow. For cool and colors and smell you would have to go to Kyoto or Izmir to find the like. The dog Ferox, remember him? They'd sawn an amphora in half, on the long axis, and one half was his bed, the other, on stacked bricks, his roof. There was another grand garden at the House of the Ship *Europa*. A stone Ceres. Demeter of the Campania. And up here, peppergrass, so sour and green.

ANEMONE

Wheat figured in gold on the steel blade of his sword, in sudden windflowers that came with the rain, clad in white linen, Hyakinthos.

BLUE-EYED SUSANS

To the reedy plangencies of a harmonium from Sheffield (John Robinson, Instruments, 1869) Buckeye sang *O lead me onward to the loneliest shade.* Sing through your nose, Quark said, with quavers and shakes. That's the way *they* do it. By gaslight in the Methodist Chapel. *The dearest place,* Buckeye obliged, *that quiet ever made.* Holy milk cow, Tumble called up from the meadow below. *Where kingcups grow most beauteous to behold, and shut up green and open into gold.*

EPPING FOREST 1840

I found the poems in the fields and only wrote them down.

37

Pascal's folks, Pastor Tvemunding said, thought it would be best if I came with them, and here we are, ready for anything. Mariana, Hugo said, heard you first and is exchanging Eve's dress for modester raiment. Well, Pastor Tvemunding said, you were allowed to run naked here as a boy, even after you qualified for the *toga virilis.* There's not a soul in miles. How come, Franklin said, after being kissed on the top of the head, forehead, and chin by Hugo, Hugo can be naked and Mariana not? Answer that, Mariana said from somewhere in the cabin, and lots of other answers will follow. Papa Tvemunding, hi! Tailless rats, hi! You've all three turned up together, what fun. She's going to kiss you, Pascal, Franklin said. So kiss back.

THE TWELVE DAYS

The *kallikantaroi,* daimons or perhaps centaurs (the Greeks still believe in them), were loose on middle earth, from underneath, for the twelve midwinter days, playing havoc. If they could be appeased and sent back to the underworld, the new year could begin. They were horses, or halfhorse halfhuman, ithyphallic, unprincipled and raw. The Greeks, even so far back in time, had the sense that life was wild impulse that needed taming, needed synchronicity, regularity, rhythm. Noise must become music, sexuality a longing of affinities, violence government, babble poetry, wild grass wheat, fear of the inexplicable religion, the puzzle of the world philosophy. But the romping centaurs have stayed on, in rituals all over Europe, and the dance of the hobbyhorse is their last vestige. At the beginning they are indistinguishable, let us surmise, with the idea of daimons in general: spirits who possess or guide or tempt. Tell you about the hobbyhorse? Well, it's man in a horse suit, many variants. He does a dance in which he gets sick and falls down. A lady horse comes and revives him with her attractions. Then something that was wrong has been set right again. Springtime can come. Crazy, said

Franklin. Folklore, said Pascal. Neat, said Mariana. I think I see what you mean, said Pastor Tvemunding.

39

With a floppy and sidewise gait, goofy of eye and with idiot teeth, an agile cripple, sinking in his pace, the hobbyhorse falls down. Poor. Old. Tired. Horse. Doctors try pills and enemas. The old horse moans, the old horse groans, like to die. This is the one dramatic role rustics up and down the map get to play. They practiced their reins, their careers, their prankers, their ambles, their false trots, and Canterbury paces. They wore horse bells, plumes, and braveries, and bragged in the opening dance to tabors and fifes, bagpipes and clacker sticks, of having a mane new-shorn, and frizzled, and of having a randy wayward giddy leaning toward the tupping of a mare. And dances himself silly. He falls. The women show him eggs. But he is old, he is tired. Hope on High Bomby he is not, nor a coach horse of the Pope, who can mount thirty mares one after the other, whickering and neighing, with his black yard still hard as a hoe handle, his tail waggling, a fine roll to his handsome eye, and his ballocks throbbing with lewdness. Oh no, that's all past. He's a sick old horse fallen in the road. But then a young mare is brought for him to see. He looks, he neighs Whee Hee. The mare says Tee Hee.

40

The daimons, Papa Tvemunding said, were the agents of Fate. It is my understanding that Yeshua cancelled Fate.

41

Oh no! Franklin said. Not Sunday School out here! It's all a blur, Pascal said. Hugo said, Use your imagination. Olive groves. The olive leaf is dark green on top, light grayish green on its underside. So if there's a breeze, you see sudden, rolling, tossing changes of color. Like foam on breakers at the shore. I'm seeing it, Franklin said, closing his eyes. Me too, Pascal said. OK then, Hugo went on. Yeshua. Hair probably black, black and shiny with perfumed oil. Sidelocks in curls down by his ears. A hat? Yes, let's give him a big round straw hat, shallow-crowned, for walking in the broiling sun. A beard. Imagine him as a comely man, wonderfully attractive, big-nosed, very Mediterranean. Tall and sturdy: he was a carpenter. Though God knows, for all we're told, he could have been chubby and bald. Big floppy trousers, like a Turk, or modern Cretan. Sandals. And a kind of coat: a caftan, I suppose. He would have spoken Aramaic, and probably Greek. That was the common-market language of the Roman empire. He could read Hebrew, which no one any longer spoke: we see him doing it in the synagogue.

A ROW OF ZINNIAS

Listen to the ringdove, Pastor Tvemunding said. It's the angle of light in its retina, Hugo said. They'd brought a table out on the meadow where it flows into the cabin's grounds. Wonderful that you brought tea, Mariana said. Hugo never thinks to. These intellectuals assume everybody likes coffee. What a glorious, sweet afternoon. I hear more than ringdoves, I hear unchanged voices over in the larchwood. Happy voices, Pastor Tvemunding said. Hugo, I've read far enough into your thesis to see that the faculty is going to adjust its glasses page after page, wondering if it's reading what it's reading. But I imagine they'll kick through with a degree. I like it. It stands to reason that something so universal in Mediterranean belief as daimons would get into the gospels, and be removed, except for the traces you indicate, by scribes who didn't understand what they were excising. There was the worship of angels at Kolossai. Your theology is going to be carped at. You require an organism for spirit, allowing for no occurrence of mind except in something, even if it be an organization of matter still unrecognized by science. And you allow for no knowledge of the future in the mind of God, as the future hasn't yet happened, and is not something of which there can be any knowledge. That's good logic, isn't it? Hugo asked. Yes, his father said. Sounds absolutely useless to me, Mariana said. Hugo, what are you looking at? The light, he said. He was looking at Quark in a French sailor's suit, standing behind his father. He gave Hugo a wink, which meant: Nobody but you can see me. He mouthed *light frequency*. He sniffed the teapot, and signalled for Tumble, whose slender honeybrown body was clad only in briefs which Hugo had last seen on Franklin. Buckeye was probably on the roof of the cabin: he dared not look. The whole crunch of theology, he said, is to what extent do people imagine that creatures of another realm, higher or lower, or invisibly within ours, interact with our lives?

GUYOT, 1900

It is not enough to describe, without rising to the causes, or descending to the consequences. A complete account of vision would contain far more than a description of the sequence of chemical reactions that begins when a rhodopsin molecule absorbs a photon.

SCALIGER ON ACTS XVII:18

Ethnici non credebant diabolum esse; Socratis daemonium vel deum vel genium esse credebant.

45

Steam seeping from the brass throttle, the red lantern glowing brighter as the dusk thickened to dark, the balloon eased to fifty meters above the larchwood, most of which was already in deep green night, with some clearings and tall trees still suffused with the last thin pink of sunset. Buckeye, pushing back his Norwegian forager's cap on his curls, tried another sip of coffee. *They* drink it, he said. It's a bean, Tumble explained, from a beautifully slender tree in the Indian Ocean islands. It came up here over long trade routes years and years ago. The bean's roasted and then ground, sometimes powdered. Hot water makes it into a tisane. Add granulated cane sugar, and it's a drink. Tastes more than a little of lion piss, wouldn't you say? Ah, but the bouquet, the aroma, Quark said, rolling himself into his blanket for the night. Hugo the theologer likes it, and his da. Mariana pretends to like it. Tumble pretends to like it. I *do* like it, Tumble protested. HQ, you know, isn't really interested in this bunch. A cute old man, his tall randy son who can't keep his generator in his pants, one sprightly girl and her little brother, and his friend. So Hugo is writing some gibberish, and teaches the old languages, which he mispro-nounces, and has a loving heart, what's the bother? Pass the molasses cookies. Maybe it's all for Pascal, Buckeye said. He's the deep one.

A GARDEN IN POMPEII

Hello, Quark said. He was behind a beech, looking around. Hugo saw a por-tion of blue student cap, an eye, a quiff of hair. Where is the balloon? Hugo asked, and then in a temper, why do you bother with it? Asking questions won't do, Quark said, trying to be very serious. Be silent, be bold, be of great heart: that's the message. But the other morning, Hugo said, you talked to me about Pompeii, the old olive, the dog. You cannot imagine what curiosity you excite. We can't read minds, Quark said. We got an *admonitum* on the thread for talking too much, and for borrowing Franklin's underpants. From whom? Hugo asked. What's on the other end of the thread? The *Consiliarii*. Hugo looked more puzzled than ever. We have only heard their voices, Quark said. They give us messages to deliver, charges to look after, things like that. Where are you when you aren't here? Hi! said Tumble, looking around the other side of the beech. Where are we when we aren't here? I wonder if we know. It is left to us to rig out our expeditions. We got the balloon out of a book of pictures, and we get our clothes where we can, and our food, as when we're inside a system we have to live in its structure. Are you always ten-year-old boys! Oh no, Tumble said. We have been wolf puppies when a mother lost hers. Dolphins. Magi from Persia. Watch it, Quark said. We don't remember all of our assignments. And once they're done, it wasn't us, some-how, who did them, you know? Actually, Tumble said, they keep things from us, practically everything I sometimes think. Pompeii, Hugo said, to hold onto that, because you remember it. Do you know what happened to it? Happened to it? Quark asked. Our information, like yours, as best we can tell, is not magic, as your language has that word. Did something happen to

Pompeii? Have you no way, Hugo asked, of finding out?

47

I agree with you, dear Mariana, Papa Tvemunding said, about the light up here. It finds something in our souls. As for Hugo's youthful adventures on the Arctic Circle, I imagine the version I got years ago, as it must seem to you, but only yesterday to me, Hugo has grown up so swiftly, is slightly different from the one you've heard. I'm fascinated by what you tell me about little Pascal. A kind of genius, is he? And for Franklin, my charming Franklin, to be bringing him out: that's a sweet wonder. I have had an entire troop of Scouts suddenly fill the house, when Hugo had the prescience to march them in. Once, even, when Margarita was alive. Tents in the garden, bedrolls on every floor.

FICUS

All three kinds of fig trees are in leaves and growing one like another, save for their height, color, and sweetness of the fruit, having many arms or branches, hollow or pithy in the middle, bearing very large leaves divided sometimes into three but usually into five sections, of a dark green color on the upperside, whitish beneath, yielding a milky juice when it is broken, as the branches also or the figs when they are green: the fruit breaks out from the branches without any blossom, contrary to all other trees of our orchard, being round and long, shaped like a small pear, full of small white grains, of a very sweet taste when it is ripe, very mellow, and so soft that it cannot be carried far without bruising.

49

Come up! Buckeye called down to Hugo. You can see the nacelle, the engine. Hugo, naked as Tarzan, had come out early to walk around the woods, as he always did of a morning. The balloon was suddenly above him before he was aware that it was anywhere near. Up he climbed, feeling giddy as the rope ladder swung away, rung by rung, and began to sway wildly before he reached the taffrail. Tumble and Quark were still rolled up in a blanket, arms around each other. I'm on watch, Buckeye explained. Quark woke, grinned, disentangled himself from Tumble and the blanket, impulsively gave Hugo a kiss and hug, and went to the taffrail to pee over the side. Hugo took in the strangeness of the nacelle: the brass-and-walnut levers, the Edisonian phone and telegraph, the neat cabinets, steam gauges from the age of Isambard Kingdom Brunel, and none of this was out of style with the Danish togs draped over ropes, American jeans, French underpants, Finnish sweaters, an Italian coffeepot. Breakfast, Tumble said, his thick hair a wreck, eyes sleepy. Croissants, to be heated in the engine. Espresso. Fig jam, from the country store over the hill. Butter. The four of them sitting, knee against knee, filled the floor of the basket, with room for cups and saucers in the ring of their toes. I can't stay long, Hugo said. They're beginning to wonder about it all. Pompeii, Quark said. You asked. We asked. They have the records at HQ. They have everything at HQ, if you know who to ask. It's awful. There was a day, I forget the coordinates, when the sky was all white, which was dust and smoke, and then it was yellow, slowly turning black. This was the volcano Vesuvius, it had erupted. Ashes in the air, miles high, which sifted down for days on the garden on the Via Nuceria, so deep that it covered the great olive, and Ferox's doghouse, the flowers, the very roofs. A flower garden one day, an ash heap the next. Fig jam and butter, Tumble said, they tickle the back of the throat. But I knew that, Hugo said. Then, Buckeye said, why did you ask us to find out?

A BLUE SUMMER SKY

Franklin! Mariana! Hr. Tvemunding! Hugo! Pascal said, running from the meadow. Up in the air! There's an absolutely scrumptious hot-air balloon over the larchwood. It's all decorated with signs of the zodiac, and circus colors, and fancy patterns. I waved, and whoever's in it waved back. They were hauling in an anchor, so they must have been tethered over there. Hurry, or you'll miss it.